Soft Gold

Soft Gold

A Tale of the Fur Trade

JIM REILEY

Turnpike Press of Northfield
Northfield, MN

i

𝒯urnpike 𝒫ress of 𝒩orthfield

P.O. Box 491
Northfield, MN 55057
jimtpike@charter.net

This is a work of fiction. Names, places, characters, and incidents are products of the author's imagination and are used fictionally. Exceptions: Simon McTavish, William McGillivray, Alexander Mackenzie, John Jacob Astor were leading men in the fur trade. The North West, Hudson's Bay, and Sir Alexander Mackenzie Companies were the leading business entities of this period.

ISBN 0-9740382-0-2

Manufactured in the United States of America

This book is dedicated to the women in my life:

Betty, Melissa, Mary, Jill, Jodi, Jaclyn, and Anne
(my late wife, two daughters, and four granddaughters)
But especially to Betty — she planted the seed and
provided the sun that brought this saga to life.

Acknowledgements:

Patricia Wellingham-Jones, my editor, stayed the course with encouragement, sharp spurs, and her firm belief that there was a story here to be rescued — which she did.

The staff, interpreters, and Rangers at Grand Portage National Monument who generously shared their perspectives of the fur trade.

The professional assistance given by the staff at the libraries of Northfield Public Library, Carleton College, and St. Olaf College.

Book style and composition by Rick Esse.

Cover design by Rick Esse and Michael Blaha.

Maps by J. Mack Reiley.

Unsnarling my computer misadventures; Jim Pokorney and Burt Johnson.

"A Red, Red Rose"

O my luve's like a red, red rose,
  That's newly sprung in June
O my luve's like the melodie
  That's sweetly played in tune.

As fair thou art, my bonnie lass,
  So deep in love am I;
And I will love thee still, my dear,
  Till a' the seas gang dry.

Till a' the seas gang dry, my dear,
  And the rocks melt wi' the sun
I will love thee still, my dear,
  While the sands of life shall run.

And fare-thee weel, my only luve!
  And fare-thee weel, a while;
And I will come again, my luve,
  Though it were ten thousand mile.

Robert Burns
Scotland
1759-1796

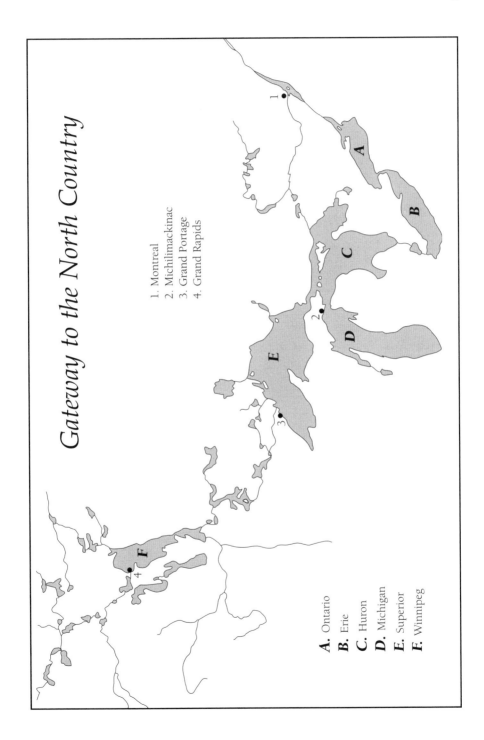

Gateway to the North Country

1. Montreal
2. Michilimackinac
3. Grand Portage
4. Grand Rapids

A. Ontario
B. Erie
C. Huron
D. Michigan
E. Superior
F. Winnipeg

Introduction

Northfield, MN
October, 2000

I like my third floor apartment. If I can't sit on the balcony and watch approaching storms, I can do it through the picture window and sliding glass door. This morning it was fog. Not run-of-the-mill stuff, this was real London pea-soup fog.

Sitting at the dining room table, I fumbled for the coffee mug hiding behind the morning newspaper. My spine shivered with a creepy feeling I was being watched. From the mist the outline of a man emerged. He eased through the double glass of the sliding door as though it were nothing.

Jeez! What's going on here? Get those feet moving, Jim, move! Synapses were not firing, the feet remained on the carpet. Well, damn it man, yell! Yeah, let out a primordial scream ... Nothing!

The outline started to fill out, I was looking at one big dude six feet tall, two hundred pounds of muscle, not fat. Hand shaking, I set the mug on the table and I'm sure my mouth was hanging open. What did I brew in my coffee to bring on this vision? Take a sip, and this will pass. The coffee didn't change a thing. This mirage was real. It stood between the door of my apartment and me. Not panic time yet, Jim, but close to it!

"Well now, Mr. Reiley," the apparition spoke in a pleasant yet authoritative voice with a decidedly Scottish accent, "are you not going to ask me to sit down and join you? A cup of tea would be nice. I take mine straight, no cream or sugar."

I stumbled to the kitchen, put the kettle on to boil. I found a box of tea bags and a mug (in Minnesota we like our tea or coffee served in a mug, part of our Viking heritage). This had to be a mirage, but he knew my name. At best he was a dream, at worst a sign of my mental disintegration.

The whistling tea kettle brought me back to reality, or was it reality? I poured the water, dropped in the tea bag, and carried the mug to the table.

"What is this thing dangling in the mug? What am I to do with this?"

Like a robot in a futuristic Hollywood creation, I jigged the tea bag up and down. When the color seemed right for a mug of brisk Mandarin Orange Spice, I took my seat at the table, and he took his first sip.

He slammed the mug on the table. I wanted to yell at him, "Easy, buster! That's a valuable mug." I was too thunderstruck to say anything.

"I asked for tea. What is this slop? Bilge water would be better than this. Damn your eyes, Mr. Reiley, no more tricks! Understood? Fine!"

When he looked up his face was a dangerous shade of red. Lightning flashing from his blue eyes got my bony knees to knocking, again. I called up some nerve and said, "That is the only tea I have, and if you would take another sip I think you would find it enjoyable."

He pushed back from the table as if to rise, but instead made himself comfortable and established as the man in charge here. Five minutes ago this was my apartment. Now it was his place, his presence dominated. My mind returned to how I might execute Army General Order #11 - 'Get the hell out of here!'

"Mr. Reiley, let me introduce myself. I am Duncan Ross, formerly of the North West Fur Company, but now like you, I am retired. I was told you were a teacher some years in the past with a keen interest in history in general and the fur trade in particular. You have been teaching about the fur trade for something called Elderhostel. And you have taught the fur trade story for another Elder something (Cannon Valley Elder Collegium). But they are not important."

He shifted his position in the chair, made a sour face, and took another sip of tea.

"What is important is for you is listen to my story and get it down on paper. You know a little about the fur trade gleaned from reading and study, but I have lived in the trade for a quarter of a century. I feel hands-on experiences are more valuable than mere book knowledge, would you not agree?"

"Mr. Ross, experience is always the . . ."

"In short, you listen, I will talk. I am not gentle with anyone who would interrupt my saga with questions or comments. Understood? Fine!

"Before we go any farther, let me apologize for the unwarranted remarks I made about the tea you served. I have a reputation for speaking directly and, at times, quite undiplomatically. My mentor frequently referred to me as his 'loose cannon'. You will have to adjust to my ways. It is a little late for me to change."

"Oh yes," he added, "I have no objection to note taking as I relate my stories. It would be a good thing to do. You have no idea of what I am going to tell you, nor do you have a sense of the order in which I will tell you of my adventures."

This man, this ghost, this mirage, this . . . this Duncan Ross seemed friendly enough. After his initial explosion over my tea he certainly knew how to make himself at home. The chance to hear first-hand a man tell of the past, nearly two hundred years by my calculation, was too good for a historian to pass up.

I sneaked a sideways look at him. He had a full head of dark, red hair and a neatly trimmed beard to match, both showing touches of gray. He was dressed in the style of the early 1800's typical for a man of substance. The coat was navy blue as were the pantaloons, the stockings an egg-shell hue, and the stock at his throat was pure white. His clothing was of quality materials and tailoring. I tried to visualize myself wearing pantaloons, stockings and stock. No way!

Mr. Ross made quite an impression on me because of his directness and ease in taking charge of a place that only a few minutes ago was totally strange to him. There was something intimidating about this man, I thought to myself as I went back to my office for the tape recorder. When I returned to the table he was sipping his tea and seemed lost in deep thought.

As he looked up he sputtered, "And what the hell is that? If you are going to make notes I expect a pen and a piece of paper will do nicely, Mr. Reiley. We have no need of gadgets."

Was it the tea, or was it his way of abruptly turning from one situation to another that brought a truce to the scene? I shrugged, put the tape recorder on the sideboard, took up a pen and began my notes as he related his first adventures in the fur trade.

Bear in mind, this is Duncan Ross telling his life story, Jim Reiley is only his scribe

Chapter One

I was alone. I expected my Uncle Simon would meet a fifteen-year-old boy upon his arrival in a strange city. There was no sign of him. Which way should I go? Whom should I ask for directions? But, directions to what? Was his place of business even in this part of Montreal?

I found myself hoping it was elsewhere. This part of Montreal in the summer of 1788 was shabby and noisy. The few people I saw since sneaking off the *Virginia Planter* were no improvement over the men I had been forced to live with during the eight week's crossing over a stormy Atlantic Ocean.

With the sea bag over my shoulder and bindle (blanket roll) under my arm, I walked into the city. I had not gone more than fifty paces when a young man fell into step beside me. He was not in any way impressive; not very clean or neat in his dress although he did not wear the clothes of a working-hand or a mariner. We walked on a short distance when he said, "You must be Duncan Ross. Simon McTavish said I was to meet you when you got off the ship."

"Yes, I am Duncan Ross. How is it you know Mr. McTavish?"

"I work for him, or I should say the North West Company. The same outfit you will be working for. Am I right?"

"I guess so. What's your name?"

"Nathan Edwards. McTavish and my old man are friends, but the bastards never asked me if I wanted to be an apprentice."

We continued walking in a direction Nathan determined. He did not bother to tell me where we were going or what we would do when we got there. He was older and a bit taller than I and had a pockmarked complexion. I didn't care for the way he took over my situation. Yet what was I to do? He knew my Uncle Simon. The fact I was expected in Montreal could only mean Nathan Edwards was my contact with the one person in this whole city who knew me.

As we trudged along I took note of our surroundings. We had not gone into the main part of Montreal, but to a large warehouse upstream from the pier where I landed less than an hour ago. Inside the dark, unlighted building Nathan said, "Toss your sea bag and bindle there and get to work."

"I don't see anything to do in this empty place."

"Keep your britches buttoned, Duncan Ross. You will work at what I say."

With that unsatisfactory answer he opened a large door on the other side of the warehouse. A line of two-wheeled carts, each pulled by a work horse and driven by a tough-looking man, began to inch its way to the door. As the cart halted, the driver slipped off his perch atop bales of something very smelly. When his feet touched the ground he slung a bale on his back and carried it inside the warehouse.

"Duncan, do you see that scale hanging from a chain where you're standing? Have the man hang the bale on the scale, weigh it, note the number and initials stenciled on the bale, and record them in that ledger on the table. You can do that, can't you?"

"Yes, I can do that. What are you going to do, Nathan?"

"I am the supervisor."

A very unfriendly way to get a young man started on his apprenticeship - if this was what an apprenticeship was all about. No explanations of what I was weighing, who these men were; they worked without a word to anyone, themselves or me. Just a steady toting of bales from the carts to the scale. After an hour of unbroken activity, Nathan called out something in a language new to me, it was probably French.

Whatever Nathan said caused another round of activity among the cart drivers. They gathered outside in the shade of the warehouse. Each man produced from a fancy little bag hanging at his waist a small clay pipe, a twist of tobacco, flint and steel. In no time the air over the group was blue with the smoke of strong tobacco and filled with a melodious stream of French punctuated with laughter. I saw a man steal a glance at me, immediately the other men did the same, then followed a flood of comment in this new language. Nathan called out again. The men promptly knocked the dottle from their pipes, slipped them back into those little bags, and resumed carrying bales from cart to warehouse.

Another two hours of work, another two smoke breaks. The line of carts had all deposited their bales. A few words from Nathan and the carts pulled into line and headed upstream away from the city.

"McTavish will be pleased to know I got some work out of you as soon as you were ashore. He's a Scotsman, you know. They're tight with their money and generous with orders when it comes to work."

"Can we get started? I am anxious to meet my Uncle Simon."

"Christ! Old man McTavish is your uncle? Why didn't you say so?"

"You seemed to know everything, so why bother with a little detail like that?"

That didn't go down well with Nathan. We walked on into the center of the city without any more conversation. In front of a shop that sold maps, charts and tide tables we halted, then climbed a set of steps at the side of the building. At the top we entered a door with neat black letters saying simply, 'Simon McTavish, Esq.' Inside an older man sat at his desk and kept on with his writing. The only notice he took of us was to sniff the air as though he smelled something not to his liking. In a pained voice he said, "I shall inform Mr. McTavish of your presence. And what names are to be given him?"

"Mr. Nathan Edwards and Mister . . . what did you say your name is?"

"Please tell my uncle that Duncan Ross is here."

"Of course, Mr. McTavish has been expecting you. Welcome to Montreal, Mr. Ross. Was your crossing a pleasant one? I do hope it was. I will inform Mr. McTavish immediately that you await him."

I could see from the corner of my eye that this upset Nathan. The clerk addressed all of his comments to me. Not that it really mattered, but my working with Nathan would be hard for him to accept, and maybe for me, too. We continued to stand; we had not been invited to sit on expensive looking chairs. The door opened and out walked Uncle Simon.

"There you are, Duncan. I am so glad you are safely arrived in our city. Nathan, you may excuse yourself. Come into my office, Duncan, I am filled with questions. Nathan, I said you are excused. I am sure there is work you should attend to."

The office of Simon McTavish, Esq. was not as big as I expected, but was furnished in subdued yet expensive style. He worked at a large desk of well-polished wood; I would guess it to be walnut. His chair was also large and well made, and covered in leather. I thought a man as important as Uncle Simon would have a desk piled high with papers and ledgers. Not so. His desk had only one or two papers, nothing else save an ink well and a stand with quill pens lined in order.

I was not asked to sit but told to gather my sea bag and bindle and follow him down an inside stairwell. As we left the room, Uncle Simon stopped to tap on the window beside the doorway. When we got to the bottom of the steps, awaiting was a beautiful, black lacquered carriage, a span of handsome horses hitched to it and driven by a man in livery aided by a footman dressed the same. Uncle Simon paused at the step into the coach and spoke to the footman who folded back the canvas top of the coach.

"Now, Duncan, I want to hear all about your crossing. It was from the port of Dundas, was it not?"

"Yes, Uncle Simon, I left from there. We were nearly eight weeks in making the voyage."

"Ah, Duncan, there is one little thing I want to apprise you of. When we are together it is quite proper for you to address me as Uncle Simon. But when we are in public you should address me as Mr. McTavish. Understood? Fine!"

"Yes, Mr. McTavish."

"Very well, Duncan, you learn quickly, and I like that. Now, did you enjoy being on the broad Atlantic? I believe this was your initial experience at sea. How was it?"

"I do admit to be being sea sick, very sick the first few days. But the ship's master, Alfred Lorton, kept me so busy I had no time for anything else."

"Busy, you say? How can that be? I gave explicit instructions to my agent that your passage was to be paid in advance of going on board. What kept you so busy, pray tell?"

"Mr. Lorton said I owed additional money for my passage, that the agent had not paid enough. He said I would have to work to make up the amount owed."

My story of the treatment received at the hands of the master of the *Virginia Planter* tumbled out like a spring freshet. I did not detail all of my experiences, but did tell Mr. McTavish enough to give him a sense of the humiliation heaped on me by that petty tyrant. While this conversation took place we rode at a stately pace on a main street in old Montreal. Mr. McTavish nodded to some people, tipped his hat to others, especially to the women we passed, and seemed to enjoy our drive. The scene was most contradictory. Here he was being the grand man about town while he listened to the very thing he did not want to happen to a member of his clan - humiliation!

As I concluded my tale of mistreatment, he called to the driver and in a rapid exchange directed him to turn back to the waterfront and hurry to the place where the *Virginia Planter* was berthed. We had barely stopped when he was out of the carriage, unassisted, and called me to follow. He marched up the gangway, strode several paces on deck, and called in a loud voice heavy with authority, "Mr. Lorton, I would have a word with you. Present yourself to me immediately."

There are not many people who would not respond to a command given in such a commanding manner. Mr. Lorton was not to be challenged on the deck of his own vessel. He emerged from his cabin pulling on his coat and ready to rough up anyone who dared to call out to him in this fashion. One glimpse of Uncle Simon and he changed his manner immediately. "Alfred Lorton at your service, sir. What can I . . ."

"My nephew tells me a sum is owing on his passage from Dundas to Montreal. Is that right? And what is that sum?"

"I don't rightly know the exact amount, your lordship, I will have to ponder that question."

"Ponder, hell. Give me the amount now, or I will have it dragged from you after you spend a day in the keep of the Montreal sheriff. Do I make myself clear? Speak up, man!"

"Well, your lordship, I figure the lad owes me four and eight. Yes, I do figure it now. He owes me four pounds and eight shillings."

"Very well, Mr. Lorton. Will you count with me as I lay out the sum here? This hatch cover will serve our needs."

I could see from where I stood the greedy eyes of the ships' master light up at the sight and size of the wallet Mr. McTavish withdrew from inside his waistcoat. My uncle counted out the bills and laid them on the hatch cover then tucked the wallet back in his coat. As Mr. Lorton reached out to take them, with a lightning-like slash of his cane, Uncle Simon knocked his hand aside.

"What the hell did you do that for, governor?"

"Why, Mr. Lorton, did my nephew not work out that amount on this vessel for the last eight weeks? I think the bill with you is paid. This money is rightly the lad's. Do you not agree, Mr. Lorton?"

The gleam of greed in Mr. Lorton's eyes was replaced by hatred and fear. He stood there, blood dripping from his smashed hand, unsure what his next move would be. I stepped to the rail near to the rack of belaying pins, but my gesture was unneeded. My uncle took two quick steps toward Mr. Lorton and, with the heavy brass ornament on the end of his cane under the man's chin, lifted the ship master's head up and back until he was looking at the rigging overhead.

"Now, Mr. Lorton, you listen and listen well. I am Simon McTavish and I control the movement of all ships in and out of the port of Montreal. You have cargo on board that is consigned to me?"

"Yes," was all the man could manage.

"You will have it on this wharf by noon tomorrow. You will place it under guard, and it will be under a cover to keep it bone dry. Understood, Mr. Lorton? If there is one parcel from my shipment missing or one drop of moisture on my goods, I will have this stinking scow burned to the waterline. Understood?"

"Yes."

"Were I in your shoes, I would have my vessel underway downstream by sundown tomorrow; my men get nervous with their matches and fire pots. Do you have any questions, Master Lorton?

"Duncan, gather up the bills lying on the hatch cover. They are yours. My business here is concluded. I bid you *adieu*, Master Lorton, but remember well my instructions. I shall return at sunset tomorrow and you, my good man, had better be underway. Come, Duncan."

We went back to the carriage without haste or concern. My uncle was a very controlled man even in the midst of a tense situation. And, oh my, was he ever quick with that cane! Some time I hoped to have the chance to examine it closely, but not with him nearby. I had an idea that cane was one of Simon McTavish's better kept secrets. He gave instructions to the driver and we resumed our stately pace to the bowing and nodding, to the life of an important man on a pleasant afternoon outing.

A chuckle escaped from my uncle, "I must confess to you, my lad, I do not control all the shipping in and out of the port of Montreal. But don't you see? Mr. Lorton thinks that I do, and that is what is important. He perceives me to have that kind of power, therefore, I have it."

"I'm certain Mr. Lorton's hand will remind him of that."

"Make no mistake, Duncan, I do have influence in this city. One of my secrets I want to share with you - after all, that is what apprentices are to do, learn from their masters - I try not to be specific about whatever power or influence I really have. I let people complete that unknown factor in their own minds. They usually come to the conclusion I have intended. And there, my lad, you have learned the first lesson in the business of fur trading."

"What is that lesson, Mr. McTavish? I seem to have missed something."

"Why, keep your opposition guessing; keep them off balance. That is the trick, Duncan. Anticipate! Figure out what your opposition will do before he makes his move."

We reached a residential part of the city about a mile from the old, walled portion of Montreal. The driver pulled up smartly in front of a small two-story house of stone and frame construction. It was set off from the road with a garden that appeared well-tended. A small addition at the side of the house held some sort of commercial business. The footman had my sea bag and bindle under his arm as he followed my uncle and me to the front door. The footman pulled on the bell cord and, after a slight pause, the door was opened by a plump woman dressed plainly but cleanly with a contented look about her. At the sight of Mr. McTavish she became subdued and deferential.

"Monsieur McTavish. Welcome to our humble abode. Will you not come in?"

I followed my uncle into a cheery room that bespoke of good housekeeping and frequent family usage; this was not the kind of room reserved for Sundays and funerals. The footman set his burdens inside then retreated to the carriage to wait with the driver.

"Madame Dessault, how good to see you. May I present my nephew, Duncan Ross? He will join your home as per the arrangements I have made with you. Is that agreeable?"

"Yes, Monsieur, we shall always carry out our part of the arrangements."

"Is Monsieur Dessault in his shop? I would speak with him. Duncan, will you join me? I think you should meet the man of the house, and he, of course, will be wanting to meet the young man who will become part of his family."

Walking through the room we turned to the door into the shop attached to the house. To my surprise and pleasure I found that Monsieur Dessault was a craftsman in leather. The man who was not much taller than his wife, but half her girth, turned to look at me with rather cold eyes and glanced at my shoes. I sensed I passed neither inspection, me nor my shoes. He and my uncle engaged in some conversation. My uncle turned quickly, said his good-byes, and steered me by the arm back to the house and Mrs. Dessault. Again his good-byes to her. To me he said, "I will leave you here, Duncan. This will be your home, and I trust you will enjoy becoming part of the family. We will find time tomorrow to begin your instructions."

With that he and his fine carriage with its fine horses and fine attendants were gone. I stood for a minute wondering about my next move, but Mrs. Dessault had already decided. I was hustled to a room opening off the kitchen and built as part of the leather shop, a combination of storage room and work room for house-keeping chores. She began to fill a large tub with water from a keg supported on a strong wooden frame. Hot water was carried from a kettle on the stove in the kitchen. Mrs. Dessault laid out a towel and soap, and smiled as she closed the kitchen door.

Instructions were not required. I stripped from my traveling outfit, and knew instantly why Mr. McTavish had ordered the top of the carriage folded back. I smelled! Eight weeks of rare bathing aboard ship without many opportunities to launder my meager clothing assortment, plus a sweaty afternoon in a warehouse full of stinking animal pelts must have given me an aroma definitely not *floritura de jardin*. Though the soap furnished by Mrs. Dessault was strong enough to peel one's hide, the towel rough, and the air brisk, I felt myself to be in the lap of luxury. Real soap, real warm water, and something real cooking in the kitchen. Montreal might be a pretty nice place after all.

During my time in the tub, the lady of the house had gone through my bindle and sea bag. The blanket roll was now outside pegged on the line to air, most of the clothing thrown on a heap ready for the next laundry, and the few remaining clean items laid out for me to put on. I felt like a new lad, ready to tackle a hearty supper, and to get to know my new parents, Amibel and Luana Dessault.

Amibel Dessault had more than just his leather working skills to liken him to my father. He was terse and clipped in his speech. He said over the years they provided a home for Mr. McTavish's apprentices, and I would be happy to know I would share the room over the leather shop with another in the same situation as mine. Not being the only addition to this little family, I burned with curiosity to learn who my companion in the loft would be.

Almost as if he were in a stage play waiting for his entrance cue, Nathan Edwards burst into the room and immediately turned on me. "A fine friend you are! You might have asked me to ride home with you and Mr. McTavish. I saw you in his carriage."

"Nathan, Mr. McTavish determines who rides in it."

"Tell it to the sea gulls. I know what sort of a Scotsman you will turn out to be. Just like all the others, big-feeling and too stuck-up for your britches."

Any further exchange was cut short by Mrs. Dessault who, in her fractured English, managed to tell us that supper was ready. As we trooped to the table I noticed that the Dessault's daughter, Denise, joined us. Immediately I made comparisons in my mind with my sister. Denise was a year or so younger than Louise, though judging from the way she filled out the simple dress she wore, more of a young woman in full bloom. Where Louise was quick and sprightly, Denise seemed slow and restrained. On the whole the atmosphere was friendly as even Mr. Dessault entered into a general round of conversation. We worked our way through the meal - I was never sure what we ate - but it was hot, tasty and served in generous portions. I could see Nathan and Denise exchange secret glances and roll their eyes. Something was going on here. Was she was being too friendly? Nathan too possessive?

Mrs. Dessault suggested that it had been a long day for all. A trip to the 'necessary' at the end of the backyard and I was ready to mount the steps over the shop for a night of sleep in a bed that did not pitch and roll, did not reek of unwashed bodies and tarred ropes, and slops the cook had forgotten to heave overboard. I was more than pleased to see that Nathan and I had single beds. The dread of having to share a bed put a damper on the good feelings I began to acquire after my arrival in this pleasant little home. Over my bed on a shelf nailed to the wall I laid out my personal items, the diary I had started to keep, the swatch of plaid material in the tartan of Clan McTavish my mother had given me as a connection to my Highlands' home.

Nathan kicked off his boots, removed a few pieces of clothing and fell onto his bed. "You will find old Dessault is an early bird and thinks everyone else should be. The old lady will have something ready to eat but, let me tell you, it ain't anything like what we had for our meal tonight."

"Supper was pretty good, Nathan."

"Well, don't think it will always be like that. Some nights she dishes up some awful stuff. I don't know how much old McTavish pays her, but I'll bet she makes a fortune on the food she's paid to provide us, but never makes it to the table."

With that exchange Nathan and I were off to sleep. Only I couldn't sleep. I wasn't exactly homesick; I had gotten over that about a week after going on board the *Virginia Planter*. I had too many things to think about. Like Nathan Edwards asleep in his bed not ten feet away. He was different, so tense and aggressive in his attitude toward me. It was as though he looked for a fight. If that's what he wanted, I wouldn't disappoint him. Enough speculating over a thing that might never happen.

Were you not surprised by the friendly way Uncle Simon greeted you? By the way he handled that scheming Alfred Lorton? He went out of his way to bring you to this place, to make the arrangements with the Dessaults, and to pay them in advance for my stay. (I saw the exchange of money between him and Mr. Dessault.) What you should be thinking is learning to speak and write in French. I heard very little English today.

Morning came with a shout from Mr. Dessault at the foot of the steps to our loft. I was down in the kitchen and at the table when Nathan stumbled into the room. He had no words for anybody but sat hunched over his bowl of porridge and only looked up to glower at me as though I was responsible for all the things gone wrong in his life. As we started down the road to the main part of the city, Nathan walked with his hands stuffed in his britches muttering about the miserable way the Company treated its apprentices. I was more interested in the sights and sounds of the city. The air was fresh, the sun was up, the leaves a blend of vivid reds and golds.

We went directly to the warehouse where we worked yesterday afternoon. Waiting for us was a line of carts and drivers with the same burdens as yesterday. Nathan opened the large doors, and the process stopped dead in its tracks. There stood Uncle Simon, a dark scowl on his face.

"Nathan, who told you to put Duncan to work here? Two men are not needed to perform these tasks. Nathan, see that you do them. Duncan, come with me."

Uncle Simon and I walked the few blocks to his office. As we stepped along he said, "Nathan is the son of an old friend from my days in Albany. Did you know I began my career in the fur trade by serving an apprenticeship in Albany?"

"No, Mr. McTavish, I did not know that. Were you the same age as me?"

My question was ignored. "Nathan's father did me a good turn to help me through a bad patch there. A few years ago he came to Montreal with Nathan in tow, slyly reminded me of my debt to him, and suggested I take Nathan into the Company as an apprentice. I complied, but Nathan takes more on his shoulders than he should, and is unresponsive to those who have tried to help him. At the end of his three years with us he will be on his way back to Albany."

We reached the outside entrance to his place of business and found two expensively dressed gentlemen waiting for him. Uncle Simon told me to go up to the office and wait there with Mr. LeGorce. As I mounted the stairway, Mr. McTavish walked off to a coffee house with the men, laughing and talking as though they were old friends. My uncle, I was learning, could turn his emotions off and on very quickly. Just ask Alfred Lorton. I wondered if that poor soul managed to get his mashed hand looked after. I suspect he bound it up himself, then directed the unloading of his vessel. I also suspected that if I walked to the dock area late this afternoon there would be no sign of him or the *Virginia Planter*.

Again my greeting from Mr. LeGorce was warm and friendly. "Mr. Ross, I am certain that Mr. McTavish would want you to sit down and write a letter to your family in Scotland."

"Yes, I want to do just that, but I have no paper with me, and lack even a simple pen."

"I can provide what you need."

This is what I wrote to my family:

Dear Father and Mother and Louise

It makes me feel so good to tell you I am in Montreal sitting in Uncle Simon's office and writing to you with the paper he has furnished me. The crossing on the Virginia Planter took eight weeks, some stormy and some quite pleasant. I will give you the details in another letter.

Uncle Simon took me to the home of Amibel and Luana Dessault to live. Mother, you will be relieved to know Mrs. Dessault is a good housekeeper and a good cook. The first thing she had me do was take a bath and put on clean clothes. And Father, you will be interested to know Mr. Dessault has a leather shop attached to the house. The Dessaults have a daughter named Denise. She is about a year younger than you, Louise, not as tall, but heavier. She seems very quiet and didn't have much to say at the supper table. She said she goes into the city to a school for girls run by the 'sisters', whoever they are.

The other member of the Dessault household is an apprentice by the name of Nathan Edwards. He is English, though he said he was from Albany. I think that is in the Colonies somewhere south of Montreal. He is two years older than I, tall and skinny, and so far has not made much attempt to be friendly. I think he is sweet on Denise.

The man in Uncle Simon's office said all I have to do is bring him the letters I write to you and he will put them in the Company mail pouches going to London. Mr. McTavish has people in London working for him and they will see that my letters are delivered to you in Scotland. When you write to me, send your letters to the North West Company in London at this address, but put my name and Montreal on the cover. The people here will see they are delivered. I think that Uncle Simon made these arrangements.

Mother, I know you thought when I came over here so far from home that we would lose contact, but I promise to write often. I am well, and most anxious to get into the work Uncle Simon will lay out for me. May God bless you one and all, your obedient and loving son,

Duncan

How nicely everything seemed to be falling into place for me. If only I didn't have Nathan Edwards hovering in the back of my mind. I had just completed my writing when Uncle Simon entered the outer office.

"I see Mr. LaGorce put you to doing what I had in mind. Well done, both of you. About noon, Mr. LaGorce, I should like to have my carriage waiting. I wish to take Duncan to *La Chine*."

Another ride on a beautiful fall day in the impressive black carriage with my uncle who enjoyed the event as much as I, for he obviously owned the carriage and took satisfaction in traveling in such style. My recent bath and clean clothes assuredly added to his pleasure. Our destination was a little village about a dozen miles upstream from Montreal.

La Chine received its name long ago. The early explorers of the St. Lawrence River thought this spot - the junction of the Ottawa River with the St. Lawrence - was the gateway to China, thus the oddly named village. More a collection of plain stone and frame warehouses than a village, it was important to the North West Company's operations. From *La Chine* the big freight canoes pushed off for Grand Portage in early May loaded to the water-line with next season's trade goods. To this same point in late September or early October the canoes returned loaded to the water-line with last season's harvest of animal pelts.

As we watched from the banks of the river, a brigade of four big, birchbark canoes swept into view. With lusty songs and flashing paddles, one by one the canoes dashed to the dock at breakneck speed. At the last possible minute with a flurry of back paddling, they brought their craft to gently rest against the dock. Each man stepped out of the canoe with a swagger that only a *voyageur* could master. He drew the attention of everyone within sight. Who could resist him? Head covered in gaudy *tuque* of the brightest colors, a feather stuck at a jaunty angle; around his waist a *ceinture flechée*, a sash of even brighter colors. The *voyageur's* attitude, his sense of who he was impressed as much as his colors.

"Duncan, I am so pleased that you are able to witness this little show. We have a spirit, a sense of pride, an *élan*, if you will, in this Company. We have our faults, but we are beating our opposition at every turn. I want to develop the same spirit in you. Our *voyageurs*, as you can see, need no encouragement to strut and show off. Nothing in our operations would take place were it not for these men."

The gleam in his eyes, the cocky way he held his head, and the almost reverential way he talked of the Company convinced me he meant every word. My mind flew back to Mr. MacQuay's maps in our dingy, little classroom. Here I stood but a few feet from the beginning of those great, white spaces of the unknown labeled, 'Here Be Dragons.' Could it be these cocky *voyageurs* were Mr. MacQuay's dragons?

A call from Uncle Simon shattered my reverie. "Come, Duncan. I want you see our warehouses and how we conduct business at this end of the operation. *La Chine* in the fall and in the spring becomes incredibly busy. Do you know what the initials N.W.C. stand for?"

"I think they mean the North West Company, sir."

"You are only partially correct, Duncan. 'W' also stands for 'work'. Not one part of the total picture of who we are and what we do makes sense until you realize how much very hard and unending work goes into it."

We returned to Montreal at a leisurely pace as my uncle pointed out sights and prominent landmarks of the city. We did not stop at his office, but turned up a steep road that soon became a trail though small fields and wooded areas. At the top of the rise he called to his driver and indicated to the footman he wished to alight and for me to follow.

"This is *Mont Royale*. It gives one a truly magnificent view of the whole St. Lawrence Valley. Don't you think this would be the perfect place to build a house, a great house to match the grandeur of the view? Come, walk the area with me. I cannot get enough of this spot. I am here as often as my schedule permits."

I did as bid, but couldn't sink the thought that at times Simon McTavish was off into his own world, marching to his own drummer, unaware of any other being in his presence. I had my little hide-away above my Highlands home and never wanted to share it with anyone, well, my sister excepted. This was my uncle's hideaway and he fully intended to keep it as his.

Back to reality. Back to the carriage and the leisurely pace down the hill to the modest part of the city that was now my home. And to Nathan Edwards who just happened to be walking back to the Dessault's place as we drove past. Uncle Simon never gave a sign of recognition nor did he direct the carriage be stopped and have Nathan join us.

Nathan was running as he came to the gate into the garden at the Dessault house where I waited for him.

"You horse's ass, you crummy bastard! This is the second time you passed by as you rode with your high and mighty Uncle Simon. Well, take this."

He swung at me with a howl of rage, but without care or planning. I stepped inside his wild lunge and planted a hard fist to his stomach. As he fell to the ground I was on top of him, had him pinned, and at my mercy. I had knocked the wind out of him but I felt as if I were on a sack of bones. Instead of pounding his face I teased and taunted him, "Did you never have a fight in the school yard? Any boy knows you don't throw a punch like that without backing it up with a second one."

I let him get to his feet. When I turned to walk through the garden, he did exactly as I thought. He rushed at my back but I quickly turned, stuck out my foot, sent him sprawling to the ground. I dropped on top and this time gave him a hard slap alongside his head.

"Don't you ever try that again. The next time I'll really work you over. Did you hear what I said, Nathan? Speak up! Say, 'yes', Say it, Nathan, Say it!"

As I rolled off him and helped him to his feet he mumbled something I took to be 'yes'. I had no wish to continue this spat in the front yard of the Dessault's place, but I knew from now on I would have to watch my backside as well as my frontside around this unhappy, weak young man.

In a few more days we were into a routine that seldom varied: up early at the call of Mr. Dessault, breakfast prepared by Mrs. Dessault, the walk to the city, usually in silence, for I soon learned Nathan was not a morning person. Here Nathan and I separated to go to our different assignments.

Nathan continued receiving and weighing bales of peltries into the Company's warehouses. This job was his as long as the big freight canoes came from Grand Portage to *La Chine* where the bales of furs were off-loaded and carted to Montreal.

I reported to a Mr. Philip Lachlan in a building in downtown Montreal several blocks from the waterfront. His office was quite large and held eight stand-up desks with a clerk working at each desk. A row of windows along the one side furnished most of the light in this room.

My work was to copy records of trade goods ordered by each of the wintering partners for their posts. Mr. Lachlan explained that each partner had separate accounts and it was absolutely essential that our work be accurate, readable, and done as quickly as possible. If the fall season meant a whirlwind activity at *La Chine*, it created a similar whirlwind for the clerks in this office. Mr. Lachlan was another of those men who have little to say but missed nothing. He could spot an error in work submitted to him in a matter of seconds, and the clerk who made the error would hear about it promptly. If you were summoned to his desk it was to correct a specific oversight.

On gloomy days as they slipped from October into November the light became dimmer and the air chillier. Each desk had a candle in its holder placed where a clerk could gain some light from its flickering flame. One stove-like contraption in the center of the big room was the only source of heat. The shorter the daylight, the deeper the cold. Many evenings I walked to the Dessaults thinking my legs would never get me to the warmth of the kitchen and hot soup or stew Mrs. Dessault always had for supper.

"You don't deserve the luck you are having, Duncan. You work in a building that has some heat. You work on paper, not with stinking pelts, and you work with people. Those dumb *voyageurs* I have to put up with are no better than animals."

Nearly every night I heard this argument as we sat around the kitchen table. I had seen his handwriting and his figures several times as we took turns helping Denise with her lessons. I knew of the high level of penmanship demanded by Mr. Lachlan. Nathan could never pass muster there. Several clerks mentioned his name in the few minutes we had for a break at noontime, none had anything positive to say. He was moved about in the Company offices and warehouses in Montreal, but nowhere did he seem to fit in.

I learned within a few days of our first meeting that he had little strength or knowledge of how to take care of himself - either with soap and water or with his fists. He seemed not to have any friends, but he did have one place to find comfort and sympathy. Denise. They had something between them that kept one another going. Denise did not like her school, her teachers, her assignments; nothing about school gave her pleasure. Nathan's work seemed not to yield pleasure of any sort. I overlooked one aspect of this drawing together of two unhappy souls: sex.

Nathan came home from work late one afternoon and went immediately to our room and slammed the door. Denise had already come from school and was in her room, Mr. Dessault was working in his shop, I was in the kitchen with Mrs. Dessault. She said she noticed a rip in one of my shirts and said if I would bring it to her she would mend it. I went up to the room and walked in to find Denise in bed with Nathan. I did not need anyone to explain what I saw, and closed the door quietly and went back to the kitchen and told Mrs. Dessault I couldn't find the shirt but would give it to her tomorrow.

School for Denise was a chore, her lessons were difficult to master. Penmanship was always one of my better skills, so I helped as best I could. Nathan wanted to help with her reading assignments but he had little patience with her faltering recitations. It angered him to hear her say, "My, what beautiful writing you have, Duncan. I wish I could write like you," or, "I wish you could do my lessons in numbers and figures, but Sister Dominique would know it was not my work."

Denise had another way of irritating Nathan. She would find an excuse to get up from her place to move about the kitchen table where we worked on her lessons. She would lean close to me, over me, around me, fuss at this and that, always making physical contact.

I remembered the time I went to my room to retrieve a shirt, Denise was not quite as innocent as she would have me believe.

In an abrupt shift, Nathan began to show a more pleasant side to his usual scruffy way of talking to me. "Duncan, do you want to stay with the Company when your apprenticeship is up?"

"I don't know, Nathan. I haven't even thought about that. Why do you ask?"

"Well, I've been thinking of getting out of Montreal and heading for New York or maybe even London."

"What would you do there? Your training is in the fur trade. Could you do the same kind of work in New York?"

"You dumb rube! What are we learning in our apprenticeship? Fur trading? Hell, no. You and I are being trained to be clerks. The real trading is done in the North Country, and I have no intention of ever being sent there."

Conversations of this type became frequent at night with Nathan. My second year in Montreal was beginning, and the strangeness and tension that characterized our relations had eased. Nathan returned to his old refrain, "Duncan, promise to keep this to yourself. Promise?"

"Promise what? What is so damned secret?"

"Listen. I am leaving this dumb apprenticeship and taking passage on a boat to New York City in about a week. Well, I am not paying my passage exactly. I have a friend who will sneak me on board. I know he can get you on, too. I want you to come with me. We could have a grand time in New York."

"You don't have three shillings in your pocket and neither do I. How are we going to get along once we are in New York?"

"My old man lives there now, and I know he has money."

"You do what you want, Nathan, but count me out."

"You don't have the guts to go with me."

"I had a miserable eight weeks getting myself to Montreal, and I'm not about to toss everything overboard just to chase after a wild dream with you."

As Nathan went about his daily routines I couldn't help taking note of the evenings he did not come home for supper. We didn't speak again of going to New York. One evening in that early fall I walked home the long way by the riverfront to see what ships were docked. If Nathan was going to get out of town there were several vessels where he might find passage.

Luana Dessault never questioned me about Nathan's absence from her supper table, but Amibel was asking questions and showed his displeasure with my answers.

"Mr. Ross, your fellow apprentice has been given work out of Montreal?"

"I don't know what Nathan is doing. I seldom know where he works."

"Mr. Ross. You owe it to me and my wife to tell us what plans Nathan is making."

"I can't tell you what I don't know, can I?"

My answers to his questions did not ease the growing tension and I innocently believed the passing of a little time would bring things back to normal. My innocence ended abruptly the night Nathan came home very late. He lit a candle and began stuffing his clothing helter-skelter into a duffel bag.

"Duncan," he hissed in my ear, "I'm in big trouble, you have to help me."

"In the morning, Nathan, in the morning."

"Now. I need you now. Help me get out of the house and up to the docks in town. That's all I ask."

"What's happened that can't wait until morning?"

"I'll tell you on our way. Hurry, for God's sake, hurry!"

I got up, dressed, and waited for his next move.

"How are we going to get out of the house without the old man or the old lady hearing us?"

I thought for a minute, then outlined this plan. "I'll make like I have to go to the 'necessary' and do it slowly and make a little noise. If Mr. Dessault calls out, I'll say it's me and I have to go. Once I start down the steps you be right behind me and don't make a sound. I'll pet the dog and fool with him so he doesn't make a fuss while you ease out the door. I'll meet you out front in a minute or two."

"I'm ready. Let's go."

The plan worked. We started toward the city. When we were far enough away from the house I asked Nathan, "Now, what the hell is this all about?"

"I owe a couple of men some money."

"I could loan you a little money. Why didn't you ask me?"

"I owe them a huge amount, more than you could loan me. They aren't joking, they'll bust my head wide open."

"How did you manage to get in a mess like that?"

"I got to playing cards and kept playing, hoping my luck would change, but it just got worse."

We knew the night watch would be out on a night like this; not too cold, no rain, and a half moon to give a little light. At this pace we needed another hour to get to the city. I took the duffel bag from him and told him to move along. We arrived at the docks, keeping in shadows along the waterfront.

"There she is, that's the vessel I am shipping out on. Stay here while I slip over and give the signal."

Nathan moved quietly to the water's edge where the stern line of a two-masted vessel was moored to a capstan, gave a low whistle, and crouched down on the dock. Nothing. Another low whistle, still no response. I began to think Nathan had bungled his plan. Then I heard a hiss followed by a cough. Nathan stood up and motioned for me to join him. As I got closer I saw the faint outline of somebody at the rear of the ship. Nathan shinnied along the ship's mooring line hand over hand; I never thought he could do it. But then, I was not the one fleeing for his life. When he finally crawled over the railing and fell on the deck I heaved his duffel bag where it landed at his feet.

I saw a wave or some sort of hand signal and he disappeared from view. As I retraced my steps to the Dessaults I knew I was going to face a barrage of questions: from the Dessaults, from the Company. I thought I had parted paths from Nathan Edwards. I was the one who faced the mess he left behind.

Mr. Dessault's call came right at the crack of dawn; no questions over morning gruel, no questions at work. Didn't anyone care about his absence? When I walked into the room that night the bed had been stripped and the room swept clean with no trace of Nathan. Another day at work without any inquiry about my fellow apprentice.

The tension had eased somewhat a few days after Nathan's departure. Supper was more enjoyable with the family gathered in the usual fashion. Denise to her lessons, Mr. and Mrs. Dessault to napping and knitting, and I had found a book written in French I was trying to read.

I was bowled off my feet the next night when I got home. Before I got to my room Amibel Dessault called, "Duncan, come into the kitchen, now."

He had never spoken to me in that voice, but I did as commanded. He stood beside his chair at the fireplace. Mrs. Dessault was in her accustomed corner with a basket of handiwork in her lap, Denise at the table with head on arms silently sobbing. I assumed because of his black robe and little white collar the new person in the room was a priest. He spoke first to me, "Duncan, I am Father Dupont. I am here to tell you Denise is with child. Her parents tell me you are the one responsible for her condition."

I said the only thing I could, "I have no idea what you are talking about."

Before Father Dupont could respond, Mr. Dessault lunged at me and wrapped both powerful hands around my throat.

"You lying Scots *batard*, you know damn well what you have done to my daughter. Don't you dare to sit here and lie through your teeth. I will kill you!"

Mr. Dessault's grip was fueled by anger, my efforts to break his grip were fueled by desperation. Had I not broken his hold he would have choked me to death. When I sensed I was getting the upper hand, I struggled to my feet, and hurled him back in his chair. "Thank you, Father whoever you are, for aiding me. This man is crazy!"

My sarcasm was lost on the priest. "Now, now, my son, we must discuss our problem calmly. The wedding will be in the parish church in two weeks. I will begin tomorrow to give you instruction so you may properly marry Denise. The banns will be published this Sunday after first mass."

Mr. Dessault nodded in agreement, Mrs. Dessault cried quietly, Denise sobbed without end. Father Dupont sank back in his chair like a man who had just finished an odious task, but finished the way he intended.

"You can publish any damn thing you want, Father, but I am not marrying this girl. Why don't you ask her who the father of her child is? Go ahead, ask her."

"Denise," said Father Dupont, "you don't have to answer this young man's outburst. You have your father and mother to think about. Let me speak for you. I know you want your child to be born with the blessings of the Church. I think that you . . ."

I broke in, "Denise, you know I think the world of you, and I wouldn't do anything to hurt you. Tell me who did this."

She raised her head and looked right at me. I mouthed the word 'Nathan', she nodded agreement.

"Are you prepared to give Denise the blessings of the Church when you learn the truth, Father?"

Father Dupont got to his feet, walked to the table and put his hand on Denise's head saying we should pray. She brushed his hand aside and softly repeated one word, "Nathan."

My room never looked so good to me as it did that night. I closed the door, lay on my bed and turned over in my mind the story that unfolded. I did not spend much time thinking what a close call I had tonight. Instead I found myself thinking of Denise. That pretty child was no longer a maiden but a woman soon to have a baby by a man she would never see again. I couldn't change that outcome, it was already history.

One thing I could change. In the morning I gathered my possessions into my sea bag, rolled my bindle, and went down to breakfast. A lonely meal. Mrs. Dessault, eyes red with crying all night, set porridge in front of me and fled the kitchen. I ate, not with appetite, but with a heavy heart. I went to the leather shop where I knew I would find Amibel.

"Mr. Dessault. I want you to measure my feet for a pair of quality boots. They will be paid from the money Mr. McTavish gives you as an advance for my room and board. I will pick up the finished boots in two weeks."

He did as requested without ever looking at me, nor did he ask any questions. I shouldered my sea bag, tucked the bindle under my arm, and walked from the shop.

"Duncan, what has upset you? Your face is a story by itself."

"Mr. Lachlan, I hardly know where to begin. I must get in touch with Mr. McTavish at once. Will you excuse me to go to his office?"

"Of course, go now."

Minutes later I climbed the stairs to my uncle's office. When I stepped inside Mr. LaGorce was at his desk. "Well, Duncan, this a surprise. Have you a letter you wish me to post?"

"No, sir, I wish to see Mr. McTavish as soon as he is available."

"He is with another gentleman, but I shall slip a note on his desk."

Uncle Simon needs only the basic story, details need not concern him at this time. I went through what I planned to say for the second time when the door to his office opened. He beckoned me to enter. "Yes, Duncan, what is it?"

His brusque manner and scowling face told me all I needed to know. He was not in the mood for a personal problem. I gave the shortest yet most complete review of the past twenty-four hours. He sat back in his big leather chair and looked at me with steely, blue eyes. Eyes that did more than see, they were like pumps that drew the whole story from me. He listened as I poured out accounts of the night of Nathan's departure and my encounter with the priest. Then followed a long pause lasting a full five minutes.

"Duncan, this is what we will do. You will not go back to Amibel Dessault for your new boots. I will send one of my men to fetch them. That was clever thinking given the strain and tension of your situation. I commend you for that. But our problem is not boots, it is a place for you to sleep and to eat, is it not?"

"Yes, sir. I am upset in bringing this problem to you, but I had to since you made the arrangements with the Dessaults."

"Wait in Mr. LaGorce's office while I write a few notes."

Notes to be delivered to whom? Was I merely a piece of baggage to be shunted around Montreal? I turned over in my mind what I had learned of Montreal and what places I might find for living quarters. So far the basics, room and board, were taken care of by my uncle. Now the basics might be my problem, and I had no answers.

Uncle Simon came out from his office, handed Mr. LaGorce several pieces of paper, nodded in my direction, and returned to his office. I continued to sit while the secretary read the papers, added something to them, studied them again, and finally said to me, "Duncan, you are to go to the address on this note, show it to Mr. Dobell, and he will inform you as to where he will give you meals and shelter. Understood?"

"I don't know, Mr. LaGorce. I am very confused."

"Mr. Dobell has helped Mr. McTavish in the past. I know your uncle would not place you in a bad situation."

It took me an hour to locate Mr. Dobell at the address on the note I clutched in my hand. Mr. Dobell was pleasant man who took me to the third floor of his house to a room which, though small, was adequate and private. He told me to drop my bag and bindle and follow him down to the ground floor. We passed through a large kitchen. I discovered later that it prepared the food for an 'eating club' of Montreal businessmen in another building abutting the one where I would be staying. In a corner of the kitchen he pointed to a table where he said I would be served breakfast and supper.

Not exactly homey atmosphere, but it took care of my immediate concerns and, like arrangements with the Dessaults, paid for by my uncle.

I settled into this new living arrangement and was back working with Mr. Lachlan as though nothing had happened. Three days later another break in my routine came suddenly. Called to Mr. Lachlan's office, I was introduced to a Mr. Grovier. He was a young man in his early twenties, stylishly dressed, and as frosty as his assumed manner and put-on airs would permit.

"You will come with me, Mr. Ross. Do not walk beside me, but follow two paces behind."

"Yes, Mr. Grovier."

He walked the streets of Montreal as though on a regimental parade ground. I found it difficult to suppress my laughter as we turned into a tailor's shop. We were greeted by a round little man with glasses perched on the end of his nose and a smile frozen on his features.

"Ah, Monsieur Grovier, a pleasure to see you, sir. And how may I serve you?"

"This young man, as you can see, very much needs to be clothed in a suit appropriate to his place as clerk to Mr. Simon McTavish who will recompense you for the selections I shall make for this lad from the old country."

Led to a room at the back of the shop, I was stripped to my skivvies, measured from top to bottom, side to side. Bored with what was presented as proper for a clerk by the shop owner, Mr. Grovier departed for a coffee house. As the door closed behind him, Mr. Marx said to me, "Quickly, now, my lad. Pick from these bolts of material what you would like for your coat and britches. I can help you to put together a fine outfit and, once it is made, our uppity Mr. Grovier will never know. Mr. McTavish would not want his clerk to be dressed as a man who helps to lay people away to their final rest."

We both smiled and in no time I made my selections. Mr. Marx said I should return in two days for a 'fitting' before he did the final trimming and stitching.

"I was detained at work and could not come to your shop. Am I too late for a fitting?"

"No. Go in the back room and strip off your street clothes, and let's see what I have made for you."

Was I ever pleased! In place of the rusty brown material Mr. Grovier had selected, Mr. Marx made the coat in a light gray with britches of navy blue. He added two shirts and three stocks to the wardrobe and suggested at least two pair of stockings. He supplied what he called a *cassette*, I would have called it a *valise*. Mr. Marx said a *cassette* was practically water-tight, but I never thought to ask him why that was important.

Look at me! I had quarters downtown, I had a downtown wardrobe, I was beginning to savor some downtown tastes - my meals were the same as those served to the gentlemen in the grand dining room next door. I did not have a downtown income. Not yet, I said to myself, but that time is coming!

The first time - a gorgeous day in late April - I wore my new clothing to work I was greeted with cat-calls, snide remarks, and some genuine expressions of favor. I was as much in the dark as my fellow clerks; even Mr. Lachlan appeared not to know anything. About a week later I was summoned to Mr. McTavish.

As usual I waited in his outer office, exchanged friendly greetings with Mr. LaGorce, but could not gain any hint as to why this call to my uncle's office. Patience, Duncan, my father would have said, patience.

"Come in," was my uncle's brusque command. What had I done? This is no way for one Scot to greet another, I thought.

"Good day to you, sir, I wish to thank . . ."

"Duncan, we have no time for pleasantries. I am removing you from your work with Mr. Lachlan. Every day from tomorrow on you will report to Mr. LaGorce and carry out the tasks he will give you.

"I have decided that in May, as soon as travel on the rivers and lakes resumes, you will accompany me to Grand Portage for the Company's annual *Rendezvous*. You will serve as my secretary as we travel to and from our central depot. While there I expect you will be available to me whenever I have need of papers or records, and above all, to take notes in the meetings I will hold with my partners at the *Rendezvous*.

"We are together for such a short time, and we have a mountain of work to be completed in only three weeks. Understood? Fine! Now, off with you. Get a good night's rest, for I guarantee you will work as you have never worked before."

He clapped me on the back as he ushered me out all the while telling Mr. LaGorce to have a small desk and chair placed in the outer office first thing in the morning.

One phrase spoken in Mr. McTavish's office rang again and again in my memory, ". . . as soon as travel on the rivers and lakes resumes."

I knew what I must do, write a letter to my family. When the ice disappeared, and that could be any day now, ships tied in at the docks in Montreal would be moving. Some would go to England with mail pouches of the NWC on board.

"Mr. LaGorce, could I trouble you for pen and paper? I must get a letter to my family in Scotland. I suspect Grand Portage would not be a good place to send out mail."

He complied immediately, and this is what I wrote:

Dear Father and Mother and Louise

In a few days, as soon as the ice is out of the river here in Montreal, ships will be leaving for Europe. I want to have a letter on its way to you in time to catch the first vessel out bound. I am well, and have gone through a very cold winter, but am ready for another year of work with Uncle Simon.

This morning he informed me that I am to become his secretary and make the trip from Montreal to Grand Portage for the annual Rendezvous of the Company. This is a time in the year when all the partners who make up the NWC, the wintering partners and the agents from Montreal, can be together. The Rendezvous only lasts about three weeks. Uncle Simon told me I will be busier than any time since coming to Montreal.

I hope this letter finds you all in good health, and that you have plenty of food and a supply of peats for the cold days and nights. Many things have happened in my time as an apprentice, but none of them are the equal of being told by Uncle Simon that I will be making this trip to Grand Portage. My love to all.

Your obedient and loving son.
Duncan.

A Return Visit

Northfield, MN
November, 2000

Working away at the PC, I was not aware that Duncan Ross was in my office until the desk chair beside me moved.

"You frighten rather easily, don't you? I am here to see what you have done with my account of arriving in Montreal to begin my apprenticeship."

"Yes, you did give me a scare, Mr. Ross. As for the draft I put together after our first meeting, it is just a draft. A spell check is the only thing left to get it into final shape."

"Balls of fire, man! Are you not proud of a little creative spelling? I have spelled many a word my way and I cannot recall a person who did not understand my meaning. Let me see the draft."

He relaxed in his chair and began to read what I had written. From time to time he went back and reread parts of the draft. I tried to get some idea of how he received my efforts, but his face revealed nothing.

"This will do for now, Mr. Reiley. At a later date you may have to rework it. Get your paper and pen. I am going to take you back to the Highlands to give you a glimpse of my boyhood there."

I had a hard time keeping up with his story. It poured out in a variety of expressions; some with humor, some with sadness, and all with a touch of longing for the land of his birth.

Chapter Two

Like many who claim the Highlands of Scotland as their true home, I proudly exhibit the banners and badges of my ancestors, yet I have been back to my home only once since leaving for the New World.

We lived in the hills of the western part of the Highlands on a small croft (people in Canada would say farm). The nearest village to our cottage was about three miles to the south, the place where my father had his shop and work rooms. When I sailed for Canada it was from the little port of Dundas twenty miles to the west of that village. The breeze that blew through our part of the country came off the moors and mountains - the Highlands. The breeze was invariably cool, cold, or freezing. One of the factors that made my transition to the New World relatively easy was the seasoning the weather gave me.

My formal schooling began at age eight under Wilford MacQuay. Our teacher worked with eleven boys; four were older, three younger, and four were of my age. Our school was not much more than a stone hut with a thatched roof, a small fireplace, a water bucket, a dozen crude desks and benches, and several pieces of slate.

Outside was a bit of a school yard, a 'necessary', and a wood pile plus - if someone in the community felt generous - a few blocks of peat.

We all thought of Mr. MacQuay as an old man. Actually he was fifty-six years of age. It was the limp he walked with that made us think of him as old. His threadbare, shiny black coat and britches did nothing to give a hint of youth to his appearance. My father said, "Duncan, it is not polite to talk of another's infirmities."

"Yes, sir. But Mr. MacQuay walks with such a noticeable limp. Why is that?"

"When he was a lad of four, a soldier from the Duke of Cumberland's army gave him a saber slash on his foot while he was hiding in a tree."

"Why? Did he steal something from the army?"

"No. Mr. MacQuay's family had fought against the Duke at the Battle of Culloden. When the battle was lost to the English, the Scots had to flee for their lives. The Duke had them hunted down like dogs."

"Father, is that why we do not like the English very much?"

He did not answer, but went on to tell me more about my teacher. Mr. MacQuay was married at one time with a small family. His wife and young son died in the frightful winter that swept the Highlands in '86.

With all these unhappy events in his life, he was not a bitter man. He worked very successfully, I think, with his unruly pack of cubs. His resources were limited, but his vast store of personal knowledge and experience were ours to benefit from, if we wanted. Mr. MacQuay had managed to get two years at the University in Edinburgh, and that experience, too, was placed at our disposal.

I looked forward to school. One area that captivated me was geography, I liked to study maps and charts. Mr. MacQuay had a friend at the University who loaned him some valuable charts. I was one of the two boys asked to remain after class on several afternoons to study with him these fascinating pieces of work. They left me with more questions than answers.

"Mr. MacQuay, why is there so much blank space on this map of North America? Here where I am pointing, this space in the central part of Canada. Why?"

"The part you are pointing to on very old maps of the New World was labeled with the legend, 'Here Be Dragons'. It discouraged explorations and covered the map maker's lack of precise knowledge. But to answer your question, Duncan, it is blank because nobody really knows what to put in that space."

"Hasn't anybody ever been there?"

"I have been told that fur traders are operating there."

"I thought blank space on a map meant an area of ice and snow."

"No, Duncan. Someday fur traders will find a man who knows this vast area and will draw maps of it for them. Perhaps you should try to answer your own question. Fur traders must have someone to trade with, don't they? Wouldn't you think some Indians must inhabit those spaces?"

"Well, I don't think I would like to live where nobody knows where he is. That is much too scary for me."

Edmund Ross, my father, was highly skilled in leather and working in light metals. He did not copy the work of others; he had his own designs fixed in his mind and the skills to bring them to life. The independence in his way of crafting his wares was very much a part of his view of life - a balance of independence and of responsibility. Edmund Ross was a family man, and a respected man in his community. He was his own man - open, honest, but prickly as a Scottish thistle.

My father divided my week into thirds: three days to school, three days to help him in his shop, one day to the Lord. I had no problem with that, I liked working with my father. I liked the environment of his shop and work rooms. Men came from many different parts of the Western Highlands when they had need of his finely crafted items in leather or metal. Listening to these men, watching as they did their business with my father, and how he dealt with them was part of my education. Of course as a mere lad, I was not aware that I was learning just as much here as I was in my school. It was a realization that came to me many years later that my father was a good teacher.

School was more than just books. It was also on learning how to get along. I knew right off I should never pick on the three younger boys, but the four my age were boys I felt I could handle if any wanted to challenge me. The four older boys were my unknowns, much like a problem in our classes in mathematics when we looked for the elusive 'X'. Some of the older boys had learned lessons from being in Mr. MacQuay's classes for several years, and he had them work with the four my age as sort of tutors while he worked with the three youngest.

Stern discipline made his system work. He did not see, perhaps he did not want to see, all the little pokes and jabs exchanged as we pored over lessons. Rory McBride was assigned by the school master to tutor me. He was two years or so older and seemed to have a pick on me. I responded in kind at every opportunity. Rory and I soon fell into an undeclared war. One day in the school yard it broke into open warfare when I tackled him to pay back for an unusually hard punch in the ribs. Rory was older, taller, and heavier, but I had the advantage of surprise. I found myself picked up by the scruff of the neck, stood on my feet while the same was being done to Rory. Like two bantam roosters we glared at each other while Mr. MacQuay shook the starch out of us. At the end of the day the other boys were dismissed, Rory and I were detained.

In the school yard we both were surprised by the strength and quickness of Mr. MacQuay as he responded to our tussle; now we were surprised by his calm manner as he spoke to us.

"I am not going to lecture, I am not going to exact punishment, but by the Great Harry, I want you two to know of my keen disappointment over your fighting. And don't try to tell me this is the way Highlanders settle their differences. I hope to God you never learn what real fighting is like. Veterans who survived Culloden and the '45 can tell you. You two put on an exhibition worthy of a pair of grub worms. You are both good students and have so much you can teach each other, and even learn from each other."

"But, Mr. MacQuay, how can I learn when Rory is always jabbing me in the ribs?"

"He lies, Mr. MacQuay. Duncan lies."

"Enough from both of you, enough! Do you hear me? If you want me to knock knowledge into your thick heads I can do that. If you want to work with me I can implant it without pain. The choice is yours. But make it quickly, I have no time for dullards."

An uneasy truce descended on the relations between Rory and me. He learned that I had an easy time with numbers and figuring, he knew far more than me about spelling and writing. Deal making came easily to both; we traded our skills frequently. The truce became a sort of friendship, and it lasted through the rest of the school year. Mr. MacQuay never said another word to us about the way things worked out. Is it possible he sensed what I was slow to realize? That Rory's change toward me reflected his attraction to my sister, Louise.

Did I mention the taciturn moods of my father? The trips I made with him on our way to his shop in the village were usually three miles made in total silence. The return trip in the evening was just as silent. We rode in his pony cart. It really wasn't a pony, but a tough, mean-spirited, little horse that pulled it.

My sister more than made up for the lack of conversation with father. She liked to express herself on everything and everybody, but only to me. I returned her confidences. She relished the idea there was someone to share her inner most thoughts with, even if it had to be with a younger brother!

"You know, Duncan, you are the only person I have to talk with. Father never has very much to say, and Mother is naturally a very quiet person. If I didn't have you to share my thoughts I think I would explode."

"I feel the same, Louise, especially about Father. Did you ever wonder why he is so close-mouthed?

"I think we should draw up a compact and promise never to tell anyone all the things we tell each other. Agreed?"

"Agreed."

"Now, why is Mother not out in her garden this spring? She gives more and more of its care to you. Why?"

"Oh, Duncan, she is not well."

"Louise, I can see that. Something is wrong with her, isn't there? What is it?"

"It's female problems, you wouldn't understand. But I can tell you they leave her very weak and listless. That is why I do more of her work."

"Does Father know?"

"I don't know what he knows; he keeps so much to himself. I really can't tell if he is aware of Mother's problems."

"They seem so easy and relaxed when they are together and concerned when they are apart. Father has to know."

"I hope so. Now, little brother, I heard something you are not aware of, and I won't tell you unless you agree to hunt the eggs for the rest of the month. Promise?"

"No. I'll hunt the eggs for the rest of this week. Deal?"

"No deal, Duncan. You can stay in the dark about what I know is going to happen to you."

"I bet if old Rory McBride knew something you wanted to know, you wouldn't make a dumb egg deal with him."

"I wouldn't have to. Some day I am going to marry Rory McBride. Now, what do you have to say about that?"

"Poor Rory. I'll tell him what's in store for him. Maybe he'll run off and join the British Navy."

"Don't you dare! I'll tell him how you cried when Father and Uncle Thomas wouldn't take you with them when they went to hunt deer last winter."

And so it went. We teased and baited each other, but in the end we usually shared. There is another part to my sister's story I wanted you to know. Louise was a nice looking maiden with lots of dark hair always neatly done up, flashing eyes, and a wide smile. Louise loved to dance, and she was a very good dancer. Mother came from a family where dancing was performed with style and precision. Mostly they danced the old, traditional steps and flings of the Highlands. To them, not to do the steps and moves in the proper order and form was unpardonable. Most of the boys in my school would hoot at me if they knew I, too, could do some of the dances taught to me by my mother and sister. Where else was a man to learn how to dance?

To this day I cannot tell you much about my mother, Naomi MacGruder Ross. I first knew the meaning of love from her. She was not a demonstrative or effusive woman, she was just herself. Love emanated from her like the glow of a candle in the dark of night. I remember that words like 'calm' and 'serene' best describe her. From this woman came the strength and resolve that Louise and I would carry all our lives.

Where, then, did my combativeness and testiness come from? Certainly not from my mother. Could it be from my father, from a part I never saw displayed? Buried deep within him were the same urges that drove me. He masked his drives, I could not.

I trudged home from school one afternoon to find two big, beautiful riding horses tied to the post at our cottage. They were magnificent animals. The saddles, bridles, and stirrup straps had the look of well-tended leather and the smell of money. To whom did they belong, and why were they in front of our place?

I slipped into the house through the kitchen - we only used the front door on special occasions. My mother, seated at her usual place in the rocking chair near the fireplace, gave me her biggest smile and hinted I might find an oat cake waiting for me on the table. I was not quick enough.

"Duncan, come into the parlor. We have a guest who wants to meet you."

I did as ordered, partly in response to my father's command, and partly out of curiosity. "Duncan, this is Simon McTavish from Montreal. He would like to have a few words with you."

I made my duties to this imposing man who shook hands with me in a solemn manner and asked me to sit near him. What was this all about? Was he hard of hearing? Did he have failing eyesight? I had never seen a man quite like this Mr. McTavish. He reminded me of the horses tied outside the cottage - he looked and smelled of money. His clothes were certainly expensive as was the large ring on a finger of his right hand. The aroma that clung to him that was not of peat or damp moor grass, but was something strange and not unpleasant. His eyes made me look down at my shoes, they were the bluest and sharpest eyes I have ever looked into. I could only think of an eagle or a hawk with eyes as disturbing.

"Duncan, I would like you to address me as Uncle Simon. As you are about to learn, we are of the same clan."

"Yes, sir. I mean, yes, Uncle Simon."

I wondered what it was that drew me to this man. Did he intimidate me, did he merely impress me, or was I just a school boy in awe of a stranger? Rapid-fire instructions from Uncle Simon brought me back into focus. When I hesitated to respond, a glance from my father confirmed that my newly discovered uncle was in charge.

"I want you to take these pieces of paper, get a pen and an inkwell, place yourself at this table (the small one in the parlor holding the family Bible), and write down these figures in their correct columns as I call them to you."

Doing exactly as directed, I wrote as quickly as ever in my life. Mr. McTavish fed me a stream of values expressed in pounds, shillings, and pence, and I was to record them, add them, reduce them and write down my answers. Then he had me calculate percentages as he called out various combinations. Uncle Simon took the paper from me and in a flash had scanned my work.

"You make very neat figures, Duncan, and I see no errors in your additions or percentages. Now, on the back of the piece of paper I want you to write this letter as I dictate it to you. Ready?"

"Yes, Uncle Simon."

Again I found myself writing at top speed. He took that paper, scanned it just as quickly as he had looked at my numbers, and had the same comment.

"You do neat work, Duncan, very neat, indeed. Do you have any idea why I had you perform these exercises?"

"No, sir."

"I am a man of business, my lad, and I speak in numbers as well as words. The accuracy of either of my languages is most important. Now do you understand?"

"I think I do, Uncle Simon, but if I may ask, sir, just what business are you in?"

"Certainly you may ask, Duncan. I like to see curiosity in a young man, but only to a point. I am in the fur trading business. Really, I should call it an industry, for there are so many differing parts to it. Fur trades are only a part of what I do. I must ship and insure my peltries, I must buy and ship hundred of items of trade goods, I must hire men, I must buy canoes, and I buy huge quantities of food to keep the whole system running year round. Now, do you understand what I do?"

"Yes, but I had no idea fur trading was so complicated, Uncle Simon."

"In order for me to do all those things I must have help. That is why I am in Scotland. I want to engage the services of a young man to work with me as an apprentice in Montreal. Have you questions, son?"

"Yes, sir, I do. What is an apprentice?"

My answer was a short burst of laughter followed by a lengthy explanation of the three year period of training and work I would be expected to do for his company. He said it was the North West Fur Company, and that it operated all over the north-central portions of North America.

Hold on, here! Isn't this the very area of all the blank space on the maps Mr. MacQuay had shown me a month ago? Uncle Simon may be a clan member, but I'll be damned if he is going to get me into a place where nobody knows where they are. No sir, not me!

"Your father and I have discussed the details of the apprenticeship I have in mind for you. I want you to write a letter to me saying you will, or will not, accept my offer. Your letter, Duncan, will be like a contract between us. Understood? Fine!"

With that final statement, I was dismissed to start my evening chores. Wait 'til I tell Louise I have to write a contract. I really wanted to be in the parlor listening to this domineering man talk more about his business, not in this little, old barn. 'Punky,' my sister's name for our little horse, was not as interesting as this well-dressed man from Montreal, and I'll bet Uncle Simon wouldn't bite you the way this devil liked to do when your back was turned.

"Come, Duncan, Mr. McTavish is leaving. Come bid him goodbye."

Where did this huge man who appeared at the side of the horses come from? He must have been in the lean-to thrown up at one side of the barn, the place father used to store his leathers and choice pieces of wood for use in his shop. He was Mr. McTavish's 'out-rider'. We were peaceful people here in the western Highlands, but there was always the temptation to rob a prosperous traveler. An outrider was good insurance, backed up by the big handgun thrust in the man's waist band and the short barreled gun carried in his right stirrup boot.

The four of us stood about the horses as the out-rider made last minute adjustments. Without further ado, he made a hand for Mr. McTavish and boosted the stout man into his saddle. Suddenly there was my sister Louise with a tray on which three small glasses filled with what I knew to be my father's best whisky - the color was the clue. Mr. McTavish, the rider, and my father raised their glasses in salute and knocked back the precious liquid. A final round of handshakes, a few words of God's speed, the promise of a letter within a week, and they were off, cantering down the road toward our village.

The three Rosses, father, daughter, and son, stood in the road until the mounted men had disappeared. I ventured the remark, "Father, Uncle Simon does not sit a horse well, does he?"

His reply was cuff along the side of my head but it was only a gesture, it carried no force. A quick glance showed my father suppressing a smile. He nodded his head at the barn and I resumed my chores.

A few nights after Uncle Simon's visit my father called us to discuss this apprenticeship matter. Father added some of the details I missed when sent to the barn. If I accepted this offer, and Father confirmed it was an offer, I would leave for Montreal in the spring. I would go to Dundas where I would board a ship and, if all went well, would be in Montreal in six weeks. There my uncle would have a place for me to stay with a bed and two meals, and my laundry. I would work six days a week and be paid eighty pounds sterling a year. Ten percent of my pay would be sent home to my father to make up for the loss of my help on the little farm and in his business. Another ten percent would be kept by Mr. McTavish and invested in my name (but it would not become my money until I had completed three years of satisfactory work). The remainder was mine to spend as I pleased. Sixty-four pounds sterling! Never in my life had I imagined such a great sum of money could be mine.

My mother's voice broke through my day dreaming to say, "Edmund, our son will be gone from us for three unbroken years. What happens if he does good work, as I know he will, what is next for Duncan?"

"Why, I reckon, Mr. McTavish will offer him full-time work in his North West Company. The idea behind an apprenticeship is to train a young man so he becomes useful to the company. I imagine he would stay in Montreal."

"But, Edmund, it sounds like Duncan has done something wrong and is being taken from us as punishment. I don't like this apprentice thing."

"This is not punishment, my dear. It is an opportunity for Duncan, don't you see that?"

"How can you call that an opportunity? To take a young boy out of his home and send him hundreds and hundreds of miles from his family. I just don't understand."

"We must look at it this way, Naomi. Our son does very well with his figures and his writing, and he reads with confidence. What chance will he have in the Highlands to put those talents to use?"

"Your work is honest and respectable, Edmund, why can't Duncan work with you everyday? He can continue the business you have started. Many boys follow in their father's footsteps. Isn't that honorable?"

"Of course it is honorable, but it has no future, Naomi. Everyday in my shop I hear men talk of coal mines, iron mines, furnaces and forges, of machinery to make all kinds of goods. What I make with my hands will not have a market. Then what is Duncan to do?"

"I want Duncan to have a future as much as anyone, but does it have to be so far from home?"

"We will talk again in a day or two, but in the meantime, I don't want this discussed outside of this room."

My father's imposed silence was obeyed, of course, but I was near to bursting at school to blurt out what I might be doing. It wasn't just Father who stoppered my mouth, it was knowing I couldn't make up my mind. This leaving home for such a long time was hard to deal with, and I found myself wishing I didn't have to be the one to decide.

On the hillside above our cottage was a shelter made by some of my ancestors as they guarded their sheep and cattle. An overhang of rocks formed a shallow open-mouthed cave and people had piled loose rocks on the downhill side to give protection from the winds that never stopped blowing over this rugged land. The view remained unimpaired and the silence and solace of this place led me to think of it as my private retreat. I might have guessed Louise had also discovered this spot, and I was really not surprised when she slipped into the little cave and sat down beside me. Fifteen minutes went by without her saying anything, an unusual event, but when she started to talk, it came out in a torrent.

"Duncan, I just know you are going to tell Mr. McTavish you will accept his offer. I am right, aren't I?"

"No, Louise, you are not right. I think I am going to tell Mr. McTavish 'no'."

"You can't do that, you silly ass, you must accept his offer."

"Why, Miss High and Mighty, must I do what you say? This is my problem, and my solution."

"Your answer tells me you are not thinking straight. Can't you see you must get away from here. There's no future in the Highlands for you or for any of us. Open your eyes!"

"My eyes are open, but what do you see that I can't see?"

"You know the English are still driving our people off their lands, even burning their cottages. Many of them forced to leave the country with no chance of ever returning. Open your eyes, Duncan, open them!"

"What I see, Louise, is that I must stay and help Father. That is what a son is expected to do."

"Who expects that? Did Father say so? Did Mother say so? Where do you get this idea of 'being expected' to stay?"

"I know that is what a son is expected to do. It's the Highlands way."

"I'll tell you what the Highlands way is, Mr. Duncan Ross. It is to go to America, make some money, and bring it back so you can pay a doctor to examine Mother and treat her illness. She may have to go to Glasgow to see a real doctor, maybe even to Edinburgh. That will take a lot of money."

"But if I stay and help Father the two of us can make a lot of money right here."

"The two of you working together can never make the kind of money we will need to get the very best doctor for Mother. You would want her to have the best, wouldn't you?"

"Of course I would. Now you have gone and muddled my thinking, and I must write that letter to Uncle Simon."

"Good, you need to be muddled. You must give some thought to your mother's condition before you write that letter."

With that argument ringing in my ears, she was gone as silently as she had come. I lingered in my retreat trying to sort through all the reasons for and against going to Montreal.

By peering over the rocks I could look down on our croft. It was my home, where my father and mother and sister lived. Only a few miles away was my school, a few miles the other way was my father's shop, and in a third direction still only a few miles away was our little church. My whole world was in sight, and I was thinking of leaving all of this? It couldn't be put off any longer. I slid and stumbled down the steep hill to write a letter.

"Duncan, have you made a final decision?"

"Father, I want to know what Mother is thinking."

"I have already expressed my doubts and concerns of the many years Duncan will be away from us, but, Edmund, I am willing to have Duncan go to Montreal."

"My dear, I can only agree with your thinking. It is an opportunity. What do you think, Louise?"

"You know I have been in favor of his going ever since you explained how this apprenticeship thing works. I will miss him, Father, but he must go."

My father suggested I make my letter to Mr. McTavish brief and direct saying that I would be most happy to accept his offer and would await his instructions as to when I should go to Dundas. This I did. By the end of the month I had a return from Uncle Simon telling what I should be prepared to do. Only after the reply from uncle did Father give his permission for me to tell Mr. MacQuay and to let my friends in on my secret.

"Duncan, you are so very fortunate to have this opportunity come your way. I give you joy on this most wonderful event in your young life."

"Thank you, Mr. MacQuay. I am anxious to get started on my way to Montreal."

"I appreciate your enthusiasm, my lad, but your father informed me that you are to remain in school until the end of April. Don't you think we should try to learn more about the country you will be going to?"

"Remember the maps you showed us last year, and all the blank space in the center of several of them? How can we learn of something that is only a blank?"

"Well, Duncan, we know fur traders are in that area at this very minute. Why don't we try to find out all we can about the fur trade?"

That is what we did. I was amazed at how much Mr. MacQuay could find to teach us. I never knew that fishermen from Europe -

France, Spain, Portugal, Sweden, England, Denmark, Italy - had been trading with natives on the Atlantic coastal parts of Canada for their pelts for over two hundred years. I think Mr. MacQuay called those parts New Foundland and Nova Scotia. It is well that Mr. MacQuay kept my mind so occupied, for I would have lost my enthusiasm and curiosity had he not spurred me along.

Routines at home also helped time pass. My father thought of chores I should attend to: re-thatch the leaks in the barn roof, pick stone by the ton from the little patches and fields my father tilled, and work on the fences which for as long as I remember always needed work. My mother, with Louise helping, went over my clothing: let out seams, darned holes and worn places, patched tears, and somehow found time to add a new shirt and trowes to my meager stock of wearables. I was not going to the New World as a well-dressed dandy but as what I was - a country boy from a loving home with hardly a farthing in his pocket.

As the final days of April dripped into May, Father became even more silent and withdrawn. Louise was quite the opposite, she chattered endlessly. I realized she was just trying to conceal her concerns and sense of loss of the one person in whom she could confide. Mother was just being Mother, outwardly cheerful, never revealing her deep thoughts and worries to anyone.

My last evening at home was normal. There was no special supper, no special reading from the family Bible, no special attempts at conversation, no special prayers before being sent off to bed. This was the way the Edmund Ross family would handle the first break in the family circle.

Mother led me to the sea bag already packed and sitting at the foot of my bed. She handed me a piece of folded plaid in the tartan of the McTavish clan. It was about two feet square, and the cut edges had been carefully stitched in a fine bit of work.

"Keep this with you always, Duncan. There is room in your bag for it. This tartan will help fix in your heart and mind who you are, where you came from, and the family you are leaving behind. Be proud of your roots; many good people fought and died to keep our piece of the Highlands. You are a part of this heritage, Duncan. I know you will never do anything to dishonor it. Go with my blessings. Go with God."

Our embrace was long and silent, no tears. I pushed myself away slowly and looked into her eyes as she looked into mine. No words need be said, our message flowed to one another with our eyes. We understood as only a mother and son could understand.

That last night I slept not a wink. When my father called at first light of dawn, I was dressed and ready. In the barn I threw the gear on little Punky, hooked him to the cart and led him to the kitchen door. Mother and Louise stood there as Father and I got in the cart, he took the reins, gave a 'cluck' and we jounced down the lane to the road leading to our village. One look back, one quick wave. Was that all there was to leaving home?

My father drove as always, in silence, yet alert to everything that moved or made a sound. At the village, a nod of the head and I unhooked Punky, stripped him of his gear, put it in the shed attached to my father's shop, and led the little horse to pasture.

We had no trouble locating the drovers I was to join all the way to Dundas. The sounds of cattle being roused, of men breaking camp, throwing their bindles onto the wagon that also served as the grub wagon and carry-all. These sounds plus the odors of milling cattle brought us to their site like a beacon. My bindle and bag tossed on the wagon, I was introduced to the lead drover. He was of my father's school of few words. On the trek to Dundas he and I seldom spoke. I knew what to do. I cut a switch from a nearby tree and took a position in the line of drovers. This was it? I was leaving without another word from my father? But I was wrong. At the last moment he stepped forward, took me in a firm embrace loaded with meaning. Before this morning, my father had never embraced me, ever! He turned quickly and retraced his steps to his shop.

I followed the example of the man to my left in the line and gave a switch to the heifer in front of me. She acknowledged my direction by lifting her tail and initiating my boots to the reality of cattle droving. This, then, was my departure from the Highlands: my head held high and stuffed with dreams, my stomach empty because of nerves that kept me from eating for the past twenty-four hours, my boots cased in dung.

We drove the cattle to the edge of the village of Dundas and the head drover nodded at the carry-all wagon. I retrieved my blanket roll and sea bag. No farewells, no wishes of good luck, no sign of anything from the men I had accompanied the past four cold and dreary days. I struck out immediately for the water front, someone there would know of a vessel ready to clear port for Montreal. When I got to water's edge and looked over the bay, not a sail was in sight, nothing was tied in at the single dock in this village, and few people were moving about. Now wasn't that a pretty kettle of fish? I didn't know a single person, all I had was the name Brian Flemming, Mr. McTavish's agent in Dundas.

Can you believe my good fortune? Brian Flemming was the first man I met. He watched me walk down the hill to the bay and guessed from my not-too-clean clothing and my dung covered boots I must have come off a cattle drive.

"So you are Duncan Ross, the young man I am expecting. The vessel which you are to board is overdue in Dundas. I was told there were some violent storms south along the coast toward England, and that is the direction the *Virginia Planter* will be coming from."

"That is bad news, Mr. Flemming. Have you any place you can send me where I might find a hay loft, some place to spread my blanket roll, and a place to buy a loaf of bread? I have a few coins in my britches."

"Duncan, you are of the clan of McTavish. You will come home with me and welcome be. Come along."

We walked a short distance back from the water front to a long, low building with a small house set off to the side. Mr. Flemming called to his wife working in the garden, "Ethyl, we have a visitor. This is the young man Simon McTavish is sending over to Montreal. I can imagine he is hungry, Ethyl, what do you think we might do about that?"

What Ethyl thought was quickly transferred into action. Mr. Flemming led me back of the house, had me strip off my coat, stock, shirt, and boots. I washed in a basin of water he drew from the well, and did what he suggested - leave my boots outside. Inside a warm and cheery kitchen greeted me and a bowl of hearty lamb stew set in front of me.

"Eat up, young man, you look a bit peaked. Did you not have much to eat with the drovers? Were they good to you, lad? I'll have a word with the head drover if there was something amiss."

"No, Mr. Flemming. I was treated fairly, and we did have food, but the cooking of it was not so good. I think the men got more from a jug than they did from the meals they cooked. I appreciate what you and Mrs. Flemming are doing for me."

"Well, we wouldn't want Mr. McTavish to think we do not know how to look after our own, would we? You will stay right here with us until we can get you aboard the ship."

"That is most kind of you. Is there not something I could help you with? I had many chores to do at home, and I would like to give you a hand if there is a bit of work I can do."

The Flemmings were as good as their word, and I was as good as mine. In the morning I helped Mr. Flemming in his storage shed next to the house. In the afternoon we walked to the bay where he learned that a ship had been sighted off the south coast.

"She appears to be waiting for a change in the winds, Brian, before making port."

"Can you tell who she might be, David?"

"No. She's standing out too far. I can tell you she's a three master, and is being smartly handled. But I no can make a name on her."

"I judge it will be morning before she will alter course to make port. Come Duncan, we will go back and get you packed, for it won't take long to get her loaded with my consignment to Montreal."

One more day, one more great meal, one more night in a real bed; gifts I really was most grateful for. In the morning I dressed and had my sea bag and bindle ready to go, eager to get on that ship and start my adventure to a new world.

"Not so fast, young man. I can see from here she has yet to make her moorings. You can take time for a bowl of porridge, can't you? It might be some time before you get porridge as good as what Mrs. Flemming makes. Eat hearty, Duncan, we have time enough."

When he put on his cap and picked up his cane I was right behind him, but first, my duties to Mrs. Flemming. She went through my outfit and washed and mended everything that needed attention. On the cattle drive we had rain most of the way and I had to change clothes often. I stumbled over my thanks, but she ended my confusion with a motherly hug and told me to run and catch up with Mr. Flemming.

As we hurried to the dock Mr. Flemming explained the many things done before a vessel was to put to sea again. She had to take on cargo, replenish her fresh water casks, possibly refit sails that were damaged in the recent storm, buy a few sheep, chickens, and perhaps a porker or two. An Atlantic crossing was a major undertaking. Dundas was her final port of call and all matters of her maintenance had to be looked after here. There were no options or refuges until we made the coast off Nova Scotia.

By the time we reached the harbor the *Virginia Planter* had docked. Surrounded with activity: shouts, oaths, orders, more oaths, running feet, straining backs - how did anyone know what was happening? Mr. Flemming seemed to take this in stride. He told me to step back, stay out of the way and watch. He led a small group of men from the vessel to his warehouse where they carried bales of tightly wrapped materials to the ship. He followed the last man, went aboard, and disappeared below deck to supervise the stowage of his cargo.

Well into the afternoon he motioned for me to follow him up the gangway to get settled into my cabin and meet the men I would travel with. A heated conversation between Mr. Flemming and a rough and coarse-talking man ended with me being taken below decks to a small, cramped cabin with two berths and not much more. I was to share this cubby-hole with the second mate. As a passenger I expected to have a cabin all to myself. I was then shown another small, cramped cabin where I would take my meals. So much for accommodations, now to meet the man who made this ship move where he directed.

"Duncan, this is Alfred Lorton. He is the captain of this vessel and you will respond to his directions at all times. That is the way of the sea."

"Welcome aboard, lad. Just stay out of the way, that's all I ask of you."

I took a few steps to the rail thinking I was out of the way only to be knocked off my feet by men who ran up the ropes where I was standing as though they were on level ground. The next I knew, they were high above me working on the sails under the direction of a short, powerfully built man who shouted orders and blew on a whistle - I had to learn to call it a 'pipe'. The sails unfurled and dropped from the spars, other men on deck pulled on ropes, at the front of the ship some men tramped about a wheel with spokes and sang as they worked, the captain bawled directions to men at the large wheel near the stern.

What now? Men on deck were busy coiling ropes, tying down anything that didn't move. They had a great time watching every move I made, or tried to make. Walking about on a sailing ship as she rolled from side to side working out from port with a stiff land breeze behind her comes with years of practice. I had none, and down I went. I had to crawl to the rail to hoist myself back to a standing position, but to do what? Or go where? Was I to spend all my time at sea holding onto something I did not even know the name of, afraid to make a move in any direction?

My interest was lost as was everything I had eaten for the past ten hours suddenly poured out. I must have fainted. My next conscious moment was in my bunk with a damp rag over my forehead, and the rough voice of the second mate telling me the first thing I should learn about ships at sea was the difference between 'lee' side and 'windward' side.

"I'll clean ye up once, mate, but only once. You gonna be sick again, git yerself topside and head for the lee rail."

He cleared out of our little cabin, and left me, mercifully, alone to gather myself and figure out how I would survive six weeks of this life at sea. A stream of images of home, of school, of my trek to Dundas with the drovers flowed through my mind, but they were mixed up with things not in their right places. I slept.

The second mate wakened me at dawn the morning following my collapse, led me on deck saying I needed fresh air.

"Take my arm while we stretch your limbs with a turn about deck. You can't lay in your bunk, mate, you gotta keep moving." We did a bunch of 'turns about the deck', and when he thought I had recovered my senses he took me below to the mess room off the galley.

"Mr. Skinner, we have a man dying of hunger. What can you do for him?"

The cook took over from the second mate and continued my recovery with a bowl of hot food and a crust of hard bread.

"Now, lad, eat slowly, but eat it all. You have a big hole in your gut to be filled. Eat!"

The stew was strange to my taste, but it was hot, it went down easily and, best of all, it stayed down. Between bites I looked around the cabin. It was simply a place where four men at one time could sit down for meals from the galley just a few feet away.

Robert Skinner, the cook, was the most broken up man I had ever seen. His face was pushed off to one side, his nose broken in several places, and his eyes looked in two directions at the same time - one to the east, the other to south. He walked with a limp and could not have weighed more than ninety pounds. His clothing was anything but clean, his hair and beard were months removed from any attention. Yet behind the grit and grime there must be a decent man. I finished eating, and made my way back to the deck.

More was communicated by hand signals, gestures, and blowing that odd sounding pipe than by oral commands. Not at all what I imagined life to be like on an ocean going vessel. I made my way across the deck to the railing, hung on to it and tested my new knowledge of shipboard basics - which was the lee side, which was windward. I walked to the waist ahead of the wheel and watched the man at the helm. He kept an eye on the compass mounted directly in front of the wheel and he constantly looked overhead to the set of the sails. His ears were cocked to the sound of the water rushing by the sides of the ship, the moaning of the wind as it spilled off the sails, and the sounds of wind whistling through the rigging. I was beginning to understand what the second mate told me in the galley, "Let the ship talk to you, she will tell you what you need to know."

By the fourth day I had explored nearly all of the vessel, managed to get about on deck without falling or lurching around. By the sixth day I was thinking I had mastered the routine.

"You there! You shit-eared land lubber. Come here!"

The master called to me from the door of his cabin. He motioned me inside, slammed the door and began shouting at me, "You will start to work this morning."

"There must be some mistake, my passage was paid for by Mr. Brian Flemming in Dundas."

"He didn't pay me near enough. You're going to work your way to Montreal."

"No sir, when we arrive in Montreal my uncle, Simon McTavish, will make up what is owing on my passage."

"You will do what I say. I don't give a shit who your uncle is. I say you will work out your passage."

"You don't understand, sir. I said my uncle will make up the difference."

"You smart talking, sniveling, snot-nosed brat. I am the master of this vessel, and what I say goes."

"I think you are making a mistake. My uncle . . . "

"Shut your mouth, you don't talk to me like that. You work, or I'll feed you to the fishes."

I started to walk out of his cabin when he grabbed me and dealt me a sharp slap across my face. I managed to keep my feet, but I couldn't move. He had locked an iron grip on me.

"Now, let's go over this one more time. You will work at whatever I tell you to do, or you'll never see Montreal and your uncle. Remember, them fishes get mighty hungry."

He shoved me out the door. The second mate was at the wheel with the helmsman and heard this exchange. When the door of the master's cabin slammed shut, he slipped over beside me, guided me to our cabin below, and stretched me out on the bunk. My head hurt. I never had a blow to the head like that. I must have passed out again. When I came to it was dark, and the vessel was rolling much more than this morning. I wasn't sick, I hurt. God, but my head hurt! I tried to get up, but a hand reached out of the darkness and pushed me back on the bunk.

"Lad, me and you, we gotta talk."

I recognized the voice of the second mate.

"You gotta accept what a ship's master says. On board, his word is law. There ain't one damn thing you can do about it. Wuz I you I'd wait 'til Montreal then maybe you can do something. But here on the briny, mate, you do what he says."

For the remainder of the voyage I did just that. I accepted and I performed. I did not question my orders, or question his judgment. In my mind I was making a note of every outrage, every blow, every onerous duty I was forced to carry out. Mostly he had me doing cabin and beneath deck duties like cleaning, serving, waiting on him, tending the few animals penned in squalid pens in the fore part of the ship. I never had to climb the rigging, or do any of the constant hauling and tugging at the lines.

After one terrifying storm came the bosun's call, "All hands on deck. All hands on deck."

By this time I knew I was included in an 'all hands' call. The bosun divided the crew in two gangs, one to man the pumps, the other to pound caulking. The violent storm had loosened a lot of the caulking between the planks of the hull and in some places the water was pouring into the ship. For more than two days without let-up we pounded and pumped; the whole crew was exhausted.

Watches set, duties went on, and the ship's master continued to be his normal, abusive, half-drunken self. I learned that he had been at sea from the age of twelve, that he was part-owner of this vessel, that he called Liverpool home, but was seldom there more than one month of the year. The sea was his life, this vessel was his only real home.

I can't say that the second mate, Garth Tucker, and I became friends. He continued to look after me in his rough manner and saved me from many an angry confrontation with the captain by knowing what I would be ordered to do next, then had me ready to jump when called. The cook and I spent more time together. In this ugly little man I felt I had a friend. He sneaked items from his galley to help fill my complaining gut. Being at sea gives one a great appetite but little chance to satisfy those hunger pains.

After our successful passage of the seas around the Gaspe Coast we couldn't seem to find the mouth of the St. Lawrence River. It took almost two weeks to do the final seven hundred miles up the river to reach Montreal.

Working a sailing vessel upstream in a river with the tremendous flow of water, the currents, the sandbars, and turns of the St.

Lawrence was extremely hard work. As his cabin boy, among my other duties, I was called to the ship master's post with the helmsman, "Ross, you no-good titty sucker, where the hell is my tea?"

"Cook can't get a fire going, the wood is soaked."

"You get me some hot tea, or I'll kick your ass over the main mast."

As the second mate said, you damn well better do what the Captain orders, he is the law. I did try to carry out every order, but things seemed to be working against us. The cook had to make fire with thoroughly soaked firewood and there was little of that left on board. Our supply of fresh water was extremely low. Men were put on half rations, there was little meat fit to eat, the supply of ship's biscuit was a feast only for weevils.

The rumblings of crew took on an ominous tone. As we managed to gain a few miles up river, and the visibility cleared enough to show shore on either side of us, some men were for going to the captain to demand he put a small boat ashore for fresh water and provisions.

"Boy, what are the men talking about? I seen you with them, what are they saying?"

"I think, Mr. Lorton, they want you to heave-to so they can get a small boat over to shore for water and food."

"They do, do they? Well, you take this message to them scurvy bastards."

He gave me a powerful kick in the seat of my britches that sent me reeling across the deck and down into the waist where I ended up against the aft mast.

"Did you hear me, Ross? Give them my message. I'll kick the shit out of anyone who dares to tell me what to do. Tell them!"

We made it into Montreal; how any of us survived is beyond me. The moment we tied in I was off the vessel with my sea bag and bindle. The second mate cautioned me to be ready to make the break. He said if I lingered on board there might be trouble.

Eight weeks crossing the Atlantic Ocean! So excited when I sailed out of the port of Dundas, I never dreamed it could become eight weeks of hell. I couldn't risk a last talk with old, broken Robert Skinner, the cook. I simply walked away from the vessel with the knowledge the master was in his cabin.

My only thought as I walked away was, "At last, dry land. It's not home, but, thank God, it is dry land."

Chapter Three

Yesterday morning when I reported to work Mr. LaGorce said I should come today knowing I would not be back in Montreal until late September. That meant bring my *cassette* (the watertight traveling case for my 'good' clothes Mr. Marx said I should have), sea bag, and ditty bag. I wrote to my family knowing another month would pass before the first vessel from England could make its way up the St. Lawrence with a possible letter from my folks in Scotland. I would be on my way to Grand Portage by then, so I felt free without a care in the world.

That bit of nonsense lasted about four hours.

Mr. LaGorce and I exhausted conversation and sat in his office looking at one another in disbelief. Nothing was going as scheduled. When Mr. McTavish made plans or gave orders, we naturally expected to carry them out to the letter.

Our anxiety was ended in a rush by the footman from Mr. McTavish's carriage who stumbled into the office clutching a note. The carriage was returning to Montreal for Pierre LeBlanc the personal cook for Mr. McTavish and me. Along the road about six miles above the city the carriage had broken an axle. The driver stayed with his vehicle and team, but flagged down another equipage returning to Montreal and sent the footman with the note.

Mr. LaGorce flew into action. He hurried down the steps of the office and commandeered the first conveyance to come along. My gear was tossed in the back and with the footman we were on our way to get the cook. We had to stop at several shops for the choice foods Pierre LeBlanc had selected for Mr. McTavish. We arrived at *La Chine* more than four hours off the schedule my uncle had set for departure.

The cart driver helped Pierre and me with our bags and bundles. Pierre was told to sit beside Mr. Robitaille in the canoe behind Uncle Simon who sat in stony silence. He indicated with a gesture I was to sit beside him.

"Duncan," my uncle began in a voice loaded with sarcasm, "I just knew you had more important things to take care of in Montreal. Are you quite ready to depart?"

"Mr. McTavish, there is a very good reason . . ."

I was cut off before I could get the words 'broken axle' out of my mouth.

"Silence! When I say be at *La Chine* at a certain time, I expect you to be here."

I tried again and said, "Mr. McTavish, if you will please give me two minutes I can explain everything."

The magic word was 'please'. It was a word my uncle never used and foreign to his vocabulary, it startled him.

"Proceed, Duncan."

I quickly told him the calamities that had befallen Mr. LeBlanc and myself, the carriage, and the scarcity of vehicles for a hasty trip from Montreal to *La Chine*. My tale of woes seemed to calm my uncle. As the loading of the canoe was being completed, I took stock of the rest of the crew.

The man in the very front of the canoe, *l' avant*, and the man in the back, *le gouvernail*, were *voyageurs* with French-Canadian roots. The ten paddlers, *les mileux*, were Iroquois Indians. Iroquois were highly prized for this particular work because of their unquestioned skills in handling birchbark canoes and for their storied endurance. We were an 'express' canoe carrying no commercial cargo, extra manpower guaranteed the fastest trip possible to *Rendezvous*.

Mister McTavish continued to sit like a statue, his beaver felt hat straight on his head, the brass-headed cane gripped in his hand. What in the hell, I thought to myself, was he going to do with a cane in a birchbark canoe?

We were underway and making good time up the turbulent Ottawa River. I could hear snatches of the conversation between Mr. Robitaille and Pierre LeBlanc as they commented on the passing scenes. Pierre had made this trip several times with Mr. McTavish and knew the course up the Ottawa River to be one of the most demanding in the nine-hundred-plus mile trek to Grand Portage.

The paddlers had to lay aside their paddles and take up long poles. They had a certain rhythm and drive to their poling that kept us moving, but it was against a very strong current with the need to thrust aside chucks of ice floating downstream along with dangerous tree branches and occasionally whole trees. Paddles would not be effective against the currents of the powerful Ottawa River running at full bore.

In a voice close to normal my uncle said, "Duncan, do you see those two leather cases directly in front of us? They contain all of the papers and records I will need to lead our business discussions at *Rendezvous*. I am placing them in your hands. You will never let them out of your sight, you will keep them dry at all times, you will carry them over all portages, you will see that they are placed inside my tent at night."

"Yes, Mr. McTavish, I will try to guard them as you have directed."

"Let anything happen to either one of those cases and your life will not be a pleasant one. Understood? Fine!"

What a way to begin my adventure. Four hours late! Cut off before I could tell what delayed our departure! Threatened with bodily harm if something happened to two old leather cases! I knew Simon McTavish's manner was brusque, his style that of command, his expectations of instant compliance but damn it, he could say "I'm sorry" once in awhile.

There was no time to brood. We were almost out of daylight, and *l' avant* had ordered the canoe to a stretch of quiet water. Activity as I had never seen before began. The men went over the side of the canoe into water up to their knees, or deeper. Several held the canoe steady while one stepped to Mr. McTavish's side of the canoe and helped him to his feet. In an instant the great man was astride his back and being carried to the shore 'piggy-back' where he was deposited with dry feet. Another man was at my side, with a roll of his eyes indicated I was to do the same. Mr. Robitaille and Mr. LeBlanc were similarly carried.

Before I could blink, two tents were erected and a cooking fire was lit for Pierre. All items in the canoe - luggage, sea bags, *cassettes,* ditty bags, blanket rolls, food hampers, bags of dried peas, kegs of grease, rum and high wine, a large iron cooking pot, a kit of repair materials (gum, a roll of birchbark, lengths of spruce roots), a sponge, and the precious dispatch cases - were carried ashore. Only then could the canoe be lifted from the water (one does not drag a birchbark craft over anything) carried to the bank, set carefully on its side and propped with paddles so it could not fall over. It became the crew's shelter for the night. With the second cooking fire ablaze I realized camp for the night was made. It happened so quickly and with such discipline had I not seen this I would not have believed it possible.

Hurried trips to the woods for personal relief were completed. The paddlers cut sticks of hard wood and pushed them on end into a fire. When the sticks were glowing red the men dashed to the canoe and ran the hot end over seams of spruce gum. Using their thumbs they worked the softened gum into seams. Where seam material was knocked off in the icy water, the men dipped into a little iron pot on the fire filled with chucks of the gum and applied the new stuff to the breaks. Re-seamed, the canoe would be ready for another day of currents and ice chunks in the raging Ottawa.

How my father would have enjoyed this scene; he respected men who knew what they were about and who worked as a team. The whole day would have delighted him. I even suspect he would have approved of Uncle Simon's rough handling of me for being late. Father never liked excuses, either.

We broke camp before daylight with the call, "*Levé! Levé! Canot dans l' eau. Canot dans l' eau. Levé!*"

The efficiency of the previous night was repeated in reverse order. Last into the canoe were the four passengers again carried 'piggy-back' style. I foolishly thought it was because we were important people. Reality? The four passengers, regardless of age, physical flexibility, weight, or height, were not capable of getting in and out of a thirty-six foot birch bark canoe without one or two bad things happening. We would either capsize the craft with our clumsiness, or we would punch a hole in the thin bark with our boots, causing a delay while the puncture was sealed. *Viola!* Carry the 'gentlemen' and avoid trouble.

One thing was missing. Breakfast! I expected hot food on this chilly morning. Where was it? At the first hint of light, we were on the water and moving at a pace of forty-five paddle strokes to the minute. Two hours of this and l' avant signaled a halt in a spot of slack water. Paddles were handed to the back of the canoe one at a time. Le gouvernail dipped each paddle into the large cooking pot at his feet, and out came the ration for each man clumped on the end. Paddle/dinner plate in hand, the voyageur lapped up the porridge like a dog. He untied a gourd from his waist band, dipped it in the river, quenched his thirst. Then he took the clay pipe, twist of tobacco, flint and steel from his waist pouch and began his fume.

Pierre LeBlanc, meanwhile, had not been a spectator. He opened the hamper stowed at his feet and produced slices of bread with smoked meat, pieces of cheese, and cups of wine. That was breakfast while under way. Last night, while I was doing not much of anything, Pierre prepared our morning meal as he prepared our supper. Le gouvernail did the same for the crew.

Our rations came from Pierre's seemingly bottomless hampers of breads, dried, smoked, and cured meats, cheeses, and a variety of wines, brandies, teas, coffees, and even chocolate. The crew had no choice; what they had in the morning was the same thing they would have at night: dried peas boiled with pork grease and a little water. There was no time for hunting or fishing. All food consumed we carried with us.

The crew sat in cramped space for hours on end. The passengers? We sat on folded buffalo robes - at night stretched out as mattresses in our tents - with back rests. I was directed this morning to sit with Pierre behind my uncle and his guest, Michel Robitaille. I watched the scenery slip by and listened to the conversation between the two men riding ahead of me.

Young Michel Robitaille was the son of a wealthy Montreal *entrepreneur*. The older man was thinking of investing with Mr. McTavish in his enterprises, and sent his son on this trip to learn as much as possible of the business end of fur trading. Michel was here to learn, but he was determined to impress the great Simon McTavish with his own knowledge of affairs. He ran on like a waterfall. I expected my uncle to shut him off after an hour of this prattle but no, he encouraged him.

Once again I listened as my uncle did what he does with such silky smoothness. He pumped the young man for all the 'hard' information he knew of his father's business investments: his income, his debts, his strengths and his weaknesses. Michel was flattered, stroked, and pampered. Totally unaware of what was going on, he was pumped dry. My uncle was clever and worked the 'pump' at irregular intervals sandwiched between hours of mindless chatter about Montreal and Michel's conquests of its young society ladies.

Every night, once our evening meal was finished, I was told to get the two dispatch cases in Uncle Simon's tent, light two candles, get my writing board, pens, ink, and paper and be ready for serious work. As long as those two candles produced any light, I worked.

Seating arrangements in the canoe varied. Mr. McTavish would 'suggest' Pierre and I ride together; at other times Michel and Pierre rode together. That put me at my uncle's side and that meant get out writing tools and prepare for dictation. A few times my uncle directed the three of us to sit side by side. A little cramped, but that never bothered Uncle Simon. He rode alone like a *caliph* on his soaring rug, calling for a dispatch case, and studying for hours the papers he had selected.

One unusually fine morning (no wind, no rain, minimum number of mosquitoes) I was seated beside my uncle, writing tools at the ready. Silence. No directions, no word of any kind. I reasoned the great man wished not to be disturbed. I extracted my personal diary from one of the dispatch cases. It was my mother's suggestion on the day I left my Highlands home, she thought it would be nice that all the family would know the details of my adventures in the New World. Deeply immersed in my writing, I paid no attention to the hand thrust at me. Again he thrust his hand, this time with some force, "Give me those papers."

A long minute passed. I said, "No, Mr. McTavish."

"Did you not hear me? I said, give me those papers!"

"No. These are my personal papers."

"I don't give a tinker's damn what you call them. Give them to me, now."

""No. I am sharing my journal with no one, not even you, Mr. McTavish."

"Give me those papers!"

"No."

"Duncan, you seem to have forgotten all I have tried to do for you."

"I have not forgotten, sir. But these papers have meaning only for me."

"Young man, I know that your father . . . "

I cut him off before he could finish what he was about to say of my father.

""You really don't know my father, and I resent your throwing him at me as a threat."

"I should take my cane across your arse."

"That would not be a wise thing to do, Mr. McTavish."

This concluded our spate of words. He turned to glare at the back of the paddler seated ahead of him. I should say, through the back of the man. Those blue eyes could melt the thickest iron.

Our heated exchange ended, the miseries just started for me. Here I was, a sixteen-year-old boy, telling the richest man in North America to go to hell. My place in the canoe was one of comfort for the body - buffalo robes, back rest, lap robe when needed - but my mind was torn to shreds.

 I imagined a series of things that might happen to me: told to leave the canoe tonight, and be stranded in a trackless wilderness; get to Grand Portage and be dismissed there with no way back to Montreal except in a Company canoe - and you know who controls this Company; I would get back to Montreal, but be sacked as soon as we touched at *La Chine* and be without any money; in Montreal no friends would step forward, they would fear the retribution of the powerful Simon McTavish. The siege of silence continued all after- noon as did the self-abasement and dire consequences I invented by the minute. I was jerked back to the present by *l' avant's* call to head for shore and prepare to make camp.

I performed evening activities as though sleep-walking. Pierre prepared a delightful meal and my uncle invited me to join him and Michel in his tent. I picked at my food, and finally asked to be excused. I snatched up a pair of buffalo robes, my blanket roll and left the tent. Tramping around outside I found a smooth place to spread the buffalo robes and unroll my blankets. It was close enough to *le gouvernail's* cooking fire to gain the benefit of its smoke and the absence of mosquitoes.

I strolled the beach in the evening light. As I walked I picked up a pebble to skip across the lake, but most were 'ploppers' and sank. I walked and skipped throwing more ploppers than skippers. Walk, throw, watch, walk, throw, watch, walk - wait a minute! I didn't throw yet. Where did that skipper come from? I whirled around to find Uncle Simon standing not ten feet away.

"If you weren't so angry, you would do a better job. Now watch as I show you how to do it."

He threw an 'eight'. I threw the pebble I held, and it plopped.

"Duncan, at times you don't seem to be learning what I tell you. Now watch! Are you watching me, Duncan?"

"Yes, Uncle Simon, I am watching," said with a deliberate touch of sarcasm.

"I don't care for that tone of voice, young man."

"If you are going to give me another lecture about not turning over my personal papers, you can just forget it. I am not giving them to you."

"You are one hot-headed lad. Some day your temper will get you into a peck of trouble."

Ready with a sizzling reply, I saw my uncle pointing to a large boulder at the lakeside. We sat looking over the water not saying one word, again visions of catastrophe filled my mind. To my surprise his first remark was, "Duncan, I am pleased with the way you handled my demand that you surrender your personal papers. I think a diary is what you called them."

"I don't understand, Uncle Simon. This afternoon I thought you fully expected me to give you my diary."

"Had you given it to me, I would be replacing you as soon as we reach Grand Portage."

"Why, Uncle Simon?"

"At *Rendezvous* some of my partners will demand you show them papers meant for my eyes only."

"But those partners are of the same North West Company as you. You all work together, don't you?"

"The answer to your question is 'yes' and 'no'. Some are company papers, and some are my private papers."

"But, sir, how am I know which are which?"

"When we get to *Rendezvous* and you sit in on our meetings to make notes for me, you will quickly learn the difference, Company or private."

"All of your partners are powerful men, Uncle Simon. How is a mere clerk going to be able to refuse their demands?"

"Duncan, you never lost a minute telling me to keep my nose out of your business. If you can say 'no' to me so confidently, I see no reason why you can't handle any of the partners.

"And, Duncan, there is one more thing. Try to practice a little diplomacy when you are confronted with angry and demanding partners. I am sure your mother taught you that a little honey catches a lot more flies. Good night to you."

I continued on to my nest outside. The night was beautiful, crisp and clear, with stars crowding out the pastel shades of the fading light. I stretched out on the robes, pulled up my blanket and, with hands folded beneath my head, tried to pick out one star from the hundreds above and call it my lucky star. I fell asleep sorting stars and business papers.

The weather was as varied as Pierre's delightful suppers. Brilliant sunshine alternated with rain driven by winds with icy fingers. Rain also meant passing back and forth a large sponge among all in the canoe. Each man soaked up the water accumulating at his feet, wring it over the side and passed it along to the next. Like our trips to the woods sponging out a canoe leveled our canoe society.

In the growing excitement among the crew, experienced hands knew we were approaching Grand Portage. *L' avant* called a halt in the lee side of an island (I heard one of the crew call it *Susie*). Over the side of the canoe went the *voyageurs* and the *les mileux*, ditty bags clutched in their hands. Some actually bathed, even shaved; some just dabbled a little water here and there. All pulled their brightest *tuques* (knit caps) and *ceintures flechées* (sashes) from their bags and put them on. Many stuck large sea gull feathers in their caps. As we rounded the local landmark, *Ponte a Chapeau*, and the paddle tempo increased to sixty strokes a minute, *le grand bourgeois's* canoe virtually flew across Grand Portage Bay.

We were sighted by lookouts at the stockade. Men raced to the dock, some repeatedly loaded and fired muskets - the traditional greeting among Company men. The paddlers broke into lusty singing, mixed with shouts of greetings, threats, profanity, sexually explicit descriptions, just shouting for pure pleasure.

Many hands reached out to help Mr. McTavish to his feet, guided his steps onto the dock, wrapped his cloak about him. Grand Portage was cold, even in late June. "Duncan," I said to myself, "someday you will be *le grand bourgeois* and all these ceremonies will be performed in your honor." Directed at me now was a sharp, "Duncan, do you have the dispatch cases? We will need them immediately. Follow me to my cabin, and see that my luggage is placed in my quarters as well."

So much for day dreams.

Without a word of apology or personal concern for Gerald McClary, the wintering partner at this great inland depot of the NWC, Mr. McTavish pre-empted the man's private cabin for the duration of *Rendezvous*. I was told to get my gear to the loft over the Great Hall, the massive two story building dominating the stockaded acre and a half of the central depot. I thought I might take an hour or two to explore everything within the stockade. I should have known better.

"Duncan, where are you? Duncan, get over to my cabin. I have work you must do immediately."

"Right away, Mr. McTavish, right away."

The wintering partner's cabin was small, sparse but clean and had what I thought was the most desirable item in the whole compound - a bed with rope springs, mattress, sheets, and blankets. I was wrong again. The most desirable feature of this tiny cabin was privacy, almost impossible to find at Grand Portage during this wild session of Company activities. My uncle had not been well the last few days of the trek and wanted to lie down. I was ordered to take my work to the Great Hall.

At a table by a window I laid out my writing supplies, and became deeply involved in writing copies of the agenda for the first meeting of the partners. A few minutes later the front door of the Great Hall burst open. Loud shouts rang through the room.

"Make way! *Les hommes du Nord* from the posts of *Bourgeois* Carl MacLarren are here."

About this group of three clerks and Mr. MacLarren hung an air of accomplishment and *braggadocio*, enough noise for a group five times its size. They had been forty-eight days on the trek from their home post in the far North Country. As veterans of several summers at *Rendezvous*, they were ready for the *soirées* and *galas* that would be held in this building.

A servant dispatched to inform Mr. McTavish that Carl MacLarren was most eager to greet *le grand bourgeois* had to be called off. "I'm sorry, Mr. MacLarren, but Mr. McTavish is indisposed."

Mr. MacLarren, crest-fallen and deflated, counted on being one of the first to welcome Mr. McTavish to this year's 'adventure'. (The NWC did not follow a calendar year, it counted a year from the end of one *Rendezvous* to the beginning of the next as an adventure, not a year.)　I resumed writing, but a few minutes later was interrupted once more by the three clerks.

"Who do we have here? Why, I believe this is Simon McTavish, Junior. Am I right, you are his errand boy for the *Rendezvous*?"

"Yes, I am Duncan Ross, here to serve Mr. McTavish as secretary."

"I thought so. Too bad, Duncan! We're off to visit the Indian camps and see what this year's crop of young lovelies looks like. If we find any we think you should know about we may tell you; then again, we may not."

"That's damned nice of you, but one look at the three of you and those maidens will head for the woods and hide."

"Listen to him, would you? Can you think of a better place to meet the Indian girls than in the woods? Have you ever done that, Junior? You ought to try it, it's great sport."

"No, Edward. Can't you see he's married to his pen and inkwell. Let's go, we're wasting time with this greenhorn."

That was another part of *Rendezvous* I would have to adjust to, the never ending verbal sparring among the clerks. Often fun, it could get pretty rough.　Would my uncle ever give me a few minutes to enjoy the other parts of the get-together along the shores of this little bay tucked against rocky ridges, pine and spruce forests?

As usual, my uncle was a step ahead of me. "Duncan, when you find yourself with a few idle minutes I want you to walk about the compound and observe the work of the clerks. Walk out the Grand Portage Trail and watch the *voyageurs* as they pack out trade goods and bring back furs. You should climb the game trails up to the top of the little peak directly back of the compound. The view is magnificent and will give you a different perspective on our operations here."

Every day free of rain, blustery winds or the imperial commands of my uncle, I walked compound and portage trail and followed game trails to the top of the ridge. I did gain a perspective on the NWC that forty-two days in a thirty-six foot canoe cannot give - we are truly one big Company. Conversation between my uncle and Michel Robitaille came to mind.

"Michel, we started the North West Company at the place you are about to see and experience. We have retained the old name for the place, *Le Grand Portage*. But since most of us are British, we simply say Grand Portage."

"Quite right, Mr. McTavish. In Montreal one hears many tales of the Grand Portage."

"Tales are one thing, Michel, but I think you are capable of digesting some facts."

"And what might they be, sir?"

"As you stand on the gallery of our Great Hall you will see spread out at your feet the greatest collection of wealth gathered at one place in all of North America."

"Oh, come now, Mr. McTavish! The greatest wealth? Really, sir, I must object to your exaggeration."

"Object as you wish, my young friend. But consider this: add the value of the thousands upon thousands of peltries, and the value of the tons of trade goods passing through our central depot in only three weeks, and you will agree with my conclusion."

"I am impressed, my dear sir, but not convinced."

"But I have not completed my accounting of wealth. You also must add to the value of goods and furs the value of all holdings and assets of my partners and agents. I humbly add my own to the total. Now what sort of a figure do you come up with, Mr. Robataille?"

"I most sincerely apologize, Mr. McTavish, for ever doubting your word. I am dismayed at my impertinence. I assure you, sir, I meant no disrespect for what you have accomplished."

"No apologizes needed, Michel. Perhaps you will see fit to inform your father the extent of resources that stand behind the North West Company? He will appreciate knowing what I have just revealed to you."

No doubt Michel Robitaille had his eyes opened, I know mine were after that exchange. Uncle Simon seemed to be talking louder than his usual manner; could be that description of great wealth was meant for my ears as well. Within a week I had climbed the sugar-loaf shaped hill (the local people call it *Mont Rose*) behind the Great Hall. The scene at my feet was that of a buzzing hive of more than a thousand human bees.

Was that really buzzing I heard? It was the low, soft voices of three Indian maidens with birchbark baskets gathering red raspber-ries. I tasted these delicious berries for the first time just a few days ago. The surprise of our meeting was complete. I was afraid I might scare them away, but one stopped and asked,

"You like?"

"Sure, er yes, I mean, thank you."

Her smile was accompanied by an out-stretched basket. I gath-ered a handful of the ripe berries, popped them in my mouth, and tried to indicate how good they tasted. What I did was dribble juice down my chin. They hid giggles behind their hands, all but the one who made the initial offer. She was a little older, I thought prettier, and certainly bolder than the other two. I wanted them to stay and talk, only what would I say next? Among themselves was a steady stream in their native tongue, but the one had asked in English, so I tried some of my own. "What is your name?"

The answer was in Ojibway, but the smile was the universal language of youth.

"I saw you dance in the Great Hall with your friends," I continued. "You dance very well, and seem to enjoy dancing."

"I saw you, too."

She was one of the many Indian maidens who came to the Great Hall in the evenings after dinner when tables, chairs, and benches had been pushed to the side for dancing. I was bold enough to join in when I thought someone should do the proper steps to the traditional dances. I danced rather well - a credit to my mother's and sister's coaching. In a short time most other men left the dance floor and I was practically doing a solo. Very embarrassing, but at the same time I enjoyed myself.

This young, attractive native woman had seen my dancing. Here on the slope of *Mont Rose*, judging from the smile on her face I felt encouraged to keep her attention. I have no idea what she saw when she looked so directly at me. I know I saw dark eyes and dark hair done up in a braid reaching half way down her back. Her complexion was clear with a dusty-rose hue, her smile turned me upside down. I tried again to hold her attention.

What caught the attention of all four of us was the appearance, from seemingly nowhere, of a very old native woman who said not a word, just raised her hand. Her eyes and gesture sent an unmistakable message, "Young man with the blue eyes, stay away from my granddaughters!"

The girls turned without a sound, though the one flashed another smile as she vanished down the trail to the Indian camps along the Bay. I knew I would be in the Great Hall tonight ready to dance.

Dinner was what the partners and agents had come to expect: venison pies, roasts of fresh moose, lake trout broiled on oak planks, delicate perch that barely touched the frying pan, puddings, breads and rolls, and, of course, a steady stream of the best wines and brandies. Some of the wintering partners had tremendous appetites. No doubt they were relieved to be free of the monotonous diets of canoe travel and the months of close confinement in their log hut-ments through long winters in the North Country. The clerks dined on a greatly reduced scale, but we usually had a roast and white bread on our table.

"Ah, Duncan, there you are. Bring several candles from the Hall and meet me in my cabin. We have work to do tonight."

Why was he so insensitive to what young people might like to do? Had he never been young? I think he must have been born an old man, and never had any idea of what it was like to grow up. My uncle started the moment I pushed open the door to his cabin.

"Where are the notes from this morning's meeting? Have you prepared them?"

"No, Uncle Simon. Did you forget you had me take Mr. Robitaille to view the fishery operated by the Company on the far side of the Bay?"

"That didn't take the whole afternoon."

"No, sir. But Mr. Robitaille wanted to stop at Francois' tents, as he said, 'To study this part of the Company's distribution system in detail'."

Let me explain the place of Monsieur Francois Bouchée and his tents along the shore of Grand Portage Bay as it relates to the North West Company. His stock of goods was in cheap trinkets, watered rum, and services in the harlots' tent.

The Company paid a large portion of *voyageurs* wages at *Rendezvous* in *bons* - paper scrip and coins made by the NWC and redeemable only at its own posts. It didn't take long for the average *voyageur* to go through a year's wage with visits to the tents. When that happened, but the man still had needs to be purchased, Bouchée extended credit. The poor devils didn't know that Francios Bouchée was an employee of the Company, and their debts to him were debts to the North West Company. The only way a *voyageur* could pay off his obligations was to get back in the Company's canoe next year and work off the debt. Slavery? Indentured servitude?

"It was this operation Mr. Robitaille wanted to study."

"Damn that young stud! Could you not get him to hurry along? No. I guess not. Well, get to work on your notes."

All night long I could hear the music, the laughter, the sounds of a good party in the Great Hall while I sat and tried to concentrate on who said what in this morning's session.

After sitting in on several sessions of the partners and agents I realized these men liked to talk, to argue and dispute. It was important to Uncle Simon that every word be recorded and attributed to the right speaker. In desperation, I concocted a code of initials and short words to identify each speaker: Mr. McTavish became O.I.B. - old iron balls; Carl MacLarren, D.S. - droopy socks; Angus McReath, B.B. - big belly; Peter Locke, F.A.L. - farts a lot; James Shaw, L.A.L. - laughs a lot. All twenty some names I had to repeat in writing the minutes of these meetings got initials to identify them individually. The code did speed my work, but I feared the day it would be uncovered and my disrespect for the successful and powerful men who made up the core of the NWC brought to light.

One name I could not bring myself to encode was Jonathan Graham; he remained simply J.G.. He was not a wordy man, but when he spoke out in Company meetings partners and agents listened with respect and a measure of courtesy not freely given among this bunch of *primeurs*.

Uncle Simon took my notes, scanned them for a minute, and said, "Well, Duncan, these seem to be adequate, but I sense your mind is not focused on this work. Why don't you slip over to the Great Hall? I know that is where you want to be."

As I made fast steps toward the Hall I reversed my opinions of my uncle; the old man was human after all. Some friends among the clerks saw me and came over with jeering comments about being let out of prison. And why did they have to keep both fireplaces going with so many bodies crowded in here?

Then I saw my raspberry picker, and she saw me. A quick smile was the only sign of recognition, but when the music started again, I made my way to her side and nodded at the center of the Hall to let her know I would like to dance. Dance we did. Reels, flings, whatever was called we danced. From the look in her eyes I knew she enjoyed dancing with me, and I sent the same message.

I retreated to the gallery running the length of the Great Hall for a breath of fresh air, it was so warm inside. I walked to the far end and leaned against the side of the Hall when I was surprised by my dancing partner. She took me by the hand and we walked about the compound. Our sparse conversation was a mixture of some French, a few words of English, and the few words in her dialect I could muster. Just strolling with this delightful native woman bridged the gaps of words unspoken. At a corner of the stockade back of the Great Hall where the vegetable gardens were located we stopped our walking. She tenderly brushed her face against mine. Before I could react she was gone. Like a zephyr leaving only a trace of its presence, she was gone.

I slipped down to the dock to regroup and think through what had just happened. Visions of Denise Dessault raced through my mind accompanied by the raspberry picker. Why, I asked myself, are girls so different? Why do they have so much impact on your thinking when they do so little to change it? I gave up trying to answer my own questions and watched the fantastic show of lights flickering in the northern sky.

The majestic display went on for a long time. I wandered back to the compound and eased around to the back door of the Great Hall thinking I could make it to the loft without being seen. Everything went well. Sleep, however, was another matter. I lay there and relived every moment of the evening, but could not answer the questions that crept to the top of the pile. Would I see Her again? Did I want to see Her again? Would we rediscover the magic of holding hands and just being together? I must have fallen asleep. The next thing I knew a dirty shirt was thrown in my face by one of the clerks.

"Lover boy, time to wake up. I say, lover boy, get your lazy bones to moving!"

"Oh, let him sleep, Charles. He needs his rest. He's not up to doing any work after a big night on the dance floor."

"You dumb ass, it wasn't the dance floor that did him in. It was the walk around the compound with that pretty native girl. That's his problem, he can't do two things at the same time. He can't dance and . . . what was it you did outside?"

"Nothing happened last night."

"Christ, Robert, did you ever hear such horse pucky?"

I thought the rough banter would never end, but it did. I prepared as I would for an average day working for *le grand bourgeois*. I was kept busy until early in the afternoon, when he said, "You know, Duncan, this *Rendezvous* is almost over. I don't think you have spent sufficient time with the clerks. Pick out one of the senior clerks and ask questions. Make no plans for tonight, I will need you in my cabin after dinner."

What did that old turkey buzzard know? What did he see? Who told him what happened? More damn questions that I couldn't answer.

The afternoon passed roaming the compound asking and watching as clerks, working at a frantic pace, completed their accumulations of next season's trade goods. Dinner was over and I stayed close to the Great Hall waiting for the signal from my uncle that it was time to resume our work. He sat in a chair placed by the fireplace as if a Scottish 'laird'. He enjoyed this time, for men came with cups of high wine and a word in private, or seeking a word of reassurance from the great man. Oh my yes, he reveled playing the part of 'lord of the manse,' and I was not about to interrupt his show.

What did alter the course of events was the smooth and silent withdrawal from the crowd of a handsome Indian maiden through the back door of the Great Hall. After a few more minutes of royal chatter, Mr. McTavish excused himself and, with a deliberate show of indifference - but no signal for me to join him for last minute work - made his way to the front door of the Great Hall and strolled to his cabin.

After an interval of about half an hour I slipped outside and carefully looked over my uncle's cabin; no light showing at any of the windows, no light showing in the crack under the door. Back inside the Great Hall the musicians were getting ready for this evening's final party. My eyes roamed over the gathering throng for sight of Her. Outside the Great Hall in the compound, some of the clerks had started a fire for their own party, but no dancing partner. I walked further along the beach past fires of *voyageurs* as they, too, were beginning a last *soirée*. No sign of Her.

I continued past one after another of the big Montreal freight canoes propped on their sides and decided I was on a wild goose chase. Back to the Great Hall, back to a *gala* that no longer held any interest for me. *Rendezvous* for me ended where it had begun, alone.

It was with great relief I noted Michel Robitaille had been placed in one of the earlier canoe brigades to depart for Montreal. But who would be the fourth party in our canoe? I assumed that since four of us came from Montreal in the express canoe, four would return in it.

William McGillivray, a blood nephew of my uncle, arrived at Grand Portage from the North Country last night when I was searching for my dancing partner. He was exhausted from his dash to get to *Rendezvous* before Simon McTavish set out for Montreal. When he did get himself aroused and moving about, he introduced himself to me.

"I am happy to meet you, Duncan Ross. I know my uncle is very careful of those he selects to come here as his secretary. I congratulate you on that. But I think I should commiserate with you. I also know how my uncle can become a slave-driver at these Company affairs, right, Duncan? I don't think you should respond to that, should you?"

He followed that brief repartee with a hearty laugh, and I knew I was glad to have him with us on the long trek to Montreal. He was going back there - permanently. He was being trained to become the second in command of the mighty NWC.

From my introduction to the heir-apparent two things became very clear: to get anywhere in this Company one had to spend time in the actual trading of skins for goods, and that could only be done in the *pays d'en haut*. Secondly, through his nephew, Mr. McTavish could erase one major blot on his record in the eyes of many of his partners. Simon McTavish had never set one foot west of Grand Portage, had never spent one winter in the North Country. With William McGillivray as his right hand man, that major deficiency could be covered with the young man's experience and success in the *pays d'en haut*.

I heard William McGillivray was highly regarded in his own right as a fine trader. Who would dare to challenge the Crown Prince?

Chapter Four

The departure from Grand Portage at the conclusion to *Rendezvous* was in marked contrast to our arrival in late June. It was so quiet. All the *Canots du Maître* (the thirty-six foot freighters that could carry 8000 pounds each) had been dispatched eastward to Montreal. All the *Canots du Nord* (the twenty-five foot freighters carrying 4000 pounds each) had cleared *Fort Charlotte* and were on their way into the *pays d'en haut*. The few men left at the depot dutifully came to the dock to bid *adieu* to Simon McTavish and to his nephew, William McGillivray. Even the ragged volley of musket fire was in keeping with the acknowledgment that *Rendezvous* was over. The silence slipping down to the central depot from *Mont Rose* would not be broken until next summer's gathering of the two divisions of the NWC.

The top men of the Company sat side-by-side deeply immersed in endless conversation. I spent hours riding beside Pierre LeBlanc. Ordinarily this would mean endless jokes and laughter, but not on this return trip.

Pierre had been pierced by one of Cupid's darts during his time at *Rendezvous*, and he was scared to death. He suspected one of his visits to Bouchée's tents was the cause of his *malaise*, and he created in his mind the terrible things he'd heard came from exposure to the 'French Pox'.

"I tell you, *Monsieur Duncan*, I am very miserable *homme de coeur*. What am I to do?"

"At *Rendezvous* I heard the clerks saying there is a salve that will relieve your discomfort."

"But, *mon ami*, we are forty days from Montreal. I will not live that long."

"In about a week we should be in *Sault Ste. Marie*."

"What good will that do, *Monsieur Duncan*?"

"Lots of *voyageurs* pass through that place who have been hit by a dart. You will be able to find one who can get this salve for you."

"*Merci, Monsieur, merci.* You make me feel better in my mind."

Starting out from Grand Portage the weather was in our favor; but when we reached *Michipicoten Bay* at the east end of the big lake, our course switched to due south and all those good days dropped behind us. After a day of no real progress in paddling into the wind, *l' avant* signaled to the crew to head for a sheltered inlet he knew. Even a man as important as Simon McTavish must surrender to the greater power of Mother Nature.

While we waited my uncle groused and complained to the point William McGillivray walked away from our campsite. I took the same general direction as his and we soon found ourselves on a bluff overlooking the inlet, but sheltered by overhanging rocks.

"Well, Duncan, I see we both had enough of my uncle's ill temper. I am glad that you are here, for there are a few things I should tell you."

"I hope it is nothing bad, sir. I tried to meet Mr. McTavish's demands as best I could."

"No. No. Nothing like that. You would not have lasted through all the days of *Rendezvous* had he been displeased with your work."

"*Rendezvous* was very interesting, every day of it. I should like to return."

"What would you say if I told you *le grand bourgeois* is counting on you to be his secretary next year?"

"That would be wonderful news, Mr. McGillivray."

"Keep it to yourself, Duncan. You must act surprised when he tells you. Just keep up your good work, you dare not let down."

The winds continued to howl throughout the day and into the night. I could hear both *l' avant* and *le gouvernail* walk about the campsite as they checked the security of our tents and the canoe. We rose at the crack of dawn and morning rations were served. As we huddled in his tent, my uncle said, "Duncan, did you hear how the managers of our canoe took charge of our safety? And were you surprised that you did not hear me giving them any orders? You have learned a very important lesson."

"And what is that, Mr. McTavish?"

"When you travel in a Company canoe, you must rely on the judgment of veteran *voyageurs*. If the crew heard you telling *l' avant* how he should manage the canoe, you might be facing a rebellion. They know whom to trust."

We continued in camp. Those tremendous winds had piled up lake waters against the eastern end of *Gitchi Gammi*. *L' avant* would not consider putting the canoe into waters running eight or ten foot waves. O.I.B. came against someone who could beat him at his own game. *La Vielle* (the old woman of the winds) won this contest.

Three days later we did stop at *Sault Ste. Marie*. Poor Pierre rushed about the post and found what he needed, the precious salve. He quickly applied it in generous amounts and reported relief - divided, I'm sure, between body and mind.

The morning we were due to arrive in *La Chine* my uncle fed me a steady stream of directives for collecting and compiling the papers dealing with this year's 'adventure' at Grand Portage.

"One more thing, Duncan. Well, two things: first, I will leave for London in about three days. You will respond to any request William may make of you as though it came from me. Understood? Fine! As for the second thing, I am moving you from work directly concerned with the NWC to the firm of McTavish and Frobisher."

"Yes, Mr. McTavish, I understand."

"No, you cannot understand. That will come only after you have worked for several months at your new position."

I had no difficulty finding the offices of McTavish and Frobisher in old Montreal. They were close to the office of Simon McTavish, Esq. which was close to the main offices of the North West Company. A chummy cluster of contact points for the major factors in the fur trade of Canada. William McGillivray took Uncle Simon's office for his current base of operations, and it was there I reported.

"Come in, Duncan, why such a long face?"

"Well, Mr. McGillivray, I don't really know what my new work will be, and I don't want to get off on the wrong foot."

McTavish and Frobisher was a partnership set up by my uncle to be the agent for the North West Company in selling the peltries gathered in the North Country and funneled to Montreal through the central depot at Grand Portage. That was only half of its mission; it was also the agent for NWC in buying and shipping from Europe the many items of trade goods marketed to its native customers through trading posts in the North Country. There was another partnership in London, McTavish and Fraser.

It took me quite a bit of time to piece this mosaic together, and when I had done that, I was awed by the genius of my uncle in creating his empire.

"This must be a huge puzzle to you, Duncan. It was for me the first years I worked for my uncle."

"It is certainly that, Mr. McGillivray. I thought by the end of *Rendezvous* I had a clear picture of how the NWC operated."

"If you understand the basic structure of the NWC, you will soon see the reasons my uncle set up the partnership you are now working for, and the necessity for a partnership in London."

"It will take a long time to grasp this complex business."

"I see that some of my uncle's impatience has rubbed off on you. Work hard, ask questions, and you will be amazed at how quickly you have the full picture in your mind."

"I hope you are right, but there are days, Mr. McGillivray, I feel lost."

"Don't worry, Duncan. I will have Arthur Keevil take you under his wing."

I wasn't sure if it was under a wing or a heavy foot. Mr. Keevil and I did not get along. He seemed so picky, so fusty and lost no time in letting me know when I had erred, but never did he explain where or why.

Our strained relations ruptured after only one month. A messenger from Mr. LaGorce brought a letter to me from a vessel that just arrived from London. Mr. Keevil was right at my shoulder saying that anything that came into his office was his business. He demanded I give the letter to him. Am I going through another episode like the one I had with Mr. McTavish over my diary?

"Mr. Keevil, this a letter from my family in Scotland. There is no way it can be your business or that of McTavish and Frobisher."

"Young man, I regard that as insubordination. I shall report you to Mr. Frobisher."

"You do that, Mr. Keevil, for I too would like to talk to Mr. Frobisher."

"Your impertinence will cost you dearly, I promise you."

Two days later I reported for work to find Mr. Keevil standing with a smug look on his bony face, and a note that he handed to me with the same warmth the hangman must greet a condemned prisoner. The note simply said to be in Mr. Frobisher's office at ten o'clock this morning without fail.

"Come in, Mr. Ross. Sit down and explain your outrageous behavior toward our valued employee, Arthur Keevil. I cannot and will not countenance such behavior on the part of a clerk. Do I make myself clear, Mr. Ross?"

"No, sir. You have heard only one side of the story. Am I to assume you are acting on the complaint of Mr. Keevil?"

"Exactly, Mr. Ross. There will be no more incidents such as this or I will terminate your employment at McTavish and Frobisher."

"I do not wish to have any more incidents with Mr. Keevil. But you must understand, Mr. Frobisher, I will not surrender my personal mail to anyone in this company."

"Personal mail, you say? Mr. Keevil informed me that you refused his demand to give him documents you had in your possession while working under his supervision."

"That is correct, sir. But the 'documents' were simply a letter from my family in Scotland."

"I think we have wasted too much time on this petty affair. I will determine if further action is warranted."

This is the letter causing my confrontation with Arthur Keevil:

Dear Duncan

We were so pleased to have your two letters. The first with the good news that you had arrived in Montreal safely. All three of us were concerned that you had an easy passage, and we were also pleased to know that Simon McTavish took you under his wing and made all the arrangements for your lodging and meals. Mother was especially relieved to know your new 'mother' made you take a bath and put on clean clothes as soon as you got in her house.

Aren't you moving too fast in your work? To be asked to go to the company's Rendezvous (you must explain that to us in your next letter) after only a year on the job has Father worried. He is afraid you will not have time to learn all you should know before going so far from Montreal. Father was also upset over the twenty-five pounds you sent with the second letter. I tried to tell him why you had done that, but he does not seem to understand.

Mother is about the same as when you left last year. She tries to do all the things she has done for so many years, but she just doesn't have the strength. She has lost more weight, and her color has faded. But nothing can diminish the strong will of this woman. Father is trying to make contact with a doctor in Glasgow to arrange a thorough examination.

Mr. MacQuay asked Father about you when he was in his shop in the village. And Rory McBride asks about you, he drops by from time to time to keep me company. He took me to the dances at Skillingford last week.

We are getting along about the same as when you were with us, but we do miss you, and I miss the long talks we had about everything. We will look forward to the next letter.

Be well, and know you have our love. always.
Father, Mother, and Louise

Father was upset over the money I sent so they could engage a doctor to help Mother. I was puzzled over him receiving twenty-five pounds. I had gone to Uncle Simon with five pounds sterling telling him why I wanted to send it home, but I didn't know how to do it.

"Give me the money, Duncan. I will draw a draft on my accounts in London which you can include with your next letter. Your father can take it to any banker and get the money from him. My business dealings are well known in Scotland; any banker would be pleased to honor my draft. Understood? Fine!"

The only thing I could figure out was that my uncle added some of his funds to my five pounds. Uncle Simon was not an easy man to figure out. He never said a word about what he was doing for my mother.

Nothing came of the incident with old Keevil, but the following week I had a summons to William McGillivray's office.

"The reason I called you here is to tell you are moving to another office in the firm of McTavish and Frobisher - nothing to do with Mr. Keevil, but with your short time in Montreal."

"Short time, Mr. McGillivray? I don't follow you. What have I done to have me sent back to the Highlands?"

"Duncan, are you always ready to do battle? Let me explain, please."

So he did for about twenty minutes without interruption. I will go back to Grand Portage in May. Until then I was supposed to learn how to analyze the individual accounts of the wintering partners, the only way Simon McTavish can know who are his top producers and who the laggards.

I had no difficulty following Mr. McGillivray's explanations until he got to that word 'analyzing'. What the devil was he getting at?

"You look lost, Duncan. Am I going too fast for you to follow? Speak up, lad."

"I think I understand, but I don't see why the need to analyze. What has to be analyzed?"

My answer was one of William's long and loud laughs.

"I'm not laughing at you, Duncan. Your question was the same one I asked my uncle. Let me show you the whole process."

With a sheet of accounting paper Simon McTavish had devised, I would work out a series of ratios and tests to enable the top managers in Montreal to know which wintering partners in the North Country produced the greatest profit margins.

"Now, do you think you grasp the nature of the work you will be doing?"

The doubtful look on my face betrayed my inner feelings.

"I guarantee that two weeks from now you will wonder why you ever felt lost in our system. Duncan, nobody is to know whose records you are analyzing. Mr. McTavish, Mr. Frobisher, and myself are the only three people with whom you may talk about your work. Understood? Fine!"

I had a personal reason for enjoying this new work. Poring over the accounts of a certain partner, I could call to mind a mental picture of the man as I recalled the code I devised for his name. Would these men be back at the next *Rendezvous*? Who might be missing, and for what reason? "Stop it, Duncan," I said to myself, "you are just a clerk and these are partner's affairs you are wondering about! Get back to your ledgers."

Christmas slipped by as did the New Year's celebration. I learned to ice skate this winter at my friends' insistence. Some of my skating teachers came to the river on Sunday afternoons with their girl friends and introduced them to me. We all looked forward to stops at a coffee house for a hot toddy following a brisk two or three hours on the ice of the St. Lawrence. One vivacious girl, introduced by my good friend, Carl Schurz, and I seemed to get along quite well in spite of my occasional spills. Our open and friendly exchanges continued in the coffee houses and, one Sunday afternoon as the group was dispersing, I noticed Jeanette Turmel was alone. Her chaperon had disappeared. I asked if I might walk with her to her home.

"Why, Duncan, that is very thoughtful of you."

"My pleasure, Jeanette. But I have no idea where you live in Montreal. You will have to be the guide."

"I have been guiding you on the ice for the past several weeks, I guess I can guide us to my house, don't you think?"

"I'll take my chances, Jeanette."

"Rubbish! I have the feeling, Duncan Ross, you don't take chances very often, do you?"

I thought best not to answer. We worked our way into a residential section of the older part of Montreal where the houses were quite large, some even grand. At the gate in front of one of these houses we stopped.

"This is where I live, Duncan. Would you like to come in and warm yourself? I want you to meet my mother. Oh, don't look so frightened, she won't bite."

"Of course your mother won't bite. If she does, I'll bite right back."

Laughing and joking we climbed the steps to the front door that opened before we could reach for the handle. A gray-haired, matronly woman with commanding demeanor asked us in quickly to keep out the frigid air blasting though the big evergreen trees at the side of the house.

"You must be Duncan Ross. Jeanette has told me about you. I am Henrietta Turmel."

"Yes, I am Duncan Ross. I am most pleased to meet you, Mrs. Turmel."

"Take off your coats, hats, and mittens, children. You may leave them here in the hall. Do come into the parlor and warm yourselves before the fire."

My first thought was that Mrs. Turmel was a school teacher. My second thought was that a flood of questions would follow.

"Jeanette tells me, Mr. Ross, that you are employed by McTavish and Frobisher."

"Yes, that is correct. But I have been with that house only a few months since my return from the *Rendezvous* at Grand Portage."

"We have heard in this city of the great *Rendezvous* held by the North West Company. What place did you call it? Grand Portage, I believe?"

"Yes, Mrs. Turmel, it is called Grand Portage."

"One of my students, I must say, one of my most delightful former students, is Mary Margaret Chaboillez. She is betrothed to Simon McTavish, the chief factor of the North West Company"

"My uncle told me of his engagement on our return from last summer's *Rendezvous*."

"Simon McTavish is your uncle? I was not aware of that, Mr. Ross. I find it necessary to keep track of all the young men of Montreal society. Your name seems to have slipped by me."

Jeanette was having a hard time smothering her laughter and I was having the same problem. From snatches of conversation among friends in the skating parties on the river, I learned that Mrs. Turmel was a widow who supported herself and her daughter with an exclusive school she owned and operated. It was devoted, not to academics, but to teaching the fine points of high society's mores, customs, and practices to young women carefully selected to benefit from the examples and contacts only Henrietta Turmel could provide - for an exorbitant fee.

"Mrs. Turmel, you have been most kind to welcome me into your home, but I must take my leave."

Jeanette walked with me as I retrieved my winter garb and at the door she whispered,

"Duncan, I hope to see you again, and soon. I am dying to tell you of the shock you gave my mother. Shocking her is quite an accomplishment. Good-bye, Duncan."

"Good-bye, Jeanette. I'm sure there will still be ice on the river next Sunday."

As I slipped and slid my way downhill to the old part of the city, a flood of questions raced through my mind. Why are relations with women always so tangled and mysterious? My intentions toward Jeanette Turmel were honorable, and I thought we would enjoy each other's company without complications. But, then . . .

One stormy afternoon in late April I had an unexpected visit from William McGillivray. We exchanged greetings and made inquiries as to our respective health. He was here for a good reason; he had a problem, I was the solution.

During the winter NWC had partners at its posts in the North Country circulate a 'round robin' letter. It began in the far-distant *Lake Athabaska* region and followed the routes of canoes converging on Grand Portage. Every partner along the way had the opportunity to tell his colleagues of conditions in his department and the numbers and descriptions of articles needed for next season's trades.

The letter was carried by veteran *voyageurs* on dog sled and snowshoe. It arrived in *Sault Ste. Marie* around the end of March and then rushed to Montreal. William McGillivray was the first to see this lengthy letter and, in the absence of Simon McTavish, was expected to take whatever action was necessary.

Jonathan Graham, a wintering partner, added to his part of the letter a request from his senior clerk, Samuel Rawlinson, to 'go out' at the conclusion of *Rendezvous*. (To go out was to leave the North Country)

"This is what I shall propose, Duncan. You will go to Grand Portage in May with Mr. McTavish as his secretary; on the return to Montreal Mr. McTavish will have Samuel Rawlinson as his secretary. At *Rendezvous* you and Rawlinson will work closely to make each other aware of the duties to be traded. Then you will go into the North Country as a junior clerk with Mr. Graham."

That stunned me. I looked up to William McGillivray as my supervisor. Now I saw him as the bearer of the best news a clerk with ambitions in the fur trade could want to hear.

"Sir, I don't know what to say. I appreciate the opportunity you have outlined to me, but I am at a loss for words."

"Of course you are. I don't expect an immediate answer."

"Thank you for that, sir. When do you need my response?"

"First thing, Duncan, you must keep this to yourself. It will only complicate my decision if this gets bandied about the offices. You are the first person who came to mind when I read Jonathan's request. I think you see why this could get complicated."

"Yes, sir, I see the problem."

"Come to me with any questions you have. But only to me. Understood? Fine!"

Blazing balls of fire! Did I hear correctly? I might be going into the *pays d'en haut* as soon as this coming fall! William wouldn't be playing a trick on me, would he? No, not William McGillivray. He was what I heard some clerks at *Rendezvous* call a 'straight arrow'. Am I ready for this drastic change?

Why do you hesitate telling William McGillivray you are ready for this? You know damn well why you are hanging back, Duncan Ross. You are afraid! Face it, lad, you don't have all the answers, and you know it.

"Mr. McGillivray. How long will I be expected to stay in the North Country?"

"You must understand Mr. Graham's perspective. He needs time to train you in the duties he will expect you to perform. Once he has trained you to the point where he can leave you on your own, you will be alone."

"Won't there be other clerks in the outposts? Aren't there *voyageurs* at each of the posts?"

"You will work mostly with other clerks. As for the *voyageurs*, most of them take native wives, have families, and live outside the post's stockade. You will have contact with them, but not on a regular basis."

"What will my duties be, sir?"

"Duncan, I cannot answer that. Mr. Graham determines for himself what each of his clerks does."

"I appreciate your openness, Mr. McGillivray. May I come back to my first question, sir?"

"I will tell you this, Duncan Ross, if I didn't think you could handle this transfer I would not have wasted two minutes talking to you. Now you had a question?"

"How long will I be expected to remain in the North Country?"

"God! Young man, you are a bulldog. You never let go, do you? Jonathan Graham will be investing a great amount of time in your training. I would think a minimum of three years. Can you live with that, Duncan?"

"To tell the truth, at this point I don't know. But I knew from the beginning of my apprenticeship that the North Country is a 'must' assignment if I am ever to become a partner."

"How right you are! Shall we leave it at this point?"

Was I any more at ease after this session with the man who just last summer returned from five active years in the North Country? I did feel assured but, damn it, there were still doubts. That word 'alone' had me worried. All those clerks I had met and verbally jousted with at Grand Portage survived the North Country for several years. If they can do it, so can I.

If you don't go with Mr. Graham, what will you do here in Montreal? Be a clerk for the rest of your life? You know the methods of Simon McTavish - once you refuse his offer there is never a second chance. I am sure William McGillivray's mind worked the same way.

"Sir, I have given much thought to what you propose for me in the coming years. I am prepared to accept."

"We are pleased, and I speak for my uncle as well as myself, to have you come to this decision. Are you firm in your answer? I will give you another twenty-four hours to reconsider."

"That will not be necessary, sir. My answer is firm."

That was it. No flowery talk about great opportunities, no glossing over the unknowns.

"Make sure your personal affairs are in order. Write letters to family and friends. As for clothing, I think it best to go with what you have. Mr. Graham will have a winter outfit made for you at one of his posts. The hides and skins that make the best winter garments are not easily available in Montreal. You don't want all that bulky stuff to handle on the trip to Grand Portage.

"Keep your personal items to a minimum. Smile, Duncan, you won't be at the end of the world, but you'll be damn close!"

He thought he made a huge joke and enjoyed a huge laugh. I thought of Mr. MacQuay and those maps of North America and white spaces, and I didn't find much to laugh about.

I wrote to my family in the Highlands:

Dear Father, Mother, and Louise

This letter must be written and sent off to you as soon as possible. Another change in my work assignments is about to be made. This morning William McGillivray, Uncle Simon's nephew who is in charge of the Company while Mr. McTavish is in Europe for the winter on business, gave me this bit of news. He is sending me into the North Country at the conclusion of next summer's Rendezvous. I will be working for a wintering partner named Jonathan Graham. He has lived in that country for many years and is considered to be one of the best of the traders in the Company. I am sure I will be well trained and prepared for the different life in the North Country.

You will want to reply to my letters, of course, but I have been told to warn you they will be few and far between. Send them as you usually do, but they cannot be delivered to me until the next year's Rendezvous and I cannot reply until Rendezvous - in short a year between letters.

I think we should all look on this change as a promotion. I will try my best to make you proud of my work for Uncle Simon. Mother, you need not worry about me; many men of the Company go and come in the North Country as easily as they would make the trip to Glasgow or Edinburgh. The thing I will miss the most is our exchange of letters, but there is no way to speed the process. Perhaps on one of his trips to London, Mr. McTavish can find time to go to Scotland and tell you about my work and where I am being sent.

Your obedient and loving son
Duncan

On a Sunday in late March, by chance, I met Jeanette Turmel skating on the river. We enjoyed several hours on the ice then walked slowly to her house. "Duncan, you remember I told you that you gave my mother a shock? Well you did."

"But why, Jeanette, why? Did I say anything out of order, anything to give offense?"

"Of course not. She was taken aback to learn you are related to Simon McTavish. My mother prides herself on knowing everybody's family tree."

"I know Simon McTavish is a well-known and highly respected man in this city. I can't see why it's important to your mother to know I am related to him. Why?"

"She told you of Mary Margaret Chaboillez's betrothal to your uncle, remember? Mother and I had a fierce argument over that. I said Mr. McTavish was hiring a womb, not marrying a woman he loved."

"That's a damning judgment to make about my uncle, isn't it?"

"Not at all, Duncan, you men are all the same! For God's sake, she is only sixteen years old, the same age as you and I. Your uncle is an old man of forty-four. He wants children on which to build his dynasty. Love is the last thing he has in mind in marrying Mary Margaret."

"Why did your thinking upset your mother so?"

"She was shocked to learn I even knew the word womb. And she was shocked to think her own daughter would dream that marriages are anything but the beautiful coming together of two souls in heaven for a life on earth."

"I guess you did set your mother back, and me too. I never thought my uncle had any reason to marry other than he met the great love of his life."

"Don't you think I have heard about the *liaisons* of you North West people with the Indian maidens who come to your damn *Rendezvous*? Duncan, I wasn't born yesterday."

"I'm sure you weren't, but you shouldn't believe all you hear about *Rendezvous*."

"Nonsense! I'll bet you had one or two yourself, Mister Prissy Duncan Ross."

Balls of fire! Was my face red? Did I give myself away? No, she was just fishing, she doesn't know what goes on at Grand Portage. Or does she?

"Well, has the cat got your tongue?"

"No it hasn't, Jeanette, for there is something I want to tell you, if you'll keep quiet long enough to let me have a word."

"And what might that be, Duncan?"

Before I could begin the front door of the big house opened and Mrs. Turmel called, "Jeanette, come at once. I have need of you."

Late one afternoon Jeanette and I met by accident in Old Montreal. She had a shopping basket filled with her purchases and was hurrying home in the fading light. I was bound for my quarters and a leisurely supper, but reversed direction on the spot.

"Jeanette, how nice to see you. May I assist you with your heavy basket?"

"Yes, you may take the basket. Why have you been avoiding me, Duncan Ross? If I remember our last meeting you were on the verge of telling me something which I think was important. Am I right?"

As we walked toward her house I told Jeanette Turmel of the plan Mr. McGillivray outlined to me, and the time table I would follow. She listened as I poured out the whole story of leaving Montreal and going into the *pays d'en haut* for an extended period. At the end of my recital, she became very quiet and said nothing.

We reached her home and stood at the gate not wanting to say good-bye. Instead of speaking, Jeanette put her arms around my neck and kissed me on the lips. I put my arms about her waist, and returned her kiss, again and again. Finally she pushed herself from my embrace and, placing her hands on my shoulders, looked at me for a moment, then said softly, "I will miss you, Duncan."

Basket in hand, she was through the gate and half way to the door before I realized she was gone. "Wait, Jeanette, wait." My last words were to a door already closing.

Each night when I returned to my quarters I went over the list of what I needed for the trek into the *pays d'en haut*. The razor used since arriving in Montreal was the one my father slipped into my ditty bag when I left home; I should have a spare. My boots were holding up well; Amibel Dessault was a fine craftsman. I remembered most of the clerks from the outposts in the North Country wore moccasins while at Grand Portage, and all had some pieces of deer skin clothing which they wore from time to time. Mr. Marx with his quick needle and sharp mind could not make the clothing I would need in the land of big, white spaces.

Simon McTavish returned to Montreal ten or so days after the ice moved out of the St. Lawrence. I was summoned to his office and given specific orders to be ready to go to *Rendezvous*. Mr. McTavish, Mr. McGillivray and Pierre LeBlanc completed the roster of passengers in the express canoe.

I could look forward to splendid dining courtesy of Pierre and his hampers and baskets. To the relief of all, Pierre was his old self; jovial, full of good cheer, and making promises of special treats along our journey. On this trip all would be agreeable companions, no silly fops like Michel Robitaille. Yes, this trip would be a relaxed and a pleasant interlude.

As usual, I miscalculated.

Uncle Simon was in a foul mood from the day we left *La Chine* all the way to Grand Portage. I could not piece together the exact causes of Uncle Simon's fits of distemper, but did learn while in London this past winter, he approached the British Prime Minister, William Pitt. He tried to persuade Mr. Pitt to take the lead in the North West Company's efforts to break the monopoly the Hudson's Bay Company had over shipping in and out of the Bay. In this he failed. Let me tell you, Simon McTavish did not accept failure gracefully!

And there was Alexander Mackenzie, what a burr he was under Uncle Simon's saddle! He had been knighted by King George III and must be addressed as 'Sir Alexander'. Now, Sir Alexander mounted a serious opposition to the NWC through something called The Alexander Mackenzie Fur Company - in the trade called 'The XY Company'. This new, feisty outfit was taking a big bite out of NWC fur trading operations at the same time the old HBC was stepping up its expansion and aggressive competition.

Within two days of our arrival at the central depot, the brigade of Jonathan Graham came down the trail from *Fort Charlotte*. The usual round of greetings and shared cups of high wine were exchanged by important men. I waited patiently for my introduction to Samuel Rawlinson. The minute this was done he and I wandered to the dock to take the measure of one another.

Samuel Rawlinson was not the sort of man I envisioned. He was short, stocky, much to my surprise he was five or so years older, and seemed very shy. I was filled to the brim with questions, but set them aside. A call from Mr. McTavish brought an end to our conversation. "Samuel, get used to this. Mr. McTavish expects immediate response."

"Whom have we here? I suppose this is the young man to be my secretary on our journey back to Montreal. Well, don't just stand there. Tell me who you are, and be quick about it. We've much to do, and damn little time to do it."

I began a formal introduction, but a wave of the hand along with a dark scowl cut off the amenities. "Samuel, you will be with me in this afternoon's session with the partners and agents. You will take detailed notes and have them in readable form for my perusal before dinner."

I could not have given Samuel a more appropriate introduction than the one Simon McTavish just gave of himself. I looked at Samuel while he was being withered by the blast from his future boss. Not a trace of pain. Perhaps he hadn't time to digest all that had been laid on him.

My afternoon was just as busy as Samuel's, for Mr. Graham saw me at the Great Hall and took me in tow.

"You will remember from last summer, I am sure, all the dealing and trading that the clerks must do to fill out the requisitions necessary to the success at the trading posts of their *bourgeois*."

"The clerks run their own little trading fair here at the *Rendezvous*, don't they? I am looking forward to this part of my work."

"If you have questions, Duncan, you ask me first."

The first encounter with my new boss was pleasant and encouraging; Samuel's was an introduction to the hubs of hell. At dinner we compared notes. I could see that Samuel had a look of concern that casual chatter could not erase. He came right to the point, "How can a body ever keep up with all the talk that goes on in one of those partner's meetings?"

"It gets pretty hectic, doesn't it?"

"Some of them can't seem to get enough of their own voices, yet old McTavish just sat there and let them run on. How did you get his damn summary done in such a short time?"

"If you promise to keep this to yourself I will tell you of the system I used to keep pace with the business talked about in these meetings."

"I promise. But why all the secrecy?"

"If this ever got out, my ass would be fried in bear grease."

The system of short-hand and the code I devised to speed note taking was revealed. Samuel exploded with laughter and I joined in just as heartily. We became friends and fellow conspirators on the spot; he immediately came up with additions to my code that were even more appropriate. If this did leak out there would be two asses to fry in bear grease. Somehow I knew he would never let that code see daylight.

Rendezvous sped to its ultimate conclusion - the beginning of leave-taking among the partners, clerks, and crews of *voyageurs*. I confided to Samuel personal things of my life and my ambitions I never imagined would pass my lips. Samuel walked with me up the Grand Portage Trail after he had said his good-byes to his friend and mentor of four years. The parting of Jonathan Graham and Samuel Rawlinson was a deep and very personal event, and I did not want to witness it. The best Samuel and I managed in our leave-taking came haltingly, and would have no meaning for anyone else.

Within two days of the departure from *Fort Charlotte* I became the center of attention. It was nothing that I did, or failed to do. It was something that I was about to do.

Les hommes du Nord kept alive a little ceremony which they introduced to me at the 'height of land' - the point in the lay of the land where the water of the rivers and lakes divided to flow into the Lake Superior drainage basin, or into that of the Hudson's Bay. One of the *voyageurs* filled a basin with water, some from South Lake and some from North Lake - the dividing place - and brushed my face with a cedar bough dipped in that water. I had to promise never to kiss a *voyageur's* wife without her permission, never to let a *mangeur de lard* (a man from Montreal) cross this point for his first time without being subject to the same ceremony, and I was permitted to wear a feather in my *tuque*. It took but a few minutes for the rites to be administered, but it was cause for a keg to be tapped, toasts to be drunk, and firing salutes from the muskets carried with us.

This simple ceremony held lasting significance for whoever participated in it. It meant that you passed into a totally different life from that of the east side of the height of land. As days became months, and even longer, I realized why I did feel different. I had made a crossing into the new world of the fur trader, and into those blank, white spaces on Mr. MacQuay's maps. I had arrived!

Seven weeks ago I was in the Great Hall of the NWC hard at work to learn the duties of a junior clerk in an active trading post. Now I was standing on a rickety dock on a lake, God only knows where, with my knees knocking from the cold. And I was hungry, damned hungry.

Jonathan Graham, *le bourgeois de Lac de Truches*, headed a brigade of five canoes. Pemmican (dried buffalo meat that was pounded to powder, mixed with grease, and packed into the gut of the buffalo) was the 'fuel' for the crews, there were no other rations.

"You must eat. You know the alternative, don't you?"

"No. You mean you will send me back to Montreal?"

"The alternative is to pile rocks over your body, erect a little cross, and move on. You must eat to survive."

"I try, Mr. Graham, but I can barely get pemmican past my nose when the damn stuff comes right back up."

"You have no choice, lad, keep trying."

Pemmican wasn't my only problem. This outpost was so small. The stockade surrounding it enclosed a handful of log hutments. Even though a wisp of smoke issued from each, they all had the appearance of drabness, meanness, coldness, and this-place-was-not-meant-for-Duncan Ross. But Duncan Ross was here!

This exercise in self pity did not last long. When our brigade was sighted coming across the lake in the near-dusk of a fall afternoon, a bonfire was lighted in the compound. Men, women, children, dogs came from everywhere to welcome the travelers. What quickly dispelled my despair was the genuine nature of the welcome. This was not a show, not a staged demonstration to please *le bourgeois*. Those shouts and prayers, those smiles and tears were real. Every kiss, every embrace repeated over and over as a little community was once again made whole.

Mr. Graham's last words were that tomorrow was to be a holiday, a feast day, and all should gather in the compound at noon. This would be a party of thanksgiving for the completion of the long and dangerous trek to *Rendezvous*.

The next morning I was greeted with, "A good day to you, Duncan Ross, and welcome to my place."

"Thank you sir."

"I am expected to say a few words at this *gala*. Natives as well as *voyageurs* like to be addressed as equals, not as inferiors as so many of my colleagues do."

Food appeared as if by magic: cakes of fish with wild rice, of ground meat with ground corn were thrust at me. Others gave me gourds of sweet, mysterious liquids that barely disguised the rum. Hot somethings were snaked from the coals of the fire in the center of the compound, and when cooled they yielded flavors totally foreign to me, but truly delicious. I forgot the endless meals of pemmican on our trek from *Rendezvous*, and literally threw myself into the feast.

After several hours of this, the crowd drifted around the sides of an area where some young men gathered. A drum began to beat out a slow and stately rhythm. The dancers traced an intricate step around the fire, chanting as they danced with faces showing no trace of emotion. The dancers were completely in their world and sent to us the message their spirits received. Although only the men danced, all were included in the ritual.

"You are taken by this, Duncan. I am pleased to see that, and I know others in the community sense your joining in."

"It is a moving experience, Mr. Graham."

"Duncan, it is not fair to ask this of you, but if I can get one of the drummers to beat the cadence for one of your Highland flings, will you dance? It would mean so much have this response from you. Will you do it, Duncan?"

How could I refuse? Not that he was my master, my mentor. Because he was Jonathan Graham, a man who was comfortable with himself and wanted all in his world to share his good feelings. I danced.

The training begun by Jonathan Graham was directed toward survival skills, trading skills would come later. I was taken to a two-room log cabin of a family inside the compound. He had me meet his long-time guide, interpreter, and friend, Luis LaGarde and his wife, Annette, and five children ranging from fourteen to four.

The purpose of this visit was to have Annette measure me for a complete winter outfit in fur of mukluks, trousers, parka with hood, and mittens. In addition she took measurements for a set of deer skin clothes of two shirts, two pairs of leggings, and moccasins with easily replaced soles.

The next stop Mr. Graham made with me was at a lodge outside the compound. A woman of immense girth waddled out of her wicki-up to look me over, measure my feet, measure my stride, grunting much but saying little. She gave Mr. Graham to understand my snow-shoes would be ready in two weeks. It was early October and he was thinking snow?

The main building of the compound became the center of my life. One end was the trading room I judged to be fifteen by twenty-five feet, lined with shelves and bins with a 'U' shaped counter for examination of skins and trade items. The open end of the counter was opposite a door that led to Mr. Graham's quarters; two small rooms, one a general purpose room, one a sleeping room. At the other end of the main building was the bunkhouse for the clerks; two rooms, one of general purpose, the other with four bunks in a two-over-two arrangement. The middle of the long building had two large storerooms for trade goods; both under lock and key - the rum was kept here.

With heat from fireplaces in the trading room, Mr. Graham's quarters, and the general purpose room of the clerks, some degree of comfort was possible. It certainly was not the Great Hall. It was noth-ing like Mr. McTavish's office nor like those of McTavish and Frobisher. This building mirrored the change I was making. From being concerned with finding the next rung in my career ladder, I focused on the very basics of life - food, clothing, and shelter.

"Duncan, I suspect one of the first things you must learn is the different view we have of our customers. You have been working with what I call the 'eastern perspective'. By that I mean, the native is an ignorant, half-savage person, who can be easily dazzled by fancy gew-gaws and rum. Something along that line, am I correct?"

"Yes, Mr. Graham. I heard that all the time in Montreal."

"You won't hear it here. I will not permit that attitude to take root in my outposts. But more importantly, you won't make it through your first winter in the North Country with a feeling of supe-riority. Survival is the key, Duncan, and there are no better teachers of these skills than natives."

"I guess I am fortunate to have them to follow."

"Mistake, Duncan, a grave mistake. You must learn to act on your own with confidence. Too many times you will find yourself with no one to follow. You must know what to do instinctively."

"But how am to learn such skills if I am to work alone?"

A hint of smile crossed Mr. Graham's face as he said, "Duncan, you are getting ahead of yourself. I will see to it that you work with experienced hands until I judge you are ready to be placed in posi-tions where you will be alone. I didn't bring you all the way to my department only to lose you in the first winter."

"For that I am truly thankful, Mr. Graham."

"Nicely said, Duncan, but your thanks should go to the men who will show you how to do what it takes to become a trader, and a survivor."

With no further lectures, I began to learn by doing, by making mistakes, and in making errors of judgment. I was being reshaped by men whose lives were in the *pays d'en haut*. Their every move made them one with nature.

But Mother Nature did not halt the advance of winter just to accommodate the training schedule of a newcomer. Winter came with a rush one night, a sudden drop in temperature, howling winds, and torrents of rain that quickly became snow. By morning's light everything as far as I could see was blanketed in white. Nothing moved except for the thin wisps of smoke curling from fireplaces. No movement, and no sound. Nothing but white, unbroken, unchanging white. I thought to myself with a smile, "Well, Mr. MacQuay, where are the dragons?"

My snowshoes arrived, now came the initial test. Luis LaGarde showed me how to step into them on, to stride, and how to keep my balance. What he didn't need to show me was how to fall flat on my face or on my duff.

"Get up and try again, Mister Duncan. That's the only way you will learn."

"What am I doing wrong, Luis?"

"Everything, my young friend, everything. But you will learn. Now, get up and try again."

I finally mastered the ability to stay upright and move slowly on the snowshoes. Luis was right, I had to get out and use them everyday. If not, I would develop the painful thing the natives called *mal de raquette* (snowshoe lameness).

One morning Mr. Graham called me to the trading room, "Duncan, I want you to see these pelts. These are very special skins."

"Yes, Mr. Graham, they are beaver, are they not?"

"They are beaver, Duncan, but of unusual quality and size. Run your hands over them, stroke them, feel how soft and silky they are. These are prime, they are top quality. You must recognize that all beaver are not the same. Rarely will you see pelts of this quality."

"My God, they are soft. They are beautiful; so dark and they keep their sheen no matter what light you hold them to. So, Mr. Graham, these are prime?"

"I call them my 'soft gold'; they are the best I have seen in years. Yes, they are soft gold!"

I was alone in the trading room on a clear but very cold February day taking a count of certain items Mr. Graham thought needed to be replenished at the coming *Rendezvous*. A family of Indians I had never seen before at the outpost came into the room single file; first the man, then I assumed it was his wife, then came a young man, and last in line was a man? or was it a woman? I could-n't tell until they pushed back the hoods of their parkas and loosened the 'frogs' that kept them sealed tight about the neck. Then I saw the fourth person was a female, tall, taller than any member of her fami-ly, nearly as tall as I.

Sauntering behind the trading counter I casually laid out a twist of tobacco. Just as casually the man picked it up, sniffed it, passed to his wife who did they same. The man laid it back on the counter as if rejecting my offer. I took a clay pipe from my *sac-a-feu* (a small beaded deerskin bag tied about my waist) crumbled some of the leaf in the bowl, lighted it with a flint and steel - a trick that took me some time to master, but now I could do it like a native - and blew some smoke with a little sound of satisfaction. The man and the older woman followed, and the air in the room filled with the pleasant aroma of good Brazilian tobacco. I had been advised by Mr. Graham this little ceremony was never to be interrupted with talk or gestures. We enjoyed our *allumez*.

The older woman crossed the room to stand in front of the shelves holding bolts of cotton and woolen materials. She was joined by her daughter, though the height of the younger one did not match that of the older. They talked softly between themselves for several minutes. With her eyes the younger indicated a certain bolt of woolen material she wished to examine. I brought it to the counter, and they began to feel and judge the quality of the fabric.

The man had gone to the bin of ice chisels and selected three that he laid on the counter. The young man had never moved from the spot where he stood on entering the trading room; his eyes were fixed on a trade gun. A nod from his father and I handed it over for the young man's examination.

The aroma of trade tobacco had penetrated Mr. Graham's quarters and he slowly made his way into the room acknowledging each family member with a nod and a smile. His eyes gave me a set of directions; he would take over with the men, I to work with the women. They selected one bolt, I placed the others back on the shelf as the young woman began to carefully unroll and measure with her eyes the amount of material she wanted. I had reached under the counter for the heavy shears to cut off the purchase. A quick shake of his head was the only direction Mr. Graham gave me - don't cut anything yet.

He and the older man looked at each other. From their gestures and eye movements I figured out this was not to be 'a deal of debts' - an exchange of goods based on a promise to bring in the furs to cover the purchase at a later time. This was to be a straight across the counter exchange, goods for skins.

At a signal from the older man, the younger man stepped outside and brought in a string of four beaver pelts. They were large pelts, very dark in color, and long in the guard hairs. As they lay on the counter Mr. Graham slowly, and with a show of indifference, began to stroke them, to turn them over in the manner of an experienced trader. No words were exchanged, no expressions showed on either face, but I sensed the moment was at hand. A deal was about to be made.

Mr. Graham took the gun from the hands of the young man and showed him how smoothly the hammer of the firing mechanism worked then handed it back to him. He walked to my counter and began to refold about half of the material that had been unrolled by the tall woman, then he took one of the ice chisels and put it under the counter. He resumed his place before the man and nodded. The native walked over to the material and unrolled about half of what Mr. Graham had just rolled up. He resumed his place in front of Mr. Graham. The two stood like statues for, I thought, an eternity. The Indian gave a nod of his head; a nod from Mr. Graham and I was cutting the woolen material.

As I began to cut the young woman placed her hand over mine to stop my cutting while she smoothed the material so the cut edge would be straight and true. The touch of her hand sent a thrill through my whole system. As I looked up at her she never looked away from me. The material was rolled and laid on the counter with the ice chisels. The young man held tightly to the trade gun, and I could see a faint smile cross Mr. Graham's face. The two men stood looking at each other with unblinking eyes, it was finished.

The family adjusted their hoods and placed their purchases in a backpack except for the trade gun; the boy kept it in his possession. They filed from the trading room in the order they had entered. I stood by the door and as they passed I caught a fleeting smile from the tall one.

"Well, Duncan, that was very well done. You were right to begin with an offer of tobacco, you were right to be patient. But, Duncan, that tall one could trade you out of the very boots you are wearing."

"Do you think so, Mr. Graham. These boots are special to me, it would take a pretty good trade to get them away from me?"

"I'll grant you she was a most attractive young woman. And I would bet those were not her parents; I've never seen a woman that tall among Cree or Ojibway people? Her features were more Spanish than Indian, wouldn't you say."

"I don't know what to say, but she had blue eyes. Can you explain that, Mr. Graham? And how would you grade the four beaver skins they brought to trade? Would you rate them as your soft gold?"

"Yes, no question, they are 'soft gold'"

Luis LaGarde and I were called to the *bourgeois'* private quarters to hear Mr. Graham's plan. We were to take some of our stock of trade items to one of our outlying posts by dog sled. On the return we were to find the winter camp of the family that brought those prime skins - the soft gold. The HBC was becoming more aggressive in our area; a visit with gifts would remind that family their best interests lay with the NWC.

Under Luis' directions we assembled our food, food for the string of dogs, supplies for the outlyer, and gifts for the family. He made a check on the condition of the *cariolle* (a toboggan with a skirt of animal hides to protect the rider). At first light we were under way.

With all we packed into the *carriole*, it was necessary for both Luis and I to 'shoe' it along the side of the *cariolle*, sometimes behind it. Our run to the outpost involved only one night of camping on the trail. We enjoyed the warmth and hospitality of the outpost for the next two nights. Luis and I were back on the trail, except it wasn't a trail. It was vast open space with an equally vast area of small-growth forest. We were totally dependent on Luis' judgment and experience.

The first day and night seemed routine, but as the second day wore on, changes in the weather were evident. The wind shifted to the south, clouds thickened. Even the dogs sensed changes were coming, and coming fast. Luis said we must get into the forest and make a camp with some protection from the fierce winds. We managed to set up a camp with the last minutes of daylight. He fed the dogs, I piled branches to make a wind-break for them. We dug a cave in the snow for ourselves. With a pot of stew bubbling on the fire, the night ahead seemed endurable.

During the night the winds died to almost a whisper, and the air became so clear and cold that stars could be had by the handful - if you were so foolish to reach outside your blanket roll. Trees popping and creaking in the intense cold were warnings to Luis that we must move. To stay in our blanket rolls invited slow death. He went from dog to dog, made them get up and move about. He rubbed each one roughly to stimulate circulation. I was no help to him in this, for he said the dogs did not know me and would snap and bite. I was told to bring wood to the fire to keep it burning.

When light was sufficient, Luis strapped on his snowshoes and made a survey of our situation. He came back to report the winds and snow of yesterday afternoon had changed all landmarks. The best thing for us to do was head in the general direction of our homepost until he could pick up familiar terrain. The visit Mr. Graham had wanted us to make was forgotten. Our mission was now one of survival.

We moved through the day ever mindful of the dogs and their condition; of our condition and the extent of food supplies. We battled rising winds and the intensity of the sun glaring off the snow. To stop was to risk never being able to start again. Moving expended the energy of both dogs and men. I was the one to go down. Luis insisted I ride in the *cariolle*, suck on a piece of elk jerky, and restore some energy. He said we would trade places every hour so he too could rest and keep up his energy level. We set our course with the sun and Luis' sense of direction.

When it was my turn to snowshoe behind the *cariolle* I tried to keep to the trace he pointed out to me. The wind and sun were taking a terrible toll on my eyes and energy level. Several times I fell behind. Catching up became impossible. Had not Luis roused himself and made his way back to me, I would have perished. He spotted a clump of trees about a mile ahead, and somehow got the dogs to it. I was in and out of consciousness, of no help to him. If we survived this ordeal, credit should go to Luis LaGarde and his dogs. Their sharp noses had detected the direction of the native's winter camp, and Luis had the good sense to let them take the lead.

I was aware of movement about me, but could not see a thing. I was blind. A gourd full of something was forced between my lips, my face was wiped carefully and pads of soft material covered my eyes. I tried to move, but hands gently and firmly pushed me back onto something soft and warm. Time lost all meaning, there was nothing to relate to, no light. Just darkness.

New voices registered in my mind, for a routine was being followed. I was fed hot soups or stews, I had been stripped of all clothing, sponged and rubbed with lotions. My eyes continued to cause me pain, and became the center of almost constant attention. They were gently swabbed and bathed with warm salve. Every time I reached up to remove the pads that covered them, hands pushed mine away.

My body seemed to recover, but my eyes remained the major concern. The pads, the bathing, the careful wiping and sponging continued. I came close to ripping off the pads over my eyes when two hands clamped over mine. They were not the hands of a man, or the old woman who directed my treatments, they were those of a young woman. The last time I remembered a touch like this was in the trading post when the family of four came in with the soft gold beaver pelts. The voice was as gentle as the hands.

My dreaming and fantasizing ended abruptly with the presence of the older woman. She knelt down at my side, slowly, with great tenderness, she removed the coverings over my eyes. She bathed them with a warm liquid, dried them, and with her fingers that had such a delicate touch opened my eye lids and told me to follow her hand. I did as directed, and followed her movements. I could not focus my eyes, but I could detect movement. Dear God in heaven, I was not blind!

The lodge seemed empty of people and I decided now is the time to do some testing on my own. I started to get up, and succeeded in standing only to be pushed back on the pad of robes. Again, the soft young hands with firmness, again the realization that I was not ready for full, unfettered activity. But this time was different, I was able to see. Only a fraction of normal vision, but I could see. What I saw was the tall, young woman who had purchased woolen material at our trading post only a month ago.

Bursts of vision were followed by bursts of pain that told me to be patient, not overdo. I began to link the signals I noticed the past two days. I matched the soft hands with the soft voice. I matched the rough but healing hands with the older woman who brought me through this ordeal. I matched the strength and firmness of my guide to the latrine lodge with the young man who gazed so fondly on the trade gun at our homepost.

All these match-ups were nothing compared to the match-up with my embarrassment when I discovered I had been stripped of all clothing. Who had done these things for me? Surely this young woman so frequently in my world of recovery was not always at my side. When I realized she was the tall one who had given me such a jolt with her touch and shy smile, I wanted to crawl into a corner of the lodge and hide. She had seen me as only my mother had; buck-ass naked. She bathed me? She massaged me? She fed me?

She knelt beside me and read my mind. She knew all the feelings of uncertainty, of being stripped bare in front of strangers, of the sense of helplessness, of the delicate balance that existed between sight and blindness, she knew all these things. And she laughed, not in derision, not to degrade or belittle. She laughed in a way that said she shared my thinking and confused sense of deliverance, of my dilemma.

Without a word spoken, we enjoyed the pure pleasure of the moment. I reached out my hand to her. She took it and cradled it in her warm hands, brought it to her face and gently rubbed my palm along her cheek and neck. I pulled back and placed my other hand over hers, brought them to my lips kissing both hands. We were speaking to each other with our senses, with our eyes, our spirits.

Luis brought me a full account of all that had taken place during the period of recovery. He said in the morning we would resume our trek to our home post after I presented the gifts. I lay back and counted one by one the miracles of the past forty-eight hours. The warmth of the lodge fire, the warmth of the stew, and the release from the worry of a lifetime of blindness all combined to produce sleep.

In the morning Luis was at my side with instructions to get dressed, to plan the ceremony of gifts to the head man of the winter camp, and to prepare for a fast trip home. The dogs had been rested and cared for; the weather was favorable; there was nothing to keep us here any longer. Was there?

Chapter Five

Luis was in a playful mood and kept after me about the tall, young woman who had spent so much of her time in the lodge where I recovered from my mis-adventure and near-blindness. In the speech to the elders when I presented Mr. Graham's gifts I spoke in French, Luis translated into dialect of the people.

"You made a fine speech, Mister Duncan, very fine."

"That is the first time I ever had to speak like that. You think I did a good job?"

"Oh yes, the Tall One was especially happy to hear what you said about her."

"But, Luis, I didn't say anything about her. All I said was how much I was in debt to all who helped me through my close call with blindness."

"What you said, Mister Duncan, you would come back to marry her."

"Luis, you devil! I didn't say that. You played tricks in your translation, didn't you?"

"Now, you know I would never do anything like that, would I?"

"The hell you wouldn't. I'll never know what you told those people."

"No, Mister Duncan, you will never know."

We had been snowshoeing alongside the *cariolle* to give the dogs a break. Peering closely at Luis I saw only a blank look on his face, but his eyes were full of mischief. Luis made the transition from a *mangeur de lard* to that of *l' homme du Nord* many years ago, but he retained his *voyageur's* love of a prank and, at times, the charming insolence so characteristic of them.

"Luis, I will ask you one more time. What did you really tell those people?"

"My friend, you doubt the word of the Great Luis LaGarde? I am insulted! We will have to fight a duel. This is an affair of honor."

"Honor! You scheming *batard*, you don't know the meaning of honor. I think I will have to ask Annette about your habits."

"You wouldn't do that. That would not be fair."

"That's right, Luis, it would not be fair, nor would it be fair to tell her of the nights you were not alone in your lodge. Should I tell her of those 'affairs of honor'?"

"I think, Mister Duncan, you and I should . . . what do you call it? Negotiate?"

"No deal, Luis. I feel I must tell Annette everything."

"You drive a hard bargain. I will tell you exactly what I translated for you if you promise Annette will not hear of my visits with women in the winter camp. Agreed?"

"I'll have to think about it."

The dogs always present in the homepost compound were the first to sense our approach and by the time Luis drove his dog team through the gate everyone knew of our return. People crowded around to give welcome and news of *le bourgeois*. What of Mr.

Graham? Why was his name the first on everyone's lips? Had something happened? I rushed to his quarters in the main building only to be met by Annette LaGarde at the door.

"What has happened, Annette?"

"Mister Duncan, he has been in bed for the last three days sleeping most of the time. I remember he had a spell like this four years ago."

"Was it the same as this time?"

"I think so. When he woke up it was just like nothing had happened. By the end of a month he was himself again."

I told Annette to get some rest while I stayed with him through the night. I promised to send for her if anything developed or changed. The night was uneventful, and at first light I was in Mr. Graham's sleeping room to check on him.

"Duncan, glad you're home." The voice, weak and hesitant, came from deep in the pillows.

"You should rest, Mr. Graham. We will have time to talk when you have regained some strength."

"Are you some kind of medicine man, Duncan? If I want to talk, damn it, I am going to talk. I know what has happened to me; it has happened before, it will happen again. Help me get to the night jar, then find Annette and tell her I would like something hot to eat."

Even in his obviously weakened condition, Jonathan Graham was in charge. Something in his manner told me he should not be challenged.

The departure scene on the little dock as it prepared to send off the brigade to *Rendezvous* was much like the homecoming last fall. This time the tears were of sorrow. Tears could not hide the excitement of five canoes leaving as one, the songs of the *voyageurs* echo-ing back to us as they sped across the lake. Paddles flashed in misty light as they dipped in unison. Sparkling wake patterns made by the departing craft leveled out and soon the surface of the lake was like a mirror. With a great flapping of wings, honking and scolding, a wedge of geese, settled on the water. Was this Mother Nature's way of telling me her creatures had a claim to this lake? That we were only intruders?

As I looked around the compound all I could see were children, women, old men, and dogs. Nearly every man fourteen to fifty was in a canoe. Luis LaGarde and I were among the few exceptions.

In his last days before leaving for Grand Portage, Mr. Graham gave me a detailed list of work that must be done in his four months of absence. The welfare, the survival, of these posts was dependent on every item on that list being completed. They all related to food: its gathering, growing, catching or killing; its preparation for safe storage. An impossible task for a boy of eighteen? Yes, but Mr. Graham was not a gambler. Luis LaGarde remained at the homepost to be my guide in this important piece of work.

"Luis, Mr. Graham said I was to take charge, and made me responsible for a whole list of things."

"I understand that. Tell me, what are you going to do first?"

"Well, I thought that . . . hell, Luis, I don't know what to do first."

"Duncan, the native people know where nuts and berries, grass-es and seeds are to be found and the best time to gather them. They know the habits of large game, the deer, bear, and the moose; the same for small game. There are seasonal patterns to catching fish, they know when and where to have the greatest success."

"That's great, Luis. Let's get started right now."

"Again, my young friend, what is our first project?"

"Damn it, Luis, the first thing on Mr. Graham's list. That's where we start."

"Why don't we ask the elders what they think should be the first thing?"

The work commenced and seldom stopped until the return of the brigade in early October.

This is my letter Mr. Graham took to *Rendezvous*:

Dear Father, Mother, and Louise

This is my first letter to you from my new home in the North Country. This place is so different from any other I have lived in that it is hard to tell you about everything. We are a very small village: the head man is Mr. Jonathan Graham who years ago lived in Edinburgh. There are four clerks, I am the youngest and least experienced. Luis LaGarde is a voyageur who has lived at this post for years. He is married and has children. He is the man Mr. Graham depends on most of the time. The rest are either voyageurs or natives. and number about twenty men plus their families. Among ourselves the five Britishers speak English, the rest of the time we speak French. I am also trying to learn to speak in the native language used at our homepost.

We eat a lot of game and fish, sometimes there is wild rice and beans and squash. It is a hard place to grow anything for the summers are so short. This letter has to be written before I will begin my summer work at the post since I won't be going to Grand Portage. Mr. Graham left me with a list of the many things I will have to work at to make sure we have food to get through the coming winter.

Louise, you would laugh if you saw what I have to wear in the winter, but it keeps me warm and got me through the winter just passed. My heavy parka is made from beaver skins worn with the hair to the inside. The hood lined with wolf fur (that kind of fur won't let your breath freeze). My pants are leather, and my mukluks are really socks and boots made as one. If you see Mr. MacQuay you can tell him I am learning about those blank, white spaces on his maps. It is more

of a strange place this summer, for nearly all the men are in the brigade
of canoes going down to Grand Portage. I feel quite alone here, but
don't worry. I am well, and have a lot of work to do that is important.
                    Your loving and obedient son,
                         Duncan

When Mr. Graham led his brigade back from *Rendezvous* I
hoped he would have a letter for me. Just writing to my family about
how few people here speak English left me feeling lonely.

The number of items on Mr. Graham's list of food gathering and
storing tasks slowly shrank. Luis told me we were making good time
and the work was done in the proper fashion. He suggested that next
I have the people build up a supply of firewood. "You are young and
strong. It would be good for the people see you share their labors."

One week of cutting, hauling, splitting, and stacking was, as
Luis suggested, one hell of a job.

"Tomorrow we will take a small canoe and begin a round of the
outlying posts to see how they are doing and to make sure they are
ready for winter."

I was not paying attention late one afternoon when Luis pointed our canoe toward shore and said we would spend the night at the
Indian camp there.

"What camp? I don't see anything resembling a camp. Are you
pulling my leg again?"

"You will never make *l' homme du Nord*. Use your nose, Mister
Duncan. Tell me you smell a pot of fish stew and I will change my
mind."

As usual, Luis was right. The camp was set on a bluff overlooking the river. Not only did I fail the first test, to spot the camp, now
I failed the second. The families in this camp were the same we had

visited last winter; the same who had provided the shelter, food, and attention to my snow blindness.

"I do not recognize any in the camp, but damn it, Luis. I was blind most of the time we were there."

They extended the usual greetings of welcome; we accepted the invitation to share their evening meal. Where was the Tall One? She was not in the circle of families as we ate, or as we relaxed and gossiped. Had some brave come to her Papa, made a suitable 'bride price' and carried her off to his lodge or wickiup? Would it be polite to make inquiry? What was protocol?

"Damn it, Luis, wipe that silly grin off your face, help me."

"I can't help you, Mister Duncan."

Before this exchange went any farther, she appeared at the circle, took a gourd and served herself from the pot of stew, then retreated from the fire, sat down and ate. I just sat and admired her. I couldn't think of anything to say, or any way to get me within speaking distance of her. God, she was attractive. Do something!

I got to my feet, made some flattering words to the older woman about her stew, and said to Luis in my best *Francais sauvage*, "I had better see to the canoe. It should be brought to higher ground in case the river should rise during the night."

I waded out a few feet into the river, carefully grasped the canoe in the middle by the gunnels, and lifted it out of the water. I brought it on to the shore and just as carefully set it down. As I straightened up, she was there on the other side of the canoe. In the fading evening light she was even more lovely. We stepped toward each other, she held out her hand. I took it as she guided us to a grassy spot along the river. A breeze shielded us from mosquitoes out on night raids.

"I have worried about your eyes."

"They are fine, I have had no trouble with them."

"I am glad. Have you been well?"

"Yes, and you, have you been well?"

"Yes, I am well."

This is what you have been practicing native dialects for, to sit and make childish conversation with the most beautiful woman you have ever met? You'll have to do better, much better.

"Is your family moving its camp to the fall hunting grounds?"

"Yes. We had a very good sugar bush camp and a very good fish camp. The elders think we should make our way north to the hunting grounds."

"Will it be close to any trading posts?"

"I do not know. Why do you ask?"

"I hope it will be near one of our posts. I would like to come and see you."

"I would like that. Yes, I would like that very much."

That was a little better, but you're still not making much of an impression. Try again.

"Do you remember that day when your mother took the pads from my eyes and commanded me to follow her hand?"

"Oh yes, I remember very well. We were pleased that you would see again."

"And do you remember how we held hands and talked to each other with our eyes, with our spirits?"

"Yes, I remember."

"Should we hold hands again, like we did in the lodge?"

"Yes, I would like that."

So we did that, but that's all we did. Both heard the clearing of the throat. It made no difference who stood on the bluff above us. The message was unmistakable - your evening together is ended.

Early the next morning Luis put the canoe in the water and took his position in the rear. Much as I would like to have stayed,

Luis' actions decided everything. As we pushed out into the river's current I glanced at the bluff. Her camp was already being dismantled. She stood off by herself, clearly visible. No sign, no gesture, no wave of the hand. I consoled myself with the thought she made certain I would see her.

"What troubles you, Mister Duncan? What did you expect her to do?"

"Why should she do anything, Luis? We had a quick friendly visit, that is all."

"I think she was waiting for you to approach her Papa to begin talking."

"Talking about what? Don't be so mysterious, my friend. Talking about what?"

"Mister Duncan, you have so much to learn. When you tell a woman you will return to marry her, she expects you will act, not talk."

"Why don't you soak your head in this cool river water. You are impossible!"

For the remainder of our time paddling back to *Lac de Truches* we gave the topic of the Tall One a rest. Pressing matters at the homepost needed our attention. Mr. Graham had given Luis permission to add a room to his log cabin. Within three days it was finished. As we worked on his addition I looked over the compound for what would be a good spot for another cabin. Great blazing balls of fire, Duncan! What the hell are you thinking about? A few smiles, a few minutes of holding hands, and you are thinking of . . . Yes, exactly what were you thinking? God, she is one attractive young woman.

The return of Jonathan Graham and the five canoes from Grand Portage was cause for celebration, for both community and individuals. All eyes focused on Mr. Graham. How had he survived the grueling weeks of the *Rendezvous* cycle? Was he better? Was he worse? From what I could see, he had taken those weeks in stride. Yet there was a change in him, though I was slow to detect it. His eyes were full of hurt and anger. Why?

Everyone in the compound joined in a feast with dancing to welcome home the travelers. I felt something was amiss. The next morning as we inspected Luis' cabin addition, Mr. Graham said he wished to see me in his quarters after the evening meal.

"Duncan, come in. I have called you about *Rendezvous* and a problem that cropped up and took me completely by surprise."

"I am at a loss, Mr. Graham. Was it some oversight on my part in helping with the preparations for going to Grand Portage?"

"No, nothing like that. It was Peter Carlson who made trouble for me. I discovered he was trying to sell assignments to our posts to *voyageurs* from Montreal who wanted to transfer into the North Country."

"Was he successful? I didn't see any new faces among the *voyageurs* when the brigade returned two days ago."

"I am not sure. Peter is my nephew, you know, he used his relationship to me as a way to impress unsuspecting men that he could deliver on his promise to get them into the North Country."

This was not my affair, it was between Peter and his uncle. Peter's shameful plan forced me to think of the precarious position we Britishers occupied in the North Country. Within the North West Company, the Canadians (NWC was traditionally called Canadian; the Hudson Bay Company was called English) were outnumbered by our *voyageurs* by thirty or forty to one. Taken all together, the Bay people and the Nor'Westers were outnumbered by the natives and *voyageurs* about eighty or ninety to one. Outrageous behavior on the part of any one in either Company could put all at risk.

Not waiting for the wrath of his uncle to descend on him, Peter Carlson stole a canoe and fled from our homepost. The chances were he paddled directly to a Hudson's Bay post where he hoped to find employment.

"Luis and Duncan, the reason for calling you to my quarters is to review the damage Peter Carlson may have done."

"How could he do you any harm, Mr. Graham? He couldn't take more than a handful of pelts with him."

"True. But he had been with me long enough to do a lot of active trading. Native people like to trade with the same person. Ties between trader and native customer become binding."

"Duncan, I think Mr. Graham is telling us to get on the trail to families we know traded through Peter Carlson."

"Exactly, Luis. When do you think you can be ready? Is there sufficient snow for the dogs to pull a cariolle carrying mostly your food and gifts?"

"I don't think snow will be a problem, Mr. Graham."

We did prepare with great care, for winter trips are never taken lightly - preparation equals survival.

We made contact with two different camps in three days on the trail. The weather cooperated with our efforts as we set out for the next family. I was always amazed at Luis's ability to recall the long and involved family names in the native language, to match names to faces, and to sort out the relationships.

Our track now led away from the lake region and into a series of forested hills, difficult travel for dogs and men. Luis was certain we could find several families in this area, for game was more plentiful in this highland. As usual, he was right. By nightfall we found the camp of four families and asked to spend time with them. Again I failed a test. In winter gear of hooded parkas and mukluks, people on snowshoes tended to look alike to me. How Luis knew exactly whom he was addressing in these situations was a source of amazement.

He spoke with the man who brought the four pelts of 'soft gold' to Mr. Graham a year ago. In short, with the Tall One's Papa. I made the required greetings and tried to follow proper conduct. All the time my eyes scanned the camp. She emerged from a lodge and looked my way. No sign of recognition. What had I done or said at our brief meeting last summer? Surely she remembered our time together. She stepped into her snowshoes and started through the timber. After going only a short distance she stopped and looked over her shoulder, then resumed her track into the woods.

Still strapped in my snowshoes, with a dig in Luis's ribs to signal I was leaving, I followed her. This was my second winter on the *raquettes* and I had no trouble catching up. After shoeing side by side she indicated a clump of cedars that formed a protected area. Out of the wind, we kicked off our snowshoes and faced each other. She pushed back the hood of her parka, I did the same. I looked at that beautiful face, so finely shaped, and at eyes that were pools of blue, at the smile that captivated me completely. I held out my arms. She glided to me and we held each other close - as close as two heavy winter parkas would permit - and gently rubbed noses on noses, necks, and on ears. I tried to kiss her, but she did not know what to do.

Teaching her to kiss was one of the most delightful things I have ever done, she was a willing and adept student. Soon she was kissing me and determined to do it right. Duncan, she could kiss you any damn way she chose and it would be right! Without a word of explanation she stepped into her snowshoes, moved back on the trail, and I followed. In less than a mile two young people in front of us signed for the Tall One to return to camp.

We were invited to the evening meal with the Tall One's family. We ate in silence. Afterward, with the passing of the twist of tobacco, the older woman joined her husband, Luis, and me in a pipe. A stream of talk and laughter quickly followed. Luis sent me a message with his eyes, I went to our *cariolle* and retrieved the gifts Mr. Graham had selected for this particular family. Another sign and I was on my feet with a speech of friendship and undying loyalty of the NWC to its trading partners. I spoke briefly without interruption by an interpreter. I sat down to the nodding of heads and a meaningful wink from Luis.

When I saw the tent was set up and sleeping gear for one person in place, I assumed that I would be the sole occupant. Luis made other arrangements. Despite my hopes and fantasies, I was alone when I unrolled my blankets, and alone when I re-rolled them in the morning.

We were hardly back on the track to the next camp when Luis said, "You should have had me translate for you again, eh?"

"I thought I made a good speech, and I made it brief. What more could I do?"

"You picked the wrong person to direct your remarks to, Mister Duncan."

"I was to give the gifts to the older woman, and I did that. What was wrong with that?"

"Nothing. The older woman knew what you would say before the words got out of your mouth. It was the Tall One who wanted to hear something of interest to her."

"You have the heart of a pirate, my friend. You would have me say things that I am not able to follow through on."

"*C'est la guerre, mon ami, c'est la guerre.*"

"When we return, Mister Duncan, the first thing Mr. Graham will want to know is whether or not we will be able to hold this trade? What will you tell him?"

"I don't think there is anything to worry about. What will you tell him?"

"I have my doubts. You will learn that people don't always do what they say. I will be the first to admit I might be wrong, but not until I see them bring a winter's harvest of pelts."

Luis had one more question. "I was made to understand at her camp the Tall One let you teach her something she didn't know how to do. Am I right?"

"As usual, Luis, you are right. I am a good teacher, too. Did you know that?"

"Maybe so. But did you think that she might have taught you something?"

"That is possible, but what did she teach me?"

"That she isn't a pushover. She likes you, likes you a lot. But if you want her, Mister Duncan, you will have to speak with her Papa."

Luis had touched a tender spot. I looked at this lovely woman only through my eyes. What did she see when she looked at me? Was I just a traveling man of the fur trade who fell for a pretty woman? One who gave no indication of commitment or wanting to live with her?

As I thought about the Tall One, and I spent many hours doing that, I judged us to be the same age, maybe she was a year older. That didn't matter. I came to realize that her way of looking at things was more mature and more balanced. Had she wanted a romp on the buffalo robe she would have been with me the other night. She did not join me in my tent. Didn't that tell me something?

Luis and I expected to be called to Mr. Graham's quarters to give our reports. *Le bourgeois* wanted more than just our opinions, he wanted detailed information: inches of snowfall, thickness of ice, the conditions in the camps we visited, signs of health and contentment, signs of ill health or discontent, signs of game, of beaver lodges, and indications of problems we had not anticipated. No wonder Mr. Graham was one of the more successful among the wintering partners; he valued the importance of precise information.

The winter passed quickly, most of the people in our little community thought it was one of the mildest they could remember. We were once again into preparations for *Rendezvous*.

As clerk to Jonathan Graham traveling to Grand Portage he and I had some most interesting conversations. I learned more of his life and events that had given him both pleasure and pain.

"I was married at one time, had a fine wife, and a son who would have been about your age. Did you know that, Duncan, and did you know I caused their deaths?"

"No, Mr. Graham, I did not. Sir, you could not have caused anyone's death. I can't believe you would do that."

"It's true. I was developing a successful business of my own in the Netherlands and in France. My family lived in Edinburgh while I got established on the Continent. I sent for them to join me in Amsterdam. and . . ."

Time passed before he could continue his narrative.

"My wife and son boarded a ship bound from Edinburgh to Amsterdam. Between those ports out on the treacherous North Sea their ship went down with all hands."

This man sitting beside me, like my uncle, Simon McTavish, had a presence, a manner of command, a way of transmitting a sense of control. Now slumped over, his head was bent, tears rained from his eyes. Nothing I could say would bring comfort to Jonathan Graham.

"I have carried the burden of their deaths all these years. I have chosen to stay in the North Country. It's my penance, don't you see?"

No. I didn't see. I just knew that a fine man like Jonathan Graham could not be responsible for another person's death. I heard sometime, somewhere about this thing he called penance, but I didn't understand how that applied to him.

Recalling the constant competition among all clerks throughout the three weeks of *Rendezvous*, I went directly to the loft over the Great Hall to claim sleeping space. Just in time to get the last space, I laid out personal possessions to stake my territory. When I returned to the loft after the evening's *soirée*, my gear was piled in a corner, an unknown clerk in my place. A few candles still burned, enough light to lay hold of the intruder and set him, forcefully, on his ass.

"What the hell you think you're doin?"

"I'm getting ready for a good night's sleep. What are you going to do?"

"I've a mind to give you a thrashin, that's what I'm doin."

I gave this stranger a sharp jab in the pit of his stomach and knocked the wind out of him. He gathered his wits, snatched his blanket and made his way to the far end of the loft. We sorted out this little hoo-haw in the morning on the gallery of the Great Hall.

"Last night was not the best time to meet a man. My name is Duncan Ross. What's yours?"

When he saw me squarely in front of him with my hand outstretched, he relaxed. "You red-headed son of a bitch, I'm John Gallagher, most call me Jack. Where'd you learn to punch like that?"

"In my school yard back in the Highlands. Where are you from?"

"I'm clerkin with James Shaw. He's got posts in *Flin Flon*, what's your homepost?"

"I'm with Jonathan Graham, we're over in the *Lac de Truches* area."

"Sorry about last night, 'nother clerk told me the man who had your place was a sissy, just take it."

That gave me a good laugh, and a surprised and relieved Jack Gallagher joined in. We became friends from that moment on to the end of the great Company get together.

Another piece of business to take care of was giving my letter to Mr. McTavish for posting back to the Highlands. We met one morning at the front door of the Great Hall.

"Uncle Simon, what a pleasure to see you. Have you been well? I should like to ask you, sir, to send this letter when you return to Montreal. Have you letters for me?"

"Oh, it's you, Duncan. Ask my secretary. If there's mail for you he will know about it. Give your letter to him to post."

He turned and walked through the door without another word. What the hell had I done? Now he acted as though I was just another flunky who didn't know his place in the social structure of the Company.

I found my uncle's secretary, he gave me the letter from my sister and I gave him my letter for Scotland.

Dear Duncan

My dear brother, this is a letter I never wanted to write, but I knew that someday I would have to. Our mother died last January. She took to her bed a few days before Christmas and was unable to leave it until the angels came for her. She thought of you so much in her last days and talked of you up until the final two weeks when she was unable to speak to anyone. She was in great pain throughout her last month, so maybe it was best that you did not see her. Remember her, Duncan, not in her pain, but in her garden, in the kitchen, in her church, at the places where she could be herself spreading joy and comfort to all. Now she is in heaven and free of the body that housed so much pain and suffering in her last years.

Father has taken her passing very hard. He goes to his shop three days each week; he does farm work three days. But there is no joy, none of his eagerness to face the coming day. You know he never missed a Sunday in church. Now he does not go every Sunday. Sometimes he does not go for three weeks or more. He said he does not understand a God who allowed a fine woman like our mother to suffer so much and for so long.

I could not have managed to get through the past five months had not Rory McBride been at my side. I think in another year he will ask me to marry him.

I know I am going to cry as I write this last line.

All our love,
Father and Louise

Mr. Graham noticed I did not sit at my usual place at the clerks' table at dinner. He knew where to find me. He excused himself from fellow partners and went to the dock on Grand Portage Bay. There I sat on an empty cask with the letter clutched in my hand, unaware of the chill creeping over the Bay

"Duncan, is there something upsetting in your letter? Do you want to tell me what it is? I wish only to help, if that is possible."

"Mr. Graham, my sister just wrote that my mother died this past January. I am finding out about her passing six months later. What kind of a son am I?"

"You are a credit to your mother, and to your father. That's what kind of a son you are, Duncan. I should be proud to call you my son."

"That is kind and thoughtful, sir, but it won't bring back my mother. It won't put me back in the Highlands to be with her in her final days, will it?"

"Of course it won't, Duncan. Nobody on this earth can undo God's will, can he?"

"I don't know what God can or cannot do. I only know I have lost my mother."

"I will leave you here, Duncan. You need time to yourself. And, my friend, it is a manly thing to cry. Good night."

With those words he slowly made his way back along the dock to the gate and the Great Hall. Before he left me wrestling with my grief, he took off his finely tailored coat and draped it over my shoulders.

Jack Gallagher and his brigade had departed *Rendezvous* two days ago. My leave-taking from him was brief, but meaningful. Now it was back to the routine of my own return trek, to the pemmican, and to the little place on the lake that I called home. How softly and quietly things change. One letter and I became aware of the fading of my past even as I looked forward to a future here in the *pays d'en haut.*

"Duncan, this morning when we set out, I want you to ride with me."

"Yes, of course, Mr. Graham. Shall I bring my writing supplies?"

"You had best bring them. No telling what might come to my mind."

We reviewed many things I made into a series of notes. At our evening camp he seemed quite tired; exhausted would be closer to the truth. He ate little of our evening meal and withdrew to his tent immediately after a pipe and a few words of thanks to his *avant* and *le gouvernail. L' avant* needed three calls in the morning to rouse Mr. Graham and help him collect himself and his gear for the day's trip. Was Mr. Graham having another 'spell' of that mysterious malady that struck him last winter?

Another day with *le bourgeois*, ready to make notes or take dictation. But not this morning.

"First of all, I again want to tell you how much I am touched by your grief over the passing of your mother."

We rode in silence for more than hour, when he spoke it was in a different tone of voice.

"In the NWC, Duncan, we are a small family, are we not? Even at our annual get together when we number nearly twelve hundred men, we are still just a family. Families talk, as you know, and several times at our meetings with *le grand bourgeois* your name surfaced."

"I hope it was nothing that drew down discredit on you."

"It was no a secret over how you displaced Jack Gallagher your first night in the loft of the Great Hall."

"Mr. Graham, Jack and I have become good friends. That little dust-up was nothing."

"I know you think so, but James Shaw has a different perspective on that."

I started to respond. A gesture from Mr. Graham silenced me.

"In the North West Company, Duncan, we have one son of a bitch. He is Simon McTavish and, I think you will agree, he is a great one."

"Yes, he is. I can certainly agree."

"He is our son of a bitch, and we are proud of him. We need only one person of that stripe in the Company. There is no possible way, Duncan, that you can be the curmudgeon Simon McTavish is, now or in the future."

"I don't understand what you are telling me, Mr. Graham."

"It's no mystery. Just be yourself. Do the good work I expect from you, Duncan Ross, but for God's sake, learn to master your temper. Have I made myself clear?"

"Yes, I think so."

"Then I need say no more on this subject, do I?"

He didn't, and I didn't. That afternoon lecture stung, but I realized Jonathan Graham would not have spoken unless deeply concerned and felt I was mature enough to understand what he told me.

I wrote a hurried letter to Louise from Grand Portage, knowing this was my last chance for a letter to the Highlands for a whole year. As I wrote my thoughts were the same Louise had expressed - she didn't want to write her letter, I didn't want to write mine:

Dear Father and Louise

Uncle Simon's secretary delivered your letter to me here at the annual Rendezvous. Mr. Graham selected me to come down with him this year, he left another clerk in charge of the homepost to see to the gathering and preparations of the winter's food supply. It has taken me several days to collect my thoughts enough to write to you.

I feel so inadequate and so guilty that I am here in Canada, and so far from my home. It does not seem fair nor is it right that you two had to bear the burden of mother's death by yourselves. We will be loading our canoes with next year's supply of trade goods in three days and going back to our post on the lake I call home. It is too late to ask Mr. Graham to find someone to take my place at his trading post, and too late for me to find a way back to Montreal.

During this coming winter I will make the necessary plans to leave Canada and return to the Highlands. For now, this letter and my faltering words of grief and helplessness will have to do. Next summer, or early fall, I should be on my way home.

Your obedient, sorrowful son and brother,
Duncan

This return trek to *Lac de Truches* was not the right time to tell Mr. Graham of my plans, but I must talk with Mr. Graham before the round-robin letter arrived. He would have to write to the people in Montreal to bring my replacement to *Rendezvous*.

Again a joyous homecoming awaited the brigade as soon as we were sighted, only this time it did not reach my spirit. How could I dance and sing, feast and drink with my heavy heart? A long walk along the lake was my escape from the joyous celebration in the com-pound. But escapes have their limits. I had been sighted when I returned inside the compound and was surrounded by friends who demanded that I dance one of my Highland flings. I protested and tried to refuse as politely as I could.

Jonathan Graham made the decision for me. He quietly said, "Duncan, dance. Not because I asked you, not because your friends demand it. Dance, Duncan, dance for your mother. Isn't she the one who taught you the proud steps of a man from the Highlands? Dance for her."

 So I danced and danced. More than joining a homecoming, I honored the memories of my dear mother with a one-person wake. The laughter and happy voices carried over the miles to the rugged hills of my home. I know she would have smiled and nodded her approval.

More than a highly successful trader, Jonathan Graham was a student of people. That was made clear when I was summoned to his quarters one evening.

He told me he knew of my attraction to the Tall One, said he understood my interest in her. What followed was given to me slow-ly, with deep thought, in a manner that made me think this was the way fathers spoke to their sons on matters of significance. Mr. Graham told me not about birds and bees, but of things of more local import.

"It is the custom among the native people in the *pays d'en haut* to give their daughter to a man only after a period of testing and observation. The next step is the negotiation of a 'bride price.' Am I making this clear to you, Duncan?"

"I follow you, sir."

"The daughter isn't being sold as a chattel, she is being exchanged from one family to another. The 'price' is a way of putting some value on the services that will be lost by one family as the daughter goes to form a family of her own. Have I lost you, Duncan?"

"No, Mr. Graham. I was thinking of the difference between your explanation and my idea of what 'bride price' meant."

"Negotiating a bride price is an honorable custom, widely accepted and expected."

"Mr. Graham, why are you telling me of these customs?"

"Duncan, are you jesting? Are you saying you have no lasting interest in the young woman we know as the Tall One?"

"Mr. Graham, I find her very attractive."

"I hate to read more into your interest in a young woman than you imagine for yourself, but if you persist in your attentions to her, an understanding must be reached with her family. Are you ready for that?"

My hesitation did not escape his notice. "Well, Duncan, what is your answer? Are you ready to make a commitment?"

"No. I am not ready. I need more time to think."

"Keep this in mind, my friend. You are deliberating an affair of the heart, not a business opportunity."

"I just don't know, sir, I just don't know."

"Would it help you if I told you what I think?"

"Yes, Mr. Graham, it might."

"I think you are in love, Duncan. That's what I think."

I was speechless, dumbstruck. My God, what if he's right? My face gave away my innermost thoughts. Mr. Graham said, "I think I am right, Duncan, you are in love. Never in the three years I have known you have I seen such a look of bewilderment."

"Am I that transparent?"

"Yes, you are, and I give you joy on this discovery of your love for a woman. You cannot be anything but honest in the feelings you have revealed, not just to me, but to yourself. Indeed, this is a time of great joy!"

When Luis LaGarde and Terry Deumet returned from their visits to winter camps of our clients I would speak with him. Two days later they came driving through the gate with the dog team.

"Mister Duncan, I have a message for you."

"Message? Is it for real, or another of your inventions?"

"If that's the way you greet an old friend, I may forget what I wanted to tell you."

When Luis and I did get together the teasing continued.

"Mister Duncan, I had a very busy time on my round of visiting winter camps. I cannot seem to sort out all the things I must pass on to Mr. Graham. Perhaps I should talk with him."

"Damn it, Luis. You are talking with me! Mr. Graham can wait, can't he?"

"Well, if you're going to be that way, I will try to think of the message. You will have to be patient. I am an old man and I forget things."

"Should I ask Annette if you perform like an old man? Should I ask her if there are things you forget to tell her?"

"Where did you learn to be so mean, Mister Duncan?"

"Just one of the things you taught me about how to survive in the North Country. Now, what is the message?"

"It comes from the Tall One. She let me know she was disappointed you were not with me. That is all, Duncan."

"You said she was disappointed in not seeing me? That part of your message is true?"

"Yes, my friend, she misses you. Now, what are you going to do about that?"

"I must get on the trail to her winter camp. And, Luis, I will talk with her Papa."

"I am happy to hear that, Mister Duncan. How and when are you going to her?"

Why am I always confronted with questions when I need answers? While I was happy to have the message delivered by Luis, it only added to my torment. I wanted to pack and set out at first light tomorrow. Alone? In what direction? With what gifts to satisfy a bride price? To bring your bride back to the messy, cramped clerk's quarters to begin her homemaking? And the big question - are you ready for this, Duncan Ross, are you ready?

The ordinary things that filled days of preparation for *Rendezvous* should have settled my mind. Nothing would put me at ease until I was with the Tall One.

"Mr. Graham, there is no reluctance on my part. I am ready to go to *Rendezvous*."

"Fine, Duncan, fine! But why did you hang back when I told you I needed you?"

"Well, I was going to tell you I was leaving the NWC and going back to Scotland."

"This had to do with your mother's passing, didn't it?"

"Yes, sir. My place is at home to help my folks."

"A noble thing to do. Did they request you to return?"

"No, Mr. Graham. I know they would never ask that."

"You would be a great help to them, I have no doubt. Did you stop to think you might make them feel guilt, feel selfish about having you return to the Highlands?"

"No, I never would be a burden to them. I can think of ten ways I could help."

"And to that I would add ten more. You learned of your mother's death last July. She died in the previous January. Don't you think they have had time to adjust?"

"Yes, I suppose they have. But they need me."

"Perhaps so. Do they expect you to give up all you have worked for since you came to Montreal? To the North Country?"

"I left the Highlands promising to make them proud of what I might do in Canada, but I don't know if that is enough. What more can I do here?"

"That I can't answer, Duncan. I can tell you the NWC has partnerships open to young men who have proved themselves in this dangerous and demanding fur trade."

"I guess that has always been in my mind."

"That is something to look forward to, lad. I make no promises, but I feel certain that is where you are headed."

At the end of a long day of extremely hard work we had five canoes safely removed from winter storage and secured in place on the shore. After a few days to dry out we would paddle them to the homepost. While the canoes dried, I wrote.

Dear Father and Louise

Once again we are into preparations for the long trek to Grand Portage. I will be going with Mr. Graham. He made me his chief clerk about a month ago. The young man who had been chief clerk had a terrible accident this winter. The barrel of a trade gun exploded in his face and used him up in a frightful way. He lived for a few days after the accident. We buried him inside the stockade. I made his coffin and a cross to place at the head of his grave. Father, I think you would have approved of my work.

In my last letter I said I would be coming home this summer or early fall. I cannot do that. I cannot leave Mr. Graham without an experienced clerk to help him manage his six outposts. You know I want to be with you, but I am needed here. He did not pressure me to make this decision. I came to it myself.

Do you ever see Mr. MacQuay? He would be surprised to learn of the numbers of people who live and work in his empty white spaces. Is that old Rory McBride still in the Highlands? Wasn't he going to runoff and join the British Navy?

I may see Uncle Simon at the Rendezvous. He is such an important man he doesn't have time to visit with clerks. I hope my decision has not upset you. I think you both understand I can't walk away from my work here and the man who has done so much to help me learn the fur trade.

> *Your obedient and loving son,*
> *Duncan*

Chapter Six

Once again the spirits who govern the thinking of men were speaking to each other.

Luis LaGarde knocked on the door of the clerk's quarters and poked his head in. "There's a job to be done, and you and I will have to do it."

"I hear you, Luis, but what job?"

"In good time, Mister Duncan, in good time."

"Moose pucky! What's going on?"

He was out of the door, out of the compound, and nearly out of sight when I caught up to him on my snowshoes.

"Now, Luis, what the hell are we doing out here? Talk or I go back to the post."

"Use your eyes and your nose, Montreal city boy. You tell me where we are going."

I stopped, turned slowly in my snowshoes to sniff the air from several directions. I looked intently as my eyes followed my nose. Nothing. Another full turn. Nothing. I looked off to my right where Luis was examining tracks in the snow. A sliver of smoke hung about the tops of two winter teepees set in among a cluster of fir trees. What was Luis dragging me into?

We kicked off our snowshoes in a clear space between the teepees, and there before me was the answer to my question. She stood tall, unmoving, said not a word, but the smile that blossomed on the face half-hidden in the soft frame of wolf fur put to rest all doubts. We shyly stepped to each other, touched hands, rubbed noses, and quickly stepped back to smile like a pair of little children.

"Luis, you scurvy, old *voyageur*. How did you know she was here?"

"Mister Duncan, please. I am honored man in this community. Not to call me names."

"As you will, Luis the Great, but how?"

"The Tall One's Papa sent word they are on their way to our homepost. The old woman is not well and could not travel any farther."

"Is there something we can do for the woman? Should we try to get her to the compound before nightfall?"

With some signing and fracturing of her native dialect, I got across to the Tall One my questions, and she gave me the story. Her step-mother had not been well for the past seven moons. They have many furs and wanted to trade only with Mr. Graham. They will camp inside our compound for several days of trading and a time of rest for the ill one.

"Mister Duncan, say your good-byes. We must return while there is still light."

With a screen of trees between us and the camp the Tall One and I were in each other's arms in an instant. One kiss followed another and for a precious minute we were lost to the world. She took a playful nip of my ear, pointed to the tracks Luis and I made only minutes ago, and gave me a shove with a clear message. "Tomorrow we will talk. Now, you must leave with your guide."

Luis and I retraced our tracks to the homepost and reached the gate of the compound just as George and Terry were closing it for the night. "Duncan, Mr. Graham wants you in his quarters immediately."

"Thank you, Terry. Did he say what he wanted of me?"

"I think he is going to string you up by your thumbs for leaving the post without his say so."

"I think you are full of moose turds, Terry Deumet."

The lad may have been having fun at my expense, but I knew he wouldn't dare risk making up something where Mr. Graham was concerned. I knocked on his door.

"And how did you enjoy your little surprise?"

"You knew the Tall One and her people were close at hand. Luis knew it, and everyone in the compound probably knew it but me! Why?"

"Duncan, it would not have been much of a surprise had you known, would it?"

Mr. Graham's reason for asking me in was quite simple. He requested I take my evening meal with him, we had many things to discuss.

"Luis told me the older woman is in need of medicines, that she is not well."

"That is so, but I can't tell you what her problem might be. I did not go to her teepee."

"I was told they will camp in the compound for several days. I was going to make you leader in the trading, but I will assign that duty to George Corbeil."

"What might be your reason, Mr. Graham?"

"I want you to be present during the trading sessions, but not to engage in them. There will be a second set of trades to make and only you can make them."

"Are you talking bride price, Mr. Graham?"

"Exactly! It wouldn't be wise for you to make both trades. If you anger her Papa in the first set, you may not get a chance to make the second set."

"I see. Would you tell George to be generous? It will put her Papa in a good mood."

"I will do no such thing, young man! George has his reputation as a trader to uphold. Her Papa has his reputation as a good provider to his family to maintain. I have my stock of goods to protect. By watching closely as George works through his trades, you can see what the family wants. When you talk with the Papa you can offer what he was not able to get through trading skins for goods."

"In other words, Mr. Graham, I am on my own in making a bride price. Is that all you have need of me this evening?"

"Sit down, we have barely scratched the surface of things. I am being very unfair to you, Duncan Ross."

"I can't believe that, sir, you have always been fair.""

"You are not thinking clearly. I am making you my chief clerk. Did I not tell you I need you to go to *Rendezvous* in May?"

"Yes"

"Am I not the one encouraging you to seek a lasting union with the Tall One? Am I not the one who is making it possible for you to come to a bride price?"

"Again, my answer is yes to both questions."

"Am I not the one who will be taking you away from your beloved for nearly five months to go to Grand Portage at the very time you want to be married?"

"Balls of fire! I never put the two problems together. I am in a pickle, aren't I?"

"I will release you from your obligation as chief clerk if that is what you want."

"I don't want you to do that. I do want the Tall One, and you know that."

"Then, let's get our heads together and work out a solution."

We began by just sitting, looking at each other, not saying a word. The silence was broken when Jonathan Graham spoke. "Duncan, consider this as a tentative plan. You and Terry will go with me to *Rendezvous*. George will be in charge of the homepost. Between tasks, you and Luis go to the woods to blaze-mark the trees you want to use in building your cabin in the compound."

"I would like to fell the trees myself, Mr. Graham. I want to have a hand in making a home for the Tall One."

"You should do that. While we are gone, Luis and George will put up the cabin. When we are back in early October, you are free to go to the Tall One."

"I thought we could be married here, for I know I can complete a successful bride price. We could not live in the clerk's quarters, nor could I remain with her people. I wouldn't know what to do, and they wouldn't know what to do with me."

"That is clear thinking, Duncan, but have you a definite 'yes' from the young woman? It's good to make plans, but they aren't worth a piddling pot of piss if she says no."

"I will take care of that as soon as their camp is set up tomorrow."

With a great fan-fare of snapping and howling dogs, the *cariole* with the ailing older woman and trailed by a second one loaded with peltries came through the gate of the compound. After a short interval while camp was set up, and the older woman brought to the trading room, the Tall One signaled with her eyes she was free for the moment.

We strolled across the stockade to the dock and walked to the end where I picked up the stout pole always lying there and poked at the water hole chopped in the ice. Drawing water was easier when each person who came with a bucket or pail broke the skin of ice that formed over the hole.

She never took her eyes off me while I played with the pole. "If you don't hold me close and kiss me, I will push you in that water hole."

"You wouldn't dare."

"Try me."

What a choice she offered! A plunge into icy lake water, or gathering in my arms a lovely, warm and inviting young woman. I felt in a teasing mood and picked up the pole. It was no sooner in my hand than I flew off the dock landing just inches from the open hole in the ice. I slipped and slid my way to the shore and waited for her to walk off the dock and come to me. She never moved from her place. I stood my ground. Another contest of wills?

Walking to the end of the dock, I took her in my arms, pushed back the hood of her parka, took her face gently between my hands and looked into those deep blue eyes. "Will you marry me?" I asked in her language.

Her answer was to take my face in her hands. Looking into my eyes she said in my language, "Yes."

Of what importance was speech in any language? We understood what was asked, what was answered. We had kissed several times before, but nothing equaled the depth of meaning and promises this kiss held. The tall, slender, captivating native woman and the taller, redheaded Scotsman with his shy yet aggressive ways stood in the fast fading light and prayed to their spirits and god that this feeling of belonging be with them always.

Our time away from the group in the trading room did not go unnoticed. Everyone knew what had taken place, but rituals required action. I went to the Tall One's Papa and said, "I wish to speak with you at a time and place you shall select."

"We will talk tomorrow in my shelter at last light of day."

As directed, late that afternoon I presented myself before the Tall One's Papa. A small fire took the chill out of the air, but not from the manner of the man who received me into his shelter. He gave no indication of where I was to sit, or whether I should continue to stand. I realized this was his way of telling me he was in charge. Fine! Now let's get down to business.

Time lost all meaning. He sat, I stood. Our eyes never left each other. I sensed light was fading quickly outside the teepee; inside the small fire burned itself to ashes. The scene continued until he said, "My trades with your people pleased me greatly. I have no wants. Next winter we will talk of bride price."

The grasping of his hand in a hearty handshake was taboo. I nodded and withdrew from the teepee. It was over. The dreaded haggling over this custom called bride price was completed. Well, not completed, deferred.

Several potential obstacles were removed from my path to the Tall One. One, her Papa and I resolved the bride price; two, the Tall One had said 'yes' to my proposal. The truly big problem was yet to be confronted. How do I tell the woman I just proposed to that nothing is going to happen for half a year?

We met in the growing light of a cold winter morning. I took her hand and walked the Tall One about the compound pointing out several possible sites for the cabin to be built for us. At a slight rise at the far end of the compound she turned and faced the gate that opened onto the dock and gave a view of the lake. By this time the sun showed its rosy face over the trees and seemed to point to this site as the place. We walked slowly back to the main building.

"You must return with your step-mother and continue with her care?"

"Yes. That is no secret, we both know that must be done. Is there something else?"

"There is. I will go to the Company's *Rendezvous* when the ice is gone from the rivers and lakes. I will not return until the leaves are in color and the air turns cold."

"That will be nearly six moons. That is a long time, Dunc. A very long time to wait."

At some time in our courtship - if that was what one called brief contacts over a period of three years - we exchanged names. The name in her native dialect was quite long and, for me, a tortuous trail of syllables. It meant, 'She Who Sings With Birds At Dawn', a lovely name with words appropriate to the nature of this woman. I gave her the name of my mother, Naomi.

When I explained the deep meaning this name held for me she took me in her arms and whispered, "It is right, Dunc. I will carry her name. It pleases me." She seemed to have some difficulty to say, Duncan. Her voice was so soft, so low and pleasing to my ear, that I made no attempt to correct her. 'Dunc' was just fine. No other person said my name quite like that.

"Naomi, the very minute we return I will be on the trail to you."

"I will be waiting. But, my red-headed trader man, make a fast trail. Now hold me close, tell me those words I do not know, but I like the way you whisper them in my ear. Hold me, Dunc."

To everyone in the compound the name Tall One was known and used. My name for her, Naomi, I reserved for the moments when we were alone. Alone! In a cabin of one hundred ninety square feet inside a stockade of less than two acres, the home of about twenty people, could be called alone. Ridiculous!

"Mister Duncan, please to slow down. We can't fell all these trees needed to build your cabin in one day. Slow down."

"I can't slow down, Luis. I don't have time to be slow."

"You wear me out now, I will not have strength to build anything."

"I will speak to Annette and tell her to put something in your pemmican."

"Don't do that to me, Mister Duncan. She will expect me to do more than build a cabin. My nights are too short as it is. Don't say a word. Agreed?"

"I never thought I would hear the Great Luis LaGarde admit defeat in bed."

"It's not defeat, Duncan. Wait, your time is coming. Then we will learn who needs Annette's secret roots and herbs."

We cut many logs and dragged them to the compound. We prepared the five canoes and one hundred fifty bales of furs ready to depart Grand Portage when Mr. Graham gave the word. That word couldn't come soon enough. I tottered on the edge of exhaustion.

The passage of Jonathan Graham's brigade to Grand Portage was made without incident.

Inside the stockade of the Company's main depot the customary pattern of action took over: our crews located space within the camp of the *les hommes du Nord*; bales of peltries recorded and stored in sheds within the stockade of the great central depot. As for me? I searched for Mr. McTavish's personal secretary; certain there would be a letter from my Highlands family. I found a quiet place to read my letter. At *Rendezvous* 'quiet' is a relative term - it is never quiet at Grand Portage during the three weeks of the Company's get together.

Dear Duncan

It took Father and me several days to accept the reason why you will not be coming back to the Highlands. We agree that you made the best decision, and Rory said he was proud of your sense of loyalty to those who have been so much help to you.

Now, my little brother, here is a real piece of news. Rory and I are married. Yes, we are man and wife and we are very happy. We had the wedding at our church, you would know all the folks who attended, Rory and I wanted to have our own place, but Father has not been well. We thought the best arrangement was to move in with him. He is not sick exactly. It is his mind that worries us. He wanders off and forgets how to get back home. He insists on going to his shop so Rory takes him and brings him home.

Rory has developed quite an interest, and some fine skills, in metals. He has made good progress in that kind of work, and has expanded Father's business. He and Father get along quite well, but there is the constant worry of having to keep an eye on him. I think it is mother's passing that has him upset, he can't seem to accept that she is no longer with him, and never again will be part of this household, part of his life. Rory said to say hello for him. He misses the tussles you two had in class and in the school yard.

All our love,
Father, Louise, and Rory

One extremely hot and grueling afternoon near the close of *Rendezvous*, I stepped outside a warehouse stocked with cotton and woolen yard goods for a breath of fresh air.

"There you are, Duncan. Come to the Great Hall and share a cup with me."

It was Samuel Rawlinson. Dressed in the latest Montreal fashion, he impressed me with his style and his willingness to overlook the social chasm separating partners and clerks.

"You have friends in Montreal who asked I remember them to you when they learned I would be coming to Grand Portage."

"And they are?"

"Carl Shurz, for one, and Jeanette Turmel another."

"Those two had something going did they not? Did they get married?"

"Jeanette is married, to me, not to Carl."

"That is a surprise. My congratulations, Samuel."

"Thank you, my friend, but I should tell you Jeanette asked me to marry her, not the usual pattern wouldn't you say?"

"I remember Jeanette as being a take charge type of woman. No, Samuel, I am not surprised. Now, here's a bit of news for you. When I return to my homepost, it will be to join the ranks of the married."

No words of encouragement or congratulations, just stony silence. Well, to hell with Samuel Rawlinson.

We were but a few days from departing Grand Portage and I had not written a reply to Louise. I hurried back to a table in the Great Hall and began to write:

Dear Father, Louise, and Rory

We will soon be reloading canoes and setting out for our posts in the North Country. This has been a very busy summer at Rendezvous, but the first thing I did was to seek out Mr. McTavish' man and get the letter he had waiting for me.

My congratulations to you and Rory on your marriage. I give you joy and my prayers that your life together will be happy, always. Now it is my turn for a piece of real news. When I am back at our homepost I too will join the ranks of the married. My wife-to-be is a native woman and I have decided to give her our Mother's name. So you can welcome Naomi to the family. I wish that you could meet her, for I think she merits in so many ways the right to carry Mother's name.

Again another gathering of all the men of the Company, and again I have not had more than one hundred words with Uncle Simon. Naturally, he is a very busy man, but I think also a snob. I am a mere clerk, and not worthy of more than a minute of his time. It seems rather strange to pass along congratulations to Rory McBride, but I do that, Rory, in all sincerity. I wish you and Louise and all of the best. Someday may we find a way to join in a total family reunion.
Your loving son and brother
Duncan

The beauty of the country we passed through on the return trek to *Lac De Truches* did not register with me, all I could see were blue eyes, a slender figure, and a smile that radiated warmth and promise.

Lac de Truches never looked as good as it did in the moonlight as we paddled and sang the last few miles to the dock and a rousing welcome. Luis and I carried torches and made our way to the top of the little mound Naomi had selected.

"Well, Mister Duncan. What do you think? Will it please the Tall One? Are you pleased?"

"Luis, you and George did yourselves proud. It is a beautiful cabin. You are a fine craftsman!"

"What did you expect from the Great Luis LaGarde? When I build, I build good. I build strong. I build for my friend and his family."

"Thank you, Luis, thank you. But I don't have a family."

"Oh, my innocent boy! I see the gleam in your eye. You will have family, and soon."

"If I weren't so damned tired I would carry you down to the lake and throw you in."

Later that night we talked with Mr. Graham. Luis and I would push off in a family-size canoe after sharing the feasting that followed the return of the brigade. We had to take advantage of open water on the rivers and lakes; winter could show its face at any time. Ours would be a mixture of passion and fear of freeze-up as we paddled to the camp of the Tall One.

I crawled into my bunk in the clerk's quarters, probably for the last time, and tried to force my attention to the tasks still unfinished: my shabby traveling outfit must be discarded; the new set of deer skins Annette made was ready; gifts for the Tall One's family set aside since last spring retrieved and packed, food and snowshoes for Luis and me carefully stored in the canoe.

Never did a canoe traverse the waters and portages as quickly as ours. We practically flew like the geese over the miles to the camp of the Tall One's family. At this point my mind went blank. I received input from those around me, but did not remember my responses. Did I give gifts to the proper family members? Did I pay my respects to the elders?

Something nagged at the back of my mind as we rushed to begin the return trek to the homepost. Whatever it was, it would have to wait.

Within hours of arrival at the Tall One's camp, we were back on the water. Luis placed himself at the back, me in the front, and the Tall One in the middle of the canoe with a small pouch of her possessions.

Luis wore a deeply worried look on his usual cheerful face, and he barked at me for the slightest false move or wasted effort. Against his strong protests, the Tall One and I gave him some hours of rest by insisting he take his place in the middle of the canoe. He rested, but he never stopped his directions and orders. All our efforts were rewarded with the sight of the homepost looming through the mists.

As we stepped from the canoe the people of the compound met us, swept us off our feet, and carried us to the trading room. Annette and several of the women laid out a royal feast. After the meal, the women took the Tall One to the new cabin where the fireplace was blazing. When I tried to follow, I was unceremoniously told to go back and stay out of the way. "Stay out of the way" was the chorus I heard repeated time after time several years ago on my passage of several thousand miles from Dundas to Montreal. Now, I set out on a voyage of one hundred yards only to hear, "Stay out of the way!"

Mr. Graham came to my rescue. "If I were you, Duncan, I would get the pack with the new deer skins, I would take them to my quarters, I would give myself a thorough scrubbing, I would dress as befitting a groom. And, Duncan, I would smile."

At dusk I was summoned to my new cabin. My own cabin, and I was summoned! Things were not working out the way I imagined. I opened the door to this new life expecting a stream of laughter and words of advice from the women led by Annette. Everyone slipped from the cabin and disappeared. The Tall One was alone.

I was conscious enough to close the door and take two or three steps inside the cabin. I stopped in my tracks. I must have breathed, but I couldn't take my eyes from her. She stood in front of the fireplace dressed in soft, white deer skins. Her black hair was brushed and hanging free to her waist. No ornaments were visible nor were they needed. She was womanhood at its loveliest and most inviting. She smiled and held out her arms.

Old habits were not easily ignored. I was awake at first light and started to drag myself from my bunk in the clerk's quarters. It took a full minute to realize I was not in the clerk's quarters, I was in my own cabin the morning after my . . . what? Was I a married man? I remember no ceremony. If there was a shivaree, I missed it. Where was the Tall One? Why am I at a total loss about what is going on? Who built up the fire crackling in the fireplace? Is that coffee I smell? Who is laughing at me?

"Are you always so helpless when you awake?"

"Are you always so sassy at the crack of dawn?"

"I can't hear you way over there. Are you afraid to join me in front of the fire?"

I did get out of bed. I did go to the fire. I did sweep the Tall One off her feet. I did carry her back to the bed. I did find I had taken hold of a wild cat. I fought valiantly, but after a few minutes of tussling, I was ready to surrender. Pieces of his and her deerskin clothing flew this way and that, blankets pulled up and all talk ceased. Peace - of a sort - descended on the cabin of Mr. and Mrs. Duncan Ross. Whom would we impress with a formal designation of names in the *pays d'en haut*? We were Naomi and Dunc. We substituted intimacies for shyness, and we were lost to the world.

The next day - maybe it was the day after the next day - I made an appearance in the trading room expecting to go to work. This room was the core of the post, the center of activity this time of the year. Where is everybody?

"Is there something I can help you with? I didn't hear you enter. May I offer you some tobacco and share a pipe with you?"

"George, it's me, Duncan Ross! Yes, I'll take a pipe of your best Brazilian, and be sure to charge your account for it."

"We seldom see you at this post, I wasn't sure who you were."

"Enough! Now, George, what duties have been assigned the clerks by Mr. Graham?"

"I don't think I can answer that, sir. Mr. Graham does not like us to talk to strangers about Company business."

The way to end this nonsense was to leap over the trading counter and take George by the scruff of the neck, lead him outside and toss him in a snow drift. I didn't make it over the counter. For some reason I didn't have the energy I usually commanded. Sprawled on the floor like a just-shot goose, I suffered the indignities of my clumsy effort. I had to lie there and endure the raucous laughter of my fellow clerk.

Luis LaGarde entered the trading room dragging a freshly dressed deer carcass. "How much of this does your bride want? You look as though you need nourishment. I'll give it all to her. What have you been doing these last few days, Duncan?"

"Luis, drag that flea-bitten hunk of stuff out of here."

"George, what do you think has happened to our friend? We used to have a such a nice chief clerk."

"I don't know, Luis. Let's shove him through the door."

Terry Deumet staggered in with an armload of ice chisels from the store room. "George, what else should I bring from storage? We are so short-handed around here I don't have time to waste. Oh. Who is this man?"

"Luis and I aren't sure, Terry. He doesn't look to be in very good shape. Sad case, don't you think?"

"Let's give him some hot food and then send him packing."

"Well, now children, have you had your fun? Get to work! I am the one who will talk to *le bourgeois* about who should be sent packing."

"Touchy *batard*, isn't he?"

I left the three of them in the trading room and made tracks to my cabin, pardon me, to our cabin. I thought Naomi would enjoy hearing about the ribbing I just absorbed from the three jokesters, but the cabin was empty. Where could she be? I glanced at the board with pegs pounded into the logs near the door. Her parka was missing. Her snow shoes were missing. What had I done to make her leave?

Annette LaGarde. Of course, that is where Naomi went. Annette was the one who took her in hand the moment we stepped out of our canoe on the return from the Tall One's camp. Fresh tracks led to the door of the LaGarde cabin, they had to be Naomi's.

"Come in and close the door, Duncan, you're letting in cold air."

Naomi was here and laughing while I stood like a fool. What did I have to laugh about? It finally penetrated my mind that being here was an interruption to important things best discussed by women. I gathered my mittens and shrugged into my parka and said something not very bright about having to get back to work. At the door I paused and sent a carefully coded message with my eyes and an imperceptible nod of the head toward our cabin. The message was received in mid-air by Naomi who sent her reply - a quick shake of the head.

Work was always a safe retreat. Do you divide your day in two? in thirds? in quarters? Do you give more time to work in Jonathan Graham's world? Does time with Naomi and her world deserve the greater amount of your time?

The news brought to the homepost by a *voyageur* from Jonathan Graham's post on Sugar Bush River staggered us as much as his obvious condition as he fell to the floor of the trading room in utter exhaustion. He gave his message in words of *Francais Sauvage* mixed with gasps for breath and groans of pain from hours on snowshoes.

"Fire, *Monsieur Graham*, we have bad fire. We lose big building. We lose much food. We lose . . ."

"Hold, my man. Was anyone injured? Are all people at the post alive?"

"*Oui, bourgeois*. All people live, but we have little food."

Luis helped the man to a robe spread out before the fireplace. He eased him out of his mukluks and began to massage his feet and

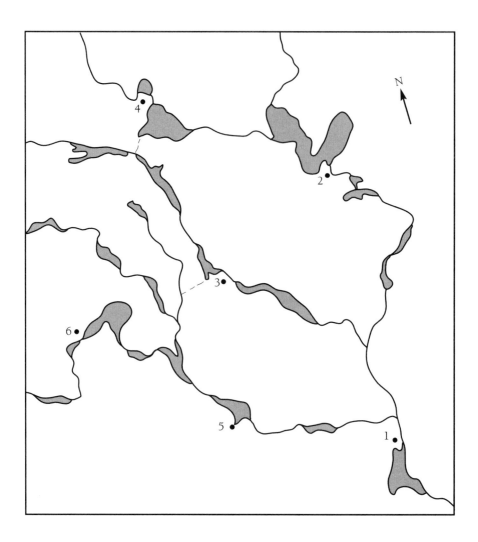

Trading posts of Jonathan Graham's Department
1. Lac de Truches (original homepost)
2. Lac aux Sables
3. Sugar Bush River (destroyed by fire)
4. Lac du Rond
5. Lac la Marie
6. Lac de Wapiti (new homepost)

legs. Mr. Graham came back from his quarters with a cup of brandy and an oat cake. Given time to rest and recover from his ordeal, the man could add little to the initial outpouring of news. Mr. Graham laid plans for a hurried trek to Sugar Bush with relief supplies.

"Luis, how many of your dogs are in running condition? Cannot you get one of your friends to make his string of dogs and his toboggan available? We will need two outfits."

Mr. Graham turned to me and said, "The collection of ten days' rations for the people at Sugar Bush is your responsibility."

When she learned what all the activity was about and the reason for our frantic haste, Naomi would not hear of my refusal to include her with the team.

"Mr. Graham, my stubborn husband refuses to listen. I will go with you. You do not know what the needs of the women at this post might be."

In spite of the gravity of the occasion, I saw Mr. Graham smother a smile as he politely refused Naomi's request. "That is most kind, Naomi, but Duncan and Luis will be able to determine what must be done at Sugar Bush."

Our group of four trailed through the gate of the stockade and set out for Sugar Bush River. We reached the post with just enough light in the cold glow of dusk to make camp within the stockade. Several teepees were set up near the burned out remains of the post's main building that also had been the quarters of the chief clerk. We held a council and from the questions and answers a pattern began to emerge.

"Mister Ross, I can tell you that the trades we have made so far this season are less than last year." That report came from the chief clerk at the Sugar Bush post.

"I don't think trades will improve in this area. We have been here four years, Hudson's Bay has been here two years, and a few independent traders have gone through our territory with some luck in their trading."

"So you think the area is finished?"

"Yes, Mister Ross, yes. The best days here are done."

On the return I alternated snowshoeing at the side of different group members. This gave me a chance to get to know the clerk who opted to go back with us. His name was Verne LaFroy, a tough man with an equally tough spouse. Tough in that they had met the worst the brutal North Country could throw at them and survived.

Mr. Graham was there to greet and commend us for making the trek safely. He, Luis and Annette took charge of getting the LaFroy family settled in the compound. I went to my cabin expecting a warm welcome, but a touch of coolness invaded the scene.

"Duncan, you disappointed me."

"How is that, Naomi? What did I do?"

"It isn't what you did, it's what you didn't do."

"What should I have done?"

"You might have protested Mr. Graham's decision that left me out of the rescue group. You never said a word."

Naomi was not teasing me, she meant every word. How could I tell her that when Mr. Graham made a decision that was final, the last word? She read my mind.

"Duncan, among my people, when a problem arises that is important to the whole camp, all have a voice."

"You mean that women speak out uninvited?"

"Of course they do."

"Strange. And good decisions are made by women?"

"Duncan, I don't believe what I am hearing! When welfare of the camp is at stake decisions must come from all. What is strange is your belief that only men are fit to decide important things."

I found myself sitting at the table with a mug of tea and a plate of hot food. Across from me was a lovely woman who spoke softly, but with such conviction and sincerity that I knew to continue my line of thinking was pointless.

I finished my meal, but something made me glance about the cabin. It was changed. The table and two stools were at the other side of the fireplace, strings of dried onions and other bulbs and roots hung from the rafters. There was more. In the alcove - which I called our bedroom - the bed with its rope mattress was gone! In its place was a large frame of boards fastened to the floor in the shape of a large rectangle. I bent down to examine this new addition to our cabin. On the wooden plank floor was a covering of small spruce branches laid to a thickness of about five or six inches, and over that three of four buffalo robes fitted within the frame.

Tacked to the logs at the head of the new bed was the piece of tartan I brought with me from the Highlands. It was free of wrinkles accumulated over years and many miles of travel. The little nails that held the tartan to the logs were not nails, but pieces of bird bone shaped, pointed, and carefully driven into its four corners. I had shown this piece of material to Naomi when I brought my personal gear from the clerks' quarters. She immediately felt the importance of this keepsake but said nothing. This was her way of telling me we had things to share, and that she liked to have some color in her life

That night as we slipped into the new bed I drew Naomi close. She snuggled into my arms and rested her head on my shoulder.

"Dunc, do you like the new bed?"

"Yes, it's very comfortable. But why the change?"

"To avoid future battles."

"Battles? Between you and me? Never!"

"I think we were headed for sad times."

"Sad times? You speak with a strange tongue, my long-legged beauty."

"Long legs are part of the trouble, Dunc. My long legs and your big body."

"Now you are speaking riddles."

"For almost half a moon you and I have slept but a short time each night."

"I am not complaining, my dearest Naomi. Not a word of complaint."

"What I am trying to say is you are so big and heavy that the rope bed we had would sag and I would roll on top of you. Then you would think I wanted to . . . Well, you know we would . . . Then every time I turned in bed you would roll on top of me and then you would think I wanted to . . . Oh, you big, red-headed man of the Highlands, you know what I am telling you."

"No, I don't understand. You tall flower with the long stems, tell me again."

She replied instantly. A sharp dig in the ribs.

"Dunc. Listen to me. I am serious. We must get rest each night. We must slow our pace of what you call 'love making'. We will tire of each other, then we will begin not to like each other."

"I hear you, dear one. What would you like me to do?"

"Tonight I would like to have you hold me, and sleep."

We did that. For three nights we just slept. I will admit, I needed the new bed as much as Naomi. It was not easy to admit that my bride was smarter than I.

One night this question came up. "Are you upset you didn't have any kind of a ceremony, something to celebrate our marriage?"

"No, Dunc, I am not upset."

This is what Naomi told me; some of it I already knew or had guessed, but most of it was new to my ears.

"The two people you assume to be my mother and my father are not my parents. My mother was of the Mandan people. She was taken prisoner following a raid by Crees who swept through our village as revenge for the death of a Cree warrior."

"Were you born in a Cree camp after the raid?"

"No. I was about four years old. The Crees were going to leave me behind, for they didn't want to be slowed by a child. My mother said I screamed so much when they tried to separate us that they brought me along to keep me quiet.

"The man you call 'Papa' claimed my mother as his share of the spoils of the raid. No one in his band challenged him. Anyone could see that the man who took my mother got me as a part of the bargain.

"My mother lived with my Papa (you refer to him as your father-in-law and I should refer to him as my foster father) as his wife, and all in the band accepted this arrangement. That is the way I grew up. My mother never let the chance slip by to remind them she was Mandan and would always be Mandan."

"You should be proud of your mother and her loyalty to her people. As a man of Scotland I can understand that."

"I am, Dunc. But my mother died when I was about seven summers old. The man I called Papa took another woman - the one you know as the old one."

"Is that not the usual way?"

"It is, Dunc, but I became the problem. I cried and carried on for days at a time. I wanted my mother, and I let the new woman know I would never call her mother."

"Did they beat you? Did they force you to change?"

"No. My Papa never laid a hand on me. No one ever touched me. They just left me alone."

"You couldn't wander off in the woods and live. What did you do?"

"I lived with my Papa as his daughter, but I was not ever made a part of the family. I lived among them, but I was never a part of them."

"But you seem so skilled in the things that make life bearable."

"It was my pride in being Mandan. I made up my mind that I would learn to do everything they did, only I would do it better."

"Why didn't you accept being a Cree woman since you did Cree things everyday of you life for the past twelve or so years."

"I couldn't, Dunc. By the time I was ten summers I was taller than any man in the band. Do you not know that Mandan people tend to be among the tallest of native people? That is one of the reasons why I like to hear you call me your 'long-legged beauty'. It keeps fixed in my heart who I really am. Besides, I like the way you caress me and my legs. Would you like to do that now?"

Of course I would, and did.

"We must begin to make plans for our future, and for that reason I have asked that Verne LaFroy be included. We will not rebuild the Sugar Bush River trading post."

Mr. Graham had called the clerks to his quarters for a review of the disaster at Sugar Bush post.

"Look at this map where I marked the locations of all six posts. As you see, the homepost is not at the center of the outlying posts, but at the perimeter. What I am proposing is that we move the homepost to Lac Wapiti. We will enlarge that post and make it our homepost. Any questions?"

"Why, Mr.Graham, why?"

"The disastrous fire at Sugar Bush forced me to look at the trend of declining business at all of our posts."

"But why move this big operation? Why not build a new post further out than Lac Wapiti?"

"In a short time, Duncan, all of our posts will have to move to develop new areas for our trading. It's better to move one post every few years than to be forced to move all at the same time."

"How soon will this move to Wapiti be made, Mr. Graham?"

"I would say within one year."

As I returned to our cabin to pass on this big news to Naomi I realized how much I opposed this idea. Naomi had turned a crude, little log cabin into a cheerful home, and I feared anything that might change this wonderful feeling of having our own place. How will she accept the notion of having to move?

"Terry, you will remain here with Luis. He will guide you through all the things that must be done to assure our food stocks for the coming winter. George, you and Duncan will go with me to *Rendezvous*. I will take Verne too. He was at *Rendezvous* several times as a *voyageur*, but never as clerk."

Later that morning as I worked alone in the trading room, Mr. Graham said,

"Duncan, you may take Naomi to *Rendezvous*."

 "I will talk with her tonight about your plan."

We were in bed, relaxed in each other's arms when I brought up the idea that the Tall One go with the brigade to Grand Portage.

"You would like the days of watching new scenery, watching our men as they paddle and portage, listening to their singing, and learning to be on guard. Their pranks and jokes involve everyone; even Mr. Graham is not left out."

"You make it sound so interesting and even fun, but I would be so useless. What am I to do for forty days and nights?"

"If you don't know what we would do for forty nights I will leave you here."

"Duncan, Annette gave me a generous cut from the moose that Luis killed and dressed out. Why don't you ask Mr. Graham to take his evening meal with us tomorrow night?"

"I'm sure he will like that."

The invitation to *le bourgeois* was made and accepted. The evening went along as it should among friends. Naomi roasted the loin of moose to perfection, the fire crackled and sputtered.

"Naomi, I accept your reasons for declining the invitation to go to *Rendezvous*. However, if you change your mind the offer is still open."

"I knew you would understand, Mr. Graham, but this red-headed man couldn't get it through his head I didn't want to go."

"He can be stubborn, can't he? Now tell me some of your background, Naomi."

"It is not an unusual story, my mother was taken captive in a raid on her village. That story was repeated over many years among many different tribes."

"Yes, I am aware of such stories. But you, Naomi, are more than the daughter of a Mandan woman. Do you know who your father was?"

I thought that a rather bold question, and was about to make a sharp protest when the Tall One answered. "Yes, I know who my father was, and I know that my father and mother lived together for several years before he was carried off by his own people."

"And who were his people? I dare say they were not natives of this country."

"No. My father was a Spanish trader who came up the big river (Missouri River) with several men who began trading posts at the Mandan villages."

"I thought there was different blood running in your veins. You have the height and carriage of a Mandan woman, and, I would add, I think your father was also a tall man."

"He was not only tall, my mother told me, he was very handsome. All the maidens in the villages tried to draw his attention to them, but he chose to live with my mother."

"A very happy story, Naomi. Did something happen to change your life with him?"

"All I know of his story is what my mother told me, for I was the only one my mother would share her stories with."

"Do you have any memories of your own about your father?"

"Oh, yes. Mr. Graham. What I recall of him is all fine. I remember good things."

"Will you share some of those good things?"

"My father loved horses, and when he rode he looked as though he and the animal were one. He used to gather me in his arms and sit me front of him and showed me how to hold the pommel of the saddle. Then we would ride like the wind."

"Happy stories should have happy endings, Naomi. I take it yours does not."

"A group of his people came to the Mandans, they were riding horses. Some of them were brightly dressed with feathers in their metal hats. Other men had flat hats and wore black robes."

"Did your father know these men?"

"I don't know, my mother never said. She said they told my father he was living in sin and must return with them. He refused to go. The men came and beat him. They took my father away. They tied a rope around his neck with the other end in the hands of one of the soldiers. They made him ride on a horse with his feet lashed to the hooks where you put your boots."

"Did you ever see your father again?"

"No."

We all sat for a long time saying nothing. Finally Mr. Graham got to his feet, thanked Naomi for the supper, and went back to his quarters. When Naomi and I were in bed she let flow the tears she had held back. Tonight I held a lonely, little girl who longed for her father and for her mother, but who knew those two people could never be more than dreams and memories locked away. Tonight for a few moments she shared her memories, but if I know my wife, they will not be unlocked again for a long, long time.

So it was settled; I would go to Grand Portage with Mr.Graham while Naomi stayed at the homepost to aid Luis and Annette. Not talking about the fact that we would be apart for a longer time than we were married didn't change anything.

Bitter-sweet described our last night together. Our evening meal was eaten slowly. Conversation became a jumble of half-spoken sentences, of thoughts left dangling in mid-air, of smiles that quickly dissolved into long faces and diverted glances. Only in bed did a sense of ease take over. Here we need not talk. Our closeness and shared warmth spoke volumes; tenderness and responses became our vocabulary.

An aroma of coffee and the sounds of a crackling fire told me the time had arrived. Dressed, fed, kissed quickly, I was pushed out the door of our cabin while Naomi made a last check of my ditty bag.

Naomi and I stood aside in the rush of organized confusion, amid the crying, hugging and kissing, and the trilling of songs about going to far places. As my canoe took its turn at the dock, a quick squeeze, a brush of her fingers across my lips, then I sat and nodded to l' *avant* to join the others following Mr. Graham in the lead canoe.

That was all behind me as I stood at the cooking fire of my crew on our first night in camp. Mr. Graham joined me. We watched the kettle of morning rations already bubbling away under the eye of *le gouvernail.*

"Duncan, I have not had the opportunity to tell you how much I enjoyed the supper with you and Naomi. It was a delight. You have married a remarkable woman."

"I shall remember to tell Naomi when we return. And, *bourgeois*, I can only agree. She is a remarkable woman. I am fortunate to have been on duty in the trading room the day she and her family came to the homepost to trade."

"So it was love at first sight? I experienced the same many years ago. And didn't I tell you after her first visit to the post that she was not a Cree, and possibly had Spanish blood in her veins?"

"Right on all counts, sir. But tell me, are Spanish people quick-tempered folks?"

"I'm not sure we should call it temper. I rather think passionate is a better word. What is your experience, Duncan? Which word would you use?"

"I don't know, sir."

"Well, I know. Your face is as red as your hair. Good night, lad."

Back in my tent I fumbled about in my ditty bag for the little box that held my razor - in the morning I would scrape away the scraggly stubble. My hand encountered an item I did not remember stowing in the bag. It was a small package of soft deerskin. I returned to the light of the cooking fire to open it. Nestled in the leather was a lock of soft, silky, black hair carefully tied with a bit of yellow ribbon. Naomi had cut her hair to give me a constant reminder that she was always with me. Mr.Graham was right, she was a remarkable woman - and I missed her.

As chief clerk I spent many hours riding in his canoe with Mr. Graham, making notes and enjoying our time together. His high regard for the Tall One, her story of an unhappy rearing, and her sunny disposition in spite of the dark times she lived through remained in his mind.

"You are one lucky man, Duncan Ross. Several of my friends in the North Country purchase Indians maidens to share their beds."

"I don't think much of that."

"I agree, but doesn't it help for you to know that you are joined to the Tall One on the basis of mutual desire? Not on a few coins or a bag of pretty beads. Eh?"

"Yes, it helps to know that."

In the Great Hall I searched for Uncle Simon's secretary to get the letter from Scotland I was sure that he had for me. No luck. I resumed my search in the compound filled with busy men.

"You clumsy oaf, watch where you're going!"

"The hell you say, Duncan Ross, back off or you might find yourself on the ground."

"I'll be damned, Jack Gallagher, you old sot. How the hell are you?"

"Long as I stay away from your big feet I'm fine. How are you?"

We strolled to the dock to get away from the din of the stockade. We gabbed like a pair of old biddies as we brought each other up to date on our respective lives. Jack was doing well as he continued clerking at the homepost of James Shaw - L.A.L. (Laughs A Lot) - in my old code.

"There is some news I think you will want to hear. I am a married man. I took a native lass to my bed just as winter set in last year."

"My congratulations, old man, not only on your marriage, but also on your timin. 'Just as winter set in'. God, what a delightful way to stay warm."

"You should try it, Jack. But then, I'm not sure you would know how to do it."

"I'll let that pass."

That night as I stretched out on my pad in the over-crowded loft of the Great Hall I took the little deer skin packet from my pocket. I kept this time just before the last candles were extinguished to touch this reminder of Naomi, I slept with it under my pillow. She was so far away in miles and time. Damn the NWC, damn *Rendezvous*, damn everything and everybody!

The next morning I caught up with Uncle Simon's private secretary, "Do I have any letters?"

The young man reached into his *musette* (shoulder bag). "Yes, here it is. And, by the way, Mr. McTavish would like you to see him."

Uncle Simon could wait. I had a letter to read:

Dear Duncan

There is good news and not so good news for you, I hardly know where to start. Father is not getting any better. He is so forgetful and seems lost and so far from us. Some days I am not sure he knows where he is living. The other day he asked me why that man - he meant Rory - was living in his house. I don't know what I can do, and aside from Rory, there is no one I can or want to talk to about Father.

Now, for the happier news. Rory and I are expecting a baby. I think it will arrive in late September or early October. Isn't that the time you are back at your homepost after the Rendezvous? Rory hasn't got used to the idea that he will soon be a father, but I am ready to be a mother. I can hardly wait. Did you marry your native woman? You said in your last letter you were to do that as soon as you got home. If you did, and I just bet you did marry her, I think for you to give her our mother's name was the right thing to do. I'm sure Mother is looking down on you and smiling, and I know she will be smiling when I

*have my baby. Oh, Duncan, were it not for Father's state of mind, I
would be the happiest woman on earth.*

*All our love,
Father, Louise, and Rory*

Now, go see what Old Iron Balls wants. I was not too excited,
for the last few times we had contact he acted stuffy and snooty.

"Well, my lad. How have you been? And have you had a profitable season with your *bourgeois*? That is the matter I wish to discuss
with you. Sit down, sit down. We are alarmed at the decrease in the
number of peltries that are coming into the stockade this summer.
Are there decreases in your shipments from the *Lac de Truches* posts?"

"Mr. McTavish, you are asking me questions which should be
asked of my *bourgeois*."

"Enough of your insolence, Duncan. I expect you to answer me
promptly and with civility."

"I beg to differ, sir. Do you recall the confrontation we had in
your canoe on my first trip to Grand Portage? I think Mr. Graham is
entitled to the same consideration of his business. The comments are
his, not mine, to give."

Now I was in the same stew as the time I refused to show him
my diary. The rising color in his face and the hand that trembled as
he reached for the watch he carried in his coat told me a storm was
brewing. Well, let it come. But nothing happened, not another word
said. I was dismissed.

Mr. Graham came to the warehouse where I was working.

"Duncan, I had a most interesting conversation with Mr.
McTavish last evening."

"I can hazard a guess as to what you two talked about."

"No. I think not. Your uncle wants me to release you from your work at my posts so you can return to Montreal and resume your work with McTavish and Frobisher. What do you think of that?"

"I don't know what to say, sir. Did you tell him I am now married, and am most anxious to return to the *pays d'en haut?*"

"I did indeed, Duncan. He only laughed and said marriage to a native woman was but a trifle, nothing to keep you from acting on a great opportunity."

"That son of a bitch! I have a good mind to search him out and reshape his nose."

"Duncan, for God's sake, stop it! You are not going to do a damn thing. You don't have to. I told him I was not in a position to release you, and that's that."

"Why does that man make me so . . . so angry?"

"Conflict and tension are only two in his bag of tricks. Get angry and you play his game. Keep your head and make him play your game. I thought you had that figured out."

One task remained before we departed Grand Portage.

Dear Father, Louise, and Rory

This summer's gathering of the Company is almost finished. I received your letter and am at a loss for words to tell you how much I am concerned about Father's condition and the burden it places on you and Rory. I told Mr. Graham what you described as Father's failings. He said that quite often the combination of advancing age and a major shock, like mother's death, combine to bring on this kind of problem. He didn't know of anything that will change the way things seem to be going with Father.

Yes, my dear sister. I did marry and am very happy. Your expecting a child must be the center of your life with Rory. I hope you and the baby have a safe time of it. Uncle Duncan, I like the sound of that.

This Rendezvous business is something that has to be done each summer. It keeps me away from Naomi for over four months, and I don't like the separation. I wish there was some way all of us could get together for I know you would learn to love Naomi as much as I do.

Uncle Simon took me aside the other day to say he wants me to come back to Montreal and resume working for him. My heart and mind are in the North Country, Montreal does not interest me. How are Rory and his metal business coming along? Do you ever see Mr. MacQuay? This vast distance that keeps us apart bothers me. I wish I could be there to help you with Father.

Your obedient little brother,
Duncan

As the canoes took turns to unload at the dock jutting out into *Lac de Truches*, I searched the waiting crowd from one end to the other. No Naomi. I consoled myself with the thought that she wanted our reunion to be private and in our own cabin away from prying eyes. As quickly as I could, I ran up the hill to our little sanctuary. I saw no smoke curling from the chimney. I found a cold and empty cabin. What was wrong? What happened? Did she go back to her people? Was she sick or hurt? Why? What?

A knock on the door brought me back from my wild speculations. "Mister Duncan, I tried to get your eye at the dock, but you weren't interested in me." It was Luis. "She went to her folks about three weeks ago."

"Why, Luis, what made her do that?"

"Her brother, well, you know the one she called her brother, came to tell her the old woman was very sick. Her Papa wanted her. Naomi knows many of the native cures for illness and he said she must go and help the old woman."

"How long will she be there?"

"No questions, please, Mister Duncan. We have not had word since she left. I can't tell you more than what I just did."

This is one hell of a mess. My first thought was to get Luis, gather some food, take a canoe and make a run for it before freeze up. Mr.Graham stepped into the cabin, noted the chill and gloom that hung over the place.

"Duncan, Luis, come to my place within the hour and we will see what can be done."

Annette joined us and we lost no time in sorting out what had happened and what might be the best thing to do.

"If I understand the Tall One's story, she was not really wanted by the people who raised her after her mother died. But she went back to them as soon as she got word of their need of her. That tells me the old woman is seriously ill, that her people would dare not play some sort of trick on the Tall One."

"I follow your reasoning Mr. Graham, but if she can't be here, I want to be with her."

"Perfectly understandable, my lad. But what will you do at her folks' winter camp? Would you be a help, or a hindrance?"

Annette broke into our exchange, "The Tall One told me she knew the cause of the old woman's illness. Her cures do take time, Duncan. If the old woman died, they will need time for burial ceremonies."

Luis added his thoughts, "If the old woman died, it may be a long while before her people can release a man to accompany her on the return trip to this place."

"Give her two weeks, Duncan. If she is not back here by then, we will send a party to investigate."

"I see your reasons, I will wait two weeks. If we send a party to her, I will lead it."

About nine days after the council in Mr. Graham's quarters Terry Deumet knocked on my cabin door. "Duncan, a dog team and toboggan is coming across the lake. Do you want to come down to the trading room and get ready for business?"

"I thought you were to be the trader for the day."

"I am, but Mr.Graham wants you to be there with me. The toboggan appears to be carrying a heavy load."

"I'll be there in a minute, Terry."

Looking around the cabin I realized what a mess it was in. I smoothed the bed, folded the blankets, tried to put the few cooking things in some sort of order. At the last minute I added a log to the fire and put the fire screen in place, then ran to the trading room.

My hopes sank as the small group grew closer; there were just two men on snow shoes following the toboggan pulled by a string of five dogs. A large mass was piled on the toboggan, but it never moved, it must be a cargo of furs to trade. The weather was atrocious; bitter cold winds blew without let-up and the bank of clouds in the north promised more of the same plus heavy snows.

When they drove their dogs through the gate into the stockade ready hands were there to aid them. The men brought the cargo inside. It was then I saw it was Naomi, bundled in robes and barely moving. I rushed to her side, her voice was weak and she was pale and drawn without a trace of the vitality that defined her.

After sipping a gourd of warm broth and gaining strength and energy from the warm shelter, she haltingly told the story. The old woman died in spite of unending care. When the burial rites were completed she insisted on starting back to our cabin. Weakened from her efforts to save her step-mother, she would not hear the pleas to remain until her strength recovered. The small group departed the winter camp, on the second day became lost in blinding snow squalls. They were on the trail four days for a planned two day trip.

Sometime during the night Mr. Graham came to sit with me. After a long spell of silence he said, "Duncan, I think there is congestion in her chest. Her breathing is raspy but it is even and not labored. She is totally exhausted, but she will recover soon."

"I never thought, Mr. Graham, that I would be in a position to do for her what she did for me nearly two years ago."

"What is that? I don't quite understand."

"Remember when Luis and I got snowbound in the winter camp of the Tall One's people? The time we took gifts to the family that brought in the soft gold pelts? I was in danger of going snow blind. Well, Naomi and her step-mother took care of me and got me through without damage to my eyes or other impairment."

"I guess I didn't hear that part of the story. So, you knew who saved your sight?"

"Naomi should be given much of the credit, she and the native remedies given by the old woman. Now I can help her get back to a normal life. As normal as life with me can be."

"I think she will survive you."

The next afternoon we carried Naomi to our cabin. Annette came that evening with some tempting hot food and took over. "There are times when one woman needs another woman to comfort her. Now, get out of here!"

The third night of her return to our cabin, Naomi feigned sleep until everyone left our place and we were truly alone.

I gathered my long-legged beauty in my arms and held her close. Gentle massaging and stroking brought total relaxation. "This is what I need, Dunc, to feel your strength and your tenderness, but that is all. There will be other nights, lots and lots of nights. Tonight, I just want to drift off with my man beside me and know that I am safe."

He's Back

Grand Marais, MN
October, 2001

The Elderhostlers attending the programs at Nor'Wester Lodge on the Gun Flint Trail enjoyed the field trip to Grand Portage National Monument. And why not? The air was brisk, the sun bright, not a cloud in the sky, and breezes off Lake Superior's North Shore were light with no hint of chill.

The interpreters at the Monument were truly outstanding. Not only were they were well versed in the history unique to Grand Portage, they brought it to life and made it seem real - like it just happened yesterday.

Late in the afternoon the group reboarded the school bus that was our 'magic carpet' for the field trip. The site coordinator took her seat at the front of the bus, I usually rode in the back. I sprawled in my seat and settled in for the hour's drive back to the village of Grand Marais. It was a long day, full of activity, and most Elderhostlers were drifting off into their own worlds - content, but drowsy.

I thought we hit a pot hole, but it was Duncan Ross who pushed me against the side of the vehicle and commandeered a generous half of the seat. I realized that no one could hear us, but if any in the group had reason to glance my way, they would have turned back saying to themselves, "That Jim Reiley is off his rocker! He's sitting back there talking to himself like a nut case."

"I am pleased that so many had a good day at my old place of intense business. And wasn't that native woman a delight to listen to? You know, the one who is restoring the vegetable gardens at our old central depot using nothing but heirloom seeds."

"Margaret always does an excellent job. Her husband, Mike, was the one who gave us the fine talk in the canoe warehouse displaying the beautiful reproductions of Montreal and North canoes.

"Did you have goosebumps when we walked along the corner of the stockade where you and the little raspberry picker had . . . ?"

 A withering look and stony silence greeted that ill-considered probe. Did you forget, Jim, what he told you about questions? We bounced along the road not saying another word until we passed Naniboujou Lodge.

"I will forget your nasty question. What I was thinking throughout much of my day at Grand Portage was of my old friend, Luis LaGarde. He was always full of good stories about his escapades at Rendezvous. More personal were my recollections of the summer I brought Naomi to Rendezvous. She was reluctant to come, and I don't think she enjoyed her time there as much as I thought she would."

"Did she never return to Rendezvous?"

"No. We talked often about Rendezvous and its importance in the affairs of the NWC, but she would not consider a return."

Our brief conversation was interrupted by a voice at the front of the bus. "All right, people, listen up. We will have about an hour in town. The bus will be parked over by the Coast Guard Station. We will leave promptly at 1730 hours. It is now 1630, four-thirty, so move it!"

That was our site coordinator, Judy, who gave those directions. She was so full of life, so enthusiastic, and such a 'natural' that we always followed her orders. I planned to browse several bookstores in our allotted time, but felt myself taken by the arm and walked along the bay to the place known locally as Artist's Point.

"I am impressed with this Judy person. She could manage the most unruly bunch of voyageurs, and it does my heart good to hear someone order you around."

"I'll agree she's good at her job, and, yes, we need a person like her."

Our track led us past the Coast Guard Station and out to the breakwater that formed the eastern half of the bay. Instead of staying on the paved path with hand rails, I turned to the clump of trees and higher ground that formed the Point.

"Do you know where you are going? I have my doubts."

"I have been to this place many, many times. My late wife took art classes in Grand Marais during several summers we spent along the North Shore. This site was one of her favorite places to sketch and paint, especially when she worked with watercolors. I was her beast of burden; I carried her easel, boxes of paints, and water jugs."

"But you didn't paint, did you? I didn't think so. You can't even make good tea. What did you do while she painted?"

"I found a comfortable place to sit and read about under-fed and over-sexed fur traders."

"Have a care, Mr. Reiley! I thought I might begin to tell you of my wife, but I'm not sure you can handle a complex story. It seems to me that your life is governed by that little thing strapped to your wrist. I want to talk about people, real people, and not be concerned with time machines."

We found an old log, sun-baked, out of the wind. That retreat added to our comfort and appreciation of the natural beauty of Artist Point. When Duncan Ross resumed talking, he was far more personal and revealing than at any time in our previous sessions.

"My wife, Naomi, the one you have learned to call the Tall One, was a strong woman. Physically, of course. But what I mean is she was strong in her beliefs, her likes and dislikes. It didn't take more than year until we could speak with ease to each other in her dialect, in Francais Sauvage, and English. Most of our conversations were jumbles of each, but we understood one another perfectly."

"I can relate to what you are telling me. My wife, Betty, had no difficulty in expressing herself."

"No more interruptions. Understood? Fine!"

There were none. He talked, I made notes, and found myself seeing a side of Duncan Ross I never expected he would expose. I was made part of his life in the most personal way.

Chapter Seven

Even though the pace of work at the homepost took a dramatic jump when the brigade returned from *Rendezvous*, Mr. Graham made sure I had more time with Naomi. Within a week the Tall One was up and walking about the stockade and soon resumed her normal routines. This signaled me to get back to my routines.

With the advantages of ideal weather, Mr. Graham took Verne LaFroy, a crew to man a North Canoe, and a stock of trade goods for the coming season to the post at *Lac de Wapiti*. The trip satisfied two needs: the resupply of the post, and a survey of the whole area before Mr. Graham made the final decision to move the home post.

Aside from that trip nothing disturbed the routine of the winter season. Nothing broke the monotony of the same food day after day, of seeing the same faces day after day, of hearing the same stories, jokes and lies day after day. Looking out on unchanging scenery day after day knowing that cold could only become colder and snow could only become deeper did nothing for the soul. Had it not been for the Tall One and her spirit, her unfailing good humor, and her patience I think I might have become someone you would not want to know.

But there was no way *Rendezvous* could be denied or delayed once the ice left the lakes and rivers. Mr. Graham again extended his invitation to Naomi to join the brigade going to Grand Portage. Her answer was the same; she stayed at the homepost. I went to *Rendezvous* and took possession of the letter from my sister.

Dear Duncan

You, my little brother, are an uncle to a pretty little niece who has been given the name of Jennifer. She is such a delight, and is grow-ing and changing daily. Of course she's perfect, look at whom she has for parents. I wish I could fill this letter with happy things and wishes for your good health and continued happiness with your Naomi.

It is Father. He grows farther and farther away from us, and he has lost strength. Some days it is all Rory and I can do to get him out of bed and to the rocking chair by the fire. He just sits there as Mother used to do, but she was alert to all that went on about her. Father sits with a vacant stare, and when he says something it is as though he is speaking in tongues. Something else I would rather not have to tell you, Mr. MacQuay died a few days before Christmas.

Rory is doing very well with the business. He talks about us moving to Glasgow because of the expanding iron industry there. I can't imagine living in a new and strange place. but he thinks our future is in iron and ship building. He even says someday we will build our ships out of iron. Can you imagine what I have to put up with? Father and his vacant mind, and now Rory and his iron ships. Your master, Mr. Graham, must be a fine man to work for and he seems to want you to move ahead.

All our love,
Father, Louise, Rory

The next item on my list of personal business was to track down Jack Gallagher. I met with a stone wall. My inquiry among the clerks in the stockade turned up nothing, but a chance meeting with James Shaw, his *bourgeois*, solved the mystery.

"Mr. Shaw, sir. I am Duncan Ross, the chief clerk for Jonathan Graham."

"Oh yes, Ross, I have heard of you. What do you want? I am a busy man."

"I am looking to find my friend, Jack Gallagher. He . . ."

"Don't you dare to mention his name in my presence!"

"Mr. Shaw, I am at a loss to understand your anger. Pray, tell me . . . "

"Tell you? I'll tell you, Mister Ross! When a man deserts his post and goes over to the enemy he ceases to exist as a man. Now, do you understand? Jack Gallagher went over to Hudson's Bay. Good day to you."

First, the letter from Louise with the sad recounting of my father's slide into darkness. Now, the unexplained behavior of a person I counted as both friend and companion. What happened to cause him to jump ship?

Even in a cold drizzle the dock that served the compound of the central depot meant a touch of freedom.

"I thought I would find you here."

Who is that? I peered through the mist but the voice was foreign to me. I was in no mood for an unwanted encounter.

"Well, am I not to be recognized? Damn it, Duncan Ross, it is Samuel Rawlinson who would have a word with you."

"My God! Samuel, what a total surprise. I thought you were rooted in Montreal never to suffer through the meager pleasures and accommodations of another *Rendezvous*."

"Let's find shelter in the doorway of an unused warehouse. We need to talk, Duncan. You have some perfectly good money in Montreal that ought to be put to work."

"I have money? Samuel, you are crazy! I am but a boy from the Highlands who barely owns the clothes on his back."

"Have you ever drawn against the ten percent of your wages Simon McTavish said would be made available when you completed your apprenticeship. Well, have you?"

"No. It would be a small dish of potatoes."

"Even potatoes sprout and grow again. Then, there are the wages Jonathan Graham pays you each year. Have you spent them?"

"Samuel, you are dumber than I suspected. Where in God's name would I spend any money in the wilderness."

The two sources of money in my name in Montreal banks amounted to nearly three hundred pounds sterling. What Samuel proposed was to give him authority to withdraw my money in his name and invest it at his discretion.

"Why not start with me and let me show you what I can do for you?"

"Prepare a paper for me to sign, Samuel. But keep this fixed in your mind, my friend, lose my money and I will take you apart one piece at a time."

""Duncan, I am no fool! I'm confident I can do you some good. I plan to keep my pieces just where they are, thank you."

Time to compose a letter to my family in the Highlands:

Dear Father, Louise, Rory
Another year, another twelve months of unchanging business but all in all a good year for me. I have been made chief clerk for Mr. Graham and his five posts. We lost the sixth post early last fall because of a fire. Naomi's step-mother died last fall at about the same time as the loss of the trading post. Naomi went back to her people's winter camp to

try to help her step-mother. Naomi is very good with natural herbs and such, but nothing seemed to help and the woman died.

When I told Mr. Graham about Rory's idea that ships will be built from iron he agreed. He tried to explain this thing he called 'buoyancy.' Mr. Graham is a very smart man and reads books all the time. I was sorry to learn of the death of Mr. MacQuay, another reader and another smart person. Rory and I should have worked harder for him.

Give Jennifer some hugs for me. This coming to Grand Portage every summer is getting to be a stale routine.

Your obedient son and brother,
Duncan

The first evening of our return from Grand Portage the Tall One and I found time for a private homecoming. At some point in the haze of sleep and satisfaction, of whispering and caressing, Naomi said. "My dear red-headed man who needs a shave, would you like to be a father?"

"Father? Me? When?"

"Now, listen to me! I asked if you would like to be a father? I didn't say you were. Would you want me to have a child?"

"Yes. Yes, I would. What would you like?"

"Why do you think I asked you? Yes, I want to begin a family."

Nothing more was said about family. Besides, talking wouldn't do the trick. We just went back to what we had learned to do with indescribable pleasure.

Leave it to the Tall One to get me away from trading room activities and plans for the future homepost.

"I know what you are thinking, Dunc, but first we have to make preparations for the little trip you and I are going to take."

"Trip? Damn it, woman, I just got back from a trip of many hundreds of miles."

"I know that, but you covered most of those miles sitting on your *derriere*. You sat most of the time, didn't you?"

"So I sat. Why are we making a trip starting tomorrow morning?"

"You will see. Now, get your *musete*, we will need it and get our snowshoes down and check to see none of the lacing is frayed."

"My dear lady, haven't you noticed? It is not snowing."

"We aren't going to take any chances. That is why we will take more than a day's rations and why you will roll two blankets separately but tied to make them easy to sling over our backs."

We slung the rolled blankets and snowshoes over our backs, and I carried the *musete*. I followed as Naomi started off at a pace that would cover many miles by the end of the day. We stopped on a bluff overlooking the lake.

"What in the world are you up to?"

Naomi slipped off her back pack and walked to the edge of the bluff. She stopped and motioned me to stay where I was, back about ten feet. With eyes closed she lifted her arms and began a prayer. It was given in silence but as I watched her face and the changing expressions, I felt something pass between her and her spirits. She dropped her arms to her side, bowed her head, stood for five minutes without moving. Then she picked up her pack and took off again in the lead.

Two hours of her steady pace and I realized we were into country I had never crossed before. Our direction was an unvarying line to the southwest. My curiosity reached its limit, "Naomi, what is this all about? Just where are we going?"

"Ah Dunc, you deserve an answer. I can only show you, we should be there soon."

Naomi stopped at the edge of a stand of spruce, unslung her pack, and gathered the makings for a fire. She built a fire ring of rocks and, as the flint and steel did their magic, the fire blazed away. The warmth of the flames matched the warmth of her smile. "I think you trust me. I like that. Now, are you hungry?"

"Don't you know, long legs? I was born hungry."

She went back into the trees with her knife and returned with two small but sturdy green sticks that she deftly peeled. Reaching into the *musete* she extracted a parcel filled with pieces of elk meat. She slipped pieces of meat on a stick alternated with wild onion bulbs. On either side of the fire she placed two large rocks and laid the sticks across them.

"While the meat is roasting, why don't you go down to that stream and bring a kettle of water? A mug of tea would go well with the meal, don't you think?"

She handed me one of the sticks, and following her lead I let it cool for a minute, then popped a piece of meat and a bulb of onion into my mouth. Pierre le Blanc in his prime could not have produced anything to equal this.

Another two unbroken hours of steady walking.

"I think we should make our night's stay here, Dunc. What do you think?"

I scooped out two shallow ruts in the duff, filled them with small branches of fir. Next I made a fire ring and collected a handful of starter wood, and then brought in two loads of larger deadwood that I broke into chunks about two feet long. I hung our blanket rolls and *musete* high off the ground out of reach of some nosy critter. With a smile, Naomi said, "Not a bad camp, I may keep you around. You can be useful."

"I'll fetch a kettle of water, then my duties are finished."

"What? You're not going to cook an evening meal? It will be cold tonight, and I would like hot food."

She took my hand, led me down a slight hill and began to skirt the edge of a swampy area. A small stream wandered back and forth through the flat stretch of ground. After a few minutes of picking our way from clump to clump of dry land among marshy spots, she stopped and asked, "Do you see all these beaver lodges?"

"Yes. What is so important about a bunch of old beaver lodges?"

"Do you see any sign of life? Is there a single one of these lodges that has a family in it? Count the empty lodges, Dunc."

I counted, and stood on a clump waiting for her to tell me what she had in mind. No answer. She took my hand and guided me back to firm ground. We promptly strode off over a slight rise to another little swamp with hummocks of dry ground in between the slews. Again the command to count the beaver lodges here, again the question as to how many lodges showed signs of occupants. We visited a third area similar to the other two where I counted more lodges. "Dunc, not a sign of life anywhere. Yet on the higher ground there are hundreds and hundreds of poplar, elder and bushy growth that furnish beaver their food."

"Yes, I saw these lodges, I saw the standing young trees all around the swamps. What are you trying to tell me?"

"What is different about these lodges? Different, yet each lodge has the same mark on it. Why?"

"Damn it woman! I'm tired of your games."

"No games, Dunc. Death is what you are looking at. Every one of those lodges was broken into from the top side, every beaver killed (all lodges should have three generations living in them this season of the year). They were clubbed to death, Dunc. My people did it."

"Of course, Naomi, they do that to get pelts to bring in for trading. We give them what they want for those pelts. That's why it's called trading."

"It's not trading, it's greed. You make our people want from you what they don't need."

My sharp reply hung in mid-air. Naomi never heard it for she wheeled about to retrace our path back to the night's camp. Once more, I became the follower. She never stopped until she reached our sheltered spot. She dropped on the ground, held her head between her hands, and her shoulders quivered with sobs I could not hear.

This was a new Naomi. When she took a few minutes this morning to stop to pray I found it unusual, I never saw her do that so openly. Now I looked down on the Tall One as I would a stranger. I started to lay the fire, and when there was no indication from Naomi of what she wanted, I struck flint and steel and got it going. I fed in some larger sticks, and when they took fire I got the kettle and walked to the stream for water. When I returned I found she had the *musete* open, and was preparing something for our supper. By this time it was nearly dark, and I could not see if she was still crying. I pulled her to her feet, put my arms around her and held her close. She did not resist. I could sense her relaxing, but she said not a word.

"Let me make tea while you finish with whatever you found in the bag."

"Fish cakes, Dunc, fish cakes. I know how much you like them. They are easy to pack and warm up quickly."

We ate slowly and silently, but not with tension or anger. When she was ready she would tell me why the tears and the hurt in her eyes.

"Dunc, it is not you as a person, but it's what you stand for that upset me and brought on the tears.'

"I am relieved to know that, my dear one, but what is it that disturbs you?"

"When my people hunt animals, they leave sufficient numbers to make sure there will be little ones to keep the line unbroken.

When you people came into the *pays d'en haut* you put pressure on my people to get more and more and more pelts."

"But we didn't take those pelts, we traded for them. It was an exchange where both parties got what they wanted."

"I know that, but you didn't encourage the hunters to leave anyone to make children among the animal world."

"It was your people who broke into the lodges, wasn't it? We didn't do it, they did."

"You forgot to say the one word from the trade that is at the root of our problem."

"Naomi, we have nearly one hundred items in our posts to trade. What did I overlook?"

"Rum, Dunc, rum! You made our people want it so much they laid aside all the things they practiced for generations that made sure all creatures of the Great Manitou would survive."

What could I tell her? Years ago we introduced rum (the NWC imported rum, the HBC imported gin) in ever growing quantities. The problem was discussed at every *Rendezvous*, and I am sure the Board of Governors in London discussed it as they made the regulations that govern HBC. Everyone talked about the problem, nobody did anything to resolve it.

At first light we broke camp after a mug of tea and a hard biscuit. When we stopped briefly at mid-day to make a fire hot enough for tea water, we were both too tired to resume the topic of beaver lodges and kegs of rum.

As we sipped the tea, snow began. It had the feel of a serious storm. Within the hour we unslung the snowshoes and strapped them on. I admired the steady pace the Tall One could maintain on snowshoes, and her unerring sense of direction. We were inside the compound as the winds increased to the point we would have been trapped in a 'white out' had we stayed another hour on the trail.

In the late spring of the following year on the dock Naomi and I had a public send off - a quick hug, a brush of fingers across my lips, and a smile that warmed my heart for many nights on another long trek to *Gitchi Gammi*. As I settled into my seat in the middle of the canoe I called to her, "I counted eighteen."

"No, you missed one, Dunc. There were nineteen. You were standing on it."

That little exchange had no meaning to anyone save us. It was my way of telling her I had not shoved aside as unimportant the lesson she gave me on the ruined beaver lodges in the slews. It was her way of telling me she had the total picture firmly fixed in her mind She had it right, I didn't.

Besides the joining of our brigade to that of William Sumner at the portage to the Grand Rapids, the summer's get together on the shore of *Gitchi Gammi* passed quickly. A letter from my sister was there waiting for me:

Dear Duncan
This is another letter I do not want to write. Father died in November. I can not give you any details because there aren't any. I went to his room to call him for the morning meal, and during the night he had just passed away. Neither Rory nor I heard anything. We buried him in the church yard at the side of Mother's grave after the service in the church. People came from all over the western Highlands. He was a well-known man and respected by all.

Our little Jennifer continues to do well and grows in size as well as showing a growing tendency to independence. Everyone tells us she looks just like me, but I think that is nonsense, she looks like Jennifer. If there is a resemblance, it is to our Mother. I hope you and Naomi have children. Rory is at ease with the idea that he is a father, but it did take a couple of months. He talks more and more about moving to Glasgow. The business has grown so much since he took it over from Father. Most of Rory's work is in metal, not so much cabinet making and the wood working that Father did so well. Rory did make Father's coffin. He said it was a family tradition.

All our love,
Louise and Rory

Mr. Graham was angry when he finally found me in one of the warehouses. "I have been looking for you for the past hour. Why didn't you answer when I called you?"

I did not try to answer, I merely took the letter from my coat pocket, held it up for him to see it was posted from Scotland. I didn't trust myself to speak, but turned to go back in the warehouse that stored cooking kettles and began to count out the number I knew we needed at our posts.

"Is it news of your Father, Duncan? You told me he has not been well. Is that it?"

All I could do was nod my head, and in spite of my efforts not to cry, the tears began to come. I tried to make myself invisible in a dark corner of the little warehouse. Mr. Graham took me by the arm and walked me to the gate away from the compound. We went quite a distance along the lake shore before anything was said. "I assume, Duncan, that your father died."

"Yes. My sister said he died last November. He wasn't sick, he just died in his sleep."

"I remember you told me of his failing mind. That he drifted off, didn't know where he was, and what he was doing."

"He never got any better. He slipped into another world that my sister couldn't reach."

"From what I hear of older people, this often happens."

"You don't understand, Mr. Graham. Once again I am way over here in this *pays d'en haut*. Father was in Scotland and I was not there to help him, or help my sister."

"Sometimes, Duncan, it is not possible to help. It does no good for you to blame yourself. I think you should write to your sister while we are still at Grand Portage, and take time to do it now. The work of the post can wait."

That afternoon I sat a table in one of the corner rooms of the Great Hall and wrote:

> *Dear Louise and Rory*
>
> *Oh Louise, why do we have to write letters like these, with one following on the heels of another, and so close together? I know I should be there with you, but here I am at this damned Company annual get together, I suppose we should thank God that Father did not suffer a long illness. I thank him for Father's sake, and for yours. With a family and the farm to look after, I'm sure you faced many full days and nights to work through.*
>
> *Naomi and I talked about starting a family, she wants children and so do I. but so far, nothing seems to be happening. To put your mind at ease, Louise, we do try frequently. Your little Jennifer must add so much to your life and that of Rory, too.*
>
> *Mr. Graham is making plans to move our homepost to a new location about thirty miles to the northwest of our present site. It won't change the address you must use for letters to me. It will add almost two days to the time for our brigade of canoes to reach Grand Portage. It also adds to the feeling I can't get rid of that we are growing farther and farther apart.*
>
> > *Your loving brother,*
> > *Duncan*

Writing the letter helped to ease the pain of Father's death, and the mad rush of last minute work in the stockade made the days fly by.

My heart sank as again my eyes searched the people crowding the little dock at our homepost. People slapped me on the back and shouted greetings as I directed the last minute chores before I could go to our cabin. Something was in the air, but I thought it was just the joy of homecoming that had everyone in a festive mood.

The glow of the fireplace gave a soft light as it penetrated the thin deer skin stretched over the two little windows Luis built into our cabin. A curl of smoke from the fireplace was visible in the light from the signal fire that still burned on the lake shore. I was home. Naomi stood in front of the fireplace to welcome me as she had the night of our wedding. Well, not quite the same. It took but a minute for me to drop the *musete*, ditty bag, and sea bag, a few seconds to shuck out of my deerskin jacket and rush to take her in my arms.

"Gently, Dunc, gently. We have a guest."

"Yes, my dearest long-legged beauty, we have a guest."

Foolish banter was a way to ease the shock of a total surprise. I reached across the table, took her hands in mine and looked into those lovely, blue Spanish eyes. There was a glow about her, her smile was wider and radiated more warmth and tenderness than I have ever seen. She was the same woman I parted from in early May, she was the same woman in early October when I returned. Yet, there were differences.

One of those differences was made known to me the moment we settled into our bed.

"Dunc, our guest must not be disturbed with the advances you make to me, the ones I want as much as you."

"Well, I guess you are right. What do you think our guest will be, a boy or a girl?"

"It doesn't matter, just so it is a healthy child, What do you want? A boy?"

"I want what you want, a healthy baby. See if you can make it look like its mother, boy or girl."

"Annette thinks I will have a boy. She said she can tell by the way I walk. I don't walk any more, I waddle like a duck."

We ceased talking for Naomi shifted her position slightly, reached for my hand and held it on her belly. "Do you feel it, Dunc? It is our child. It wants to say hello to you."

"Hello, little baby. When will your mother let you come out and play?"

"Annette says I will have it in a month. I think it will be more like two."

We slept for a little while, talked for a little while as I told her of my father's death, slept again, talked again, on through the night. My father was an elder in our church back in the Highlands, and he knew well his church and its teachings. It was my mother, however, who knew her Bible. I remember the stories she told that came from the Holy Book. One of my favorites was the story of miracles; I asked her to repeat it many times. Did we not have a miracle here in this remote *pays d'en haut*? In this crude little cabin, but now a home transformed by the presence of one we could not yet see, we were part of a miracle. My Mother could have told this story with so much realism, so much faith, and so much love. It truly was a mother's story.

"Isn't it time you went to the trading room? Just before our evening meal I have a job for you. Now, out you go."

Le bourgeois was the first to greet me. "Now, father-to-be, I guess you were surprised when you walked into your cabin last night."

"Naomi said that when we left for *Rendezvous* in early May she wasn't sure that she was with child and didn't want to say anything."

"The whole compound is happy for you two. And, Duncan, anytime you feel you must break off work and go do something for Naomi, why, you just go and do it."

The outpouring of good wishes and support matched the downfall of snow. Here it was the middle of October and Luis said we already had more on the ground than he could remember.

I got back to the cabin just as the sun sank in a cold, clear frozen line to the west. Naomi was waiting for me. She took my hand, led me to the bed and disrobed. "Easy, Dunc. I want you to rub my back. By the end of the day I am so tired."

Back rubs were one of my special talents. The Tall One showed me early in our marriage how to do it gently, yet effectively, and we traded that pleasure many times. I pulled the blanket over her as she turned on her side. I started at her neck, to her shoulders and arms, to her upper back and flanks. I reached the small of her back and she asked that I work over that area again and again. Then on to the other side and a repeat of the territory. "It's soft gold I am massaging, Naomi, soft gold."

"What is soft gold, Dunc? I do not know what that is."

How do I explain that her warm, supple, shapely back is like a prime beaver pelt? I was not ready to chance that. "It's really nothing, Just my way of telling you how lovely you are."

No response, only contented sighs and drowsy requests not to stop. To myself I said over and over, 'Soft gold, pure soft gold.'

Christmas was a quiet day for the few within the compound who knew its significance. New Year's was the holiday all celebrated - natives, French-Canadians, transplanted Europeans. This was the big event of the year and Mr. Graham was having a grand time directing the preparations. The trading room was the center. Hard work on the part of all clerks turned it into a ball room. Well, we thought it passed for a ball room. We were ready to welcome a new year.

In our cabin we prepared to welcome our overdue guest. Naomi had broken her water in the morning and by afternoon serious labor pains began. Annette took charge. I did everything she ordered and I thought I was an essential person. It was a shock to be told to get my parka and go to the celebration in the trading room. One did not argue with Annette.

Mr. Graham tried his best to get me to do one or two of my Highland dances.

"How can I dance when I'm having a baby?"

"I thought Naomi was taking care of that. Let me look at you, Duncan. My word. You aren't showing a thing. How far along in your pregnancy are you?"

Further embarrassment was spared me, for Annette entered the room with a look that said everything. I grabbed my parka and made a dash for our cabin.

"She asked me to get you. I don't know why, but Naomi wants you. Men aren't worth a pouch of acorns at a time like this, but I told her I would fetch you."

I ran to our cabin and burst through the door, "Come, Duncan, meet your daughter. Isn't she beautiful? Here, take her and hold her. Are you pleased?"

What I said I don't remember. I will remember forever taking that precious bundle in my arms and kissing Naomi at the same time. I just let the tears go. Tears of joy and relief that Naomi came through the pains and anxiety of childbirth looking so radiant, and the little one added her dampness to the occasion.

How can six pounds of gurgling, squealing, wiggling, wetting joy take over the lives of two adults? Stand them on their heads and run their daily schedules on a twenty-four hour basis? She did it, and without lifting a finger - because it was usually in her mouth.

Naomi and I knew that a name for our child was essential. What shall we call her? Naomi's suggestion was translated into her native tongue using many vowels and a torrent of consonants. In my tongue it meant - Little Bird Under Wing of Mother Bird. I suggested she be named Margaret Louise Ross. I had no problem with Naomi's choice, nor did she raise any objections to mine. Without knowing why, I began to call her 'Peggy' and the Tall One did the same. It seemed a good fit and, when I probed my mind, I remembered an uncle who called my sister Peggy, not Louise. Peggy it was.

Within six months Queen Peggy ruled over her domain on the shores of *Lac de Truches*. It was grand fun, but it did take her mother and father to the edge of sanity with Peggy's responses to all the attention. She loved it.

In the trading room I found Mr. Graham again scanning the sketches and estimates I had made for the enlargement of *Lac de Wapiti* into our homepost. The dark scowl so visible yesterday was still there today. "Duncan, this is turning out to be the kind of winter Luis predicted. Will it ever end?"

"It will end, winters always end. But will it be in time to let us get started on the building?"

"No, I'm afraid not. As soon as the weather breaks we will have to rush into preparations for the run to Grand Portage."

"I don't want to talk about that."

"I know you don't, Duncan, for it means separation from the two women in your life. Well, we will make every attempt to shorten our time there."

"Would it be possible for me to stay here and have you take George and Verne with you?"

"No, Duncan. I will have Verne and Terry remain with Luis. I think three of them can manage overseeing the summer work and begin the work at *Wapiti*."

Damn! Now I had to tell Naomi that I will be gone for close to five months at a time when I wanted so much to be with her and Peggy. Each trip to *Rendezvous* rubbed a little shine off the luster of the great Company get together.

Naomi and I fell into the habit of talking over any problem that surfaced during the day as we lay in bed. Not every night's session resulted in solutions to vexing situations, but at least they were talked over. We never went to sleep in a mood of anger or resentment, but some nights did take hours of talking.

I can't begin to describe the tug at my heart when I held Peggy and Naomi close for the final hug, thrilled to the fingers that brushed my lips, and the slobbery wet fist that punched me in the eye.

Jonathan Graham planned to meet William Sumner at the portage of the Grand Rapids. While we waited we made camp and plunged into the repairs and refitting essential to keeping an active brigade on the move.

The keen eyes and ears of a *voyageur* alerted us that a group was coming down the portage. We expected the Sumner brigade. What passed through our camp were two North canoes. Two *voyageurs* carried each canoe in the upright position, one man at either end, the usual method that size canoe was portaged. It was the *entourage* that caught my eye. In between the two canoes was a line of twelve native girls each with a heavy pack on her back. At the head and end of the line of girls was a trader. Both were the meanest, hardest men I have seen in this part of Canada. Not only were they big in every dimension, they were dirty, raunchy dirty. Not a word passed between the men and Mr. Graham or me.

"What was that, Mr. Graham? I don't like the looks of that outfit. Where do you think they were going?"

"I guess their first stop will be Grand Portage."

"What would those men do in Grand Portage with those little girls? Grand Portage is our place, only NWC business is done there."

"Not quite, lad. Did you forget Monsieur Bouchée's second tent?"

"You mean to tell me they will be forced to be . . . ?"

I couldn't bring myself to say prostitutes. Not a one of those girls could have been older than twelve or thirteen

"Easy, Duncan, there is nothing you can do. Forget it! Make one move and those men would have you filleted like a white fish."

"But, Mr. Graham, they are only girls, little girls. How could these men get their filthy hands on twelve little girls?"

"Duncan, they are what we are. They are traders. They probably came through Grand Portage last summer, picked up a stock of trade items and trinkets from old Bouchée, went up into the North Country and made a winter camp somewhere. They began to trade until they had as many girls as six men could manage in two canoes."

"Can't we stop them? We have enough men in our brigade to take them on."

"Duncan, Listen to me. You are not going to do one damn thing. I am not going to risk you or any of my men in this business deal."

"Business? You're crazy, Mr. Graham! Pardon me, but you are out of your mind."

"It is business. Those men traded for those girls, probably with their fathers, maybe even the mothers doing the trading."

"When we get to Grand Portage I am going to look up those men and have it out with them."

"I said you are not to do anything, and I mean it! By the time you get to Grand Portage that outfit will be on its way to *Michilimacinac*." (That large post and gateway controlled fur trade traffic going south on Lakes Michigan and Huron.) "They will no doubt trade a few of the girls to Bouchée, the rest will end up at 'Macinac'."

My letter from Louise:

Dear Duncan

Have you moved your homepost? In your last letter you said it was to happen. Rory has made up his mind, and mine too. We will move to Glasgow as soon as he can sell Father's shop in the village. He will keep the tools, of course, but he sees no reason to hang on to the shop. Many of the families there have already moved to Glasgow. Rory said most of the people will work in what he calls 'mills'. Do you know what he means?

I differed with him when he said we should also sell the house and farm. I can't bring myself to sell everything, and I want to keep this place. I accept the fact we will have to rent or lease it so that it doesn't fall down and become totally useless. Did you ever think you might want to come back to the Highlands? If you do, there is one problem you won't have to solve. This place is as much your home as mine.

I hope we have a letter from you telling us that you and Naomi have a child by now. Rory and I take so much pleasure from our Jennifer. She grows and changes so fast, and seems to be so contented. You never say much about Uncle Simon. Do you not see him at all when you go to this Rendezvous thing? Are there so many men there that you can't sit down and have a long visit with him? Father said he was one of the finest men he ever met. Rory said he misses Mr. MacQuay and the boys in your little school and the fun your friends had in the school yard.

All our love,
Louise and Rory

In a few days I will sit down and write to Louise, for I have so much to tell her in this letter. What will she say when she learns I am a father and have a daughter! And the name we chose to call her! What a great time all of us would have if only her family and mine could be together.

Samuel Rawlinson sent a clerk with a note for me to meet him on the dock at tea time. Tea Time. My, aren't we putting on Montreal airs?

"Good to see you, Duncan. How goes it in the North Country?"

"The North Country never changes, Samuel. What is different is me. I am the father of the most beautiful little girl you can ever imagine."

"Father? I'll be damned. My congratulations, old man, congratulations."

"Now, Samuel, you asked me to meet you here. Why?"

"I bought a share in your name from a group that purchased a whole block of open land in downtown Montreal."

"You what? What in the hell is a parcel of empty land going to do for me?"

"Buildings. Buildings. Montreal is growing, my boy!"

"Don't give me that 'my boy' bull shit, Samuel. How will a bunch of dirt make me any money?"

Samuel gave me a lesson on real estate development. "Can't you see what a sweet deal I made with your money?"

"All right, Samuel, maybe I spoke in haste."

"Why don't you come to *Rendezvous* next year with your wife and daughter, transfer to Montreal, and begin the good life with me?"

"Samuel, you are full of . . . You know I will never leave the *pays d'en haut*."

"We shall see, old man, we shall see."

Dear Louise and Rory

By the time you get this letter you may already be living in Glasgow. We were not able to move our homepost. This past winter was so severe it would have been impossible to do any building.

Now, big sister, you are an aunt to the most beautiful little girl you would ever want to see. Remember that Uncle Roderick from over near Grampian who insisted on calling you Peggy? Well, Naomi and I gave the name of Margaret Louise to our daughter, but somehow we started to call her Peggy. What do you think of that?

More and more the business of the Company is in the hands of William McGillivray, Uncle Simon's nephew - by blood. I will not see or have a chance to visit with Uncle Simon, he lives in a world of his own where the little people, like me, are not welcome. My master, Jonathan Graham, is not in the best of health, but he is still a wonderful man to work for.

All our love,
Duncan, Naomi, and Peggy

We were barely clear of *Fort Charlotte* and working our way up the Pigeon River on our way home when at the first portage I was ordered to his canoe. "I must tell you what William Sumner told me. He is 'going out' from the NWC, not for a year's leave of absence, but permanently. The reasons he gave me I find to be very disturbing."

"He just got tired of living in the North Country, wouldn't you say?"

"Not so, Duncan. He maintained he loved the *pays d'en haut* as much as when he first came to it. He said he sowed too many seeds that produced nothing but weeds, poisonous weeds."

"I don't understand, sir. I never pictured Mr. Sumner to be irresponsible."

Mr. Graham went into details. William Sumner liked his 'bits of brown', the term he used to describe native women he chose to warm his bed each fall when he returned from Grand Portage. He was generous in his gifts to them, and most generous in making rum available to them and to their families. Some of the families resented his changing partners every year, for it cut them out of access to his rum. Last year serious fighting broke out among the displaced families resulting in injuries and death. Mr. Sumner said the deaths and the savagery in the way victims were literally butchered overwhelmed him with guilt.

"Do you think he is the cause of all that?"

"Duncan, we all share in the responsibility for the introduction of alcohol into the trade."

"This is a very black picture you have painted, Mr. Graham."

"I'm afraid it is just that, my friend, black and bleak."

We were no more than six or seven days from *Lac de Truches* the afternoon *l' avant* in Mr.Graham's canoe signaled for me to direct my canoe to draw alongside. I did not see anything unusual in this request until my canoe was a stone's throw from that of *le bourgeois*. *Le gouvernail* was in the middle of the canoe, not in the rear at his accustomed station.

As we came near I heard none of the lusty, profane gibberish of *voyageurs* who knew they were but a few days from home. Now I could see tears in the eyes of each man in the crew. There was a problem. A glance in his canoe gave me the answer. The choked, small voice of *l' avant* confirmed it. "*Mon patron, mon ami, est mort.*"

When the brigade came to slack water shallow enough to permit our men to slip out of the canoes in the water and hold them in place, my canoe came alongside. No detailed directions were needed. Birchbark canoes are fragile and the body of the beloved Jonathan

Graham was precious. As the body was lifted from his canoe and stretched out reverently on the bottom of my canoe, all involved made a sign of the cross and murmured, "*Dieu vous garde, mon bourgeois.*" One man left my canoe to take his place in Mr. Graham's craft to adjust the weight in both craft. The brigade bunched together as I outlined the plan we would follow.

"George, you will take Mr. Graham's canoe as yours and lead the brigade. The other three canoes will trail after George. I will stop at our outpost on *Vermilion River* and see to a proper burial for *le bourgeois.*"

I signaled for George to have his canoe lay alongside mine and in English told him to follow the advice of his *avant* as to the management of the canoes. It would take me two days to complete the final rites for Mr. Graham. No one needed a reminder of the pressure of time.

In the morning George led off as planned with three canoes in trail. Never in my life in the North Country have I shared such a quiet night, quiet morning, and quiet parting of the brigade. No singing, no curses, ribald joking or pranks. Silence. Total silence as we set our canoes back on the water.

The people at *Vermilion River* post wondered why four canoes of the NWC passed by but did not stop. When my canoe turned to their dock and made signs that we were going to unload, a few people came to assist. One look at the sad faces of my crew answered a host of questions. The post was short-handed - most of the men had not yet returned from Grand Portage - but what had to be done was work best done by women.

While the body was prepared by their caring hands, the men of my crew got picks and shovels and began to scratch out a grave in the hard, rocky ground of the North Country. I gathered up boards and tools and made a coffin. Although not a finely finished piece of cabinetry, it served its purpose. That coffin was an honest effort to see that this man, mentor, semi-father, and above all, friend, was laid to rest with all possible respect and ceremony. He would be buried in the country he made his home for so many years as a proud Nor' Wester.

The women told me when Mr. Graham's body was sewn into his shroud. It struck me, as I helped to gently lower him into that wooden chest, how small a man Jonathan Graham was in physical size, yet so big in character, integrity, and leadership. Each nail pounded into the lid of his coffin was a nail in my heart.

We knelt in prayer, each man tossed a clod of earth on the coffin, crossed himself, then we all set to work building a mound of stone over it. I thought of the bitter irony of protecting his body from the very animals he had come to barter with - their lives for his goods.

In the spring on the way to *Rendezvous* I would stop to place a suitable marker on his grave and distribute presents to all who helped us through this difficult time. We reloaded our canoe and set out for *Lac de Truches* under skies as leaden as our hearts.

Just at sunset the next day we touched the dock at the home-post. I called all together and said we would hold a memorial service in the morning for Jonathan Graham in the trading room.

Naomi at my side, Peggy in my arms, I slowly trudged up the hill to our home. My daughter wasn't sure who I was, and let me know she preferred her mother to this strange, bearded giant with the rough voice.

"You have been away from her for almost six moons. It will take time until she will accept you. Wait until you get into my bed. It is her bed, for she slept with me every night you were at *Rendezvous*. Just wait, she will let you know."

The warmth of homecoming lasted through the evening meal. We held each other closely and I realized the Tall One was weeping. For the rest of the night we talked softly of Mr. Graham. Naomi wanted to know everything about his last days, his death, what we did to prepare him for his next life. We talked only of him.

In the morning all the people in and near the compound gathered in the trading room. Earlier, I had gone to Mr. Graham's quarters and took his Bible from where it rested on the table beside his bed. I knew he read it frequently, but was surprised to find the great number of dog-eared pages, the scraps of paper that marked other pages. I sat down and read most of those marked portions and found he, perhaps without doing it consciously, created his own memorial service.

I asked those gathered in the room to listen to his favorite readings from the book he treasured. I read a few lines, then paused. Naomi took a little time to think through what I read, then repeated it in her dialect. I could see my reading was received with respect, but it was the spoken word from the Tall One that brought expressions of understanding. At the conclusion to the readings I offered a prayer, one I had not written out. I was reluctant to pray aloud, but as I began the thoughts were there waiting for me to put into words. I suspect the spirits of my father and mother were hovering nearby.

Luis told us what the time with Jonathan Graham meant to him over the many years of their association. He was hesitant, but he gained confidence as he spoke and told us, in an expressive way given only to *voyageurs*, of his love for our departed *bourgeois*. Annette wanted to add her thoughts, but tears and sobs were her way of relating the esteem she always felt for this man. George, Terry, and Verne offered their thoughts.

Naomi and I talked quietly and at length in the cabin that night. Peggy, who could crawl with amazing speed everywhere in her kingdom, sensed the atmosphere was different tonight. Somehow she knew there would be no tumbling and play with the big red-headed person she finally readmitted into her court. She took the wooden bear Luis carved for her a few days after her birth and crawled to a hiding place only to retrieve it and move it to another all the while spouting a steady stream of sounds that made perfect sense to her.

"What does all this mean, Duncan? Will the Company send another man to take Mr. Graham's place?"

"I have never been involved in something like the death of a wintering partner. I don't know."

"What about *Wapiti*? Will you go ahead with the building there?"

"The reasons for moving to *Wapiti* aren't going to go away just because of Mr. Graham's death."

"The Company must come first, eh?"

"Naomi, you sound bitter. Can't you see our life is tied up in the Company's life?"

"I don't want to be bitter, I want to help you do what is best for everybody. That means thinking about people as well as how many beaver pelts you can trade for in *Lac de Wapiti*."

"My lovely, long-legged friend, I am going to need all the help I can get."

Another gathering in the trading room, this time Luis, George, Terry, Verne, and myself. We went over all that was done last summer to prepare for the transfer.

"We will leave George here as homepost trader, the rest of us will rush to *Wapiti*. With the men already stationed there we can get the additions to the post roughed out in two weeks. What do you say? George? Terry? Verne, Luis?"

"You are *le bourgeois* now, Mister Duncan. What you say is what we will do."

"Just a minute, George. I am chief clerk, and that is all I am. This is not a one-man operation."

Luis spoke up, "We still need a leader, and I think you must be that."

Verne who was generally quiet in our group meetings said, "I think Luis is right."

Two North Canoes, four *voyageurs*, Luis and three clerks, and full loads of supplies, food, and hearts heavy but warmed with tender farewells, set out for *Lac de Wapiti*. Mother Nature was once more smiling on us, we were not hampered with rough weather.

Once at *Wapiti* Verne quickly showed the group the stakes he and Mr. Graham had driven into the ground to outline the enlarged stockade as well as sites for new buildings.

It was the hardest kind of work and went on for eight days. The small staff in residence at *Wapiti* worked alongside as though we did this sort of thing every day. No disputes, no wrangling, just work. The women of the area kept their cooking fires going so we were never without hearty rations and endless hot tea. When we had done all that was possible, I decided a great feast was merited. We were all so tired from the efforts at more than tripling the size of *Wapiti* that I was afraid we really wouldn't celebrate. Never underestimate the capacity of a *voyageur* to party! Include clerks in that category.

The next morning a sad collection of men - some with tired muscles and weary bones or with over-sized heads, others with both - manned the canoes that set out for *Lac de Truches*. We started in snow and it never quit until we reached the old home post. Mother Nature felt a touch of sympathy for this bedraggled bunch; she pelted us with snow, but did not let the water in the streams freeze. Back home, back to Naomi and Peggy. Back to a place with a vacancy that could never be filled.

Annette and Luis came to our cabin one night to share mugs of tea and the pastry the Tall One baked with dried fruits. We enjoyed the easy give and take as only good friends can do, and we made an effort to talk around Company affairs. Impossible. The NWC loomed so large in our lives that it became the center of everyone's attention - now that Queen Peggy was asleep in our bed, as usual.

"Duncan, it is only a few days until the courier with the round-robin letter arrives. What will you tell them in Montreal?"

"Why, Luis, I'll tell them that Jonathan Graham died on the way back to his homepost. What would you have me tell them, Luis?"

"Tell them they must make you *le bourgeois* here."

Annette stuck her paddle into the conversation. "I don't care what they do in Montreal, just so they keep us together."

"I agree. My shaggy, red-headed man, you must write in your letter that the people at *Lac de Truches* have to be considered when they decide who will be the head man here."

"Luis, can they make us go to another post? You have been with the Company longer than anyone. What can they do?"

Luis' reply was more in the nature of another question than an answer. "I think they will do any damn thing they want. What will you do, Naomi, if they order Duncan to move? What can you do? Where would you go?"

An evening that began on such a note of warm friendship and sharing of simple things as tea and bannock ended up on the dung heap of Company business. All four adults around the fire in Queen Peggy's cabin sensed that some power not yet identified would some-day drive them apart.

So many things to review, so many decisions to make. I miss you, Jonathan Graham, I miss you terribly, yet I must do the best I can. You had an esteemed name in the NWC, you ran a tight ship in the *pays d'en haut*, you were so good to us at this post. I will not let you down, Mr. Graham, I will not!

Now for the circular letter. Every post between here and Montreal will read it. It must be a report of actual events, free of personal comments or observations. The important men back in Montreal should make their decision about this department of the late Jonathan Graham based on facts and merits, not on some clerk's speculations. I needed a space in Mr. Graham's quarters to do this, yet couldn't shake the feeling I was intruding. Later that night as I spread my work on the little table in our home Naomi joined me.

"You mean when you go to *Rendezvous* you will be able to get all the things on your lists for our posts? They will be there waiting for you?"

"When the system works, we will bring home everything I ordered. When it works."

"Dunc, do something for me, will you?"

"Of course, my long-legged beauty. What would you like me to bring for you?"

"It's not what I want, Dunc , it's what I don't want. I want you to bring back half the number of kegs of rum that you have on that list."

"Balls of fire! Naomi, I can't do that."

"Why can't you? You just told me how your system works. Why can't you make it work to bring back less and not more? Tell me, Dunc. Why?"

"We need that rum to conduct our trades. If we don't supply it, our native customers will go to a Hudson's Bay post or an XY post and get what they want."

"That's easy. Just give them more in goods. Another yard of cloth, a few more beads, an extra ounce of gun powder. Even I can figure that out."

"It doesn't work that way. We trade what they want. They want rum. It's that simple."

"It's not simple. It's ruining them, and you know it!"

"My hands are tied, my dear. I can't change the requests I am sending to Montreal."

"I think you could if you wanted to. Dunc, just this year ask for ten kegs less than last year. That won't make anybody angry, and it will make me think a lot more of you."

"Well, once again you win. I will try."

"I know you will. And I am sure you will come back to *Lac de Truches as le bourgeois.*"

Added to her walking, little Peggy now demonstrated consistently that she too could speak. Only she and her mother understood exactly what she said. I translated her chatter enough to know that I was now 'Papa Dunc'. Like her mother, Duncan was not a word that she fully pronounced. She said 'Papa Dunc' in a way that was hers alone. We stood on the dock as my canoe was loaded, the crew impatient to get underway. I held Peggy and had my arm about Naomi's waist. The hug, the brushing of finger tips across my lips repeated; first Naomi, and now by Peggy. In spite of the cold rain falling on Lac de Truches I set off for Grand Portage with warm feelings that lasted for days.

Over and over in closed meetings in the Great Hall I had to account for the final days, even hours, of Jonathan Graham. Several times I sought the eyes of Simon McTavish for some indication of support or sympathy. Nothing from him in any fashion; he sat, usually mute, and did nothing to temper the remarks and insinuations of the partners. To his code name O.I.B.- Old Iron Balls - I added O.I.E. - Old Ice Eyes.

On the third day of my grilling an abrupt change occurred. Now I was severely questioned, not about Jonathan Graham's death, but over my qualifications to become a wintering partner.

Balls of fire! I never hinted that I desired that to happen. Someone put my name forward without one word to me. Is this the way the big men of the Company went about settling partners' affairs?

William McGillivray took me by the arm and said to walk with him along the lake shore. "Duncan, you seemed in a trance when you heard the partners begin to debate your merits and faults as a potential partner."

"I swear to you, sir, I never tried to plant 'wintering partner' in anybody's mind."

"Do you know who campaigned hardest behind the scene for your promotion to partnership?"

"I don't know who that might be. But in confidence, sir, I will tell you I was most disappointed in Uncle Simon. From the very first question put to me about Mr. Graham's death, he never opened his mouth. Hell, he wouldn't even look at me."

"Duncan, Duncan. That is our uncle's method. He was testing you. He wanted to see how you would respond under pressure without his visible support. He works that way, you should have remembered that! He wants to see you become a full-share wintering partner, but a partner able to stand on your own two feet, not lean on him."

"What, sir, do I do next?"

"For starters, have a clerk take your measurements to send back to Mr. Marx so he can work up a full wardrobe for you. Next summer when you come to *Rendezvous* it will be here waiting for you."

"I guess my deerskins are pretty shabby compared to the fine clothes you Montreal men wear."

"Yes they are, but don't forget for five years I lived in deerskins."

Before the full meaning of being made a partner hit me, I had another surprise.

"I say, Duncan, will you not give me a minute or two?"

"Samuel. I thought you were a friend! You never opened your mouth in there. (Samuel had taken over Loren Deschamps' share as a partner in the NWC.) I would have welcomed some support, you know."

"What could I have said? You were doing quite well on your own behalf. What I have to tell is far more important than any five hundred words said in a meeting of the NWC partners."

"Out with it, Samuel. I'm not going to play games with you. Say your piece."

"My God, Duncan. It's a wonder you don't collapse under the weight of that chip you carry on your shoulder. Now, listen to me."

Samuel went into a history of Lauren Deschamps' handling of Jonathan Graham's personal affairs as his agent and as his banker. On the death of Deschamps, Samuel took over. When my round-robin letter reached Montreal he was one of the first to know of Jonathan Graham's passing. Samuel said he came to *Rendezvous* prepared to sink any opposition to my becoming a full partner. He brought Jonathan's will - Samuel was the executor of his estate - that named me as the inheritor of his partnership in NWC. If anyone had tried to block my elevation from clerkship to partnership, Samuel was prepared to counter with provisions of the will.

"Samuel, I am speechless. The partnership was mine from the beginning? All that questioning and verbal abuse about my not being old enough was bull shit?"

"I would not put it in those words. But, yes, a lot of things were said that need not have been uttered. Simon McTavish was not the only one testing you."

"Why can't those partners be 'straight arrows' and come out and say what's on their minds?"

"I can't speak for others. However, this might sweeten your disposition. Duncan, you not only inherited Jonathan Graham's partnership, you are the sole inheritor of his entire estate. You my testy, bitchy, hard-assed young man are well off. You are a wealthy man."

I felt as if I had been kicked, beaten, and mauled by a gang of street raiders. I wanted to sit down. I wanted Samuel to tell me all over again what he just said. What do I say?

What I said poured into a letter to Louise:

Dear Louise and Rory
What a cold blow, not to find a letter from you waiting for me when I got to Grand Portage. I trust this does not mean you have bad news that you couldn't bring yourself to write about. This news might knock you and Rory flat. Mr. Graham died suddenly on our return to the homepost last fall. It happened so quickly without any warning that it must have been his heart that just gave out. Oh, Louise, he was such a good man, so good to everybody. We will miss him. We already miss him, for the next thing I must tell you relates to his death.

The man from Montreal who is to settle Mr. Graham's estate is here at Rendezvous. He told me I inherited his partnership in the North West Company, and I am the inheritor of all his estate. Mr. Graham had no known family nor did he mention anyone in his will except me. This man told me I am a wealthy man, a very wealthy man. Louise, I can't believe all this has happened to me. We will be returning

to the North Country in a few days. I am so scared, I don't know just
what I am to do. I don't want any of this to change the way I live with
my Naomi and little Peggy. I want everything to stay the same.

Our love to all three,
Duncan, Naomi, and Peggy

Rather than paddle on past the NWC post on the *Vermilion River*, I ordered the brigade to stop. We went ashore to the grave site of Jonathan Graham. The men could see the cross I made, inscribed, and erected on his grave on my way to *Rendezvous* in May. The brigade had to make that stop. It gave each man a chance to say in his own way the final farewell to the only one they had ever called *le bourgeois.*

How sweet the homecoming this time. The men lost no time shouting the news, "*Messieur Duncan est le bourgeois.*" I was overwhelmed, and when I announced that tomorrow would be a feast of thanksgiving for the safe return of the brigade, I was overruled and told that it would be two *regales* - for a safe return and for a new master. That was tomorrow, tonight was foremost in my mind.

Now for my reunion with the two women who gave purpose to my life. The hesitancy in Peggy was there, not with Naomi. She held me close for the longest time, long enough for the little Queen to set up a storm of protest. When I tried to gather her into our embrace she pushed me away. A year ago it took nearly two weeks until Peggy would accept me as belonging in her world. How long would it take this year?

The double feasts of thanksgiving and celebration were a great success. We ate, we drank, we danced, we sang, we seemed to be one truly happy and contented family. The day after was one of reality. Crews and North canoes were dispatched to the outlying posts with the essentials, not just for expected trades, but also for survival. We had three heavily loaded North canoes to move goods, supplies, food, and families to the new, expanded homepost at *Lac de Wapiti*.

In a short time Naomi had the new quarters for *le bourgeois* at *Wapiti* in livable shape. Tacked to the wall above our bed was the piece of tartan that I brought from the Highlands. When the main building was enlarged, I planned the usual separate bedroom, a general use room - kitchen and dining area - and a small room with a door to the outside that I called my office. That gave more privacy for Naomi and Peggy, and kept valuable papers and records away from the hands of a naturally born artist. Once Queen Peggy learned what she could do with a stick of charcoal on a piece of paper there was no stopping her.

One evening after a hearty supper and a rough-house session with the Queen, Naomi and I were talking about not much of anything important. As was her style, Naomi asked me without warning, "Duncan, why did you bring as many kegs of rum back from *Rendezvous* as you did last year? You told me you would bring ten kegs less. You didn't even try, did you?"

"Naomi. My hands were tied. You take what you order. That's the way the system works."

"But you told me you would try."

"This spring when I send my order I will cut it to sixty kegs. But, don't you see, I had no choice this year."

"Then you shouldn't have told me you would try. I don't like you to tell me one thing and then do another. I do not like that."

For the first time Naomi and I slept with a major difference hanging between us, unanswered and unresolved. Outwardly, everything seemed to go as usual, but a cloud was taking shape.

Yet another cloud formed and produced an immediate storm. One native family traded on credit for nearly two seasons but had not brought enough furs to the post to clear their debts. They were back demanding more goods on 'tic'.

"Mister Duncan, I told them no more goods until old debts were paid."

"Emil, did they not seem to understand how the system works?"

"I'm sure they did, but they left quite angry."

"Sounds like we need to pay this family a visit."

Two days later I set off with Emil Rendall as guide and interpreter. Emil talked our way into the wikiup of the man who owed us peltries. Parley began in earnest.

"I see you have beaver pelts here. We will take only what is needed to clear your debt."

"No. I promise I will bring you pelts next full moon."

"Many moons have gone by, but no pelts."

"I promise, *bourgeois*, I promise."

I got into the exchange that was growing heated. "He is not *le bourgeois*, I am." We stood toe-to-toe, "We will take what is ours, do not try to stop us."

While I used my size and threatening manner, Emil counted out the number of skins needed to cancel the debts. We backed out of the wikiup, lashed the pelts on the toboggan we had dragged with us, stepped into our snowshoes, and were on our way to the homepost.

Naturally Naomi wanted to know why I had to be gone from the homepost for four days. I told her the reason and explained how credit was important to our success in the trade.

"If they are going to use our system, they must learn both sides - you want, we give; you pay, or we take. It's a simple system, and they must learn it."

"Just the way you failed to learn why that man will kill only what his family needs to survive. But you would have him kill all the animals. Have you learned the lessons he can teach you?"

Chapter Eight

Dear Duncan, Naomi, Peggy

What a topsy-turvy world we have been living in. Rory finished all the business matters connected to selling Father's shop - I think I told you I refused to sell our home. We leased it to Preston Shaw, his older brother, Edwin, was in your school group. And we moved to Glasgow. Rory wanted to build a new house, but I found a place in the country about four miles outside of the city. I guess I am a country girl and always will be. I made Rory spend some money on bringing our new place to be more of a family house. For a good reason, I want to have another child and maybe another after that. So you see, a large house will be needed.

I think Jennifer is quite the young lady. Rory says she looks more like me every day, but we both agree she gets her feistiness from you. We are well, and hope you and your family enjoy good health. I must hurry to post this so it gets to London in time for the dispatch cases going to Montreal.

All our love,
Louise, Rory, and Jennifer

That explained why there was no letter at last Rendezvous. Louise did not get her letter to the London offices of the NWC in time for Montreal postings. There was a second letter, but I had to put it aside until after the morning session with *le grande bourgeois* in the Great Hall. This began as a meeting of friends, but ended in angry words exchanged among men who poured out frustrations and age-old recriminations couched in words usually ascribed to horse nackers and street toughs. As you can imagine, I was right in the middle of this stew.

I consoled myself with the second letter from Louise that I took to the dock where I could read without interruption.

Dear Duncan, Naomi, Peggy

So you are a wintering partner! Our congratulations. And you are a wealthy young man. I would have to say your cup runneth over, but it is a most deserved cup. We wish you joy, and at the same time we want to send our sympathy to you on the death of Jonathan Graham. Your letters over the years have made it clear to us how much you loved this man, and how important he was in your life.

Now, rich little brother, what does all this mean? Will you and Naomi continue to live in the North Country? Will you have to move back to Montreal? I could fill several pages with questions. I like the name you have given to your daughter. I never minded the name Uncle Roderick gave to me, and I'm sure your daughter will like being called Peggy. Will things be changed in your life? I mean, will you be able to take the time to make a trip to Scotland? Surely there is Company business that you must tend to in the Highlands. You know you and your family are welcome here at any time.

Rory thinks I am going to have twins when I give birth this time. He insists he has never seen an expectant mother as big as I have become. But what do men know? I wish so many times that I could talk with Naomi about how you met the challenges of a new father. I just know she could tell me many things that would make you blush as red as your head of hair.

All our love,
Louise, Rory, Jennifer

Somehow I managed to find a few minutes I could call my own. This is what I wrote to my sister:

> *Dear Louise and Rory and Jennifer*
>
> *I am leaving this summer's Rendezvous with the realization that I have been made a full-share partner in the Company. I am in a haze or a dream for it will take several months for the reality to set in. I never knew there were so many and varied decisions to be made. And such a short time to make them. If I make any money at this partner business it will be because of work and worry on a scale I never imagined.*
>
> *I appreciated your kind comments about Jonathan Graham. We all miss him and in so many ways. Why should it take the death of a person to make you realize how important he was to you? I find myself thinking the same way about Mr. MacQuay.*
>
> *I don't really know that much about Company business to tell you what there might be in the Highlands for me to tend to, but your idea's a good one. Yes, I would like nothing better than to be able to tell you that the North Country people will visit you next month, but I can't. Your Jennifer and my Peggy would make a powerful pair of young women who could drive all of us wild if they got together. When you and Naomi would begin talking Rory and I might as well take to the hills for a prolonged hunting trip. Does Jennifer have a toy or doll that she never leaves out of her sight? One of the men at the homepost carved a little bear for Peggy and it is always with her.*
>
> *All our love*
> *Duncan, Naomi, and Peggy*

We were headed for home, what a pleasant ring that had - homeward bound!

It was the usual homecoming for all except me. Naomi and Peggy were not on the dock with the whole community involved in our greeting. No matter. They must be in the master's quarters in the big building with a private welcome waiting. I told myself to take care of business, arrange for tomorrow's feast, then go to your own place. No one there. Now, this was serious. What was the explanation? I finally caught up with Annette LaGarde. "My dear friend, where might my lady be found?"

"If you would calm that fiery temper of yours and open your eyes, you might find her coming through the gate with your daughter."

I rushed to meet them, gathered the Tall One in my arms and attempted to snatch Peggy off her feet. She was too quick. She ran and was in our place in a second. When Naomi and I tore ourselves apart and went into the building she had already found a place to hide.

"This time, Dunc, why don't you ignore her instead of trying to reestablish your place in her life the very minute you are home?"

"But, my dear, I am the same man who kissed her good-bye a little more than five months ago. Why does it take her so long to remember me?"

"Dunc! Not only were you gone from early May until early October, you were away from us all through the winter for days at a time. At one time you were in Lac aux Sables for almost a month. What does a four year old child have to remember of you except good-bye kisses?"

"I don't know how to change things, Naomi, every one of those trips was business."

"Business! I am beginning to hate the word. And, my red-headed lover, I am finding I must rediscover who my man really is too many times in one year."

"So why are we wasting time? Let's rediscover each other right now."

"It doesn't work that way, Dunc. Not any more."

To say that winter was difficult would be a vast understatement. Naomi's tension and Peggy's shyness took weeks to disappear.

In the din and confusion of departure for Grand Portage in early May we stood on the dock and went through the tradition of a hug, a brush of fingers across my lips. It meant so much to me that Peggy now insisted she be the first to make the moves. Naomi's farewell? I wanted to think it was as warm and tender as the first time, but . . .

I had renewed my invitation to have Naomi go with me or, even better, have both Naomi and Peggy go to Grand Portage. No response.

That first night in camp I nearly went out of my mind. I tore through my luggage, every piece of it one item at a time. I could not find the little deerskin pouch with the lock of Naomi's hair. How could I become so distracted in my packing for *Rendezvous* that I overlooked such a personal item like that?

My first priority upon arriving for *Rendezvous* was the latest letter from Louise. I read it three times. I could not imagine the grief that must be tearing at my sister.

Dear Duncan, Naomi, and Peggy
Oh Duncan, this is again a letter I don't want to write, and I know you will not want to read. I had my baby. It came about a month sooner than I expected, and I had a difficult time to deliver it. The poor little fellow never had a chance, he lived for four days. His passing has hit the three of us so hard. Jennifer has been the center of our lives, but I think the death of her brother will be with Jennifer always. She and I became even closer as she watched me grow and prepare for the birth of this child. And, of course, Rory is devastated with this sad turn of events. Life is so cruel, Duncan. I can't think of anything more to tell you.
All our love,
Louise, Rory, Jennifer

There was a time in my life when I thought important things could always be put off until tomorrow. How foolish; I had a letter that must be written.

> *Dear Louise, Rory, Jennifer*
>
> *My dear sister you are in Scotland grieving the loss of your little boy, and I am so far away. You know my thoughts are with you and Rory. But what can one tell little Jennifer? She was with you as you went through your pregnancy every step of the way. Then, to have a little brother taken from her life so quickly. I cannot imagine her loss. You know I want to sit down and talk the way we used to talk through our problems and questions. I miss you.*
>
> *In another day we will have to load the canoes and head back to our homepost. I can't believe another whole year has slipped by. I know Naomi would want me to add her words of sorrow to those I have tried so inadequately to write to you.*
>
> *All our love*
> *Duncan, Naomi, Peggy*

Forty-four days of tough and demanding travel from *Fort Charlotte* to *Lac de Wapiti*. Another rousing welcome by the whole community - save for me. When I finally broke away to go to my quarters I found them empty.

A rousing homecoming? Not at our place. Rather than gather with the people welcoming the returning brigade, Naomi chose to take Peggy and went to search for a certain bark she wanted for a medication she was concocting.

Some time ago I estimated that twelve hundred men of all ranks worked for the NWC. Each man in the Company found that his life revolved about one word, *Rendezvous*. Even the great Simon McTavish was forced to bend to its schedule, its importance, and the consequences of not being present at the annual get-together. I had no problem understanding and accepting *Rendezvous*, but I failed to have Naomi see why I was locked into that huge event on the shores of *Gitchi Gammi*.

The departure in May was a repetition of the whole winter. Polite, proper, and cold. I tried again, for the third time, to have Naomi go to *Rendezvous*. When it came time to get in my canoe I choked back tears when only Peggy gave me the family's traditional send-off; the hug, the brushing of fingers across my lips. Naomi stood tall, unmoving, and silent.

> *Dear Duncan, Naomi, and Peggy*
> *This spring when the winter was well behind us, and the signs all pointed to new life and new beginnings we turned back to old places. Rory and I moved the grave in Glasgow of our little man-child to a place between the graves of Mother and Father in the churchyard near our old home. It was a heart wrenching thing to have to do, but Rory and I both felt he should be with friends. The very best of friends, his grandparents.*
>
> *I hope your news is more cheerful, for you really didn't say much in your last letter about Naomi and Peggy. Is there any indication that your family may be growing? Rory has established himself in the iron business in Glasgow, and he is still talking about ships built with his iron. He is always trying new ways of making the stuff, casting it, hammering it, rolling it. He has some other men thinking along his same lines that we are moving into a whole new era of making things. Of course, made with his iron.*
>
> *I wish I could meet Naomi and Peggy, I'm sure we could become more than relatives, we would be friends.*
>
> > *All our love,*
> > *Louise, Rory, Jennifer*

What would I tell Louise when I wrote my return letter? That could wait. I was to meet with Samuel Rawlinson after the morning session with Mr. McTavish. What can be on his mind that we must meet so early in this summer's meeting?

"Duncan, I have met a trader who comes to Montreal from New York at least once every season to buy furs, huge quantities of furs. He's a German, calls himself John Jacob Astor, tough as a nut, crude as hell, but smart. He needs some financing to move his fur purchases. I immediately thought of you. Are you interested?"

"Not so fast, Samuel. Is he a good man to deal with? Lots of men talk big, but act small. Which is he?"

"He's big, he acts big, he knows the fur business. He doesn't like to be public any more than necessary. That's why he is looking for private money to move his enterprise along."

"Sounds interesting. How much are we talking, at what terms, and with what security?"

"Splendid, Duncan, you asked the questions I would have asked."

We thrashed over this Astor deal for several days before I gave Samuel permission to put some of my money into the scheme. I told him I was 'in' for no more than 15% of my total worth, and he had to put an equal amount of his money into the venture.

Back at the homepost and settled in for the winter, I began to put an idea to the test. I would read stories to Peggy. My mother used to read to me nearly every evening, and my father read from the Bible every night just before we went to bed.

All the books Jonathan Graham accumulated in his many years in the North Country were now in our place. I looked them over carefully, but found nothing that resembled a child's book of stories. Be creative, I said to myself. Peggy will not know what you are reading, it will be the story that interests her.

We had thrown a bearskin on the floor in front of the fireplace and that became Queen Peggy's sole property. As she stretched out on the skin, I stretched out beside her on a buffalo robe with a book. I turned a page and began to make believe I was reading. What I began was a story my mother told about the 'woods' people'. I spoke to the fire; out of the corner of my eye I could see Peggy taking in every word. Her eyes grew heavier the longer I told my tale until I found a sleeping child beside me.

"That was a nice thing for you to do, Dunc."

"Now it's your turn, Naomi. Stretch out beside me and let's talk."

"Talk, Dunc, nothing more."

"Agreed."

We did talk much the way we used to before tension took over. I started by telling the Tall One the way I felt about being married to two wives: to her and to the Company.

"Dunc, I try to see the way you have come to place the Company in your life. What I also see is that you have not learned to make a place for me and my daughter in your life."

I almost corrected Naomi to remind her that Peggy was my daughter, too. That might end what seemed to be a beginning.

"Naomi, I work hard to take care of the Company interests in my department for it takes care of me and my family, don't you see. With you and Peggy it is different. I love you, and I love Peggy. I do not love the Company, it is only a part of life for me, but you and our daughter are my life."

"I do not understand this word 'love'. You use it with such confidence, and you use it so frequently. I know it has meaning for you, I am not sure 'love' has meaning for me."

The next night Peggy stretched out on her bearskin and looked at me as if to say, "I want another story from you." I continued with my creation, the woods' people. I had to turn a page now and then to make the reading seem believable. In less than an hour I carried the sleepy Queen to her bed. I asked Naomi to stretch out in front of the fire.

"Naomi, remember last night I tried to tell you how I had to balance living with the Company and with my family. I had an idea I want to share with you. Why don't you and Peggy go to Grand Portage in May?"

"This is not the first time you asked me, is it? Well, the answer is the same. No."

"You don't have to make your decision tonight, there's all winter to think about it."

"How will going to your *Rendezvous* help me to understand why you seem not to have very much time for me?"

"This NWC is a very big outfit, Naomi. In your time you have seen two or three trading posts and I imagine they all look alike to you. If you would just go with me to *Rendezvous* you would get a better idea of what a huge outfit the NWC is."

"Dunc, my answer is still no."

That was where things stood as we were on the dock in May saying good-bye. This time the traditional parting was from both Peggy and Naomi. The one gave me her hug, brush of fingers over lips with some emotion - she was losing her story teller. The other's send off was cool and mechanical. I tried, but had not succeeded in bridging the gap that still yawned between us. I resolved to try again in the fall when I returned from Grand Portage.

Dear Duncan, Naomi, and Peggy

We missed the letter you always write to us when you are at your Rendezvous. I hope this does not mean some trouble has befallen. Rory has been so busy this whole year in trying to put together a company or what he would prefer, a partnership, with other men who share his vision in the future of the iron industry in Glasgow. He gets so busy at times he seems to forget he has a wife and daughter. Do you ever get that busy?

Both of us have been spending time with Jennifer to get her started on her letters and numbers. We want her to go to a school in another year or two. Like most in the Highlands, we think girls should have some schooling as well as boys. Are you going to teach Peggy to read and speak English? We are all well, but we are always aware of the empty feeling when we recall the little boy who was with us for such a short time. I pray there will be a letter from you this fall.

All our love,
Louise, Rory, and Jennifer

The frantic pace of affairs at Grand Portage prevented me from getting off a letter as quickly as I would have liked. I was a partner for such a short time and already growing displeased and touchy about the endless bickering over trivial items connected with our business.

I was not alone in my frustration. A small group of wintering partners became aware of my changing attitude and my willingness to challenge *le grande bourgeois*.

"It's a shame, Duncan, you were not a partner when Alexander Mackenzie was one of us. What I remember about 'Mac', when he was a wintering partner, he preached about his idea that NWC and Hudson's Bay should merge. We should cease this foolish competition that saps so much of our energy and resources."

"Will you not join us, be our spokesman, and see if we can't force McTavish to think of other options for NWC?"

That ended this particular *Rendezvous*, but not until I wrote to Louise and to Samuel Rawlinson.

Dear Louise, Rory, and Jennifer

Let me apologize for not writing to you at the time of last Rendezvous. I let Company affairs take over my thinking; you and Naomi both have reason to be down on me. She thinks I do the same when I am working at our homepost. This was a troubling meeting of the Company. Some of the partners are unhappy with Uncle Simon's leadership. And to add to our woes, we suffered a severe decline of prices on our furs in the London markets.

I will be happy to get back to Lac de Wapiti and my family. Is Rory still pressing ahead with his ideas about the iron industry? Maybe he and I should trade businesses so we wouldn't have to spend so much time at our work. You are fortunate to have school as a possibility for Jennifer. Anything like that for Peggy will have to be done by me. I don't see myself as a school teacher, do you?

Our love to all,
Duncan, Naomi, Peggy

Dear Samuel

Where the hell are you? I can imagine that some important piece of business required your presence other than at Grand Portage. That does not excuse the absence of a letter along with an annual review of my investments. Remember, you are my agent.

You will soon have the details of this summer's Rendezvous, but I can tell you there are definite signs of unrest with you Montreal people, especially Le Grande Bourgeois. My regards to Jeanette and other friends.

Duncan

More of the old and familiar drill: forty-four days and nights in canoe and overnight camp; pemmican twice a day; homecoming followed with the traditional feast of thanksgiving; winter's coming and then winter's here. It never varied.

Naomi, who was always quick to pick up on any changes in my moods, asked about a week after my return and after a night of 'reading' stories of the make-believe woods' people. "What is it, Duncan? What's making you seem even more distant than usual?"

"You won't like me to say it, my dearest friend, but it's business."

"You said it. Now, what makes it so difficult?"

"Some of us think my Uncle Simon is not doing the things a leader should do to keep the NWC ahead of our competition."

"This will give you something different to think about, Dunc. I have decided that when the ice leaves the lakes and rivers I will go to *Rendezvous*. That is, if you ask me."

"I'll ask you right now. Naomi, will you go with me to *Rendezvous*?"

"Yes, But don't ask me what changed my mind. While you were gone this past summer I talked it over with Annette. She and Luis are more than willing to keep Peggy."

"That is just great, Naomi. Pray that we have an easy winter and nothing gets in the way of our trek to Grand Portage."

It was an easy winter followed by a routine assembling of the brigade, assignment of personnel, checks on food supplies, and the emotional leave-taking. Naomi had anticipated this and prepared Peggy for it by taking her to the LaGarde cabin a few days before actual departure. We stood on the dock and said our good-byes; she gave her mother a big hug and kiss, I got the hug and brushing of my lips with her fingers. That was it. No tears, nothing emotional. She stood with Annette and Luis as though we were just another bunch of people in canoes paddling across the lake.

Naomi agreed that the tent erected by my *voyageurs* for our use was appropriate, but when it came time for the evening meal, things changed. She insisted we eat with the men.

The second night of camp, Naomi went to *le gouvernail* of my canoe, and in her subtle way said she would like to learn how he cooked pemmican. The next night they cooked it together and somehow wild onions made their way into the iron kettle of bubbling *rub-baboo*. The next night it was another seasoning that made the crude meat dish a little tastier. Other crews got wind of the changes in the pemmican rations. To avoid an uprising, Naomi changed cooking fires each evening. What a diplomat, and what a charmer.

Other changes appeared; their songs were toned down in 'shady' places, and most *voyageurs* made an attempt to get some quality into their singing. Personal hygiene got a boost, razors and combs and a light touch of water became part of the morning routine.

It certainly did not compare to any of the many trips I made to *Rendezvous* with Jonathan Graham, or with Simon McTavish for that matter. Naomi was an influence, no doubt. The best thing was the natural way she brought these changes into the daily routines, mine included.

"Duncan, I should like to have our tent erected at a place I have picked out on the high ground to the east of the stockade."

"But, my dear, I am a partner and expected to take my accommodations near to the others of my station."

"Take your accommodations wherever you like, Dunc. I prefer the site I have selected."

I made camp with Naomi, and it worked out rather well, much to my surprise. I insisted that we take our evening meal in the Great Hall, for the dinners were one of the things about *Rendezvous* I thought would most impress my lady from the North Country. That did not work out as anticipated. Of the twenty-two nights we were in

Grand Portage, we dined in the Great Hall about half of them. As for the *soirées* that followed dinner nearly every night, she stayed for only five or six.

"Naomi, I am puzzled. You seemed to enjoy the long and difficult trip to *Rendezvous*, am I right on that?"

"Oh yes, Dunc, and I thought the constantly changing scenery was a delight. I had no idea we lived in such a big world."

"But, my dear, as soon as we got to Grand Portage you changed. Here, as the wife of a wintering partner, everything is yours to command. You wouldn't have to do a single thing ."

"Dunc, you disappoint me. I'm not some piece of delicate dinner ware. How can you ever believe I would enjoy doing nothing? I am a wife and a mother. I must feel I am alive and useful. Don't put me on a shelf to be taken down, shown to and admired by your friends."

"They do admire you, Naomi. You are the center of attention wherever you go and whatever you do. You are a lovely young woman, and I am proud to call you my wife."

"Oh Dunc, how can I explain? I have enjoyed some of the dinners in your Great Hall, I have learned to dance in your style, and I enjoy that. But don't you see? I am admired for what men see, not for the real person that I want them to know."

"I hear you, Naomi, but how can people get to know you when you spend such a small portion of your time with them?"

"Dunc, I think I have seen more of this *Rendezvous* thing than you have ever seen."

"How can that be? You forget the eleven times I have been here."

"It's what we want to see. You see things that are important to your business. I see things that are important to the little people who make your big company successful."

In between sessions with the partners and fleeting moments with my wife, I found time to collect the letter from Louise.

Dear Duncan, Naomi, and Peggy
We were so relieved to learn it was not a serious problem that kept you from writing to us. Haven't we all had a little more than our share of ills and misfortunes? Rory has involved himself deeper into iron experiments and new processes. Often he tells me he could use you and your ease in the use of numbers. He says he gets ideas about iron making without difficulty, it is when he has to reduce them to figures he gets lost.
*   Would the iron business have more attraction to you than smelly old furs? It would get you back to the Highlands if you would return and began to work with Rory. Jennifer is finding that letters and numbers are fun. She must have some your talent mixed in with Rory's. My talent? I still like to dance, and I think I still can do it rather well, and I still have the figure for it. What has happened to your figure, little brother? You haven't told us much of Naomi and Peggy for several letters. We have contact with them only through you and your letters.*
                    All our love,
                    Louise, Rory Jennifer

I felt tugged by my sister to come back to the Highlands and pulled by Samuel Rawlinson to go to Montreal. I began to feel like a lost soul. Where did I belong? Naomi made it clear about what her answer would be to leaving the North Country. No!

I made time for a quick letter to Louise:

Dear Louise, Rory, Jennifer
This has been a special Rendezvous for me, one that I was afraid would never happen. Naomi came with me. She is a good traveler, I knew that would be no problem. Some of the events at our annual get together pleased her, and she takes part in the evening dances we hold in the Great Hall after the dinner tables are cleared. I think you

would see that Naomi is as fine a dancer as you. You two could trade - she to learn Highlands steps, you to learn her native dances.

Some of the events at Rendezvous were displeasing to her. She does not think the differences in the treatment of the voyageurs and the partners is at all fair. She says voyageurs work like animals and the Company treats them like animals. But Rendezvous is finished until we meet again next summer.

We have not come to a decision about schooling for Peggy. Every day is some reminder of how different her childhood is from what I remember of the Highlands upbringing I had. She is at home in this world of fur trading posts but knows nothing of other places and other people.

My right-hand man at the homepost and his family offered to keep Peggy while we would be gone for nearly four months. Both Naomi and I are most anxious to see her. It will make the forty-four day return trip all the harder to make - it won't go fast enough.

All our love,
Duncan, Naomi, Peggy

Our time at *Rendezvous* was over; the brigade gathered, provisioned, and loaded with next season's trade goods.

The light-hearted way Naomi handled our spring trip to Grand Portage was replaced with long days of near silence. Her mood was more in keeping with the shorter hours of daylight and the chill more evident each night. "Dunc, I am truly glad I decided to join your *Rendezvous*. I think I did see some of it through your eyes, but there is much about this gathering that you choose not to see."

"And what might that be?"

"I would like to think one part I saw is one you have never seen, and I hope you will never see."

"Naomi, what are you getting at?"

"Monsieur Bouchée's second tent, Dunc."

"Oh that. Yes, I know it's there along side his trading tent. What about it?"

"Dunc! How can you be so indifferent? That second tent is a brothel, is it not?"

"Yes, my dear. It is a brothel."

"And it is a part of your Company's profit-making operation, yes?"

"Yes."

"The women that Bouchée employs, Dunc. Do you know they are little girls as young as thirteen? He does not have women to service your men, he has little girls. And you know that?"

"I have been told he uses girls. Yes. I guess I know that."

"What have you done to end this shameful practice? Tell me, Dunc. What have you done?"

"Nothing, my dear, nothing. Bouchée's operation is not a part of my concern."

I foolishly thought her outburst of anger over what she saw so nakedly displayed in the tents of Bouchée was the end of her negative impressions of *Rendezvous*. I was wrong. Several days later came this set of questions. "Why do all of you, and I mean the partners, bow and scrape at the feet of this Simon McTavish? You will agree that many of the partners treat him like a king."

"Some do, some don't. He is not our king, he is but one of the partners. He is the one who formed this NWC, and showed all of us how to make money."

"Well, you may be right about that, but let me tell you something else about this Simon McTavish."

"And what can you tell me about him that I don't already know?"

"Do you remember when you introduced him to me?"

"Yes. He was quite taken with your charm and beauty. Did that not please you?"

"No, my dear husband. It infuriated me! You all remark about his blue eyes and how they intimidate and dominate. Well, his eyes are blue and alive, but as he murmured his silky words over our introduction his eyes were undressing me. Do you admire that in your leader?"

"I'll call him out! I beat those blue eyes until they run with blood!"

"You'll not do a thing, Dunc. It's over. I am honestly pleased to know you are ready to defend me and my honor. But you are missing the point of my anger."

"Missing? What am I missing?"

"Does he not have a different native maiden meet him in his cabin many nights of *Rendezvous*?"

"Yes, that is no secret. We all know of his trysts."

"Dunc. He eyed me the same way he would size up the young girl selected for his night's tumble on the blanket. Now you know he was looking at me as someone who could be 'useful' to his pleasures."

That was a low blow to absorb. My own uncle, even though of clan, not of blood, had so little regard for me that he felt free to regard my wife as a trophy to collect. Naomi had gotten those disturbing impressions of *Rendezvous* out of her system, and now we would enjoy the balance of the trek to Lac de Wapiti and our reunion with Queen Peggy. But it wasn't yet finished.

"One of the things you always liked to tell us of *Rendezvous*, you and Mr. Graham, was of the wonderful dinners that were highlights of every evening."

"Yes, they were remarkable, and I am so happy to have you to share them with."

"I tried to share, Dunc. As one who thinks she knows something about preparing food so that it more than just a necessity, I found them interesting as well as a pleasure to eat."

"Something troubled you, didn't it?"

"Yes. Some of your partners are animals. They stuff their faces; they don't eat for enjoyment and companionship, they simply stuff in huge amounts and then brag about it. And drink! Dunc, I think fully half of those men are drunken slobs. The ones that are able to stand and dance still manage to get their groping hands to work for them. Disgusting, Dunc. Disgusting!"

I sat beside the Tall One in our canoe and counted the days until we would be back at the homepost. Nothing she had told me so far was really off the mark. Most of her observations were mine at one time or another in my annual trips to *Rendezvous*. It was her passion and perspective that shook my view of how the powerful NWC went about its business.

"Dunc, the man you insisted that I meet, Samuel Rawlinson. Who is he?"

"Samuel? He's an old friend from the days when we were just clerks dreaming of one day becoming partners."

"You must have had a lot of big dreams that you must talk so much."

"Naomi, Samuel is the agent who takes care of my affairs back in Montreal. I need to talk to him every year at *Rendezvous*. Do you have a problem with him too? Seems like everyone you met in the Great Hall caused you some sort of discomfort."

"Now Dunc, you know I enjoyed much of my time there. It wasn't all discomfort. I couldn't understand what Samuel was trying to tell me."

"And what might that have been?"

"He thinks we, you, me, and Peggy, should move to Montreal. He said you could make a fortune there and I would become the Princess of Montreal."

"Samuel likes to talk big, but he is correct. You would become the toast of Montreal."

"Why would I want that, Dunc, what is wrong with the way I am?"

"Not a thing, my dear, not a thing. He thinks in Montreal with your beauty and commanding ways you would be the reigning princess of high society in that city. Is that so bad?"

"Of course it's bad. I am myself, not some creature in a make-believe world. Look at me, Dunc, touch me! Am I real or am I a fantasy? Well?"

By the time we worked our way through all Naomi had to tell me of her three weeks in Grand Portage we were both ready for the homecoming at *Wapiti*. Three days later we had our reunion; joyful and tearful with hugs and kisses and little eyes searching for presents. Nobody was disappointed. The best part of our return was to finally have Peggy to ourselves. After several hours of her non-stop chatter, both of us looked across the compound to LaGarde's cabin wondering if they wanted a little girl for one more night.

Naomi's gift to Peggy was an instant success; a headband of intricately designed beads of every color sewn on the softest leather. She had her mother brush out her hair and work it in a way that complemented both the wearer and the headband.

"Peggy, an old woman at Grand Portage made this just for you. She was sick and I was able to find some roots to make a special tea for her. When she was better she said she would make something for you, for she knew I had a little girl."

My gift was not the kind to generate instant pleasure. When our little talker finally wound down and gave signs of sleep, my selection was ready and put to use. In the round-robin letter to Montreal last spring I ordered an illustrated book of children's stories.

Instead of stretching out on her bearskin, Peggy had to prop herself against me so she could see the pictures in the book. The stories matched the illustrations, but when I started to read from the book I ran into a storm. "I want to hear about 'woods people', Papa Dunc. Read me about them!" So I was back to being creative while Peggy studied the picture on each page. She was contented, and I was no longer a red-headed stranger who came and went in her life.

The ensuing winter was routine; no catastrophes, no emergencies. The chill I detected last winter was still with us, not quite as icy. Some evenings Naomi rested her head on my shoulder and we talked over her summer at *Rendezvous*. Rather than draw her farther into my world, last summer's trip widened the gulf between us. There were some bridges. Other nights her head rested on my shoulder with an invitation to nuzzle, kiss, caress, to make love with the same passion we'd known before.

"Oh Dunc, my dearest Dunc. You make me feel so complete when you come to me like this."

"I have that same feeling, my long-legged beauty. Complete is the word."

"We are so fortunate. I feel we have been blessed by the Great Manitou."

"Blessed? How is that?"

"I think most men and women spend a life together and find they only take pleasures from each other."

"But isn't that why they live together?"

"Yes, but I think we are blessed, Dunc. We have learned to give pleasures. I think that is why I am so attracted to you. You, my man, give me pleasures."

"You have taught me how to do that, and I would not want it any other way."

Spring came right on schedule, ice went out of the lakes and rivers, and my brigade was on its way to *Rendezvous*. I knew even as I invited Naomi to go her answer would be a firm 'no'.

Dear Duncan, Naomi, Peggy
What a year for us! Rory and his friends brought their little company to life in Glasgow. Already they have orders for more iron and iron products than their foundry can produce. Can you believe it, Duncan? In business only a year and already he and his partners are talking expansion. I am happy for him, but I know I will see even less of him. I am so glad I have Jennifer for company, but then next year she will begin schooling. Why is it that women never seem to come out winners?
I suppose Naomi came to Rendezvous with you. One of these days you will have to keep on going east from Grand Portage until you run into Scotland. We want to see you and your family so much, to have Jennifer and Peggy get to know each other.
All our love,
Louise, Rory, Jennifer

Get your letter written to Louise. Then if you get the opportunity to exit *Rendezvous* ahead of the pack, you'll be ready to go.

Dear Louise, Rory, Jennifer
Your last letter was full of cheery news. I'm happy to learn of Rory's success in the iron business. Our brigade will be on its way back to Lac de Wapiti in about two days. I have the feeling this is going to be a long and difficult winter and I want to be home before the storms begin to blow in.

Naomi did not come with me this year. We talked over the idea of some sort of schooling for Peggy. The only option would be to send her away, probably to Montreal. Neither of us want that. I suppose I could teach some basic reading and writing. Naomi didn't think much of that. What will she ever do with that kind of knowledge in this North Country? Naomi said she will increase her efforts to teach Peggy the skills that a woman needs to be able to do for her family in this wilderness. As Mr. Graham told me years ago, survival is the main thing to learn up here.

Sometimes I find myself thinking about working with Rory. Wouldn't that become a community joke among our Highlands friends? Duncan working for Rory after all the time we spent knocking each other about the school yard.

All our love,
Duncan, Naomi, Peggy

What bad luck! We were only one day away from the homepost when we became wind-bound. *L' avant's* decision was wise. He thought the brigade must get off the water before severe cross-winds capsized the canoes. Our evening camp was subdued. Each of us thought of the warm welcome awaiting the brigade only hours away. *Le gouvernail* did not bother to start the morning ration over his cooking fire - we could be home and have our morning meal there. At first light *l' avant* gave his usual,

"Leve, leve, allez y, canot dans l' eau, leve!"

Every man was up and moving to the canoes, no laggards this morning. We made the usual noisy entrance to the homepost - loud, boisterous, and mostly off-key singing, shouts and the rush of the home folks to greet us. No one was on the dock to greet me. As I made my way to our quarters I noticed a young native man lounging nearby. He seemed familiar, but I couldn't match his face with a name. No matter, my interests were on the two people inside.

"Papa Dunc!" The human cannon ball nearly bowled me over. What a difference two winters of reading stories made in Peggy's greeting.

"Come Peggy, you must get your parka and the wooden bear that Uncle Luis made for you. We have not a minute to lose."

"Naomi, what is going on here? Am I not to be welcomed into my home?"

"Oh Dunc, I can't take the time to explain now. My brother, well, my stepbrother is here to take me to his winter camp. He thinks his wife is dying, and he has come for me. He thinks I will know what to do for her."

"How long will you be gone? Why do you have to take Peggy with you? Naomi, certainly half an hour bringing me up-to-date will not be time lost."

"Dunc. Do not delay us, we must be underway. You know how quickly the weather can change. Come, Peggy. Go to the canoe, now!"

I gathered Peggy in my arms and walked to the dock with her. Naomi's brother was already in his canoe. It was loaded but had a place for Peggy in the middle and for the Tall One in the front. I knelt down and carefully set Peggy on Naomi's winter parka, folded to make a seat for her. I pulled her bearskin over her legs as she reached to brush my lips with her fingers.

I stood and took Naomi in my arms. She didn't resist, but buried her head on my shoulder. I cupped her chin in my hand, slowly and gently forced her to look at me.

"You're not coming back, are you?"

No answer, no words of any kind. Just tears.

"Naomi, how can you walk away without saying something?"

For an answer she lowered herself into the front of the canoe, took her paddle and pushed off from the dock. Expert paddlers, in moments they disappeared down-stream and around a sharp bend in the river.

On a dock at a remote trading post deep in the *pays d'en haut*, years ago, I asked the Tall One to marry me. On a dock at remote trading post deep in the *pays d'en haut*, I watched as the swirling currents in the river erased my visions and my dreams.

Chapter Nine

An autumn evening in the *pays d'en haut* comes quickly. Luis LaGarde took me by the arm and firmly led me off the dock to my quarters. "Mister Duncan, you have been standing here for a long time. Don't you think you had best come inside?"

"Ah, Luis, my good friend. Did you say *adieu* to the Tall One and to Peggy?"

"It's quite cold, Mister Duncan. We should go in."

In my quarters a welcoming fire was blazing in the fireplace, but Annette and Luis looked at me as a stranger. "Luis, do you not feel well? And Annette, why have you not said a word?"

Annette's reply was to bow her head, and Luis just stood and stared.

"Now this has gone far enough! What is wrong with you two?"

More silence. After some difficulty in getting her words to come, Annete asked,

"Mister Duncan, did you not say farewell to Naomi and Peggy? Do you not know it will be for the last time? They are gone, Mister Duncan. They are gone for good."

"Naomi would not answer when I asked her questions, Annette. Have you information I am not aware of?"

Her answer was a spell of crying, of words that tumbled out unintelligibly and without meaning.

"Annette, Luis, sit down. Let's see what we can put together"

I began to piece together the whole story of Naomi's sudden departure. "As you know, the minute I touched the dock here at our homepost I ran to our quarters to greet Naomi and Peggy."

"We saw you do that, Mister Duncan." Luis said, "We saw you come out from your quarters carrying Peggy to the canoe. We saw you hold Naomi in your arms for a minute."

"Yes, we saw you do these things, but we could not know the words that passed between you and the Tall One."

"She said her step brother had come for her because his wife was near death."

Luis picked up on his version of what events had transpired. "I am not sure, Mister Duncan. I want to believe Naomi, but she sent for her step-brother to come for her."

"How could she do that? Wasn't she working with you two gathering the winter's food supplies?"

"Oh yes, Mister Ducan, but I think she asked Joseph Gray Squirrel to carry a message to her brother."

Luis volunteered, "If you want, Mister Duncan, I can fetch him and he will guide you to the winter camp of her people."

I pondered this suggestion for a long time. Finally, I said, "Thank you for that, Luis. I will not ask him or anyone to take me to the Tall One."

"I'm sure he would want to do that for you."

"Yes, but it wouldn't do any good. She will not come back, and I won't force her. She has gone. I guess that's the way she wants it."

Luis broke in to add, "Your long times away from her when you had to go to *Rendezvous* began to make her unhappy. The same in the winters when you had to go to the outliers to tend to Company business."

Annette found her voice, "It's not just Naomi, Mister Duncan. It is Peggy who made her do this thing."

"Peggy? You can't blame a six-year-old girl, Annette, I won't hear of it!"

"Mister Duncan, the Tall One does not want Peggy to grow up in the fur trade. She is afraid of what will happen to her when she is no longer a girl and becomes a woman."

"But, Annette, that is just what Naomi did. She grew to her womanhood in the fur trade. She came to me on her own. No one browbeat her into becoming my wife."

"You didn't have to flee from an unhappy life. Naomi did. She had to get away from her mother's captors. She had to feel she was free. You offered her that freedom."

"But, Luis, Annette, she is going back to the same place she fled from. How can that be called freedom?"

"Don't you see, Mister Duncan, she is fleeing from the fur trade and what she fears it might do to Peggy?"

Annette had collected herself, dried the tears, and reviewed her version of what took place over the years.

"It's Peggy, Mister Duncan. Naomi thought the little one would always be picked on because she is different."

"Different? Annette, you are speaking in riddles."

"No, my dear friend. Do you forget how the Tall One had to grow up surrounded by people who were shorter, people who spoke a different dialect, who followed different customs and beliefs?"

"I can't see how that would affect Peggy."

"Peggy has blue eyes, not dark brown eyes of natives. She has your red hair, not black hair of natives. She has features of her mother's Spanish blood, not native features. And if she grows to be as tall as you or her mother, that's another way she will be different."

"Do both of you see those as problems?"

"I'm afraid so, Mister Duncan. There will be problems for Peggy in the North Country all her life. I suspect she will have problems in the white man's world as well."

These dear friends, these two people who had taken me into their hearts as family, who had welcomed Naomi and Peggy the same way, opened my mind to harsh, uncompromising realities. It was my sister who wrote to me at the time of her infant son's death, "Life is so cruel, Duncan."

I don't know exactly when I discovered the piece of tartan tacked to the logs above our bed was missing. Apart from clothing, nothing else was removed from our quarters. Hell, Naomi could have taken anything she desired and be welcome to it, but she chose only the tartan. It was her message that some part of me would forever be with her. Perhaps she had a double meaning in taking the tartan. It would be something to give to Peggy connecting her to her father.

Naomi and Peggy departed in early October, now it was February. I could not say what I did, where I went, what decisions I made in the intervening months. Life seemed a prolonged sleep-walk.

I added a note to the round-robin letter addressed to William McGillivray telling him of my intention to leave the *pays d'en haut*. Next, a sealed note to Samuel Rawlinson telling him of my decision.

Samuel
You are cursed with foresight you never knew you possessed. I am leaving the North Country. We will meet in Grand Portage at this sum-

mer's Rendezvous, and I expect to return to Montreal with you in a Company canoe, so begin to make the arrangements now. What of my partnership in the NWC? Do you want to undertake the search for a suitable candidate willing to pay the true worth of the position? I suppose you will want a commission to complete the deal. I am agreed to that.

You have repeatedly offered me some sort of a working arrangement with you in your private bank. We will discuss your proposition in detail as we return to Montreal. You and Wm. McG. are the only people privy to my decision. Keep it that way until our summer meeting.

Duncan

Those two notes to Montreal drove home again the hollowness of my life since October. I saw myself as a shell; whole and hearty on the outside; inside, I was a wreck. Another difficult task still lay before me. I must tell Luis and Annette I was leaving, not just *Lac de Wapiti*, but leaving their lives. Over a second mug of tea and serving of the bannock Annette had just removed from the fire, we sat in the LaGarde's cabin and began to wrestle with the dragon.

"As you saw, Luis, I sent the courier on his way to *Sault Ste. Marie* two days ago. He carried the round-robin letter plus two personal notes from me. All of them headed for Montreal."

"I saw, Mister Duncan, and I can guess what you said in your notes."

"Perhaps so, my friend, perhaps not."

"You told the big men in Montreal that you were leaving the North Country. Yes?"

"Yes, Luis, as usual, you are right."

"Duncan," Annette was quite agitated as she spoke, "did you have to make up your mind so quickly? Give Naomi a little time. She might change her mind."

"My dear Annette. You have known the Tall One for nearly nine years. How many times have you known her to change her mind once she has decided on something?"

"You will have to admit, Mister Duncan, she could change it any time."

"She could, but she won't and we all know that. If she feels what she did is best for Peggy, not even the Great Manitou could alter her thinking."

We speculated about what Naomi might or might not do for a few more minutes.

"I will leave this place and you wonderful people when the ice breaks in May. My decision is final. It is the hardest thing I have ever had to decide."

That statement delivered with such finality put a damper on the rest of the evening. We struggled to find other things to talk about, but the spell was broken. Acceptance replaced the hurt in their eyes, the pain of leaving was reflected in my eyes. The third mug of tea, laced with rum, helped me to collect my weary body, my troubled thoughts and make my way to the lonely quarters that felt like a prison.

I had a private moment with each of my clerks. I wanted to tell them of my appreciation for their loyalty and hard work. Of the support they gave me as we worked through the transition from Jonathan Graham to Duncan Ross in management of the five posts in the department. I think my message was received, responses were brief and mostly unfinished - men seem not to do this sort of thing well.

Next, I went from home to home of the *voyageurs*, to say goodbye to them and their families. Life in the *pays d'en haut* bound you tightly to one another, the glue that binds could quickly dissolve. Another the curses hanging over people living in the North Country.

The time had come. Luis, Annette, and I stood on the dock as my canoe came along side. No words, just warm embraces and tears. *L' avant* of my canoe was not only skilled in the ways of canoes on lakes and rivers, he was wise in the ways of mortal men. The minute I settled in the middle of the canoe he gave a signal and we sped down the river. The spirited song drifting back to those on shore was the *voyageur's* dual message - farewell and promise of return. For me their singing had but one meaning - farewell.

What would this *Rendezvous* hold for me? As I turned over in my mind the events of the last seven months I realized this would be my last Company get-together on *Gitchi Gammi*.

My sister's letter awaited me.

Dear Duncan, Naomi, Peggy

There are two big stories to tell you, and I can't decide which is of greater importance. Jennifer has completed her first year in school, and she loved it. She can hardly wait for the next term to begin. I don't remember that you were ever that eager to get back to school. I'm certain that Rory never felt Jennifer's enthusiasm for school.

The other thing is Rory. No, nothing happened to him. It's that his company has done so well. He has had to hire several more men to help with the paper work. He asked me to tell you he is serious about wanting you to come back to the Highlands with your family and get into this iron business. He thinks you could make a comfortable living and become an important man in the Glasgow community. Will you give it some thought? It would please both of us to have you and your family living close by.

Again, I have a complaint, little brother. Your letters don't tell us very much about Peggy and how she is growing. I hope things are well with her and with Naomi. Is there an addition on the way?
All our love,
Louise, Rory, Jennifer

About the time I began to think Samuel would be absent from this summer's meeting he arrived with a stranger in a brigade of freight canoes from Montreal.

As Samuel and I strolled along the pebble beach of Grand Portage Bay I unrolled the whole story of the separation from Naomi and my daughter. The account didn't flow, it came in bits and pieces between long pauses. Though Samuel's response was guarded, he saw the total picture clearly and quickly.

"Duncan, I see two problems that are related, but we must think of them separately. You can't bull your way deep into the *pays d'en haut* and force a reunion with your wife and daughter. It would be impossible for you, Naomi, and little Peggy to live independently in the communal world of her people."

"You paint a bleak picture, Samuel, but what of Naomi?"

"Duncan, hasn't she made it clear she will not continue her life and that of Peggy in your world?"

"Well, yes. What will she do?"

"I don't think either of us can answer that, Duncan. What I fear is that Naomi will learn that she is not truly welcomed in the circle of families of her Papa or step-brother."

"One time Naomi told me of how difficult it was to grow up in that setting because she was different. Why, Samuel, why would she chose to go back to that situation?"

"My friend, I can't answer your question. All I can suggest is you review all the conversations you had with your wife and see if you can call to mind anything she might have said that would give you a clue."

"One thing she told me was, 'Like my mother, I am Mandan, I will always be Mandan'."

"That is something to hang on to, Duncan. Right now I think we had better get to the Great Hall and begin the steps that separate you from this NWC."

Throughout the three weeks of *Rendezvous* we picked up my saga, explored the multiple problems from all angles we could think of, but always came back to two conclusions - Naomi would never return with Peggy as the wife of a fur trader and I had to leave the North Country.

My leaving the Company did not stay a secret. The partners began to focus their eyes and probing questions on the new man who accompanied Samuel to Grand Portage, Askel Leggitt. He and Samuel hammered out an agreement that gave him my seat among the wintering partners. "As is my practice, Duncan, I have forged a most favorable deal for you. I am good at this sort of thing."

Did I have twinges of regret over leaving all this behind me? Yes. Grand Portage was the place where I felt I had passed from boyhood to manhood, here I was given large responsibilities and free rein to carry them out. Here I crossed the height of land that placed me in a world I would never have imagined. This place was the gateway to a woman who gave of herself honestly and passionately, and the daughter born from that union.

Without much thought at the time Samuel made the offer, I accepted his invitation to make a temporary home with him and Jeanette in Montreal. Then it struck me. I once thought Jeanette Turmel was the prettiest girl I knew in Montreal, and a bit flirtatious.

The reunion of Samuel and Jeanette was warm, barely, and her welcome to me as a guest in her home a bit chilly. "I am most appreciative of your hospitality, Jeanette."

As for Jeanette? She hadn't changed; she added to her good looks to the point she was a strikingly handsome woman - a confident, grand lady of Montreal's higher levels of society. She belonged here. I didn't.

Dinner that first evening with the Rawlinson's was a challenge for me. This was the first time I was exposed to the full splendor of fine dining with a couple who represented the elite of Montreal. I was not ill at ease, my appetite did not flee in fright, but it was different. My yes, it was different. Only weeks ago I was more than ready for a meal of *rubbaboo*. Here a great variety of dishes superbly prepared by professionally trained chefs were served by servants who anticipated our every need.

Samuel and I retired to a room he called, "A little place for men to talk privately over coffee." How could we carry on a meaningful discussion when surrounded with such displays of wealth and grand furnishings?

My thoughts were interrupted by a servant who slipped into the room and silently refilled Samuel's cup. As she turned to do the same for me she gasped, spilled coffee from the silver server on me, and fled the room.

"What the hell! Excuse me, Duncan, I am going to the kitchen and discharge that maid immediately."

"No, Samuel, don't do that. I am responsible for her accident."

"You? You didn't do anything. I will not have a guest in my house treated like that. Well, in Jeanette's house."

"Listen to me, Samuel. Her name is Denise, is it not?"

"Yes, old man, how is it you know a maid in Montreal when you have been in the city only half a day?"

"I took room and board with her parents when I came to Montreal to begin my apprenticeship. I failed to recognize her as she assisted with the serving of dinner. She recognized me, and evidently was unnerved when she faced me at close quarters. This is my fault, Samuel. It would be unworthy of you to discharge her for the fright I caused."

As I saw it, Samuel had the large view, the imagination to seek and find areas and people who could benefit from his skills and resources as he ran his private bank. He wanted me to be the disinterested observer and analyze the prospects for success, to be his alter ego. I would be the one to challenge his enthusiasm with cold, hard information, statistics and financial assessments.

We fell into patterns of work as though we had done this for years. We could speak frankly, we could argue, but we kept personalities out of the mix. I was amazed at Samuel's daring, his lightning fast decisions, and his luck - at times. On other occasions my input, expressed forcefully, saved him from costly errors.

I had little time to solve one of my own problems, permanent housing. Samuel insisted and Jeanette seconded the idea that I continue to live with them. A generous offer, one not easily declined. Their style of living was good preparation for achieving the proper mind-set for my work.

"Duncan, I must make a trip to *Sorel*. (A village about thirty-five miles downstream from Montreal.) I'll be back in four days."

Dinner the next evening with Jeanette was pleasant, nothing more. She pleaded the need to write letters and retired to her rooms. I brought work home that demanded my full attention and went to bed with an unresolved, complex deal on my mind.

From a deep sleep I became aware the door to my room was opening. I had no weapon at hand, but my fists had served me well in the past. I detected movement but not its exact place in the room. This intruder knew his business, no false moves, no sounds, a professional break-in artist. At the side of my bed she let the night dress slip from her shoulders and drop to the floor. Sneak-thief? No, Jeanette.

"Is this the welcome I get? Move over, I'm getting cold standing here."

"Jeanette, what the hell are you doing here?"

"You are the one who is to be 'doing' and don't be all night in starting."

Jeanette was all woman. God, was she ever! Warm, responsive, and passionate. Some time in the night she left the bed then returned later and relit the fire she had kindled in me. Dawn came and went in a house enveloped in silence.

"Jeanette, your servants are going to think you take your duties as a hostess a little far, don't you think?"

"I have waited years for the chance to get you to myself. I gave the full staff the day off. This was too good an opportunity to let slip by. Now, aren't you happy I did it?"

"Exhausted might be a better word, not happy. I have betrayed a good friend. That does not make me happy, Jeanette."

"Oh posh! Don't turn into a Puritan on me. I have to take my pleasures when I can. Samuel seldom takes his pleasure in me. Once every two months or so is his limit. What's yours?"

"We are not going to test my limit, Jeanette."

"We don't have to. You more than passed my test last night. When will we spend another delightful night in bed?"

My answer was to get up and begin morning preparations. Jeanette followed, gathering her gown and robe. "You are going to wait for breakfast, aren't you? I'm as good in the kitchen as I am in bed."

"I have no doubt on either score, but I think I will pass on breakfast this morning."

There were no bitter words, no recriminations as I left the house, just a satisfied and confident woman who was sure she had her man where she wanted him.

I had searched for a place of my own after arriving in Montreal. However, the ease, comfort and convenience of living in the Rawlinson's house took the urgency from my searching. Now I renewed some contacts. Before the day was over I found a place that met my requirements.

"Are you punishing me because I am straightforward in my desires? You needn't make this move, Duncan."

"What I am about to do is for the good of all. You, Samuel, and me. I'm not a Puritan, Jeanette. Didn't last night prove the point? We know this is an impossible situation, it can't go on."

"My dearest Duncan, you have no idea how lonely my life will be when you are gone. Samuel spends many evenings downtown and frequently does not come home for a day or two. You are all I have that is alive and appreciative of me and my charms. I do have charms, don't I?"

"My dear, you have charms that would tax any man's skills and endurance. You are all woman. And that, my dear, is the heart of our problem. *Adieu, Jeanette, mon cheri.*"

I knew I gave my best and undivided attention to our projects at the bank yet I felt something was lacking. Samuel had a real talent for reading the thoughts of others. "Duncan, we have an opportunity

to underwrite a new enterprise holding promise of substantial profits."

"Sounds like the very thing you are always looking for, Samuel.
Is there a problem?"

"Yes, a big problem. The enterprise is in London, we are here in
Montreal. How would you suggest we handle this problem?"

"That is obvious. I must go to London and get our foot in the
door. Are you agreed?"

He more than agreed. He had assembled all the information
gathered about this start-up operation, compiled a list of contacts in
England to confirm and test my findings. Best of all, he had me
booked as passenger on a first-rate ship about to make a direct
Montreal to Liverpool sailing. This assignment was the cure for my
restlessness, would it cure sea sickness? A needless concern, I
enjoyed every day aboard the vessel.

There were seven passengers: two elderly couples who kept to
themselves for the entire trip - they were returning to England after
years of missionary work in Lower Canada. Then a man who let all
know he wished to be left alone. That meant the remaining passenger, John Trostle, and I must make an effort to be congenial or the trip
would be exceedingly dull.

John was in business, alternating his time between New York
City, Montreal, and London. He was a grain broker with years of
experiences to relate and had a good grasp of the problems and
prospects of business between Canada and the United States.

"Duncan. If you complete a deal with the principals you are to
meet in London, your private bank will be truly international.
Interesting, but loaded with risks, wouldn't you say?"

"Risk is an integral part of doing business, John, we both are
aware of that. But do we not know ways to hedge, to ease the odds
of risk?"

"We can control some risks, but what of those we cannot control?"

"Something lurking in your conversation has me curious. What do you see that I have overlooked?"

"Just two words: Napoleon Bonaparte. Sooner or later England must confront him or become a second-rate power. If that happens, Canada may be drawn into Europe's conflicts. What will that do to your pending international deals?"

"Truthfully, John, I had not considered that. Do you think things are that close to open warfare?

"I just have a suspicion that bad things are going to happen."

This was the nature of our daily meetings and the easy way we exchanged viewpoints.

"Duncan," John and I were doing our morning rounds on the main deck, "I have been thinking of the scope of your bank's area of operations. Have you ever considered getting into business in the United States? It's far more convenient than England and the potential for this fresh, new country is truly astounding."

"What advantages do you see, John, aside from being new and undeveloped?"

"My dealings in the States put me in touch with a cross-section of many different people. They tell me the resources there are unlimited."

"Now, you have not only stirred my curiosity, you have my interest aroused. Where would one begin to tap into this wealth?"

"I should think that you and your partner would do well to establish New York connections."

My crossing was not the dreaded five weeks of misery and boredom I envisioned, but a delightful voyage made so by the good cheer and openness of a shrewd and observant man.

At Liverpool we parted company. I caught the stage for London and was in the city the following evening. That night for the third or fourth time I went over the folio put together by Samuel and our staff. The next day I began contacting individuals and exploring the potential for profits in Samuel's idea. The deeper I probed and the more men I questioned, the less my enthusiasm for making this deal. I did have another long-standing project - Scotland.

A few days after arrival in Montreal last fall I wrote a hurried note to my sister. I rushed to the office of Uncle Simon hoping that my letter was included with the dispatch cases of the NWC on their way to London.

Dear Louise and Rory and Jennifer

This must of necessity be brief, for a vessel to clear Montreal bound for England leaves in two days. I have left the North Country permanently and will be located in this city for the coming year. Your letters to me should be addressed as always. Instead of being sent on to Grand Portage I will get the letters in Montreal.

Naomi has taken Peggy and fled to the winter camp of her stepbrother. She does not want Peggy to grow up in the environment of the fur trade. I know this is an inadequate explanation of our problem, but until I can sit down and talk with you it will have to do. Do not worry about me. I am adjusting to this sad situation although the hurt of it sinks deep into me.

I hope that you, Rory and Jennifer have had an easy winter and Rory's business continues to grow and prosper. I have been given a lesson in the true meaning of family, and I shall always be concerned to know what is happening in the lives of yours.

All my love,
Duncan

On my many explorations of London I located the offices of McTavish and Fraser, went in, introduced myself making much of my family ties to Simon McTavish. My contacts were with highly trained and experienced clerks. The name of McTavish impressed them, as did a six foot, red-headed Scotsman with a commanding air telling them how to care for his mail. When I asked for assistance and advice on the best way to get to Glasgow, they responded quickly. Clerks made the arrangements while I sat down and penned a hurried note to Louise that was dispatched at once.

> *Dear Louise and Rory and Jennifer*
>
> *Prepare yourselves, you will shortly have a visitor. I have been in London for the past six days on business. I am now free to make a dash to the Highlands for a brief visit. We will have so much to talk over and so many pleasant hours getting to know you and Rory all over again. And Jennifer, I am most eager to meet her. In two days my plans call for a stage to Liverpool, then coastal vessel to Glasgow. I guess if I yell loud enough for Rory McBride some kind soul will give me directions. I can't wait.*
>
> *All my love,*
> *Duncan*

Before I departed London a letter to Samuel had to be written and sent off immediately.

> *Samuel*
>
> *In a few days I will be on my way to the Highlands for a brief visit with my sister and her family. If possible, I will leave Glasgow for Montreal. If not, I will go back to Liverpool and arrange passage from there. I think it best to forget the London people and the deal you hoped we could make with them. I will, of course, bring the details of my analysis of their merits, but I think you will agree that it is best we look elsewhere for a London investment.*
>
> *Duncan*

More than fourteen years with only letters to maintain contact was all Louise and I had to hold on to. Now it could all come tumbling out as we sat face-to-face around a kitchen table. Just like the old days.

Rory, experienced man of the city, had his people checking on all vessels coming into the port. When a stranger fitting my description made an appearance on the docks I was taken in hand and escorted to his place of business.

"Duncan Ross, you old scoundrel. How are you? It is so good to see you. My God, let me look at you! Am I ever glad I beat up on you in our school yard, for I don't think I would want to try to knock you down today. You look great."

"Well, Rory, you didn't disappoint me. I knew we would go at each other as soon as we met. You are looking well and prosperous. An ample vest is always a give-away."

"Let me help you with your *valise*. My carriage is just outside the door. We can have you at the house within the hour."

Rory handled the horses in an expert manner. It gave him a chance to show off for my benefit. The greeting from Louise confirmed that warm feeling of being home. We didn't say a word, didn't hesitate. We threw our arms about each other and danced an impromptu fling right there. It was so good to see her, to turn back the clock, and once again be a Highlands lass and laddie lost in the joy of a family reunion.

"Where is this Jennifer person? I must see her."

"She will be coming from school in about an hour. She begged not to have to go to school until you had arrived."

I anticipated that when we got through the initial reunion there would be a long period of awkward silences as we struggled to find the starting point for conversations. Louise started talking and never stopped for all the time I was with her family. That was an exaggeration, of course, but she made it so easy to put together the stream of details we demanded of each other.

"It took a long time for me to realize, Louise, that Naomi and I lived apart as much as we lived together, perhaps more apart in terms of months out of each year."

I went over the cycle of a whole year from one *Rendezvous* to the next. Rory wanted to know, "Wasn't there someone from your home-post who could go to this gathering at Grand Portage? To act as your representative and report back to you?"

"When I was a clerk, Rory, I was replaceable. As a partner, I had to be present. The same for the winter trips to the outliers, only a wintering partner could make decisions there."

The lead questions were of Naomi and Peggy. I put aside the questions about what it was like to live in the North Country until Jennifer could be with us. I wanted her to know of the conditions her cousin lived in, and the things a little girl in the vast *pays d'en haut* did to fill in her days.

"Speaking of the devil," Rory said with a laugh, "she's here. Prepare yourself, Duncan."

I expected a shout, a crushing embrace, pure energy unleashed. Into the room walked a tall, somewhat gangly young lady with a winning smile. She looked at me in a most straightforward manner, polite, curious, but not impressed.

"I am most happy to meet you, Uncle Duncan. How was your voyage to England?"

"I don't answer questions, Jennifer, until I have been given the traditional hug and kiss due a man of the Highlands."

That broke the ice, and damn near broke my back as she hurled herself into my arms. Now the real reunion began as questions and answers flew back and forth in the kitchen. It seemed only natural for us to gather there, for this was the way we would have done it in our old home.

When I had given detailed descriptions of Naomi and Peggy to Jennifer I found I had a difficult time resuming my narrative. Tears appeared without warning; one word or phrase, and they just happened. When I told Jennifer of the tales of the 'woods' people' I created for Peggy, she insisted that I tell her one every night before she went to sleep. I thought I could never get through that, but somehow did, and never missed a night for all of my time in Glasgow.

Louise arranged for a friend to come to their house and stay with Jennifer as the three of us made a circuit of the old home places. With Rory driving, Louise narrating, my eyes, ears, and mind filled with recollections of year's past. We gave ourselves a 'grand tour' of the compact world of my boyhood.

The first stop was our little church and adjoining graveyard. It was a visit with the soft whispering of winds among the pine trees, of solitude and unspoken words. I touched the headstones of my mother and father with a feeling of warmth to my fingers, not the cold, hardness of stone. The headstone of the little boy who had brightened the lives of Louise and Rory for such a brief time brought home as nothing had ever done the true meaning of separation from Naomi and Peggy.

Our next stop was the homestead, remarkably unchanged, even to the wisp of smoke curling from the kitchen chimney. The barn still stood, but the lean-to at the side was missing. I declined the offer of Louise to go to the door to see if any one was home to receive visitors. That was more than I felt I could handle. From there we drove slowly to the school house. It looked to be well cared for. Rory and I identified places in the yard where memorable skirmishes had taken place.

After we left the school Rory picked up the pace and drove the team at a brisk trot to reach the village where father's shop and work rooms were located. We found lodgings and a meal at a small tavern in the village square. In the morning we went to the shop, again not wanting to enter. I regarded it as my father's place, and the new owner had undoubtedly made changes. I made this trek to the Highlands to see things I knew and remembered, not things that had been changed.

From the village Rory drove us over the same roads I helped to drive cattle many years ago. In Dundas we found both Brian and Ethyl Fleming at their little house.

"What a surprise, Duncan Ross, how nice of you to stop to see us. I must apologize for Ethyl, she has been slipping away from us a little at a time. Strangers are upsetting to her."

"I am heartily sorry for the fright I gave her, Mr. Fleming. Will you please give her my regrets? I am happy to see you are up and about. I shall never forget your kindness and patience with a half-scared lad about to leave for the New World."

Rory was having a hard time managing the horses, so I said my good-byes and joined them in the carriage. Late the next afternoon we were back in Glasgow.

After supper Jennifer wanted my help with her assignments, and she did want another chapter in the life of the 'woods people'. Louise listened at the door, and when we gathered in the kitchen she said, "Duncan, you amaze me. I remember mother's stories but not with the details you recall."

"Well, big sister, I had to have some way to shine. You were always the dancer, the one who gathered attention and praise. I was the one who sat in the corner neglected and forlorn."

"Oh, you poor lad. Will another cup of tea ease your pain?"

It was fun to be home.

Rory gave me extensive tours of his iron making and machining operations. He also found time to show me the ship building yards and rival iron works that covered the Glasgow water front. Back in his well-appointed office he began a serious review of the reasons why I should make the Highlands my permanent home, and get myself into the many opportunities for profitable business in Glasgow.

Time passed very quickly in the warmth and hospitality of the home Louise and Rory had made for themselves and for Jennifer. I had to get back to Montreal. Not just for pressing business reasons, but for my own well being. I had disturbing thoughts about the risks of going back to one's roots, it is possible that one can go too deeply. I found myself falling into the trap of thinking I could turn back the clock, make things the way I imagined them, the way I wanted them to be. Reality swept through my dream world like a blast of cold air from the North Country.

My last conversations with Louise became personal, as I expected they would. "Louise, I can't put my finger on one reason, one happening, one event that brought about the disintegration of our union."

"I might suggest you and Naomi felt great attraction for one another and responded to it in a natural way. Then you found that your infatuation turned into love. The former does not permit a couple to adjust to absences, the latter does make such an allowance, but it takes time, Duncan."

"So many things crowded one against the other. Naomi's growing interest in the details of the trade and the practices we followed to make those trades. Then the trip to *Rendezvous* gave her insights into the Company that turned her away from the fur trade as a way of life."

"I'm not going to make judgments about what you and Naomi did. There's no right or wrong. My question, little brother, have you made every effort to bring about a reunion with your beloved women, Naomi and Peggy?"

"I think I know Naomi well enough, Louise. Her decision was final."

"Perhaps it is, perhaps not. Maybe in a hidden recess in her mind was the hope you would come charging after her. Once she knew how much you cared for her and Peggy she might reconsider."

"Being here in your home has made me realize how much I do care and how much I miss them. Although the differences in our houses are too great to describe, the similarities in the warmth and sense of contentment of our homes are just as great.

"That's quite true. I can't see you giving up, Duncan, it's not your way."

"I haven't given up. I realize I cannot do a single thing here to change things. Louise, I must get back. If there is hope of reunion it will be found in Canada, not in the Highlands."

"I know what you are telling me. I don't want to hear it, for having you with us has brought so much joy and true happiness to my family. You have captivated Jennifer, and I am so pleased to have our daughter meet her Uncle Duncan. Now, she will have her own remembrances of you to keep with her always. Besides, you will return, I know it."

Rory found passage for me on a vessel bound for Halifax and on to Montreal. The voyage from Glasgow began with a delay *enroute* to Liverpool. The six people embarked at Glasgow gave signs that they would be pleasant companions once we had settled into daily routines on a trip of about forty-five days. The two added to the passenger manifest in Liverpool provided the excitement - a young couple who threw off signs of upper class, perhaps even royalty, with two servants and a ton of personal effects. Two days out from Liverpool the woman disappeared and was not seen again until carried off the ship in Halifax. If *mal de mer* removed her presence from among the passengers, we all hoped the same thing might put her spouse below decks. He was insufferable! Nothing pleased him, agreed with him, or caused him to be polite or considerate. The one positive thing he did was provide entertainment. Nearly each day between Liverpool and Halifax, weather permitting, he came on deck in a completely new outfit. What a fashion plate - what a pain!

We cleared Halifax harbor after discharging the high society couple and their servants and mountain of luggage on the dock there and set a course to Montreal. Instead of going directly to my cabin I stopped in the lounge to see if any of the passengers might be there. Some pleasant conversation would be in order.

I did not find a soul in the little room. What I did see was that the Liverpool dandy had misplaced one of his hats, an expensive hat of the latest style. My attention was caught immediately by its weight. It was light, noticeably lighter than a beaver hat. My God, this hat is made of silk! Look at its color, beaver felt could not be dyed in that hue.

I could hardly wait to tell Samuel of this discovery. I decided to keep the hat since it fit me perfectly and the young man would never miss it. The implications of this silk hat were frightening to a man in the beaver trade. Scary as hell would be a better way to describe it.

The arrival in Montreal was a huge event in the life of the other passengers. For me it was devoid of emotion; no friends on hand to celebrate my arrival, just getting my luggage, hailing a carriage, and taking a room in downtown lodgings. I hired a riding horse from a stable and spent the next day refreshing my eyes and mind with the changes I could see in Montreal. The following day I called on Samuel at our bank.

"Duncan, I am extremely upset, even angry, over the way you absented yourself from our business. I'm not sure I have time for trivial conversation. Good day to you."

I got to my feet and planted my six foot frame inches from his flabby body then said in a voice coming through tightly clenched teeth, "Sit down, Samuel, sit down and listen to me carefully. One wrong move and only God knows what might happen!"

I produced the silk hat, handed it to him, and waited for his reaction. He hardly looked at it, just handed it back to me.

"Samuel, you have in your hand an example of bad things headed your way."

"I have no need of or regard for anything you may wish to tell me. Now, will you remove your bulk from my passage to the door? I have important matters needing my attention."

"Believe me, Samuel, there is nothing that could be more important than this hat."

"I am no fool, Duncan, and I resent your treating me as such. How can a mere hat be a threat to me?"

"A huge percentage of your personal wealth and assets of our bank are tied up in the fur business, especially in the beaver trade. Open your eyes, Samuel, this silk hat represents a change in the trade that is beyond your scope and means of control. For God's sake, man, wake up to the future that lies before us!"

Perhaps I was too blunt in my attempt to get his attention. I wanted to suggest he begin liquidating his connections to the beaver trade. The ever-rising costs of getting peltries out of the North Country and delivered to Montreal when added to the threat of silk as a substitute for beaver felt spelled disaster of catastrophic proportions.

Was I the one who over-reacted? The silk hat seemed right to me and I continued to wear it about Montreal. Nobody stopped me on the street to comment, to ask questions. Did these people lack vision, had they no imagination? The fur trade came close to making Montreal into a one-industry town. Could they not see what was coming? Damn it, I knew deep down I was right about the threat silk hats posed to beaver felt hats.

Chapter Ten

This summer's gathering the North West Company would be at the newly constructed central depot at *Fort Kaministikwia*. It was to be built on a grand scale, the only scale NWC did things. Although consumed with curiosity over this facility, I would have to wait until early October to hear first-hand a description of the new site of NWC's *Rendezvous* from my partner.

Montreal in July resembled an oven. Stalled on the work laid out on my desk, I decided to stroll along the waterfront and catch the breeze coming off the river. A good idea, but I was too slow. "Mister Ross," my chief clerk, Galen Planche, said from the doorway, "Mrs. Rawlinson asks if you will receive her. What answer do you wish me to convey?"

"Oh shit! No, Galen, don't tell her that. Say I would be pleased to see her. Escort her to Samuel's office, it's more stylish than mine and she prefers style."

"Dear Duncan, how sweet of you to receive me. I am in the area with the carriage and thought I could induce you to ride with me into the country in search of cooling breezes. I warn you, I must hear yes."

What a choice! The grubby waterfront or riding in an elegant carriage with a handsome woman who was expert at baiting the trap - delicate perfume, a filmy and revealing summer gown, a beguiling smile.

As we rode to the outskirts of the city Jeanette kept up a running commentary of absolutely no consequence. "Enough, my dear lady. Will you get to your main reason for this search of cooling breezes?"

"Duncan, how dare you think I have an ulterior motive in asking you to join me."

"I dare, Jeanette. Now what is at the back of your mind?"

"The same thing that has been on your mind ever since Samuel left for *Rendezvous*."

"Games! Must we always play games?"

"I want to play, not a game, at an evening in my bed."

As I strolled back to my rooms in the old part of Montreal late that night I had to admit that Jeanette was right - we were good at 'it'.

Ending my business relationship with Samuel Rawlinson was not easy. Complications and details were overcome with hard work and stiff negotiations. The personal connection was not so easily severed. I depended on him even as I became very critical of him. Samuel, a natural leader, told me frequently, "Duncan, nothing succeeds like success." Another of his favorite bits of wisdom, "Money makes money."

I remembered something my Uncle Simon said to me when I suggested at Grand Portage that it was not always necessary to be the winner in a business deal. "Duncan Ross, never again let me hear you say anything as stupid as that! Coming in second only places you at the head of the line of losers. You are of the Clan McTavish, lad, we strive always to win."

I never dodged responsibilities. When Samuel was at *Rendezvous* the burdens of our private bank were on my shoulders. Why not carry burdens of this magnitude for your own enterprises? Why not, indeed!

At the livery stable I selected a spirited but manageable horse and rode to the summit of *Mont Royale* on a lovely summer day. On the grounds of my late Uncle Simon's estate I hobbled the horse and strolled the mountain side. The great house was standing just as it was the day he died - magnificent but unfinished. It was rumored about town the property had been sold, the structure to be demolished, and a new mansion built on the site.

Turning my back on my uncle's dream was an omen. Looking out over the St. Lawrence River valley I saw it through my eyes, not those of Uncle Simon. He saw it as something to be possessed; I saw it as something to turn away from, to leave before it trapped me.

I was about to mount the horse for the ride back to the city when some powerful inner force compelled me to walk to the large oak trees at the side of the unfinished mansion. There I found the grave of Uncle Simon. How appropriate to bury him at this site, the place where he was building the grand house that would match the grandeur of the scene.

"Farewell, Uncle Simon. You opened so many doors for me, and I thank you for that. In spite of the hours we worked so closely together I had the feeling that I never knew the real you. And you, dear clan member, never tried to know the real me."

The decision made to quit Montreal, to separate myself from the fur trade, to end my brief but profitable efforts in banking and investments needed only action. It was final, it was irreversible, and it left me feeling good about the life I would leave behind - without regrets. Both Jeanette Rawlinson and I knew, though we never spoke of it, that we were using each other. Ours was an empty affair, momentarily rewarding, even exciting, but shallow and lacking in commitment.

Closing down my financial relations with Samuel was a draining and exhausting experience. Nothing of importance remained, it was finished. I was free to go. But to do what?

Two weeks later I was in New York City talking with John Trostle. He had aged considerably since our last time together two years ago.

"Duncan, my weary old body insists on running down hill, but I still have a few hills to climb."

"Perhaps a trip at sea would be the best place to get back in control, John. Have you considered that?"

"The best medicine for me would be to find an enterprising younger man to take over my business and just let me fade into the background."

"I can imagine finding such a man would not be easy. Have you tried placing a notice in one of the city's newspapers? Are the members of your club aware of your plans?"

"Duncan, to tell the truth, when you walked through that door I felt the answer was standing in front of me."

"I'm sorry to disappoint you. What walked through the door, John, is possessed of a pair of restless feet, and would not be of help to you."

"I understand, but what will you do?"

"You told me on our crossing to Liverpool two years ago that the fur trade was an 'extractive' industry similar to coal or iron ore mining. I want to distance myself from businesses like those; financial affairs are in the same category."

"Noble thoughts, my young friend, but my questions remain. What will you do? And where will you do it?"

"I don't have answers, John."

"I see you as a reasonably intelligent man. You could 'read law' with any number of fine barristers in this city and within a year or two 'hang your shingle'. You know, start your own law practice."

"An interesting suggestion, and I thank you for even regarding me as capable in the law. But, John, what to do about these restless feet?"

"The eastern seaboard holds no lasting interest for you?"

"No, John, I must move on."

"You should not tarry in New York, then. Get yourself to a place like St. Louis on the edge of the frontier with unlimited possibilities. Go there, go with all possible speed. And, Duncan Ross, don't look back."

I went. From New York to Philadelphia and on to Harrisburg by stage coach. Then came a long and tiring ride by horseback over the Allegheny mountains. When I got to the village that gave itself the imposing name of Pittsburgh, I almost gave up the great plan all because of a crude, little flat-bottomed river boat. It was the only way to get to St. Louis, short of hundreds and hundreds of miles back on a horse.

Winters in the challenging *pays d'en haut*, summer after summer in the rough and tumble of the NWC's *Rendezvous* were episodes in your life you met and adjusted to. "Get on that damned boat! Once a Nor'Wester always a Nor'Wester," I told myself - without conviction. I packed my city clothes in a wooden crate, dressed in deerskins -

many years since I wore such garments - and strapped a sheath knife about my thigh. I prepared for the worst and stepped on board.

Some days were pleasant and smooth on the Ohio River, others were as bleak and dangerous as anything I had ever done. Within two days I was taking my turn at the 'sweeps' (long wooden oar-like paddles that guided the boat where experienced hands thought it should run). Every morning, after a night tied to the shore, we had to row the craft into the main current. Other than that the major task was one of control, the flowing river did the propelling.

When we reached the junction of the Ohio and the Mississippi Rivers, I parted from my companions. They would continue down to New Orleans, I would hire a horse and ride up to St. Louis. Not a bad bunch, on the rough side, but basically honest men who didn't ask many questions. None of them could be called 'educated', but they gave me lessons in the geography of the middle of the continent. They knew all of the major rivers and which parts of the country could be reached on them. One lesson was deeply implanted in my mind: the Missouri River was the key to reaching the Mandan villages. What other lessons would I learn when I got to St. Louis?

"Duncan Ross, you redheaded son of a bitch. How the hell are you?"

"And who the hell are you?" I took the measure of the man who called out to me at the livery stable and swung down from the horse I had been riding since daylight. He was a little taller, a little thinner than I. Something was familiar in this man. Then it struck me. "Jack Gallagher! My God, I thought you would be a governor of Hudson's Bay Company by this time. What brings you to St. Louis?"

"Brings me here? You old beaver-skinner, I live here. What brung you here?"

"My answer will take all day and half the night. Steer me to a place where I can get a room, a tub, and some real food."

"Forgit about all them problems, Duncan me lad, you're a'comin home with me."

"Jack, I can't impose myself . . . "

"Duncan, you're in St. Louis, and this here's my town. What I say goes!"

We rode out of the city a couple of miles to the west and on a slight hill with a view of the river we stopped at a cluster of buildings. In the middle was a substantial two-story frame house with a yard full of children. I soon learned that some of them, five to be exact, were his children, the others were neighbors. "Hey, Billy, git over here and take them horses to the barn. This here's my oldest, and he's a good 'un. Billy, this man likes to be called Duncan."

It took a while to meet all of his family, but I did and was taken with their open hospitality and good cheer. His wife, Eleanor, was a bit shy but her reception was genuine and I felt very much at home. After a fine supper we sat around the table and talked. Everybody spoke at once but somehow we managed to understand one another.

Jack had drifted down to St. Louis after he separated from Hudson's Bay Company. "That jumpin from NWC to HBC was not the best move I ever made. After a couple years in the North Country the Bay sent me to the Mandans to set up in opposition to our old outfit, the NWC."

"Sounds like you had a choice location there."

"I did the HBC some good work, but all their damned record keepin got to be a burr under my saddle. I talked a smart, young clerk with me in the HBC post in Mandan country into settin up a small, independent trading post. He would run it, I to supply the trade goods and git the peltries to markets in St. Louis. Next thing I knowd, me 'n Eleanor 'n family were on a keel boat driftin down to St. Louis. End of story."

"Quite a story, Jack. Did you get back into fur trading here in St. Louis?"

"Well no. I got into supplyin traders here. I'd stake a couple of trappers headin out to the high plains with grub and trade goods and we'd split the profits when they come back the next year with pelts. Had me some good years, some not so good."

"So, Jack, you're back in the fur trade, only indirectly."

"Guess you might say that."

"You said my crate of personal gear might be carried in one of your wagons. What is that all about?"

"General cartage business is 'nother of my outfits. I own two livery stables in town, and I got a couple farmers on shares workin some good bottom lands west of town. Hell, Duncan, you can't move any direction in this here country but what you'll cross my trail."

"I will have to say, Jack, you have done yourself proud in St. Louis. And a fine wife and five children. Yes, indeed, you've done right well for a clerk who liked sleeping on the floor in the Great Hall."

"I forgot 'bout that, Duncan. I'll bet you could do that agin, set me on my ass. But don't try. Billy and his brothers and sisters would have you trussed like a hog afore butcherin."

Like fur traders everywhere, Jack and I fell into stories of years past. We went over the high points and rough spots of some of the men we had crossed trails with in the trade.

"Jack, did you learn a lot from your *bourgeois*? I called him 'Laughs a Lot', but I forgot his name."

"Name was James Shaw, an he was a right smart teacher. How 'bout you? Who taught you the most?"

"Well, I had several years with Old Iron Balls (Simon McTavish). I worked closely with the Crown Prince (William McGillivray) for a time. The man who really opened my eyes was Jonathan Graham."

"You set great store by that man, you thought he was the best of the winterin partners. And didn't you git all his holdins when he died?"

"Yes, but I got more than money. He taught me about people; to treat everyone as an equal. There was none of the snob in Jonathan Graham."

"Why didn't you stay in Montreal and build yourself a fine mansion like some of the partners?"

"I wouldn't be comfortable in that kind of life. Hell, Jack, I'm like you, just a country boy at heart."

"Country boy? Shit! You wuz born to make deals."

"Maybe so, Jack, but for personal reasons I had to get away from the fur trade and the NWC. Having a pile of money sitting in Montreal did not make me feel comfortable. In fact, it made me damned uncomfortable."

"How so? You worked hard in the North Country. You otta feel good about havin money and not a care in the world."

"Working hard is only part of my story. Along the way I made some mistakes."

"Damn it man, if you strayed off'n the straight and narrow it don't seem to hurt you none."

That remark from Jack set off a full accounting of how I met the Tall One, of our marriage - I didn't think this veteran of years in the *pays d'en haut* and his native wife required a lengthy explanation of how 'country marriages' were formed - and the daughter that came from that union.

When the conversation reached this point I made some flimsy excuse and went outside to gather my composure. It was probably twenty minutes until I returned to the kitchen table. Jack and Eleanor had the children in bed. The three of us picked up where we left off; my separation from Naomi and Peggy and my three years in the Montreal business environment.

"Naomi came to me to live in our trading post as my wife and I can't describe the happiness we enjoyed. When our daughter was born, I thought I was the luckiest man that ever lived."

"That's a beautiful story, Duncan. But why are you here in St. Louis?"

"Well, Eleanor, on my voyage down the Ohio River I got a lesson in geography and learned that the fastest way to the Mandan country was to follow the Missouri River."

"You're in the right place to git to the Mandans," Jack added, "but why there?"

"Naomi's mother was a Mandan. When she took our daughter and left me I felt she would try to get back to her mother's people."

"I don't mean to pry, Duncan, but why did your wife leave?"

"She became convinced the fur trade was not the place she wanted our child to grow and mature into womanhood. And, Eleanor, the long absences from her when I had to go to *Rendezvous* were a source of constant friction."

"Sounds like you've cut yourself a cold trail to pick up on, Duncan. Mandan country is mighty big. You'll be needin help."

"Jack, all I can ask of you is to point me to the men who know about travel on the Missouri."

"Point you, hell, I'm a'goin with you! And I ain't takin none of your sass. I got me some business with the Mandans."

"I can't ask you to walk away from Eleanor and your family and all the things you have going for you in St. Louis."

"What you can do is git your gear together and be ready to haul ass up river."

This man made all the arrangements, went over my pack and sea bag, outfitted me with a small hand gun and a long barrel hunting rifle. Luis LaGarde's words flooded back to me, "Preparation equals survival, Duncan, the *pays d'en haut*, she is a cruel bitch." The Missouri River was another 'bitch' and not to be taken lightly.

Our craft for the trip from St. Louis to Mandan country was a 'keel boat'. Larger and heavier than a *Canot de Maitre*, it could be as cantankerous and required a set of skills and an amount of muscle that equaled the demands of a large birchbark canoe.

I gave Jack money to pay for our passage, but neither of us was the kind to sit and watch as others struggled to make signs of progress on a river that exacted something for every mile of upstream distance. About the second day at an oar or with a pole in hand, I knew easy living in Montreal had to be paid, not with bank notes, but with sweat and blisters, and sore, aching muscles I forgot I owned.

"Feels good to sweat your jacket, doesn't it?"

"Agreed. Too many fancy meals, too little real work."

"Not to be a hero on the poles, Duncan, we'll be a good many days on this ark. You've already changed a few minds."

"How's that?"

"I heard some of the men talk about that redheaded foreigner. Soft in the body, soft in the head, and talks funny. That's how you come acrost when you stepped on board."

"I'm not looking for trouble, but I'm not backing off if one of them wants to challenge me."

"Duncan, ain't a one of them that's fixin to call you out. I know these river rats, they work in packs of three or four. That's what you gotta look out for."

Black flies and mosquitoes worked in clouds and swarms and did not know the difference between the Ottawa and the Missouri Rivers. They surely knew blood tasted on the bodies of hard working men was the same no matter where it could be found. I won't try to describe the heat. Our only relief came after sundown and from the breezes that occasionally made the use of a sail practical.

Our western course made a big change when we passed what Jack said was the Kansas River as it joined the Missouri and we took a more northerly track. The next major river to add its burden of silt and water would be the Platte, that marked territory of the Omaha tribe. I was glad to have Jack as my guide and companion, for he had made this trip several times. He knew the landmarks and something of the native people who lived in the country we were passing through.

Late one afternoon I was resting in the shade of the cabin after a four hour stint on the oars when I saw a man prime his long gun, set it on the roof of the cabin, and intently track and sight on something on the west bank of the river. .

"What do you see? Going to get us some venison for supper?"

"Naw, I'm goin to plink that injun shadowin us."

I was on my feet and knocked the gun from his hands.

"You redheaded bastard, what the hell you doin?"

"I just saved your life!"

He let his right hand drop to the knife at his waist. My left hand grabbed his wrist while my right took a good hold in his hair and dropped him to his knees.

The scuffle lasted all of five seconds, but brought the whole company of the boat's men to the scene.

"What the hell's going on here?"

"This here man's loco, he knocked my gun away just as I drawd a bead on a damn injun. Bastard said he saved my life!"

"Take his knife and I'll let go of his hair."

"You one of them Indian lovers? Ain't nothin wrong with knockin off a thieving red belly."

"You saw one, but there's a hundred back in the hills within sound of your gun. Kill that one, and this whole crew could be scalped."

"You're full of shit, mister, ain't that many injuns within fifty miles."

Jack climbed to the top of the cabin, cupped his hands to his mouth, and gave a long, tremulous yell that echoed off the hills to our west. In a few minutes his yell was repeated back to him. He called again, another reply. We all looked at one another, some siding with the would-be shooter, some looking to Jack. He dropped from the roof, pointed to the west bank of the river, and said, "How many do you count? Maybe not a hunnert, but a damn sight more than I wanna fight."

The gun that started this incident laid on the cabin's roof. I retrieved it, handed it to the man, and said, "Go ahead, shoot. If you miss, you have lots of other targets. Show us what a good shot you are."

"You wanna git me kilt?"

"If I was sure it was only you, I say yes. But not a one of us will ever see the sun come up if you fire that gun."

"Enough, Duncan! The whole crew just learnt a lesson. If any of you put this boat at risk, you'll have me to deal with."

Most of the crew agreed with Jack and told him so with a few words or a nod. I was the one who had prevented a bloody massacre, but not one of the crew would even look at me. For the remainder of the trip to Mandan country no one spoke to me. Once again I felt like the bastard at a family reunion. I said something to Jack about this.

"Don't lose sleep on it. Most of the men knowd you done the right thing. They don't cotton to a stranger showin em up."

As we did every night, we tied up to the river bank, assigned watch duties, and started cooking fires.

"What's your plan when we git to the Mandans?"

"To tell the truth, Jack, I don't know. I was told there are several Mandan villages."

"It ain't gonna be easy, but let me ask round the tradin posts. Might scare up a lead or two. Gimme me a good description of your woman and girl child, that'll help."

"This sounds crazy, Jack, but I hoped that when I found Naomi and Peggy I would get a little school started in their part of the country."

"Ain't nothin crazy 'bout that. Makes sense to me."

"The other day we were talking about which men taught us the most, remember?"

"Yeah, you had some good 'uns."

"One I never mentioned was my teacher back in a little school in the Highlands. His name was Wilford MacQuay. I think more than any one, he expanded my mind and made me find answers to my own questions."

"You wuz lucky. My teacher in the Carolina hills beat the hell out of us if we flubbed a lesson."

"Old Iron Balls would never have taken me on as an apprentice if Mr. MacQuay had been that kind of teacher. He made us feel that when we didn't learn a lesson, we didn't fail him, we failed ourselves."

"I got the feelin you could be 'nother MacQuay. We'll work on a plan when we git you and your women together."

"While you nose around and ask questions, why don't I do the same?"

"Fine! But you be damn careful, Duncan. You didn't exactly makes friends with all hands on this here tub."

"The crew said they were going as far as the Yellowstone. That's a good bit to the West, isn't it?"

"It is, but mind me, keep your eyes open!"

Our arrival at the first of the Mandan villages was not the big event I had imagined. Ever since the Lewis and Clark group and the John Jacob Astor crew went through here a few years ago, traffic on the Missouri increased to the point that one keel boat's arrival was not exciting news.

Jack's name and face were still remembered in this trading area. In no time he arranged bunk space in a small warehouse that was a part of his trading post, and paid some Indian families to give us our evening meal. I drifted over to the NWC post but didn't recognize any of the clerks nor did I know *le bourgeois* assigned there. I did pick up a little gossip that up in the *pays d'en haut* the NWC and the HBC were close to war with each other. Dirty tricks turned into nasty tricks and some men had been killed.

On a fine morning after three fruitless days of looking and asking, one of the guides I engaged said I should talk to a family on the Knife River that had some knowledge about a tall woman with an eight or nine years old child always with her. That was the only flicker of progress in our inquiries. The guides said it would be an overnight trek, and I gave Jack a brief outline of what I had learned and where I was going and with whom.

The first night in camp was quiet and uneventful; the guides had little to say and seemed to shy away from me. At first light I rolled out of my blanket ready to begin the second day of working up the Knife River. It would be a day alone, the guides and their canoe had disappeared.

When Jack learned who my two guides were and where I planned to search, he immediately hired a dugout with four paddlers and started up the Knife.

"Buzzards circlin and raisin hell drawd us to your camp site," he told me later, "you wuz out cold, the side of your head laid open by a bash from a gun butt, your body like a sack of taters from the poundin them bastards gave you. You had your pistol clutched in one hand, your knife in the other. One of the varmints that lit into you lay down the trail in pool of blood with a slug in his chest. Another was staggerin round holdin his shoulder and arm with a big gash leakin blood."

He went on to recount how he and his crew got me and the wounded assailant into his canoe and started back to his post. News of his return and his cargo spread rapidly throughout the Mandan villages. With the help of three women at his trading post they stripped me of my blood-soaked clothing, bathed me, and bound the head wound. It was some time before I learned that my attacker had been given similar attention. Most people avoided me, I was bad medicine.

Jack was sitting beside me in the warehouse when Naomi walked in with our daughter. She knelt, brushed her fingers lightly over my lips, and went to work. She had Peggy help remove the cloth that bound my head wound, asked for a basin of clean water and some clean cloths. She washed around the wound while the girl carefully picked foreign matter from the ugly lump on my skull. From the pouch at her waist, Naomi took out some moss, spread it over the suppurating wound, and rebound it with clean cloths. She directed Peggy to stay at my side and talk to me, knowing I could not answer, but that I might hear the child's voice and give some sign of recognition.

Naomi led Jack out of the warehouse and this was their conversation as best he could remember it.

"I am Naomi, this is Peggy."

"I am Jack, Jack Gallagher. Duncan and I met at Grand Portage when we wuz both clerks workin for winterin partners. I don't need to tell you, but your man's a straight arrow, one to walk the trail with."

She smiled at this but offered nothing. She asked Jack to talk loudly when he was in my area. He was to talk to me, to others, but talk. "Let him always have the sound of familiar voices."

"Had you experience with others in Duncan's condition? You know, men who wuz beat up, laid out cold. Will talkin make him wake up?"

"I think he will drift in and out of the deep sleep he is in. Somebody should always be with him."

"God, woman, I hope you're right. This here's too good a man to lose. We gotta fight his fight for him."

Some time later as Jack recounted his conversations with Naomi he said only once did she smile when she attended to my wounds. Most of the time she said very little. Even when speaking to her daughter she was short and sharp in her directions.

Peggy came every morning to be with her 'Papa Dunc'. She helped her mother bathe me, to tend the head wound, to rub oils and salve on my bruised and battered body. Naomi would then leave to gather leaves, berries, roots, bark, grasses, the things made into the oils and salves she used daily.

Jack said he tried to talk with my wife and daughter as though they had known one another for years, but it was one sided conversation. "Naomi, me and Duncan talked for hours on the long, slow drag up the big river. He's cut himself away from the fur trade, wants nothin more to do with it."

"Then why are you here?"

"I come here on business, Duncan come for just one reason, to find you and Peggy."

That put an end to their conversation. Naomi left to gather her natural, healing materials. Peggy was with me and telling a long story about some people she called the 'woods' people'. At some point she left, running for her mother, and when she couldn't find her, she turned to Jack.

"Mister Jack. Come! Papa Dunc opened his eyes. He moved his head. Come!"

They walked to my side, she knelt and brushed her fingers lightly over my lips, buried her head on my shoulder, and sobbed over and over, "Papa Dunc, Papa Dunc, Papa Dunc."

I rewarded them with a weak smile, a little movement of my right hand, and said, 'Peggy' - it sounded more like the croak of a raven, but it was speech. I was back with them but knowing I faced a long and difficult recovery.

The next day Jack saw to it that I lay propped on a buffalo robe in the shade of a cottonwood tree. "Some fresh air will do you good. Do all of us good. That bash on your head don't smell like lilacs."

Voices and shapes began to come together. I remember being in the lodge of the Tall One's people when I suffered from snow blindness. I could see, not clearly, but my vision improved a little each day. When I tried to move I was painfully aware that this time was different. Then the distress was confined to my head, to my eyes. Now my whole body sent searing flashes to my brain. Frightful pain accompanied each move; changes in position were adventures in hell. My breathing and ribs were at war with one another, and when I made water there were traces of blood.

I was conscious enough to realize it was Naomi who was tending to my battered body and I felt like a different man. Penetrating pains and limited movements were forgotten. Naomi was here! She had stripped off my shirt and was about to spread a soothing salve over the ugly bruises on my back and shoulders.

"My long legged beauty, I want to hold you close and tell you how much I have missed you."

"Don't touch me!"

"Naomi, this is Dunc you are talking to. I'm the man who came many miles and suffered a severe thrashing to find you."

"Mister Ross, I am here to help you recover from your beating, and nothing more."

"Mister Ross! What nonsense is this?"

Silence was her answer, silence described her departure.

A few days later I felt strong enough to get on my feet and move about. With the help of a cane, I made it from Jack's trading post to the trading posts of the HBC and the NWC, to the river bank and the several docks that were in constant use, to the clump of trees on a little hill that gave a view of this part of the Mandan villages.

As my world enlarged, so did my understanding of what had happened. Two young, native men I engaged as guides offered to take me to a lodge on the Knife River where a tall woman who had healing powers lived with her daughter and a native family. For reasons I could not fathom, these men led me into an ambush. I remember being set on by three men, but they were not natives.

In the explosive minutes when I stumbled into the trap set for me, I recognized the man on the keel boat I had stopped from shooting. I remember firing my hand gun at the first attacker and fending the second one off with a slash across his arm and shoulder. Aware that one was behind me, I turned to give him a taste of my knife when my world went blank.

A large canoe eased up to one of the docks and Jack Gallagher jumped out. My place was pointed out to him, he came running with a shout.

"Well, old man, you've slept long enough! You look like death warmed over."

"And you look like something the natives set up in their fields to scare the crows away. Where the hell have you been?"

"Had me a little business to take care of up stream. Looks like you're gittin lots of care, better'n what I could give."

"Thanks to you, I've had the best from the Tall One, but how did you know where to find her?"

"I lived among these people for six years. They respect me for they know I respect them. When they saw you wuz with me they figgered you're a good man and needin the care of the mystery woman who lives on the Knife."

We slowly made our way back to the village, chattering like blue jays. Instead of going to our place, Jack steered me to another warehouse, a small windowless structure with two men lounging at the door. Jack engaged them in their dialect. They went in the shed and dragged out a native man bound hand and foot.

"Recognize this critter? He's one of the two you hired to take you up the Knife. Somehow he got a little roughed up and don't feel so good."

"How many were there? I remember seeing three men jump me."

"You put one away for keeps, cut one, but the third un run off."

"Can't we untie this man? He didn't take part in the beating, he just led me into the trap."

"Sure! But it'll go bad for him. His partner's out there waitin to git him. He thinks this here bastard didn't share the money they wuz paid to lead you into the trap."

"Jack, I have an idea your piece of business up stream had to do with this mess I got into. Right?"

"Right. But don't be askin questions. What I want to know is why you look so down in the mouth when you are makin such good recovery from the thumpin them bastards give you."

"I guess I never told you of my first reaction when I realized it was the Tall One who was tending to my bruised body."

"No, you never did. Well?"

"She wouldn't talk, she wouldn't even look at me."

"She must be feelin some deep hurt to act like that."

My thoughts centered, not on recent history and those who wrote that chapter for me, but on Naomi and Peggy. They had not been in the village for three days. My recovery was coming along quite well, I thought, but now that I could move about and my head was not a source of constant pain, I wanted to try again to talk with the two women I had come to find.

Jack sensed my unrest. "Tomorrow you git ready for a trip up the Knife to the lodge of your Tall One."

"Fine! I must talk with Naomi."

With four men I hired, Jack and I set off for the Knife River. We reached the site of the home lodge of the Tall One and Peggy, but no sign of anybody. The place had not been abandoned, that was obvious, but where were my women?

"Mama, it's Papa Dunc. Hurry, Mama, hurry."

Peggy's voice floated from the high growth at the back of the lodge. Peggy, then Naomi, then an old woman, two boys about six and eight, then a husky, well-set-up man emerged. We looked at one another for a long minute, then Naomi spoke, "Jack, Duncan, this is my new family."

Some words were mumbled, heads nodded, but no real message exchanged. Tension filled the air. It was natural that Jack and I would feel some distance from the others, but there was even greater strain among those who emerged from the woods. Peggy broke the awkwardness of the meeting. "Mama, look! Papa Dunc needs some of your medicine, his shirt is wet with that seeping stuff."

"I see. Take your shirt off and sit here while I get some fresh cloths and salve. Armand, bring a kettle of water from the river and hang it over the fire. Peggy, poke up the fire."

A flurry of activity followed on Naomi's orders. All but the man; he turned and stalked into the woods. Jack brought a full kettle from the river while Peggy brought the fire back to life. Naomi tended to me with Peggy helping. The silence became unbearable. Finally I spoke, "Naomi, this is a difficult time, but can we find a few minutes to talk?"

"Anything you have to say can be said here."

"How can I tell you what I feel deep within me if you won't look at me? Has my beating made me so repulsive that you must turn away?"

"This is the manner I wish to follow, I have no need to look at you. I can hear your voice, that is enough."

"Why your absence from the village? What have I done to cause you to stay away?"

"I have duties to my family. I am needed here more than I am needed at your place."

"Mama, that is not true! Armand forbids us to go there."

"Naomi, is what Peggy says the truth?"

"My daughter speaks out of turn."

"Peggy is our daughter, Naomi. Your insistence in calling her 'my' daughter is part of our problem, is it not?"

"You chose to leave us, Mister Ross, you have no daughter."

"You have the story backward, you left me."

To continue in this vein was hopeless. Outwardly, Naomi was still the tall, slender composed woman who gave a sense of well-being and control. All but her eyes, now they were those of a frightened and confused woman. She was the one closer to me than anyone I have ever known, who shared everything I had to offer, and made me feel needed. Yet I was not reaching her. I was talking to a stranger.

"Naomi, can you not remember the scene at the homepost at *Lac de Wapiti*? You said your stepbrother came for you to return and help his ailing wife."

"I went because he asked me."

"You sent Joseph Gray Squirrel to your stepbrother with a message to come for you and Peggy."

"That is not true!"

"It is true, Luis and Annette knew what you did! You were helping with the gathering of the winter's food, but you found a way to send a messenger to him."

Naomi turned and fled into the lodge. I was stunned with the vehemence of my words, and shocked at the look on Peggy's face. She had never heard her mother speak falsehoods, and she had never experienced my sudden anger. This was total disaster. I came here hoping to bring about an end to our separation, now I faced unknowable consequences. Peggy had followed her mother into the lodge, but returned a few minutes later with a pouch and a blanket roll.

"We must leave at once, Papa Dunc. Mama is afraid of Armand. I will take care of you."

We worked our way down to the Missouri River and to the Mandan village that served as the home base for Jack and me.

"Peggy, you said your mother was afraid of Armand. Does he beat her, is he rough with her?"

"He doesn't beat Mama, but he is mean in the way he talks to her. He said she must be punished for trying to live like a white woman."

"But Peggy, he knows of your mother's blue eyes, her Spanish features. He knows she is not fully Indian nor is she fully a white woman. He must see these differences."

"I think he does, Papa Dunc. He just doesn't like any of the things mother kept from our life with you."

"Things like what, Peggy?"

"She tacked up the pretty piece of material she always kept with her. Armand made her take it down. I had to hide the headband Mama brought from Grand Portage for me. He wouldn't let her sew any beads or quills on our clothing."

"I'm surprised to hear this, Peggy. Your mother was always quick with her selection of the colorful decorations in our cabins and our clothes at the trading posts we lived in."

We took our supper in the Mandan village with the native family Jack had made arrangements with for meals. The evening was pleasant and a change from the smoldering tension during our time at Armand's lodge. Now we were around a fire enjoying the companionship of friends. Jack was a master story teller, and his blend of Carolina mountain twang with Mandan dialect held his listeners for several hours.

As the shadows darkened Peggy snuggled up to me, laid her head on my shoulder and fell asleep. How many nights have gone by since I carried Peggy to her bed and brushed her forehead with a kiss? Too many, Duncan, far too many!

After a short interval Jack and I found ourselves alone at the campfire. "My redheaded friend, I think you miss your Tall One. I'm right, ain't I."

"As usual, Jack, you're right. I do miss her very much. It's not just her, it's the good cheer she carried with her where she went and kept about her like a light blanket or shawl. We had our differences, but we were always willing to thrash out our problems. Believe me,

Jack, what you've seen is a complete change in Naomi's behavior. She is not the woman I married."

"I see. But why did she leave you?"

"This sounds like I'm trying to weasel out of an answer to your question. I think she left, not just me exactly, but the life I lived in the fur trade and my expecting she would like that life."

"I kin imagine that livin with you wouldn't be easy, but wasn't it better'n what she gave up to live with you?"

"I thought it was. Then she went to *Rendezvous* for one summer and that seemed to change everything."

"*Rendezvous* would be hard to explain to any one. I didn't like the looks of that man she's livin with now, Duncan, he seems like a mean bastard."

"Peggy is telling me what sort of a life she and Naomi are forced to live with this man called Armand. Yes, he is mean, Jack. But she stays with him. Why? Can you tell me why?"

In the morning Peggy dressed my open wounds and rubbed lotions on the bruised places. Jack was a silent observer. When the two of us were alone he said, "The attention you git produces results. Are you up to the trek down river?"

"Yes, I'm ready. I can handle it."

"Good. I need to git us on a keel boat or we're gonna spend the winter here."

"But Jack, I'm just half of your problem. Peggy told me on our way from Armand's lodge that she wants to go with me."

"Now that's a piece of news. Were you surprised?"

"Yes and no. I never had it in mind until Peggy told me how unhappy she was in the lodge of Armand."

"Well, what's holdin you back? Tell her you want her to stay with you. That ain't hard to figger out."

"Naomi will never let her leave."

"Seems to me your Tall One made a decision for herself. She ain't considered the girl child. If Peggy wants to go with us, then she should."

The next day Peggy, two native men and I were in a canoe headed up the Knife River. Naomi took in the situation in a minute.

"I know why you are here. The answer is no."

Again the downcast eyes, the voice that was always so soft and gentle was edged with steel. "Peggy must remain with me, it is Armand's wish this be so."

"Armand be damned! You and I are Peggy's family, not him. You are not happy with him, that is plain for all to see, and it hurts Peggy deeply to have her mother lie to her."

"I have nothing more to say."

"It's Peggy's decision to make, and she made it. We leave in two days for St. Louis. She asked me to bring her here to gather a few things she wants to take with her."

"Go, Peggy, and gather what you want."

"Naomi, it's time to set aside our differences and think about Peggy. We want you to come with us."

"My place is here."

"We can make a new beginning without any connection to the fur trade, make a home where our daughter can grow and be happy. To be free of the tension and fear that is everywhere in this lodge."

Peggy emerged from the lodge with a bundle carefully wrapped in a deer hide and holding the wooden bear Luis carved for her when she was only a year old. Tears streamed down her cheeks when she saw her mother make no move to take her in her arms. I had memories of a smiling, alert little girl. This child wore the saddest look, drained of all emotion save the look of longing she fastened on her mother.

"I have something for you."

Naomi disappeared in the lodge and came out holding a folded piece of colored material. It was the tartan my mother gave to me as I left my home in the Highlands. Now, another mother gave it to her child as she was leaving home. But the true meaning of the exchange was not present. It lacked warmth, it lacked the unspoken message only mothers can give to their departing children.

"Take this."

Naomi hurried to the edge of the woods, turned and looked at the two of us, and disappeared. No words, no hugs, no tears. Never in my life did I expect Naomi would repeat her leave-taking in such a cold, heartless manner. First, on the little dock at *Lac de Wapiti*. Now this second parting without a word, and from the daughter who had become the center of her life.

Jack the organizer, Jack the provider had us on board a keel boat making the last run of the season to St. Louis. We three were the only passengers, the other eight men formed the crew on the heavily loaded craft.

A routine was quickly established and Peggy fit in easily. We tied up every night and made a fire on shore if the weather allowed. She delighted the men with her cooking skills, her roots and herbs that made ordinary dishes extra-ordinary. Within a week I took my turn at the oars and poles several hours a day.

There were periods for catching up on three years of separation. Jack joined us from time to time. As the father of five children, he sensed when Peggy needed to talk, and when she needed to be by herself.

"Papa Dunc, it was a long time before I realized Mama did not have a plan. We spent a hard winter with her stepbrother. That ended in the spring when Mama persuaded him to guide us to Mandan country."

"That was always in her mind, Peggy. She never gave up memories of being a Mandan."

My daughter continued over many days, and sometimes at night, the account of the flight from *Lac de Wapiti* to the Mandan villages. "Her stepbrother left us as we got near the Mandans. He said as a Cree it would be too dangerous for him. He said it would be bad for us to be seen in the company of a Cree.

"The Mandans were polite to my mother, gave a little help and gifts of food, but never really took us into their circles. Armand began to pay attention to us, especially to Mother. He was a shield between us and the people who were not happy to have us in their village.

"Armand took us into his lodge with an old family woman, an aunt, I think, and his two sons. The boys were from his living with another woman, but I did not know what happened to their mother. They were not allowed to talk about her. It was not a happy place. I cried for you and talked about you all the time. Armand put an end to that.

"We couldn't speak in French. We were never to say a word in English. He said we must not talk of friends we left behind. I missed Luis and Annette. I missed playing with their children, I missed hearing laughter, I missed my mother's smiles and the songs she sang to me.

"It was dull living with Armand. He was a good provider; we always had game and fish, grains and things from the village farms that he would trade for. But he never smiled, never spoke directly to me."

This recital, which came in bits and spurts over eight weeks of travel between Mandan country and St. Louis, spanned nearly three years of her life. I could not understand that the strong, forceful woman I loved and to whom I gave the name of my mother would permit these harsh measures.

Peggy had to tell me everything. It was though a dam had burst within her and she had to make me to see what her life had become. "Mama said many times as we fled from the homepost that we had to forget the white trader's ways and get back to 'native ways': the foods we gathered and cooked, the way we dressed, and even our prayers to the spirits that guided our lives. Papa Dunc, how could she turn her back on our happy times, the dancing, the singing?"

"I can't answer, Peggy, for I have the same problem as you. Why did your mother change so completely?"

How could I possibly fill all the voids in our daughter's life, replace three years of fright and loneliness, of life without color or laughter? Peggy had been cheated of a big slice of her childhood. I was in some ways responsible for these bleak pages in her story.

The minute we went ashore in St. Louis Jack took over; popped us in a carriage from one of his livery stables and set out for his home. What a joyous reunion with his wife and children! Peggy and I were made a part of this family instantly. Without any planning, Billy - Jack's oldest son - organized some sort of game. Peggy was in the middle of it, having a chance to be once more a child who knew how to have fun, to run, laugh and shout without a harsh word directed at her.

Jack and I had lengthy discussions about my plan for a school on a piece of land in the hills to the west of St. Louis where I could begin my new project. The site was about a mile from Jack's home. Once free of the confining and limiting atmosphere of the Montreal financial scene, flights of fancy took over. I had a burning desire to do something with my money other than make more money.

"Jack, I told you of my visit with my sister and her family in the Highlands, didn't I?"

"Many times, my friend, many times."

"Seeing my niece and the way she blossomed in her school made me realize what Peggy was missing."

As the school began to take shape in my mind, I made lists of needed items and the sequence to be followed in making the many parts of the school come to life. The years with Simon McTavish were good training for this part of the project. I'm quite sure Jonathan Graham would have approved of the way I was spending his money.

I wrote a long overdue letter to my sister:

Dear Louise, Rory, and Jennifer

No, I haven't dropped off the edge of the world, I am in St. Louis and have Peggy with me. I did find my women in Mandan country, but Naomi chose to remain behind with the man she is living with.

You can send letters to us at:

Gallagher's Livery Stables

St. Louis

Louisiana Territory, United States

What I am starting to do is build a school in this area for both boys and girls. I want Peggy to have the same chances that Jennifer is having. I will be the teacher to get things started, then maybe I can get you to come over and run the school. Rory could become important in business in St. Louis, Peggy and Jennifer would become the best of friends and drive us all crazy with their plots and pranks.

I spend many hours wondering why Naomi refused to come with Peggy and me. I never thought she could separate herself from Peggy, and I think she is not really happy with her new man. I waited too many years to unite with my women.

There is no way I can tell you how long it will take for a letter from you to reach me, but please try. Letters from Scotland will mean so much to Peggy and to me.

All our love,
Duncan and Peggy

In a short time I had log buildings underway, fields marked off, an orchard started, a well dug, and a daughter who, like my sister, was into everything. Jack and Eleanor supported my plan and provided my first students.

One of the men working on the buildings was a black man, the first I had ever met. "Mister Ross, me and my woman want our two children to go to your school. We could pay you with work at the school and on the farm. What do you say, sir?"

"I say bring them. We will be happy to have them."

"I might bring you more than children, Mister Ross, I could bring you trouble, big trouble."

"I think I can handle that, Mister Crawford, not to worry." Even before the first class, I now had eight students.

Every day was a challenge, for I really didn't know what I was doing. I had Mr. MacQuay's classroom as a model, and I planned on having the older students help teach the younger ones. Where he had only boys to teach, I had boys and girls.

On one of my many trips into town to purchase supplies I chanced upon a young man with a sketch pad on the bank of the Mississippi River working quickly and confidently. He had a full head of sandy hair indifferently stuffed under a straw hat. I might also say his clothing, though relatively clean, was indifferent - at one time it might have been the work of a competent tailor. I looked over his shoulder, liked what I saw and told him so. "I'm not sure I appreciate your interruption, sir, but since you have stopped my work for the moment, what can I do for you?"

"Take that chip off your shoulder and come across the street to the coffee house and hear me out."

He drew himself up to his full five and a half feet, looked up at me, drilled me with his dark brown eyes and said, "I'd welcome a coffee, sir."

We talked easily and openly. I told him of the school I would be operating, where it was located, and what I had in mind for him. He would teach my students art, not just to make pretty pictures, but to develop talents which, under his practiced eye, could take them in many directions. One coffee became two as we explored the possibilities of my school.

"Give me a day or two to mull this proposition over in my mind, Mr. Ross. You know you took me completely by surprise."

"Mr. Archer, as you have learned, time is not to be wasted in getting my school up and running. Can I have your answer by the end of this week? You know where I am to be found. Good day to you, sir."

The next day I saw the artist ride in to my school site on the most inartistic nag I had ever seen, certainly not a horse from one of Jack Gallagher's liveries. As he lowered himself to the ground I saw he held a violin case in a most protective fashion.

"Good morning, Mr. Archer. Glad you are here. I want to show you what we have started and what is planned."

"And a good morning to you, Mr. Ross."

We walked and talked, looked and questioned. I was sure in my mind I wanted this young man to agree to what I had in mind to offer him.

"Mr. Ross, I am able to give you two days a week of my time. In turn you will provide a place for me to stay overnight, four meals while I am here, a stable for my horse, and space I may call my own for sketching and painting."

"I am amazed and delighted at your thoroughness in laying out your demands, Mr. Archer. I am agreeable to all of your terms."

"Good. Now, sir, if you will show me where to hang my coat, I will get to work. I can see another hand is needed."

Poor Eleanor had another mouth to feed, and no advanced warning. Thomas Archer returned her kindness after the noon meal by sketching her youngest child at play with neither mother nor child aware of what he was doing. Would he adjust as quickly to teaching as he adjusted to this lively family?

Thomas insisted he come to the site two days each week to work until the buildings were completed and made ready for the children. In time I would learn more of his background. For the present, I was satisfied to have him here and making himself part of the family

We were ready to open the school. The main building had three rooms for class work, two bedrooms - one for Peggy, one for me - and a 'commons' room with a small kitchen in one corner was finished. Outside were two necessaries, a shed for supplies and a supply of firewood. Further down the hill was the place where I had started a barn and barnyard. On all sides were fields yet to be plowed and planted. To the east was the beginning of an orchard.

"You look so tried, Papa Dunc, why don't you stop work for a day and let Thomas and Mr. Crawford take over? Uncle Jack is away, but I want you to take Aunt Eleanor and me to town, there are things we need."

"What makes you think I can rest when two women are going to spend all my money?"

"Oh, we'll be careful. And if you are a good boy we may buy you a stick of peppermint candy."

A day with those two and I brought home a wagon load of their purchases and my brain stuffed with suggestions and ideas for the school. We were walking out the road from Jack's place to ours after supper.

"There is one thing missing, Papa Dunc."

"And what might that be? Another shopping trip?"

"No. You should have another teacher, and it should be a woman. The girls, and the boys too, should hear some one other than men."

"So you think men can't teach?"

"Oh, Papa Dunc, I mean it! We should have a woman teach us as well as Mr. Archer and you."

Nothing more was said about Peggy's suggestion, but she had planted a seed. I knew I was a good teacher, Thomas exceeded my fondest expectations with his art. His time grew from two days a week to four as we added music to the program of letters, numbers, reading, art and geography. Thomas and I had our limits and were approaching them quickly. We had finished a year as an active school, yet here was my prized pupil pointing out a glaring weakness.

As winter gave way to spring and the days became longer, some evenings Jack and two or three of his children would drift over to the school. While Peggy joined with them in some games Jack and I would share a pipe like old fur traders are wont to do. "I could never quite get across to Naomi the way I had to divide my time between her and the Company."

"Ain't easy to do. Same problem I had with Eleanor when I was running the Bay post up in Mandan country."

"How did you solve it, Jack?"

"Didn't. Just kept on talkin and we sort of stumbled into answers that we both seemed to accept."

"And I thought I talked too much. Now you're telling me maybe I didn't talk enough?"

"What I wanna tell you now, I'm on my way to the Mandans, got tradin business to take care of. I'd ask you along, but you got your hands full here. Got a message should I meet up with a certain tall lady?"

"Why yes, Jack. If you happen to see the Tall One tell her Peggy is getting along just fine. Tell her there is place for her here if she wants to practice her healing skills and make her medications. She would be welcomed and live free of the fur trade. She might want to teach our students about all the living things, plants and animals, from her perspective. I would be pleased to have her come."

"Now you ain't gonna go and git your redhead to boilin if I tell her what you said in my own words? You sound too much like a school teacher!"

"What did you expect me to say?"

"You might say, you love her, you miss her. But no, you're too damned stubborn to say what's in your heart."

"I don't think I am stubborn."

"The Lord save us! Every day you put on your stubbornness like a piece of clothing. I kin abide you're bein stubborn, Duncan, but it's your pride what gives me pain. I'm gonna have to tell the Tall One your real message my way."

"I would be obliged if you would tell Naomi just what I told you and nothing more."

"Obliged my ass! Your wife had the sense to see there wuz no future for Peggy in Mandan country. Why else would she let her come down here with you? Sure, she's got pride in being a Mandan, partly, but her pride is mixed with her common sense. You've got pride a plenty, but it's mixed up with your stubbornness. I ain't got any more to say."

"Jack, I'll think on what you just said. Have a quick and safe trip to Mandan country."

In the second year of the school's operation, late in the fall, I was splitting and stacking wood for the coming winter. Stripped to the waist and sweating like a mule I heard a familiar voice, "Ease up, old man, you ain't a youngster no more."

"Welcome home, you old horse thief. How was your trip to the Mandans? What can I do for you? You always need help."

"Got a bit of freight on my wagon, more'n I kin handle. Git your arse out front and lend a hand."

We walked around the school building to Jack's rig, a pair of big Belgian workhorses hitched to a heavy freight wagon. There was just one person wrapped head to foot in a traveling cloak seated on the driver's bench staring ahead and making no effort to help.

"Jack, there's not one damn thing on this wagon that can be called freight. What's the game this time?"

The mystery person turned slowly to look down at me with her blue eyes, she smiled and held out her arms.

Post Script

Northfield, MN
November, 2003

Bridge Square in the center of Northfield on the east bank of the Cannon River is a pretty place - made so by the local Garden Club. As I walk to the library in town or to the library of Carleton College I frequently lay out my route so I would pass through the Square. A relaxing place to encounter friends, to munch popcorn, or just sit on a park bench and let water surging over the dam at the old mill soothe away the cares of a busy, crazy world.

It was late afternoon and the sun that made an early November day into a Minnesota classic was going to rest in a western sky composed of colors that could drive an artist wild. The chill of evening reminded me I should move on to my apartment to enjoy the book I checked out an hour ago.

"Not so fast, my friend. Will you not linger and enjoy this beauty with an old fur trader?"

Duncan Ross settled his big frame onto the park bench, gave me a long, searching look and said, "Mr. Reiley, I am never disappointed when I join you without warning. You scare as easily as a snowshoe hare that realizes the shadow cast over it is made by a timber wolf."

"Damn it, man. It isn't that you aren't welcome, but you ought to give some sort of a signal, don't you think?"

"A signal! And rob myself of the pleasure I get from jolting you?"

"Can we walk back to the apartment and resume our work? I will have tea for you in five minutes."

"I will pass on that, but thank you. Why don't we enjoy this time of the evening here while I relate more of my story?"

I sat with him in the dusk confident that I would remember this flood of reminiscences - some of them I had heard at other times. The street lights in Bridge Square were soft and did not intrude on the serenity of the place. Without the need to concentrate on note taking, I took advantage of this meeting to focus on my friend. I was careful not to stare, but locked into my mind the features and expressions on his interesting face. They were as complex as the person himself, but one thing was revealed to me tonight. Duncan Ross was both a lonely man and a contented man. His eyes in the fading light showed all too clearly those emotions as he talked of his wife and daughter.

There was a long pause in the narration. I took that to mean our time together was finished. I got to my feet, picked up the library book, and said, "The offer of tea still holds. Will you walk home with me?"

I talked to an empty bench.

Walking up town in the afternoon was sheer delight in the warm sun and gentle breeze. Walking back to the apartment after my chance encounter with Duncan Ross in Bridge Square at dusk with a stiff breeze out of the north was anything but delightful - it was cold! I was glad to step into the comfort of the kitchen, and think about supper. Instead, I found myself drawn to the office.

Standing there looking out the window was Duncan Ross. An hour ago he was dressed in his usual fashion, but seeing him now was a shock. He was in the full dress, top to bottom, of a Scottish laird wearing the tartan of Clan McTavish. To me, Duncan Ross was always impressive because of his size, his red hair and beard, ruddy complexion, style, and commanding air. In the attire of his native Highlands he was magnificent. God, what a man!

"While waiting for you, I took the liberty of reading the last draft of your work on my return from Mandan country and the events that followed. You have made quite an improvement over the previous drafts."

"Thank you, sir. Let me repeat the offer made at Bridge Square for a mug of tea."

"I think not. Tea won't help me to discover the rationale behind my wife's decision to stay behind with the man whom my daughter said treated her with scorn and contempt. Naomi thought she could live in the past. I always thought it was only possible to live in the present and perhaps plan for the future."

"Mr. Ross, did you ever consider that your wife had the past living in her? She did not have to return to the past, it was always deep within her."

This question brought a long silence. So long that I feared I had gone too far and stumbled into a private recess in his mind with silence his rebuke for my error.

"Mr. Reiley, that is a profound thought. I did not think a young man of your age capable of such wisdom."

My first response died on my tongue. I am now over eighty and I have several times judged Duncan Ross to be in his late forties - he had his young men reversed. Then I remembered to add two hundred years to his age. I ventured to extend an expression of my gratitude for sharing his saga.

"I appreciate the door you opened for me into this most personal portion of your saga, Mr. Ross."

"I will think fondly of Naomi as long as I live. But you must promise that whatever you write about my wife will be done with the utmost care. Her impact on my life may be more than I can relate, and beyond your capacity to commit it to paper."

As I digested this proscription on my thought processes he said, "Are you not surprised at the full regalia that would be worn by a laird of my native land? Do you not approve?"

"I approve most heartily, Mr. Ross. You are an impressive person and your Highland's attire only adds to your commanding presence. Is there a special occasion for you to dress in this manner?"

"Nothing special, lad. I just thought you should see me in a different light."

"Well, you certainly have ...."

His raised hand and pointing finger cut me off in mid-sentence.

"Do you not hear them, Mr. Reiley? The pipes! Can you not hear them? Are you deaf, man? I hear them clearly and they are calling to me."

We stood looking at one another, he with his challenging manner and mystery hidden in his blue eyes. I looked at him in awe, with respect, and a sinking feeling that we had come to a critical moment. With a smile flickering on his tightly compressed lips and a softening in his eyes, he squared his shoulders, raised his head and, as if on parade to the skirling of bagpipes, Duncan Ross marched with deliberate, stately steps from the office. He turned to the passage leading to the dining room and went out through the closed, heavy sliding door to the balcony just as he had entered three years ago.

Of course, he was gone. For a long time I stood on the balcony in the fading evening's light and deepening chill. Was this it? Was this his way of moving back to his past? Or, perhaps, into his future?

Glossary

voyageur	traveler, usually of French-Canadian roots, tough, resourceful, playful, 'workhorse' of the fur trade
bourgeois	proprietor, the man in charge, the 'boss', supervisor, owner
mangeur de lard	'pork eater', derisive term given to voyageurs from Montreal
homme du nord	man from the North Country, a voyageur who 'winters over'
canot du maitre	a Montreal canoe, usually 36 ft long, capable of carrying 8000 lbs.
canot du nord	a North canoe, usually 25 ft long, capable of carrying 4000 lbs.
canot batard	'bastard' size, usually 15 ft long, used mostly by native families
avant	leader, man in front of a canoe to guide and direct it, usually the 'crew chief'
gouvernail	man in back of canoe to steer it, often doubled as cook for a canoe's crew
milieux	men in the middle, duties usually confined to paddling and portaging
pays d'en haut	the 'up country' beyond Lake Superior to the Northwest
allumez	smoke break
leve	get up, on your feet, move it!
a la facon du Nord	in the custom of the North Country
mal de raquette	snowshoe lameness
mal de mer	sea sickness
sac a feu	beaded bag, 'fanny pack'
ceinture flechée	sash, the brighter in color and more elaborate the design the better
entrepreneur	risk taker, the source of working capital
rubbaboo	thick soup made from pemmican and flour